The Forgotten Witch

Editors: Rosie McCaffrey, Judy Jewell, & Jennifer Bottum
Formatter: Susan Veach
Cover Design: Rena Violet
Page Art: Irina Beliakova, Jessica Lamson, Libby Sharp, & Francesca Scillia

ISBN: Hard Cover: 978-1-7376966-1-2
ISBN: Paperback: 978-1-7376966-2-9
ISBN: E-Book: 978-1-7376966-3-6
ISBN: Hard Cover Special Edition: 978-1-7376966-5-0

This book is dedicated to
my family & friends,
who support me
100% in everything I do.

Special dedication to my wonderful Mother and Father,
my husband JT, and our two amazing children
Aidan & Sadie.
You are my magic!

TABLE OF CONTENTS

Ley Lines Of
Scotland
N
W
E
S
Ring of Brodgar
Stone Circle
Cape Wrath
Callanish Stone
Circle
Stone Circle
Loch Moy
Stoneyfield
Oban
Iona
Luss Loch Lomond
Mavishall
Lindisfarne

PROLOGUE

The rain came down in sheets as it did most days in the month of July in Cambridge, England. Susan raced out of Anstry Hall and across the lawn with nothing more than an old, quickly degrading newspaper over her head. By the time she made it to the small pub down the road, she had tiny bits of disintegrated newspaper littering her hair. The pub was dry and inviting. Old, tinted glass shades hung over each small grouping of tables, casting a rosy glow. A huge oak bar in its rich brown color spanned the length of the pub's back wall, and people stood around in little knots, drinking and laughing. The Emperor was full, as it normally was on a late Friday afternoon, and the noise that reverberated off its walls was a low hum of voices, cut through by bursts of laughter here and there. Susan spotted her small group of girlfriends in the back corner and had almost made it to the table when a man pulled out a barstool from behind her and abruptly slipped and fell on the river of water that was coming off her slicker.

"Oh my God! Are you alright?" she asked, her American accent falling into harsh contrast with the smooth tones of the British accents in the room. She helped the man back to his feet.

He was tall and looked to be a few years older than her, with dark brown hair and sea blue eyes. A Cambridge University tag that read "Lecturer" hung from his tan argyle jacket, stating he was an aide to a professor from the chemistry department.

He brushed himself off in an attempt to save what dignity he had left now that his pants had been soaked in a very awkward arrangement.

"I am so sorry. I had to walk here and I guess I brought half the storm in with me," Susan apologized, handing him the hat that had made its way to the floor when he had.

"It's fine. I needed the motivation to leave anyway," he said, motioning down at his water-stained trousers. "And this is quite good motivation, anyone who didn't just see that will think I've pissed myself."

Susan laughed and gave him a smile. "Well, the least I can do is buy you another drink to ease the embarrassment," she insisted. "I better not. I think I may have had one too many as it stands,".

"Well, maybe another time then," she said, outstretching her hand. "Susan Price, nice to meet you."

"Roger Kent, pleasure," he replied, taking her hand.

From that moment on, they had become inseparable. It started with long walks and nights of movies with popcorn, then turned into a cozy two-bedroom townhouse with large Victorian windows that let the afternoon light pour in from the sleepy street. Proposals were made and vows taken and soon Susan was pregnant.

It was 4:18 a.m. on January 19th, 1991, when Susan's water broke. Roger raced down the stairs and brought the car around, picking Susan up on their frozen front step. It was bitterly cold that morning, falling somewhere below zero. As they drove to the hospital, the car lights broke through the darkness, illuminating tiny ice particles that floated in the frozen air. Even through the pains of her contractions, Susan thought the early morning air looked as if it was full of sparks of magic.

By the time they arrived at the hospital, Susan was beginning to push and within a half-hour, she was holding her tiny baby girl in her arms.

They had decided on the name Helen after Roger's grandmother. It meant "light" and it suited her well, as she was an easy baby and even more of an easy child. As she grew, she spent most of her days playing in the garden or drawing pictures in one of her many pads of paper.

When she started school, she picked up reading quickly and grew into an avid reader. She preferred spending free time either with a pencil and paper, creating art, or escaping into the worlds waiting for her in books than playing with the few friends she had made.

Roger was offered a professorship in the chemistry department at Harvard University in the summer of 1999 and Susan was overjoyed to return to the States and be closer to her parents. They had only met Helen twice and she was delighted that they would now be able to watch her grow up.

That fall, they packed up their lives and moved from Cambridge to Boston. Roger had a hard time adjusting at first to the faster-paced life in the States, but after six months he finally settled in and they made their home in a beautiful little suburb named Belmont. Susan took up the head librarian position at the

Belmont public library, happy that the flexible schedule allowed her to balance a career with motherhood.

Their story was that of most middle-class families striving for the American Dream. Forty-hour work weeks, play dates, weekend trips to the country, school plays, high school dances, graduations, and before they knew it, Helen had grown up. When she moved out and went to college, they sold their home in the burbs and opted for a cozy bungalow in Florida. As their life together began to wind down, Helen's was just beginning. It was the natural progression of life and they felt they had played their hand well.

Chapter One

IMPULSE

Helen draped her legs off the large rock she sat upon, letting the cool water slip over the tips of her toes. The water lapped the edges of the rock in a rhythmic motion as she sat looking out over the vast lake in front of her. The sun was beginning to set in the mountains, its rays creating a golden rim around the water's edge and lighting up the grays and blues of the pebbles along the shore. Helen sat and watched the stillness that lay before her, wishing to be one of the rocks that scattered the shoreline in peaceful solitude.

Twilight didn't creep in but rather fell fast into night, leaving the air thick with the sounds of birds flying off to roost and a chorus of the peepers that had come out to sing their nighttime ballads.

The light of the day had gone, leaving shades of blacks and grays. Helen felt a chill run down her spine. It was not the twilight seeping into the valley that made her feel this way. She could sense the presence of another. The hairs on the back of her neck rose as if a storm was about to roll in.

As Helen stood up, she glanced into the water. A figure stood behind her in the lapping reflection of the lake. A bolt of fear shot through her and before she could turn around, she was pushed into the darkness of the water.

Small beads of sweat rolled down the side of her brow as she sat upright and tried to catch her breath. This dream had been plaguing her for as long as she could remember and, like clockwork, had her up earlier than she wanted. She looked over at the small digital alarm clock on her nightstand. It read 4:50 a.m.

She fumbled around for the switch on her lamp. Once lit in its soft glow, she propped herself up and grabbed her phone.

She scrolled through her work emails, seeing what lay ahead for the waking hours before getting caught up in the time-sucking social media trance. She noticed an email from Coney Estates, a company she was assigned to a few years back. She had helped them with a marketing campaign. It was a small foreign company that sold foreclosures and estates. They had properties all over the world but focused mainly on central Europe.

The email was a bit jumbled but from what she could gather they were looking for a new website—not her forte. But she'd enjoyed working with William, the older Welsh man who ran the company, so she didn't mind throwing a few ideas out there. She'd hand them over to Kevin when she headed into the office. Kevin was a web designer and one of Helen's only true friends. They had been hired at the same time five years ago and had quickly bonded over their shared social awkwardness. They were oddballs, the two of them.

Kevin will love working on this little gem, she thought as she logged in and began scrolling through the ancient rolling webpage. After a few minutes, she came across a picture that caught her eye. It was a very old white stone cottage nestled snug against a lush green mountain. The title above read "Charming Scottish Cottage Nestled In The Rolling Hills of Oban." She clicked on the image. The cottage was being auctioned off right that very moment. She glanced to the right-hand side of the page and saw that the starting bid was $11,000. There were zero bids. The auction was ending in three minutes.

"Zero bids? That can't be right," Helen murmured to herself as she stared at the page. *Must be a problem with the refresh rate*, she thought. She hit the refresh button and waited. Still no bids. A bar at the top of the screen popped up; 1 minute and 23 seconds it flashed, trying to entice a last-minute bid.

Then something came over her, an unexplained feeling of need for this place she had never even seen before. It was a feeling like an integral part of herself was being separated and she couldn't let go of it—to lose the bid was not an option.

She clicked on the bid box and typed $11,001.

This was crazy. This was rash. Unexplainable.

The timer counted down the seconds and then the screen turned white. A gray window popped up saying: "Congratulations, you have won this bid. Please contact William Evans with estate number 1597."

She won! A feeling of utter excitement raced through her. Then as soon as it came, it was replaced with an overwhelming feeling of panic. Her head began to spin at the thought that she'd just spent her life savings on a house in Scotland.

"Oh my God, Helen, you insanely crazy woman. What have you done?" she said to herself as she began to come up with ways to wiggle herself out of the deal she had so hastily agreed to. This was the money she had saved to put down on a condo so she could get out of her shitty apartment. But she knew there was nothing she could do right now. She would have to reassess this when she got into the office and could call and talk to William. She had no doubt the old man would let her back out of the purchase when she explained everything to him, or at least she hoped.

Helen got out of bed and made her way into her tiny apartment kitchen to make a cup of coffee and a few slices of toast. She stared at the coffee pot, willing it to work faster but alas it took its sweet time in brewing her morning energy, as it always did. Once the coffee was done and the toast buttered, she sat at the small table in the cramped kitchen.

She had lived in this same apartment since she graduated college. She had always needed her space and was a perpetual loner, never really fitting in or even wanting to. She did, however, have a few boyfriends in college, but those relationships were short-lived when they realized that art was the real love of her life and not them. Love didn't come easy to her and most of the time she ran in the opposite direction when things started to get serious. It wasn't that she was bad at dating or even talking with men; it was the fact that loving someone always felt so terrifying. Laying her heart in the hands of another seemed like a recipe for disaster. Pretty soon she gave up on dating altogether and focused on her art degree. Art nourished her in a way relationships just couldn't. It gave her a kind of contentment that was steadfast and unwavering.

When she graduated, she was hired by a marketing company and had been working for them ever since. She'd never imagined she would be using her talents to sell diapers and lipstick. At least it paid decently, and she had evenings and weekends free to work on her own paintings. It wasn't much but she was happy. Although, she thought, if she really was happy, would she have just bought a crumbling old cottage in a country she'd never been to on the spur of the moment?

After her second cup of coffee was drunk and her toast picked apart, she mindlessly moved through her morning routine as anxiety slowly filled her every thought. She slipped her laptop into her bag, put on her worn pair of wingtip shoes, and headed out the door for work, forgetting to even grab a jacket on her way out.

The office building where she worked was only a few miles away from her apartment but most days Helen took the bus. It was within walking distance if she felt up to the task, but today she was running low on fumes. The bus was crowded as always and she chose a seat next to an old woman with her nose in a book. As she sat down and laid her bag snugly between her legs on the floor, she looked over to see what the woman was reading. The title read *Folklore of the Scottish Highlands*. The busyness of the bus had momentarily broken her train of thought and her anxiety had faded into the chaos, then it all came rushing back to her: the auction, the house, her savings account. What had she done? A confusing mix of excitement and worry filled her to almost overflowing. Was it a sign, this book?

"Are you alright, dear?" the old woman asked, noticing that Helen looked unwell.

"Yes, I'm fine. Your book, is it any good?"

"Yes. Very interesting stuff here. My father was Scottish and I was told many of these tales as a young child. Reading them as an adult is a whole new experience," said the woman.

"Are they ghost stories?" asked Helen.

"Some," said the woman. "The one I'm currently reading is

about a kelpie. Have you heard of them before? They are water spirits capable of transforming into hypnotic black horses. Of course, the kelpies aren't friendly, since they will lure you to your doom by drowning you in the water. Not the kind of creature you would want to come across while walking alone in the Highlands I'd say. These Scots told some dreadful dark tales, but they're all quite fascinating." The old woman said, as she smiled at Helen and then dove back into her book.

"Yes, I'd say so," Helen said with a small forced laugh. While the woman had talked, all she could think of was what a terrible mistake she'd made and how fate appeared to be rubbing her nose in it. A muffled ring announced the next bus stop and Helen got up, grabbing her bag and saying goodbye to the old woman.

"Have a lovely day, dear," the old woman's voice rang out after her as she pushed past people to exit the bus.

"Enjoy that book," she called back.

Her office was just a stone's throw from the bus stop, and as she stepped out onto the street the city was there to greet her. Everything about the place was fast-paced and busy, from the sounds of traffic to the myriad of smells that assaulted her nose. After years of living and working in the hustle and bustle, she had learned to block out the sensory overload that engulfed her.

She stepped through the rotating door and into the lobby where people rushed here and there. Helen decided to take the stairs today to avoid the crowds at the elevator.

Upon opening the door to the third floor, she saw Kevin in the break room already grabbing for his first cup of coffee. She rushed over to her desk and unloaded her bag, trying to hurry before anyone else went in and started talking to him.

"Kevin, oh my God! You won't believe what I did," she spat out as she reached him in the break room, not giving him even a sliver of a chance to ask "What?" before going on. "I had that damn dream again last night. I swear, at this rate I am never going to get a decent night's sleep. Anyways, I decided to get a jump on the day and go through some work stuff I've been putting off. There was an email from Coney Estates, that little company I helped with branding a few years back. They were looking for someone to help them update their website. So, I thought I would have a look. As I was scrolling I came across a listing for a tiny cottage in Scotland up for auction. I don't know what came over me but I bid on it, and WON!"

"Oh my God, Helen!" Kevin said, spilling his coffee on the break room table. "What the hell were you thinking?"

"I don't know. I saw the picture of the cottage and it called out to me. I acted on impulse and then immediately regretted it. And just like that everything I had saved up for the down payment, gone in the click of a button. I have to get a hold of William and see if I can back out of the deal. What time is it in Wales?" Looking down at her watch, she knew that she wouldn't be able to call until after her morning meetings were over.

"It's going to be okay, I'll do what I can to help you get out of this. Just take a deep breath," Kevin reassured her as he rested his hand on her shoulder.

"Thanks, Kev. I better go get ready for the Holloway meeting, I can't afford to screw this up. I need to get my head back in the game," Helen said.

After all the morning meetings were over, Helen decided it was time to call Coney Estates. She searched in her bag for the auction number.

It felt like an eternity before anyone picked up on the other line. It was an older woman with a very thick Welsh accent.

"Coney Estates, how may I help you?"

"Hello. This is Helen Kent calling for Mr. Evans."

"Yes, Ms. Kent, he has been expecting your call. Let me get him for you," she said in a sweet, mild voice.

Helen waited, her stomach in knots. Flipping and flopping.

"Hello, Ms. Kent," said a jolly voice on the other end of the line. "May I be the first to congratulate you on the fine new home you have acquired. I believe you will find Fernbeg to be quite a diamond in the rough."

"Fernbeg?" Helen repeated.

"Yes, that's the name of the cottage you have won in the auction," William said matter-of-factly.

"About that, I was a bit hasty in placing my bid. Is there any way that I can step down so that another bidder may take over and purchase the cottage?" Helen asked, holding her breath while incessantly tapping her finger on a notepad as she waited for his reply.

"My dear," William spoke softly into the phone, "these bids are final. Did you not read the fine print at the bottom of the listing? Once a bid is placed, you are under legal contract to buy the property if you win. There's not much I can do."

"But I can't just pick up and move to Scotland," she said, with a bit of angst in her voice.

"Most people who buy properties at such an economical cost fix them up and resell them for a much larger sum. I suggest that you come for a visit, hire some local handymen and fix the old girl up. Then you can put her back on the market and make a pretty penny. You just let me know when you're planning on coming and I will send someone to pick you up and take you to the cottage," William said optimistically. What he didn't know was she'd just spent every last penny she had and would have nothing left to fix the cottage up.

Feeling in a complete and utter daze, the conversation ended without her even registering it. Sitting at her small desk in her tiny white cubicle, she stared at the wall, her palms sweaty, heart racing.

"How did it go?" Kevin asked, breaking her trance.

"Not well. It was a factual contract and the only way out of this mess is to fly over, fix it up, and resell it," she explained, tears breaking free from her eyes and flowing down her cheeks. Crying was something that she very rarely did, and never in public. But she was just so overwhelmed. Where was she going to get the money to fly to Scotland in the first place? She couldn't afford to take the time off work, and who knew how long it would take to fix up the old, crumbling cottage. Feeling exposed, she rested her head in her hands, peering down through her fingers at her tears falling on the desktop. Her impulsive choice had completely altered the direction of her well-laid plans for the next few years.

Kevin yanked her from her chilly leather office chair and embraced her with a loving hug. "Hey now, it's going to be alright. We can figure this out. Why don't you take the rest of the day off and we can talk through a plan tonight? I'll tell Tom you had a family emergency and needed to leave."

Helen agreed, packed her laptop back into her bag, and left the office early, but this time she didn't take the bus.

Chapter Two

POSSIBILITIES

Helen thought a walk home would help clear her head. The streets were not bustling with people like they normally would be when she left work at five. Instead, there was a low flow of pedestrians, mostly mothers with small children and people of retirement age. They all moved at a much more leisurely pace compared to the hustle and bustle of rush hour.

She watched as an elderly man in a tweed jacket held the door open for his wife. They entered a small wine and spirits shop on the corner of Westmore and Parkview. It was a shop Helen had frequented many times, the only shop around that carried Ankida Ridge, a wine she was very fond of. She noticed a new poster in the large front window of the shop advertising a fancy Scotch they were now carrying. As she squinted to read the fine lettering on the bottle, her heart stopped. "Oban" it read. Not believing what she was seeing, she crossed the street to get a closer look.

Your eyes are playing tricks on you. You're seeing things, she thought as she made her way up to the storefront window. But her eyes did not deceive her. There, in fine golden print over a black velvety background, were the words "Oban, 14-year single malt Scotch from the Scottish Highlands."

Helen gasped. *If this isn't a sign I don't know what is. First the woman on the bus with the book and now this. It has to be a sign. Too many coincidences for it not to be.* She thought. Stepping back from the window, she turned on her heels and started at a much faster pace toward home, but first, she needed to make one quick stop on the way.

Only a half a block from her apartment building was a small bookstore that she was quite fond of which offered a broad selection of travel books. She decided that if she was going to do this, then she would do it right. She opened the wide wooden door and walked in. The shop smelled of old books and incense and the sounds of chimes greeted her as she entered. She headed back to the travel section which was nestled in the far back corner, tucked between historical fiction and myths, legends, and folklore.

She found a small section on Scotland and began to dig through it.

"May I help you, dear?" came a soft, kind voice from behind her. Helen turned around to see the owner of the shop, Mrs. Jewell, a short older woman with snow-white hair wearing a blindingly bright yellow dress.

"Yes, please. I'm taking a trip to Oban, Scotland, and was hoping to find a book with a little bit of history on the place," Helen said.

"Oh, Oban is a beautiful place, tucked in next to the sea and with quite a bit of history. I have just the book." The little old woman stood on her tippy toes and thumbed through a shelf above her head, teetering back and forth. She pulled down an older-looking book. "This should do nicely," she said, handing the book over to Helen.

The worn dust jacket read: *Ward Lock's Red Guide to Western Scotland - Oban, Fort William, Skye, and The Hebrides.* Published January 1, 1970.

"It may be old but I'm sure not much has changed," Mrs. Jewell chuckled.

"Thank you for your help," Helen said as the old woman shuffled past her to another shelf nearby.

She pulled a small leather-bound book down and blew off a layer of dust that made Helen think it must have been there since the bookstore opened. That, or they were just very bad at dusting.

"I think you may find this interesting. It came from an estate in Argyll, just a few miles away from Oban. They had a large sale of books and we happened to win a box lot online years ago. Most of the books in the lot were nice first editions or older rare books that are hard to come by here in the States. But this book never sold. It seems to be a handmade journal of sorts. It might be a nice little travel diary for you on your trip."

Helen looked at the book. It was beautiful. The brown leather was tooled with a fancy flower border that had tiny acorns adorning it. The craftsmanship was meticulous and she couldn't help but think of all the time and effort it must have taken.

Smiling, Helen told the woman she would take both books and headed to the counter to pay.

"Thank you again," Helen said as Mrs. Jewell handed her a bag with the books in them.

"Have fun on your trip and enjoy the beauty of the Highlands! It's one of the most magical places I've traveled to. I'm sure you'll love it. Oh, and don't forget to try their famous Scotch!" Mrs. Jewell said with a bubbly little laugh.

"I'll be sure not to miss that," Helen said, giving her a mischievous smirk as she headed for the door.

Helen arrived home at 3:45 pm. It had been an eventful day and she was exhausted. She turned on the coffee pot and brewed an extra-strong pot of Sumatra to wake herself up. She had a long night of planning ahead of her after all and she needed to be on top of her game.

Kevin showed up at the stroke of five and they sat down at her small kitchen table, on which was laid out one large notepad, a pen, and Helen's laptop.

"Okay, how much did you have in your savings before you bought the cottage?" Kevin asked, getting right down to business. Helen grabbed a bank statement from a large pile of mail on her counter.

"$11,289.82."

"You said you paid $11,001 for the cottage, correct?" Kevin asked, jotting down numbers on the notepad. Helen nodded. "Well, that leaves you with $288.82 plus your next paycheck?"

"Yes, so grand total of $2856.82 is all I have left to my name. Thank God I already paid the rent this month," Helen said jokingly. She didn't know at this point if she should laugh or cry.

"We need to make a list of what you're going to need on this quest of yours," Kevin said, trying to lighten the mood. "First things first, let's see what we can do about finding a reasonable plane ticket."

He grabbed Helen's laptop and flipped it open. After what seemed like hours of clicking through all the normal travel websites, he came across a flight through Celtic Airways for $558 roundtrip, open-ended. The only catch was that it left in less than twenty-four hours.

"This seems to be the best deal. All the other flights are well into the thousands. Think you can pull it off? You have a bunch of time saved up. Just tell Tom it's a family thing and you need a few days off. I'm sure he'll be fine with it seeing how you've never taken a vacation day in your life," Kevin teased.

It was true Helen never took time off, but there was never a reason to. Now that her parents were retired and lived in Florida, they only came to visit on holidays that she normally had off anyways. If they realized what was going on, they would be furious with her. They were pragmatic, well-organized people who were the furthest thing away from spontaneous. There was no way she could go to them with this until she had things more under control.

Their boss, Tom, was a wonderful man and was always very kind to Helen; she knew taking the time off would not be the problem. The real problem lay in the fact that she was scared shitless of stepping outside her comfort zone. Flying halfway around the world by herself and fixing up a cottage in Scotland, where she didn't know a single soul, sounded like a nightmare to her. But there was a spark of excitement that followed the fear and it was just enough to push her into purchasing the ticket.

"What if you come with me? We could make it a sort of adventure," she suggested as she fumbled for her credit card.

"If I had any time left, I would in a heartbeat, but I used up my last few days for my brother's wedding last month."

Kevin had asked Helen to be his plus one for the wedding, but she'd politely declined. She didn't want to risk stepping over the friendship line with him as he was the only true friend she had and she cherished that. She hadn't wanted anything to come between them and feared a wedding may do just that. Plus, relationships were just not in the cards for her right now. So, instead of spending a fun weekend on the Cape with Kevin's family, she'd opted for Netflix and takeout.

As she purchased the ticket and saw that she would be leaving in 23 hours and 18 minutes, her head began to spin with all the things she needed to do in such a short period of time. First of all, she needed to send her boss an email and tell him she would be taking a few days off. Then she would need to go to the bank, cash her paycheck, let them know she was leaving the country, and get a few hundred pounds for petty cash. Lastly, she needed to send William an email letting him know when she was arriving.

"Kevin, can you do me a favor and check in on my apartment and water the plants while I'm gone? Get my mail, that sort of stuff? You know where the key is."

Kevin agreed as he broke open a bag of chips and continued jotting notes down on the pad of paper.

"What are you doing?" Helen asked.

"Writing you a list of everything you're going to need for this adventure. Follow it to the T," Kevin said.

As the night came to a close and they both had gone over the plan a half-dozen times, Kevin decided to head home. Helen walked him out into the cool night air and gave him a hug goodbye. He pulled her close and hugged her back, giving her an extra big squeeze before letting her go.

"Things will be okay. You got this!" Kevin said.

"Thanks for all the help, Kev. It really means a lot to me," she said.

"My pleasure," he said as he stepped backward and bowed. Helen giggled and waved goodbye.

Back inside, she looked over the notepad on the kitchen table. It read:

Essentials For Your Adventure:

1. Plane ticket/passport
2. Suitcase packed with warm clothing/raincoat
3. Cash/credit card
4. William's phone number
5. Toiletries
6. Cottage address
7. Phone and charger
8. Camera
9. Boots
10. Headphones
11. Laptop
12. Snacks for the trip
13. Universal plug-in adapter
14. Have a good time and be open to what may come your way!!

Helen smiled as she read his list. He was a wonderfully organized person; she admired him for that. As much as she tried, her life was a bit of an unorganized mess. She always joked that being in clutter was the only way a real artist could work.

She decided, though, there were a few more items to add to Kevin's list: a drawing pad, pencils, paint, and brushes. If she was going to be traveling to a country with some of the most beautiful landscapes in the world, then she would be taking full advantage of it. Plus it would help her relax and destress a bit while she was there.

She went into her closet and pulled out an old black pull-behind suitcase. Her parents had purchased it for her first solo trip to England to visit her grandparents when she was a teenager. At this point, it was at least ten years old. She dusted off the years of neglect and flung it onto her bed. She unzipped it to find an old tube of chapstick and the smell of her grandparents' house. That trip was the last time she had seen them both before they passed and the smell of their woodstove still clung to the fabric liner. Pushing aside the emotions that opening the suitcase had evoked, she began to fill it with the items on Kevin's list. Before zipping it shut she slipped in the book on Oban and the leather-bound journal from the bookstore. Now, it was time to get some rest. Adventure would be waiting for her with the rising of the sun.

Chapter Three

FEET ON THE GROUND

In nervous anticipation, Helen checked Kevin's list and her bag for what must have been the hundredth time, then stepped off the bus with her worn suitcase and her laptop bag and entered the airport terminal.

Boston International was a chaotic place, full of people rushing in and out, either trying to catch a flight or a cab to hurry them on to their next destination. As soon as she entered, she was swept up in the sea of people, the current taking her toward the check-in aisles.

The check-in went quickly, but the time she spent waiting to board the plane seemed to be ages, long enough to feel the panic she was trying to keep at bay. Just as she was deciding this was beyond crazy and she should turn around and go right home, her phone buzzed in her pocket. It was a message from Kevin.

Hey, Globe Trotter! Happy Travels. I snuck some Dramamine in your laptop bag. Take it when you get on the flight and knock yourself out. It's a long flight and if I know you, you will just sit there working your way up to a complete meltdown before you land. Message me when you are officially a Scot. LOL. But in all seriousness let yourself have a bit of fun. You got this, just think about all the hours you spent watching House Flippers. lol

Helen smiled. It was just what she needed to calm her nerves.

Over the loudspeaker came a woman's voice: "Flight 108 boarding for Glasgow, Scotland, at Gate Ten."

Helen stood and made her way to the gate. She joined the line of travelers with boarding passes in hand as they walked past the flight attendants and boarded the plane.

Four rows from the back and next to the window was her seat. She tucked her laptop bag into her foot space and scooted into her seat. Settling in, she glanced around to see her fellow travelers. An older man in a slate-gray suit sat two rows ahead of her; he had a raspy voice with a thick Italian accent. *Businessman*, she thought as she watched him unfold a laptop and get to work before the flight had even fully boarded. Sitting across the aisle from him was a middle-aged couple. They were obviously tourists with their travel guides and maps laid out on their drink trays. They looked excited, smiles on both their faces as they chatted and pointed at the maps. Helen wished she felt half as excited as they looked. From the two seats in front of her, Helen could make out the beat of dance music. A teenage girl and what looked to be her little sister sat with their headphones on and looked through the safety guides that were tucked into the back of all the seats. A tired-looking woman with a young child no older than two sat to the right of Helen. The baby had the fiercest red hair she'd ever seen. She feared this might be a very long and loud flight if all the things she had been told about redheads were true. However, the baby seemed in good spirits and smiled at Helen as she played with a book.

As the doors closed and the flight attendants stood in the aisle giving their safety speeches, Helen began to feel her heart race, and the panic returned. Her head spun with thoughts about everything that lay ahead of her. It took everything she had to hold back the tears that were welling up inside. *One small bit at a time*, she told herself in an attempt to calm herself down. It did not work. The last time she had taken a long-distance trip was when she was eighteen and she had forgotten how much she disliked flying.

As the plane began to lift off the ground, she searched in her bag for the Dramamine Kevin had slipped into it. Finding the small box at the very bottom, she ripped it open, popped one into her mouth, and chased it down with a bit of water she had left in a bottle in her bag. She hoped it would knock her out as quickly as possible. She laid her head back on the seat and looked out the window, seeing her life below growing smaller and smaller until it was just a blur of grays and blues as she drifted off to sleep.

Helen woke to the cries of the little red-haired baby beside her as the pilot announced their descent. She looked out the window as they broke through the thick cloud cover and saw a lush green landscape peppered with rocks and a few stray houses here and there. Then the green began to fade and the houses grew closer until they merged into a large gray city, Glasgow.

Thankfully the Dramamine started to fade as Helen made her way off the flight. After a long wait in the security line, she made her way down to the baggage claim before heading to the south exit where she was to meet a man who would take her on the journey to Oban. As she neared the exit, she began looking around. Heads bobbed in and out of her view of the far wall where all the drivers were lined with name signs. Down toward the back right corner was a short older man with a brown tweed jacket, green corduroy pants, and a paperboy hat pulled over a thick head of gray hair. He held a tiny sign in his hands that read "Kent." Helen walked over and introduced herself.

"Hello, I'm Helen Kent," she said as she stuck out her hand.

"Henry O'Brien. Nice to meet ye, Ms. Kent. William told me you're an American?" he asked, shaking her hand firmly.

"Yeah, I am, although I lived in Cambridge, England, until I was eight, and then we moved to the States. Hence the slight accent," Helen said, smiling.

"He also said you required an escort to Oban," Henry said, as he grabbed her faded black suitcase and walked out the double doors leading out into the taxi terminal area.

They walked across the street and up one floor of the parking garage. Henry made his way over to a small black Volkswagen parked near the exit and popped open the passenger side door for Helen before putting her bag in the back. As he got into the front seat, he grabbed what looked to be a small gray stone with a hole in its center. It hung from a piece of twine off his rearview mirror. He kissed it.

"For luck," he declared with a wide smile that showed off a gold tooth in the back of his mouth. Helen gave a tiny chuckle. She liked this man already.

As they made their way out of the city onto route A82, they began the drive to Oban. Helen told Henry the story of how she won the cottage in an online auction and how everything happened so quickly she'd had hardly any time to prepare for the trip.

"It's a lovely little cottage," Henry assured her. "I've lived a few miles down the road from it most of my life."

"Oh really? So, you must know all the stories about the area then?" She was eager to hear all about this new place she would be staying at for the next few weeks.

"Oh yes, many stories!"

Henry proved to be the perfect guide, and she enjoyed the lively conversation and stories he had to share about the areas they drove through. He considered himself an amateur historian so the conversation was endless as they made their way toward their destination. She felt quite comfortable with him and his sweet grandfather-like charm. Henry was the kind of person who you felt like you had known for years after only being around him for a short while. Helen was grateful that William had sent a friend to take her to Oban and not some random Uber driver.

Coming upon Loch Lomond, Henry decided to stop in the small town of Luss so they could stretch their legs and grab a bite to eat. It was past lunch and Helen looked in need of a bit of food. He brought her to a cute little place near the loch called The Coach House and they ordered coffee and sandwiches. As they waited for their food, Helen looked out over the beautiful town. The houses were mostly made of gray fieldstone and adorned with window boxes full of flowers. Separating each yard were either well-groomed hedges or stone walls with thin, velvety moss filling each crack and crevice. The roads were small and gentle looking, like little black streams that weaved their way around the town, unlike the four-lane highways she was accustomed to. Things seemed simple here: no large buildings or busy chain stores, just small family-run shops and eateries amidst the houses, working together. It felt almost like stepping back to a time when things were simple and life moved at a slower pace.

When their food arrived, Helen had not realized how hungry she was. As a matter of fact, she didn't even realize what time it was. In the daze of the Dramamine hangover and the excitement, she had completely forgotten about the time change. As she relished every bite of the delicious cheddar and onion sandwich, she began to realize that ever since she'd stepped out of the airport and into the Scottish air, she felt a bit different, like something in her was waking up. There was something about this place that just felt right to her.

Henry broke her contemplation by asking if she would like to walk down to see the loch before they got back into the Volkswagen and headed on to Oban. They finished up lunch and paid the bill before making their way down the cobbled stone street that led to the loch.

"This loch is one of the most beautiful in all of Scotland," Henry said, looking out over the long, dark loch that sat cradled in between the hilled landscape. At the shoreline was a long stone wall that created a nice place to rest or sit upon while enjoying the view. The body of water was so large it was difficult to tell where it began or ended.

"My granny was born and died here. Me and my brothers used to visit in the summers, ye know? My granda loved scaring us wi' the tale of a monster, like a huge crocodile, that lived in the loch," Henry said as he looked out over the water.

"Did he succeed?" Helen asked.

"Scared the hell right out of us," he answered with a laugh. Helen chuckled.

There was a cool mist coming off the loch, creating a low fog that almost sat upon the water. She could see where a tale like that in a place like this would be scary for a young boy. They sat and took in the view in silence for a few more minutes until Henry patted her on the shoulder and suggested they get back on the road.

Walking back up to where the car was parked, they passed a stone house completely covered in moss on the north-facing side. It was a bit smaller than all the others on the street and stood out with its bright fern-green door. A small black sign hung over the door with golden letters that read "Luibh-eòlaiche."

"What's that place?" Helen asked as she slowed her pace and pointed over to the small cottage.

"Oh, that's the local herbalist," Henry answered. "Most towns in this area have one. It's a bit of a tradition. A lot of us older generations still believe in the ways of the cunning folk."

"Cunning folk?" Helen echoed.

"Oh, my wee American, you have much to learn," Henry said, laughing his big belly laugh as they found their way to the car.

Helen took one more glance back over her shoulder at the little shop as they got into the car and drove out of town.

Chapter Four

OBAN

For a number of miles, the A82 became a small ribboning road along the loch's shore. There were several times when Helen caught herself gripping the edge of the seat tightly as a tour bus whizzed by, pushing Henry's small car close to the jagged cliff-side of the narrow roadway. The car trip stretched out over another hour or so. Henry regaled Helen with tales of his youth and the wondrous adventures he had with William, who turned out to be Henry's cousin. Helen liked listening to him speak in his thick Scottish brogue; it made her feel at ease.

As they neared their destination, he pointed out some of the more notable landmarks.

"If you look over there, you'll see Oban coming into view. Oban was founded in 1794 when our famous distillery was opened. Best whiskey in the Highlands. It was home to lonely fishermen and a few merchants before the distillery came and modernized the town. Now we're a travel destination and our summers are filled with the hustle and bustle of busy tourists, but our winters are calm and peaceful once everyone finds it too cold here. Gives us time to rejuvenate and go back to our simpler ways. Thank heavens for that," he said, turning a wide corner that took them onto the main route into town.

The first stretch of the town was a cluster of buildings all adjoined in a 1960s fashion with their drab gray brick and basic architecture. As they pulled onto George Street, the road that bordered the Sound of Kerrera, the buildings became older, the brickwork meticulous and made for beauty rather than square footage. The village framed the bay's edge with its quaint shops and eateries while the fishing boats and sailing vessels peppered the azure water.

Henry slowed down and found a parking spot by the side of a large white building. It was a plain but very beautiful old inn made of what looked to be plaster over stone. A sign on the face of the building with fine print read "Oban Inn Est. 1790." The inn had been painted snow white with black trim outlining its windows and doors, giving the building a dramatic look that made it stand out. There was a grouping of tables and chairs for people to dine and drink at as they looked out over the water in front of the inn. This was where Helen was to meet a lawyer named David Loft, hired by William to make up the final paperwork and handle the affairs of the estate sale.

Helen and Henry found their way over to a clean table facing the water. Henry went into the inn to acquire a couple of pints of beer to enjoy while they waited.

Helen decided it would be a good time to call Kevin and let him know she had arrived safe and sound. The phone rang three times and then went to voicemail. Doing a quick calculation in her head she realized that it was still quite early in Massachusetts.

"Hey Kev, I'm here in bonnie Scotland. So far so good. I have a wonderful guide who's getting me a pint of beer as we speak. I'll try you again in a few days. No worrying about me if I don't call right away. I have no idea what the cell reception will be like around here. I'm going to be just fine. I think Scotland suits me."

Henry came back with two pints and it wasn't long before David Loft arrived. Dressed in a nice suit and with a sharp haircut, he certainly looked the part of a lawyer, Helen thought.

"Hello, you must be Ms. Kent. Hi, Henry," he said, sticking out his hand in greeting to Helen and giving Henry a nod.

"Yes, nice to meet you, Mr. Loft," she said, giving his hand a firm shake. They both sat down.

"I have a few things for you to sign and wanted to go over a few items written in the deed," he said as he looked over a stack of paperwork he'd taken out of a large brown briefcase. He placed a handful of papers in front of Helen. They consisted of a few legal documents for the purchase of the cottage and the deed to the house and land. "Now, it has a few quirks. The deed reads that the cottage sits on fifty-two acres of land adjacent to the McKenzie farm. The land is not to be farmed by anyone other than the McKenzie family. They have farmed the cottage's land for centuries and hold those rights. The other stipulation is that it not be divided up and sold for land. I had them turn the electricity and gas on, but the phone won't be hooked up until next week," he said, pointing at the places for her to sign.

"I think that all sounds simple enough. I believe I can manage," Helen said as she signed the papers and gave Mr. Loft a smile.

"It's been sitting empty for nearly five years now, so it's in a bit of disrepair. It comes fully furnished and has a very lovely garden.

Once it's been weeded and given some TLC, I think you'll find it's quite a beautiful little place," said Mr. Loft.

"Can I ask you a question? Why did no one here buy it? Why did it end up on an online auction?" Helen asked as she took a swig of the cold beer.

"Well, you have to understand that people in these parts are very superstitious and there's a bit of history with the place. It's said to have once been owned by a woman who communed with the fairies and that the house is still visited by them."

"Fairies? Aren't they harmless little pixies that like to roam in the woodland and hide under rocks? Why would anyone be scared of them?" Helen asked.

"Oh no, my dear, most fairies are evil creatures that are only self-serving and bring about destruction wherever they go. Fairies are not to be trifled with," Henry interjected in a very serious tone.

"You're kidding me, right? I won that auction because no one in this town would buy that cottage even being dirt cheap because of some made-up fairytale?" Helen laughed.

Henry and Mr. Loft looked at each other with worry in their eyes as Helen piled the papers up in front of her.

"Henry, why don't you take Ms. Kent to the shop for a few essentials and then over to the cottage to settle in?" Mr. Loft said, handing a key over to Henry. "I think I have everything I need to send back to William. I hope you enjoy your new home and find many years of happiness there." He shook Helen's hand again and loaded up his briefcase with the papers. Giving Henry a pat on the shoulder, Mr. Loft turned and walked down the street, disappearing into a group of tourists taking pictures in front of the water.

"He's right. You're going to need a few things before we head out. Let's pop into the shop around the corner before we leave,"

Henry said to Helen as they stood up and pushed in their chairs.

They walked two blocks down, weaving in and out of bustling tourists, then entered a small grocery shop with a mini hardware section and a small pharmacy. At the front of the store, an older woman in a baggy shift dress stood at a cash register that looked straight out of the 1950s. She seemed to be skeptical of everyone who walked in the door, sizing them up to see if they were a potential thief or pickpocket. It was an all-in-one kind of shop, a place where you could find just about anything you might be looking for. It reminded Helen of an old 5&10 shop down the road from her grandparents' house in Vermont. She used to beg them to take her there when she came up to visit. She loved that little shop and all the fun treasures she found there. Once, her grandfather bought her a Jacob's ladder toy and she remembered playing with it the entire trip. This shop was very similar and smelled of licorice and pine just as the one in Vermont had.

Henry grabbed a basket and began throwing things into it. A pack of candles, a box of matches, toilet paper, a loaf of bread, a block of cheese, a small bag of sugar, and a box of tea. Helen added a bag of coffee, a flashlight, a chocolate bar, paper towels, and a roll of trash bags. Henry looked at her and smiled.

"Is that all you're going to eat, a chocolate bar?" he asked.

She thought twice about her choices and decided to add a box of cereal, a couple of boxes of pasta, and a jar of sauce.

"That should do it!" she said, throwing him a smile.

As they checked out, the old woman looked them up and down as though questioning if they had stuffed their pockets with goods while her back was turned.

"Hello Nina, how's yer day going?" Henry asked. She just looked at him and scoffed. Not saying more than she had to, the old woman asked for twenty-eight pounds. She frowned at Helen as she paid and said thank you.

"Don't let her bother you, she's grumpy like that with everyone," Henry said as they made their way back to the car.

Driving back through the town, Helen could imagine what this place looked like before it had been modernized and turned into a tourist trap. She spotted a structure on top of the hill that overlooked the town. It almost resembled the Roman Colosseum, in its large round structure and columns that reached into the sky.

"What is that?" she said, pointing a finger up at the large ruin on top of the hill in front of them.

"Oh, that's McCaig's Tower on Battery Hill. It's quite fascinating, a giant of a thing. Would you like to go and get a better look at it?" Henry offered.

Helen would have loved to explore the site, but she could feel the jet lag setting in.

"Thanks, but I think we should save it for later, don't you? Don't want to get all my sightseeing done in one day. Plus, I'm beat," she said, staring out the window at the enormous monument.

As they left the town, the houses became more spaced apart and the landscape opened up into rolling hills of the most beautiful shades of green. The artist in her tried to seize the imagery in her mind so that she could remember the way the colors melted and folded into one another. Maybe someday, if she was lucky, she would be able to capture it on canvas.

The winding road stretched out as far as the eye could see, and the large hill before them was speckled with sheep grazing, creating a polka-dot look to the landscape. Helen gazed upon the beauty as they drove, feeling the mounting excitement of the adventure that lay ahead. However, her excitement slowly turned to unease as they drove farther and farther away from Oban.

"How far away is my cottage exactly?" Helen asked.

"Oh, it's quite far, about sixteen miles. Don't worry, I'll come and check on you in a few days. I live just over that next hill there." Henry pointed, giving her a smile that was supposed to be reassuring.

But Helen sat back with a pit in her stomach. Maybe it was the beer or not enough sleep that was taking over, but the thought of being trapped in a house she didn't know and too far away to walk into town was terrifying to her. Then it happened, the rush of reality hit her. The excitement of being in a new country and the company of Henry had kept her from thinking about the altogether life-changing decision she had so hastily made. It had taken her almost five years to save all that money and she'd planned to use it for a down payment in the coming fall. That seemed like a lifetime ago now. Everything had changed. All her "life plans" were now completely thrown off course and she had to be here in another country fixing the mess she had gotten herself into.

But she was (usually) a rational person. She knew there was no use getting upset about what was already done. She needed to focus on the task ahead, getting the cottage fixed up, back on the market, and getting home.

Chapter Five

A NEW WORLD

They crested a large hill and as they made their descent, Henry announced, "There she is, Fernbeg, your wee cottage."

Helen looked down at the most enchanting place she had ever seen.

There, at the bottom of a lush green hill, was a little white stone cottage sitting snug in its valley. It looked out over rolling fields and then upon a loch reaching out to the sea. As they drove closer, she could see the little stone walls that bordered the lawn of the house, or what they called the garden. The sight of it made her breath catch in her throat, leaving her speechless.

Henry pulled into the small stone driveway and parked the car. As Helen opened her door and stood with both feet firmly planted on the ground, the wind picked up and blew around her in a spiral gale as if to say hello and welcome her.

Henry grabbed her bags out of the car and walked them to a short front gate that led to the garden path which in turn led to the front door. Helen grabbed her bag of groceries from the backseat and slowly followed. She took it all in, from the flat fieldstone she walked on to the moss lining the stone wall that bordered the house. The gate had once been a pale blue, but the paint had worn off, leaving the thin wood grain peeking its way through after being hidden away for years. It looked old and tattered, yet it was alluring in its own way. The garden was in ruins and not much was visible other than weeds and overgrowth; however, there was the most delightful grouping of ferns around the border of the inner walls. The ferns must have been deliberately placed as they were planted there in rows, hence the name of the cottage, she assumed.

The cottage was also in disarray. The paint was chipped on the stone and the trim was worn and rotting in spots. The shutters were either hanging from only one hinge or altogether missing. But the roof looked good; the gray slate with its light green moss growing in the cracks of each shingle seemed sturdy and unwavering. There was an overgrown bush of ivy growing up the side of the cottage and knitting its way across to the front door. Helen liked the way it looked; it gave the place a kind of charm.

Henry set the bags down in front of the fern-green front door and turned to Helen, handing her the key.

"Here ye go, my dear. It's bad luck for someone other than the new owner to open the front door for the first time."

Smiling at Henry, Helen took the key and stepped forward. It was large and made of old brass with an intricate Celtic knot design at the top. Almost like the old skeleton keys in The Hardy Boys or Nancy Drew novels. As she inserted the key and turned the lock, a bolt of energy shot up her arm and into her body. Stunned, she jumped back and dropped it onto the ground.

"Oh my God, what was that?" she cried out. Henry rushed to her side.

"What happened?" he asked.

"I stuck the key into the lock and when I turned it, it felt like a bolt of lightning went up my arm and into my chest," Helen said as she bent down to grab the key off the ground, her body still ringing with the energy.

"Oh, these old houses. Sometimes you can pick up a bit of static electricity in this kind of weather. You might have gotten a bit of a shock from the doorknob," Henry said, looking at the house apprehensively.

With a bit of hesitation, Helen grabbed for the doorknob a second time but before she had the chance the door creaked open on its own.

Feeling a cold chill run down the base of her neck, she pushed the door open wide and walked inside. Fumbling around for a light switch, she finally found one on the entryway wall and turned it on. The bulbs buzzed overhead and the house seemed to wake from a long slumber. The hum of electricity echoed in the house as she stepped through the sitting room and into the kitchen, looking around.

The kitchen was quite large with wooden floors that looked as if they had come from a shipwreck, all water-stained and battered. The inner stone walls were white-washed and filled with dark wooden shelves and a few cupboards. In the center of the longest wall was a large stone fireplace with a kettle hook and bread door. A sizable, dark wooden table with two chairs at each end and long benches on each side was set directly in the center of the room, creating a place to eat and prepare food. It looked as if it could easily seat ten people. There were exposed beams with cast iron pots and pans hanging from them along with bundles of dried herbs and flowers so thick with dust and cobwebs they looked a hundred years old. In a far corner was a very old refrigerator that Helen doubted even worked and there was one small counter on the front wall with a window over an enamel sink. Helen walked over and looked out onto a view of the valley that led to the loch. A chill of excitement ran down her spine in anticipation of adventures to come.

Henry walked in behind her and set her bags down. "I see you've found the heart of the house."

Helen smiled back. "Yes, I guess I have. Now let's hope the rest of the house looks as good as this room."

However, that was not the case. Each room they inspected seemed a little worse off than the last. First was the bathroom which, upon entering, they could tell had at least one leaky pipe from the amount of water on the floor. Then came the small sitting room, where the plaster had begun to come off the ceiling in spots. One of the floorboards was broken, leaving a hole the size of a basketball in the floor, and the window to the back of the room was broken. The bedroom was no better. Broken floorboards and another cracked window awaited them along with a bird's nest on the top of the dresser and what looked to be some critter's bed in the other corner of the room.

The tour was beginning to depress Helen. Room after room was in such bad disrepair that she knew she'd need outside help to fix it.

Henry took her to the last room in the back of the house. The door was shut but a thin stream of light seeped through the cracks and painted the edges of the door as if they were lined with gold. Helen opened the door and the two of them peered in, amazed.

It looked as if the room had not been touched by the hands of time. The walls were lined from floor to ceiling with bookshelves packed tight with books. The wall to the left of the door held two large bookcases with a stone fireplace sitting neatly between them. The mantel had the same beautiful Celtic design as the key, delicately carved so that it became the focal point. In the center of the room facing the fireplace were two overstuffed emerald velvet chairs. Their backs had the appearance of half-open clamshells and their big armrests looked to be perfectly placed for elbows holding books. The setting sun cast a golden glow in through the two large windows on the far wall. It gave the room a magical feel and everything seemed to shine and sparkle where the light touched.

Unlike everything else in the house with its layers of dust and cobwebs, this room seemed untouched. It looked as if it had been cleaned yesterday and was awaiting an important guest. It was very odd, Helen thought, but she attributed it to the fact that the door had been closed and it must not have gotten as much airflow and dirt blown in as the other rooms that were exposed to the elements from the broken windows and the holes in the floors. Whatever the explanation, Helen was just relieved it was not another room in major disrepair.

"Well, look at this!" Henry said in amazement as he squeezed past Helen and walked around, gazing up at the hundreds of books lining every empty space on all four walls. "There must be over five hundred books in here, it's magnificent!"

The shelves were lined with a variety of books, some of which appeared to be quite old and others newer.

"How can it look like it was just used yesterday? Hasn't this place been unoccupied for five years?" Helen asked, removing a book from a shelf and running her finger over the top ridge, inspecting it for dust. Nothing.

"I would say fairy magic," Henry said. "These hills are well known as being home to the fae. And like I told you earlier, this house has a history with them."

"All this fairy magic seems like complete nonsense to me. Do you really believe in all that?"

"Well, it may be nonsense to you. But I do very much believe. I've seen the workings of fairy magic with my own eyes when I was a wee boy. One of my father's prized workhorses had taken ill and the vet said they couldn't save the poor creature. Without this horse, my father's farm wouldn't be able to be worked and to get another horse adjusted to the farm would take weeks. Being autumn and harvest season, there was no time. As it lay on its deathbed in the stables, an old woman came to my father's door. She said she could save the horse but that the healing of one would mean the demise of another. My father thought it was a small price to pay to lose another one of the farm animals if it meant she could save the horse and his livelihood. So he took her to the horse and she gave him a tonic held in a small glass vial. She told my father to walk the horse out into the field and let him stay there through the night. He needed the moonlight for the tonic to fully work. My father did as he was told and by the next day, the horse was fully recovered. But my mother took ill with polio and never walked again. You see, the old woman had made a deal with a fairy, and it tainted her magic. From that point on all her magical healing powers were stained with darkness and my poor mum was the first to find that out," Henry said as he pulled a worn copy of *The Great Gatsby* off one of the shelves and fanned through its pages.

He placed the book back on the shelf and walked to the large window at the far end of the room, continuing, "After that, she stayed hidden away not wanting to hurt anyone else. For each ray of light, darkness would come with it, and that was the curse she carried from meddling with fairy magic. Some people in town called her a healer, others called her a witch. Maybe she was a bit of both. She owned this house once, and when she died she willed it to her niece who lived here until she passed of old age. This house is said to have been passed down from generation to generation of Darrow women for over four hundred years until there were none alive to pass it down to. Now it's yours, my dear. I think you'll bring the light it's needed for many years."

"Oh Henry, your poor mother. That's awful," Helen said.

Henry gave her a gentle squeeze on the shoulder and they walked out of the library and back into the kitchen.

"Do you have everything you need for the next day or two?" he asked.

"I think so," she answered, looking over at the bag of groceries and her two bags sitting atop the kitchen table.

"I double-checked that the stove had gas and that the water is on. The phone should be connected in the next few days. I'll come back to see how you're doing in a day or two. The McKenzie farm is just on the other side of the hill if you have an emergency."

Helen walked him out into the garden and waved goodbye as he got into his car and headed back on the road toward town. It was now dusk, and she watched him for as long as she could see the lights of the little car in the distance. Once he was out of view she turned and walked back into the house.

Now that the sun had gone down, the stone walls of the house began to cool and the cold seeped in. Not being adept at starting a fire, she rummaged in her bag for a thick sweatshirt and a warmer pair of socks. Thank goodness Kevin had reminded her it would be damp and cool here this time of year and had added warm clothing to the list. Thinking of Kevin, she checked her phone to see if she had missed any calls from him.

"No service, damn. I guess I won't be needing you around here then," she said to her phone as she placed it face down on the large kitchen table.

Once she was snug in her extra layers, Helen decided to make herself a cup of tea and have a bit of bread before bed. Jet lag had fully set in and she was ready to crash. She walked around the kitchen, looking in each cupboard for where the mugs were hiding. The first one she opened had three cans of kidney beans, one can of sweetcorn, and four cans of peas, along with a half-full box of pasta. She pulled one of the cans down from the shelf to inspect it; the expiration date read best by 3/2004. *Not going to risk that unless I get really hungry*, she thought as she put the can back into the cupboard.

The second was full of herbs in mason jars and spices in small shakers. She found six small, hand-thrown mugs in the cupboard beside the hearth. They were glazed in earth tones of greens, browns, and sky blues. As she took them out one by one she saw they fit together like an extended painting and the glazes created the exact landscape that she saw through the kitchen window. *Oh wow, I wonder if the woman who lived here before me created these?* They were too intimate to be made by anyone other than someone with great appreciation for this very spot, Helen thought.

Deciding on the mug that showed the dip in the valley where the mountains met the sea, she grabbed the kettle and went to fill it at the sink. When she turned on the tap the pipes moaned and spit and then a rusty-colored liquid came out into the sink basin. After a few minutes of running, the water turned clear and she felt safe pouring it into the kettle. Then she tried to turn on the stove; three attempts without even a spark. It was an old thing, the kind you needed a match to light the burners, she guessed. *Ah, hence the matches Henry grabbed. Clever man*, she thought. Taking the matches out of the bag and praying she didn't blow herself and the cottage up, she struck a match, and with a pop and burst of blue flame, the stove was alight.

As she sat and waited for the water to boil in the ancient-looking tea kettle, she wondered what it would have been like to live here back in the days without electricity or modern conveniences. She had always felt as if she should have been born in a simpler time. She liked solitude and the gratification of doing something "the old-fashioned way." Her mother used to pick on her when she was a young girl saying, "You're an old soul, Helen."

When they lived in Cambridge, she was always in the garden playing or sitting under the large oak tree reading a book while the kids from her school played at the local park. Making friends was never easy for her, but that was okay because she didn't mind being alone. Things didn't change much when they moved; her accent and being a shy child left her the outcast once again, and while all the other neighborhood kids were out at the local swimming pool or the ice cream shop, she was home with her books and art supplies.

As she grew older, she came out of her shell a little more but preferred the shadows. In high school, she was the nerdy girl who was always in the art room and spent more time with her dog than the kids her own age. She couldn't see how they had time for such insignificant things like dances and sports games. There was so much to learn and so many new pieces of artwork to create. She had always felt a void, a longing for something unknown to her. She was missing something but just didn't know what it was. Art somehow brought her closer to understanding why she felt the way she did.

Now, as an adult, she found herself still looking on from the outside, always the weird girl who would rather spend time with her paint and canvases than with people. Avoiding parties and happy hours. *Maybe this will be good for me, maybe being out here away from people will help me gain a new perspective so that I can put myself back out there more. Time to think about what I really want to do when I fix this place up and sell it,* she thought.

The kettle let out its rapid howl of a whistle, startling Helen out of her deep thoughts and back into the damp kitchen. Getting up from the table, she poured herself a cup of tea, her first cup of tea in the first house she had ever owned. At that moment she felt a deep connection, rooted in the soil the tiny cottage sat upon. A feeling of knowing, a feeling that could only be described as home.

Chapter Six

FERNBEG

The first night in the cottage was a long and cold one. Helen decided not to sleep in the bedroom with the broken window, fearing that the critter whose home lay in the corner may come back to spend the night. Instead, she slept on the small floral couch in the living room. It was awkwardly lumpy and smelled of mildew. But even when she had settled, the cold kept her awake along with skittering sounds coming from the bedroom. She didn't want to come across whatever was roaming the back rooms of the house so she didn't move from the sitting room until morning. The stone house was drafty with all its broken windows and floors and she was chilled to the bone when she woke from her uncomfortable slumber.

She took to the kitchen as soon as she was up and put on the kettle to make some instant coffee, not her first choice but the only thing they sold at the local shop. She would have much rather been drinking her favorite Green Mountain coffee, but it was better than nothing.

As she tried to enjoy the semi-palatable cup of coffee, she took out a pad of paper and pen and began to write a list of the things that needed to be fixed. She broke it down into two categories, things she could fix herself and things she would need to hire someone else to do.

Things I can do:

1. Paint the gate, trim, and outer and inner walls
2. Fix hinges on cupboard doors
3. Weed garden and flower beds
4. Refinish some of the more worn furniture
5. Put something over the broken windows
6. Get a fire going

Things that need to be hired out:

1. Fix broken floorboards
2. Fix leaky pipes
3. Fix rotting outer trim
4. Fix shutters
5. Fix side stairs
6. Fix broken windows
7. Find someone to catch animal living in my bedroom

The list was not looking in her favor, so she decided that she would try and fix the things she could and ask Henry about finding someone to help with the others. As for today, at the top of her list was getting something over the broken windows and learning how to start a fire to heat up the cottage. At this point, she could see her breath and her bulky sweatshirt was not enough to keep her warm.

Helen zipped up her jacket, slipped on her boots, and dug out a knitted hat from her bag, pulling it down over her dark hair. She opened the front door and stepped out into the crisp air. Autumn was slowly working its way into the coastline.

There was the faint smell of salt from the sea in the heavy, dewed air and a thin layer of fog hovered over the grass and traveled its way down the valley to the loch. The thick gray clouds foretold little chance that the sun would be out to help warm the house.

Helen looked around. The cottage was tucked into a fold of the land with fields all around. There were no trees in the yard that might have dropped a few branches to use as kindling, so she walked down her small driveway and around the stone wall searching for a woodpile the previous owner might have left. Walking her way completely around the house, she found nothing but discovered a small pull-behind cart. One of the wheels was a tad flat and the handle had been bent at an odd angle, but it would do. She looked in both directions to decide what woodland area looked the closest and decided on the small patch of trees off to the east that bordered an old stone wall. The trees looked considerably older and a bit more haggard. This left Helen thinking she might find more fallen branches there than the patch of trees to the north that looked to be younger saplings.

She seized the cart by its bent handle and slowly began walking toward the trees. The cart started to feel a bit heavy as she tugged it up the hill toward the woodland. It wasn't long before she broke a sweat and the heat from the workout took her chills away. Winded, she stopped, turning around to see that she was about halfway between the cottage and the tree line. She guessed the trees were a mile away but with the amount of time she had been walking and the fact they didn't seem much closer than when she started, she feared she had a dreadful sense of distance.

Finally, after what seemed to be hours of walking but had only really been twenty-five minutes, she arrived at the small patch of trees. Stopping at the tree line, she let go of the cart and propped herself against it to catch her breath. Just as she had hoped, there was an ample amount of small twigs and branches littering the ground. However, no large limbs were there to be harvested. This posed a problem, as the small twigs and branches would burn up quickly and would not do much for heating the cottage.

Looking up into the webbing of branches, she spotted a long-dead branch hanging almost low enough for her to jump up and break off. It looked to be at least five feet long and was thick enough not to burn up quickly. After several failed attempts, the branch hovered just a foot higher than she could reach. Feeling defeated, she sat at the base of the tree and rested her head in her hands.

If only it was just a bit lower, I could have gotten it. Maybe if the wind blows, it could knock it free. Come on wind, blow! she thought as she picked her head up and looked at the branch once again.

Just then she heard the low moan of wind making its way through the woods. The leaves began to rustle and the trees swayed and creaked. A small whirlwind whipped leaves and dust up around her as it built up speed and blew more ferociously. Helen looked up into the canopy of branches and feared one might break free and strike her. Abandoning the cart, she ran out into the field, the wind propelling her forward until she was safely out of reach of the trees. Just as she turned to look back at the wooded area, the old dead branch broke free and fell to the ground, breaking into five large pieces on impact. Then, just as suddenly as it had come, the wind stopped.

Helen cautiously walked over into the wooded area to inspect what had just occurred. She stood looking at the broken branch scattered across the ground in amazement. It was as if the wind had heard her and answered back. *No, that's not possible. It was purely a coincidence, a fluke,* she thought. Grabbing for the cart, she began loading it with chunks of the heavy dead wood and twigs. Once it was full to the point of being almost too heavy to pull, she started back to the cottage.

It took over an hour to make it back since the overweight cart was difficult to operate with one wheel so low on air. She had to take multiple breaks to adjust the wheel and catch her breath. By the time she reached the garden gate, she was more than warm enough from the workout and decided to leave the wood in the cart until a bit later. She was hungry and in need of water more than heat at that moment.

Inside, she opened the bag of groceries from the shop and began taking them out one at a time, looking over what she had to eat and deciding what cupboard was best for keeping the food safe from mice. *Add to the list of things to do: get mouse traps!* She decided on a dry bowl of cereal and went on another search in the kitchen for bowls. *This kitchen keeps getting bigger and bigger, I swear. I don't remember this many cupboards when we first arrived, but I guess I wasn't searching through them at the time* she thought as she clambered around.

Finally, she came across the bowls in a cupboard to the side of the sink. When she pulled a bowl down, she saw a thin black leather notebook resting on the back wall of the cupboard. Standing on her tiptoes, she grabbed the edge of the book and dragged it closer. A thick layer of dust came with it, causing her to sneeze and her eyes to water. Setting the dusty notebook aside, she decided to eat out of the box instead and save the notebook for some light reading later since there wasn't much else to do here in the cottage with no TV or internet come evening.

Finishing up her unsubstantial meal, Helen decided that her next task would be to find something to cover the two broken windows. *Cardboard would do nicely*, she thought. She went into the small living room where she remembered seeing a box next to the fireplace filled with old newspapers. Removing the pile of worn, yellowed newspapers from the box, she inspected it and decided it was inadequate, much too small for the window in the bedroom. As she bent down to deposit the papers back into the box, she noticed a headline on the front cover of one of the papers. It read: "Maoth Blair Farm, the story of 5 generations." There was a picture above the headline of a large rolling field. She was sure she'd seen the same field stretching into the distance beyond the trees where she'd got the wood. *That must be the McKenzies'* she thought. Interested in knowing a bit more about her neighbors, she took the paper with her to the lumpy floral sofa. Wading through the long article, she came across a passage that made her breath quicken.

From father to son, this farm has been passed down through 500 years of history. It has seen feast, famine, multiple monarchs, and even the infamous Oban Witch Trials of 1597. It is said that the McKenzie family harbored an accused witch in their sheep barn, but despite their attempts to hide the woman, she was found and brought to her untimely demise by the cruel hysteria of the time.

"Witches! Of course, because fairies weren't enough," Helen said out loud to herself, with a laugh that was only partly sparked by humor. Every time things of this manner were mentioned, she felt uncomfortable.

The amount of history each house here held seemed so unreal. Most of them being hundreds of years old and passed down through generations, there were bound to be many stories. The building she lived in back home was built in the late eighties and had little history at all. There were no stories her building could tell other than the middle-aged couple with their weekly fights and the older woman in apartment 3b that liked to sunbathe naked on the roof.

She put the paper down and walked over to the stone fireplace. Where most modern living rooms might have a flat-screen television as the focal point, here the room was centered around the cool gray stone of the hearth, skillfully laid more than a hundred years ago. When she touched it, she could feel a sort of energy pulsating in the stones as if to greet her, welcome her. Even though the house was cold, worn down, and in disrepair, she started to sense something that she hadn't noticed the first time she walked in. It was a feeling of familiarity, almost as if she'd run into an old friend long forgotten until their unexpected meeting. The cottage was small and far away from the village and people, but Helen felt safe within its sturdy stone walls.

A low whistle of wind blew through the house. She felt the cool air making its way in through the broken windows and cracks in the floors, as though the house was breathing.

Helen soon again felt the chill setting in. Now was the time to fix those windows and start a fire.

Chapter Seven

HOUSEGUEST

Making her way back into the kitchen, she assessed the items she had on hand and decided on using the trash bags on the broken windows. She knew it wouldn't keep the cold out or the heat in, but it would at least block a bit of the draft that seemed to be spreading. She searched the kitchen for something to secure the bags when she came across a small drawer full of miscellaneous things.

"Well, I'll be, even the Scots have junk drawers," she joked to herself. Rooting through the mess of odds and ends, she found a small tin full of tacks. *This will do,* she thought as she pocketed the tin and headed for the bedroom with trash bags in hand.

Upon entering the bedroom, Helen let out a startled scream when she witnessed something quickly make its way from the heap of bedding and books on the floor to underneath the bed on the far wall. It went too fast for her to make out what kind of animal it was, but whatever it was, it was much larger than a mouse.

Taking a step back into the hallway, she grabbed for the broom and waited to see if the animal would reappear, thinking she had left. She waited for what seemed to be a good ten minutes when finally she saw movement coming from the front corner of the lacy bed skirt. At first, only a small black nose poked out, sniffing the air, using its nose rather than its eyes to determine whether the intruder was gone. Helen lifted the broom above her head, preparing to hit the creature if it came toward her. Then, cautiously, the little critter came out from under the bed and made its grand appearance.

Helen's face lit up when she saw what it was, and she slowly lowered the broom and tucked it back into its resting place in the corner of the hallway. Standing there in the middle of the bedroom was a small, wiry gray dog. The poor thing was skin and bones and didn't look much older than six months, still just a pup. Well, that certainly explained the skittering she'd heard and the messes she had found in a few of the rooms.

Slowly, Helen bent down and stuck her hand out for him to sniff. He looked at her with fear and backed away, tucking himself back under the bed again. She walked into the kitchen and came back in with a small piece of bread. The dog popped his head back out from under the bed and sniffed the air in her direction. Smelling the food, he slowly made his way back out.

"Hey there little guy. You poor thing, you look utterly dreadful. How long has it been since you've eaten? You're nothing but skin and bones," she said softly as she bent down and outstretched her hand with the bread in it. He cautiously moved toward her and took the bread from her hand. "Let's go get you some more to eat," she said, standing back up and walking into the kitchen. The small dog gingerly followed, making sure there was still an ample distance between them.

Once in the kitchen, Helen took out an old chipped bowl from the cupboard and filled it with water, placing it on the floor next to the table. Then she sliced some cheese and broke some bread into small chunks while the wiry dog sat in the kitchen doorway sniffing the air above its head. She put the bread and cheese into a second bowl and placed it beside the water. It only took a few seconds before the dog had his head in it and did not come up for air until every last piece was gone.

Helen sat and watched the dog eat and wondered how he'd come to be here. The cottage was miles from other houses and way too far from town for it to be a stray. *Curious*, she thought. When the dog had finished, he approached Helen and gave her hand a tender lick as if to say thank you.

Helen had always had a soft spot for dogs. She remembered when she was thirteen bringing home a stray she had found behind the movie theater in town. Her mother was furious when she found it hiding in Helen's room, but her father talked her into letting Helen keep it. Sheba was a wonderful dog, her constant companion, and they shared many adventures together.

But there is a sadness that comes with owning a dog since they don't live nearly long enough. Helen remembered the day they had to put Sheba down. It was the day before she left for college. She had started having issues with her backend and that night she lost the use of her back legs and was no longer able to stand. Helen couldn't bring herself to go with her father to the vet, so she gave the dog a hug and kiss in the car, and then her father drove off with her. It was something she still felt guilty about to this day. Helen's heart broke. She couldn't stand how empty and lifeless the house felt without Sheba in it. She carried the loss with her for years and decided to never own another dog again. Just another confirmation to her that love always led to heartache.

Yet here she was, in a cottage in Scotland with another stray in need of her help. She could never turn it away. She reached down to give the dog a pet, but he stepped back, still timid.

"It's okay, boy, take your time. I'm not going anywhere," she said, pulling her hand back and getting up from the chair.

The windows still needed to be fixed before any more cool air ventured into the cottage. As she walked back to the bedroom, the dog slowly followed her. She managed to tack the trash bags up tight enough that the window frame was sufficiently blocked from a good portion of the wind that was streaming through. Then she began picking up the room. She lifted the overturned nightstand, picked up the pieces of broken glass from the window, dusted off the bureau, and cleaned up the pile of bedding the dog had been sleeping on. Once the room was clean and the floor swept, it looked fine enough to sleep in. She found a spare set of sheets and blankets in the closet so that she was able to make the bed to sleep in for that night. The dog watched her closely from the doorway while she worked.

Once Helen had finished cleaning, she decided to go outside and gather up the firewood to bring into the house. The sky had darkened to an ominous gray and rain seemed imminent. When she opened the front door, the wind blew with such vigor that it slammed it back into her face, as if to say *Stay inside*. Just then came a crack of thunder so loud it shook the ground and sent the poor dog running from the doorway back into the house.

"Well, that's my cue," she said, running out the door and to the front gate where she had left her pull-behind cart full of wood. She grabbed for the handle when another loud crack of thunder rang off in the distance and echoed across the hills. Pulling the cart as fast as she was able, Helen managed to get it up to the front door just before the rain began. She flung open the door and tossed twigs, branches, and logs into the house in a desperate attempt to keep everything dry. As she unloaded the last log, the rain hammered down upon the slate roof and a small river poured down over the doorstep and soaked her to the bone. When she finally got inside, a pool of water circled her feet.

Helen took off her sweatshirt, rang it out, and hung it on the old ladderback chair that rested against the wall by the door. You could tell the chair had been set there as a place for someone to sit as they took off their shoes, as there were marks of wear on the floor and wall where the chair had been pulled out and pushed back many times. She sat there to catch her breath, cold and wet. The little gray dog came out from the kitchen and sat next to her. She reached down slowly and he let her stroke his soft, wiry fur.

"Well, boy, looks like you and I are going to try and start this fire, or I fear we'll both freeze tonight."

She got up and started bringing the wood over to the fireplace. Then she gathered some of the old newspapers and balled them up, throwing them into the fireplace and adding a few twigs and large sticks on top. Getting out the box of matches from the kitchen, she struck one and lit a newspaper ball. The flame sparked and jumped and then began its dance, catching the other balls of newspaper and a few of the smaller twigs before dwindling out to a smoldering bit of ash.

"Crap," she said and tried again, balling up more papers, this time adding smaller twigs first and then only a few large ones on top of those. With the strike of another match, the paper caught quickly and she watched as words and images melded away into jumping flames. Soon there was a small fire going and she added more kindling until the flames had grown big enough to place one of the larger pieces of wood on top. She watched to make sure that it would stay ablaze before setting the box of matches on the mantel and standing back to admire her creation. It was almost art, she thought. All the pieces needed to be put together just so to create its beauty, and what beauty it was. There was something about the glow of an open fire that gave everything around it a peaceful appearance. It was something that she had often tried to paint but never seemed to capture quite right.

Now that she had accomplished a fire that was already warming the house, she went into the bedroom and changed out of her wet clothing. She put the kettle on in the kitchen and sliced up a bit more cheese and bread, but for herself this time. Loading everything onto a small plate, she made her way back into the sitting room and curled herself up on the faded floral sofa in front of the fire. The dog had already made his bed on the round wool rug by the hearth.

Helen sat and enjoyed the thunderstorm as warmth licked around the room until there was a loud pop and a hissing bang, then all of the lights went out. The fire was the only thing that lit the room now as the storm had brought nightfall a little sooner than expected. The dog sat up quickly and ran to her side, frightened by the loud noise.

"It's okay, boy, the lights just went out," she said, reassuring herself as much as the dog. "Let's see if we can find the fuse box."

She got up and walked slowly, not yet used to the layout of the place, and made her way into the kitchen. On the table was the flashlight she had bought and the candles Henry had added to the basket. She turned the flashlight on and then started to search for some candle holders. Finding nothing in the kitchen, she made her way back to the library room where she remembered seeing some on the mantel.

As she opened the door, the room seemed to be lit from within. No lights were on or candles lit but the room glowed. Maybe it was the large windows that gave it this effect in the setting light. The books all shone brightly on their dark walnut seats, awaiting their chance to be chosen. Everything in this room seemed to be different somehow from the rest of the house. It was by far the focal point of the cottage, there was no doubt about that.

After locating the candlesticks, she decided to search for a book to keep her company while the electricity was off. Looking around at the endless choices, Helen noticed a set of books on one of the top shelves. They seemed to sparkle and shine, giving the illusion they had been dusted with a thin layer of gold. She was unsure why they stood out, as they were plain leather covers with no fancy frills or gilded edges like some of the others in the library. But they seemed to call to her, inviting her to take a closer look.

Setting down the flashlight, she slid over the ladder, which was attached to an extended rail that ran the length of the library's longest wall. Climbing up it, she reached for one of the curious little books. As she gently plucked one from its resting place, she noticed that the dark wood stain on the shelf had been rubbed off in the place where the books sat. They had obviously been a favorite of whoever had owned them. She held the book in her hands. The leather cover was smooth and cool to the touch and the book seemed to weigh little to nothing, yet it was thick and sturdy. The leather was tooled and embellished with a vine of thistles that wrapped its way around the four corners, but there was no title on the cover.

When she opened it, she realized it was a journal, not a book. The pages seemed to produce a luminous glow that made them easy to read even in the dimming light. The jet-black ink on the snow-white pages looked so crisp and clean that it could have been written yesterday, but the date at the top of the page clearly read September 5th, 1597. The handwriting was elegant, each letter perfectly penned and spaced out, making it easy to read. Helen was completely mystified by how familiar the journal looked to her—even the writing seemed similar to something she had seen before but she couldn't quite place it. She fanned through the pages and landed on an entry midway through. The first line was written in handwriting that looked to be more rushed than on the previous pages. The first line read: *As the days grow shorter with the changing of the season, so do my days on this earth. It is only a matter of time before they discover where I am.*

Eager to keep reading this extraordinary treasure she'd just found, she hastily made her way down the ladder. Her foot missed a rung and she slipped, hitting her shin hard and dropping the flashlight. As it hit the floor, she heard the bulb pop and was plunged once more into darkness.

"Damn! Bloody lights," she spat out. She placed the journal on the side table as she bent down to pick up the broken flashlight and felt her way back to the kitchen in the darkness to get some ice for her leg.

Sadly, the journal would have to wait until proper light was available again to read. After a maddening search for the candles and then the matches which she had left in the living room, she discovered that the fire had burned itself out to a smoldering slumber. At that point, she gave up and decided it was time for bed.

Finding her way blindly into the bedroom, she tripped over the dog, who had taken up his old residence.

"My God, this day couldn't come to an end soon enough," she snapped as she slipped herself into the cold bed and pulled the covers up over her head.

It had been a long couple of days and, at this point, she hadn't accomplished anything in terms of fixing up the cottage. From the look of things, it was going to be slow going, and this whole thing might drag out longer than she had thought. Being isolated with nothing other than her self-doubts and constant worry to keep her company was taking its toll and she needed sleep.

Apparently sensing her dismay, the dog hopped up onto the bed and curled itself next to her.

She smiled and gave him a pat. "Goodnight, boy."

Chapter Eight

DREAM

The water lapped over the tips of her toes as she listened to the rhythmic sound of the waves on the shoreline. The day birds sang their lullabies as the night birds woke to sing their cheery praises to the darkness. Everything in nature was a balance of light and dark. The creatures of the day did their daytime work so that the creatures of the night had what they needed for the tasks set upon them in the dark. She considered herself a creature of the in-between. She was the dusk, the perfect mixture of light and darkness.

As she sat upon a low ledge overhanging the stony shore, the lush green hills cascaded down behind her where the sun had begun its descent down into its slumbering place. Her hair hung down, flowing over her shoulders and down her back in big auburn curls, the wind blowing them out to mimic the movement of the waves. She had called to the wind as the day had been hot and all the creatures were in need of a cool, tender breeze. It obliged and danced around the valley, sweeping up the coolness of the water and blowing it over the hills and down the meadow.

In her lap was a small book with tooled vines and thistles embellished into the leather. A gift from a very special person in her life, he had made it for her by hand, pouring his love for her into each and every curved line that twisted and turned its way around the cover. She picked it up and held it close as she looked out over the water. This spot was where her heart was most happy, where she connected with the elements around her in a way she could not do anywhere else. It was her spot, her altar.

The sound of lapping ceased and the water suddenly stilled, becoming mirror-like. No birds sang and the gentle wind had ceased, leaving the air hot and stale. The natural darkening of the day rapidly increased and it became almost night in a matter of minutes. At that moment she knew she was close. Evil is the only thing that can cause such darkness to descend and frighten all living beings into stillness.

She looked down into the water, and in the murky darkness she saw a figure step up behind her. She was pushed as she turned around, falling longer and deeper than the small ledge she had sat upon.

She was falling from a cliff. She saw its edge and the jagged stony shoreline approaching, rushing up to meet her.

Just before she hit, she closed her eyes and surrendered to her fate.

Waking up in a cold sweat, Helen sat up quickly and flipped on the small bedside lamp. Thankfully the power had been restored during the night and the cottage hummed with electricity once again. The sudden abruptness of the light startled the poor dog and sent him to leap down off the bed and hide beneath it.

It was nothing new for Helen to wake up like this in the middle of the night. It seemed that traveling halfway around the world made no difference; the recurring nightmare would find her no matter where she was. She pulled her bag up from beside the bed and dug out a sketch pad. She had been drawing this dream as a tool to help her process it, as instructed by a therapist she had when she was a child. At this point, she must have filled twenty drawing pads with images from this dream, and it didn't seem to get her any closer to understanding it. It did, however, assist her in coping with it in some ways. Opening up to a blank page, she pulled out a charcoal pencil and started to sketch. This time the dream had been different. Things had changed. This time she had the journal from the library in her hands. The dark presence was female. The edge of the water was a cliff. But something else had changed; she felt more in control, calmer than before. She gave into the fate that lay ahead of her instead of fearing it. The overall mood of the dream was still dark, yet a bit lighter than before, and that was how she drew it.

Not being able to get back to sleep, Helen decided she would grab her bag with sketchbook and watercolor paints and set herself up to paint the rising sun over the cottage.

Getting out of bed, her leg still felt a bit sore from the fall the night before. There was a bruise forming on her shin the size of a golf ball. She was thankful it hadn't been worse and wouldn't prevent her from doing a little exploring later in the day.

The little dog came out from its hiding spot under the bed and followed her into the kitchen as she put on the kettle.

"You up for a walk before the rain comes, boy?" she asked as he looked longingly at the empty bowl on the floor. "I can't keep calling you 'boy.' If you're going to stay, then you're going to need a proper name! Let's think… Scamp? No. Chester? Definitely not. Hmmm, that dark wiry hair of yours looks quite windblown. What about Storm?" At that, the dog walked over and gave Helen's hand a small lick. "Storm it is then," she said with a smile. "Now, let's get you a bite to eat before we head out into the wild, shall we?"

After cutting up a bit more cheese for the dog and a slice of bread for herself, she sat down and had her morning dose of instant coffee. Sitting there on the table was the old black leather notebook she had found in the cupboard the day before. When she picked it up, it felt warm in her hands. She flipped it open and began to thumb through the pages. It was full of herbal remedies, a recipe book of sorts. The handwriting was delicate and neat, each word written as if a perfect piece of art in itself, the measurements so precise that no one could mistake amounts.

There were cures for bee stings, back pain, rheumatism, headaches, fevers, colds, and such. Toward the back were other remedies for things like broken hearts, lost soulmates, unruly neighbors, barren cattle, and fruitless fields. As she read on, she realized she was holding a book of handwritten spells. They were clearly scribed by more than one person, as there were various types of handwriting and dates on the tops of the pages spanning nearly two centuries. It was a collection of things learned and passed down. Under each spell were names, places, and dates. One page was marked with a red silk strand lying in the crease. The page was yellowed, stained, and worn as if it had been turned to and used many times. In dark blue ink, the page read:

For Safekeeping Against the Wicked

Gather 4 jars of the same size.
Place rice at the bottom of each jar
then add salt from the sea.
Atop of that a bit of lavender
and sage.
Seal with wax and place in the 4 corners of your home.

Recite this as you place your jars:

The wicked who would do me harm
May he take the throat disease
Globularly, spirally, circularly
Fluxy, pellety, horny-grim.

Be it harder than stone,
Be it blacker than coal,
Be it swifter than the wind,
Be it heavier than lead.

Be it fiercer, sharper, harsher, more
Malignant,
Than the hard, wound-quivering holly,
Be it sounder than the stained, lustrous,
Bitter salt,
Seven, seven times.

Helen felt a chill run down the length of her spine. In her hands was not a book of herbal remedies but a book of spells. She knew that there was talk of a woman being in league with the fairies, but she had thought all of it was nonsense.

Yet she couldn't deny that strange things had been happening to her since she arrived at Fernbeg. The jolt she felt when opening the door, the wind in the woods, the library, and now this. Her logical mind had written them off as her imagination running wild. She was in another country all by herself in the middle of nowhere; of course she was going to be on edge and find everything strange. Maybe this book was nothing more than the writings of an eccentric old woman with too much time on her hands and a little too much faith in all these fairytales.

But as much as Helen wanted to believe that was true, deep down she knew it wasn't. She felt as if the book was calling to her, urging her on, and before she knew it, she was flipping through the pages, looking for a spell to try. She tried to dismiss it as curiosity or boredom, but the real reason was the sensation she got when she held the small book. It was as if she could feel the power within its pages.

"Okay, Storm, change of plans. I think we're going to stay in and try out a little magic. What do you say?"

As though he had perfectly understood what she said, the dog let out a small whimper, left the kitchen, and headed back to bed.

Helen looked through the book until she found something that seemed simple—a spell of light. The spell called for a small vial of salt, a white candle, and rainwater collected from a storm.

She went outside with a cup and collected some water that had gathered in the bottom of the cart overnight. Back in the kitchen, she rummaged through cupboards until she found a small box of salt. Taking one of the candles from the piles of goods from the shop, she sat down at the far end of the table and read the spell:

A Spell of Light

Take one white candle and dip it into the rain from a storm
Then set it in the center of a circle of salt
Chant this verse 3 times:

From the light of the storm
Bring unto me
The light of the heavens
So mote it be

Doing exactly what the book said, Helen waited for the candle to light for several minutes, but nothing happened. She let out a laugh of relief, feeling quite ridiculous for thinking such things could actually happen.

She got up, pushed in her chair, and walked into the bedroom to try and get Storm to go out for a walk with her. She could see his fluffy gray tail poking out from under the bed.

"Storm, do you want to go out for a walk?" she said in a gentle tone, trying to coax him out of his hiding spot.

The dog slowly crept out from under the bed and approached her. He looked up at her, his eyes glowing an orange brown. Then he tilted his head, looking past her and into the hallway.

"Come here, boy," she said again. He brushed against her legs then headed past her and into the kitchen. "No more food just yet, let's go for our walk first," she called after him, following him into the kitchen.

When she entered, Storm was sitting in the center of the room looking up at the table. There, hovering above the large oak slab, were six candles. All six were lit with a silvery-white flame.

Helen gasped, and in that instant, the candles fell to the table and extinguished themselves.

She rushed over to look. All six were untouched by fire, wicks intact. When she picked one up to examine it, she felt a rush of excitement course through her.

"It couldn't be," she said, thinking she must be going insane. Her imagination had been running wild since she got here but this was just crazy.

Just then, she heard the rumbling of a car engine close to the cottage. From the sitting room window, she saw Henry pull up to her dooryard. He got out of his car and walked up to the front gate in the heavy, dewed air. Helen opened the door wide for him to come inside.

"Oh dear, I fear I've left you far too long on your own," he said, glancing at the pull cart by the front door as he stepped inside. "You look like a frightened rabbit and this place is chilled to its core."

"Oh Henry, you have perfect timing. I don't think I could have stood a minute more in this house alone. I think all this time by myself is driving me a bit crazy," she said, fiddling with a hair-band that adorned her wrist like a bracelet.

Rushing ahead of him into the kitchen, Helen quickly brushed the ring of salt off the table, grabbed the book of spells, and tucked it into a drawer before Henry made his way into the room.

"Would you like a coffee or tea?" Helen asked.

Just then Storm came trotting into the room.

"Bloomin' heck!" Henry said, jumping back as he looked down at the dog.

"Oh, that's Storm, he was the houseguest living in my bed-room. We've come to terms with our living arrangements. It's kind of nice having another soul here with me. Makes me feel not so alone," Helen said, looking down and giving the dog a smile.

"You do know this is not a dog?" Henry asked her, not taking his eyes off Storm.

"What do you mean? Of course he's a dog. What else would he be?" She reached down and scratched the fur behind his ears as he beat his wiry tail on the wooden floor.

"A wolf pup," Henry answered, still regarding Storm warily. "Your little houseguest is no dog but a Highland wolf pup."

"You must be kidding?" Helen said in disbelief. "But he's sweet as pie and he's taken to me so well. He even slept with me in bed last night. He can't be a wild wolf, maybe he was someone's pet who got lost? He certainly seems domesticated."

Storm trotted over to Henry and sniffed his worn leather boots then looked up and gave his hand a lick.

"Well, I'll be damned. I have known a few people who claimed to have hybrids but these guys were thought to be hunted to extinction hundreds of years ago," he said, giving him a pat on the head. "Helen, I do believe you are an animal charmer, my dear."

"Really? Well, he didn't just appear out of nowhere. There must be some roaming the Highlands still," Helen said

"Well, as far as the government is concerned, they've been extinct since the late sixteen hundreds. Some must have survived and stayed hidden away. I've seen pictures of wolves in history books and there is no doubt about it, he is a wolf pup. He's marvelous," Henry said, looking down at Storm.

"He is that," Helen said with a smile.

Helen made them both a hot cup of tea and they sat at the table and talked while Storm napped on the rug under the table.

"Let me get a fire going for you. This cottage is quite drafty and it'll help take the dampness out of the air," Henry offered.

"You know, I gathered that wood myself and successfully started a small fire last night. I felt quite accomplished."

"I can see that," he said, balling up the papers and tossing some small kindling into the pile. As he struck the match and lit the small fire, he looked around at the disrepair of the room. "This won't do," he said. "We need to get someone in here to fix these windows and holes in the floor right away. I'm sorry, I shouldn't have left you here the other day without starting a fire for you and getting some of these windows boarded over. This time of year, you could freeze with this kind of draft. Not to mention, you'll be eaten out of house and home by the mice."

"It's okay. I managed. I wrote a list yesterday of all the things that need to be done, and most of them I'll need help with. I don't have a lot of money to hire a professional, but I thought maybe you might know some local handyman who might be able to do it a bit cheaper?"

"Mr. McKenzie's grandson does a bit of that here and there. I'm sure he'd be more than happy to come and take a look. I can phone him later for you when I get home, see if he can come tomorrow and get these windows fixed."

"Oh Henry, that would be wonderful. could take me into town today to the hardware store for some supplies?" Helen asked as she sat on the overly cheery floral sofa soaking up the warmth of the fire.

"Of course. We can head out whenever you like," Henry said, adding another log.

Chapter Nine

SOUND ON THE WIND

When they arrived in town, the streets were bustling with tourists strolling along the main stretch by the loch and dining at the shoreside restaurants. They parked and walked a block to a small store called Miller's Hardware. The storefront was part of the older buildings in town with painted brick walls and old wooden windows and door frames. The store's sign was painted in a dark rustic navy blue with bright white trim that looked very nautical.

"Now, what are we looking for?" Henry asked as they went inside.

"Well, I need paint. Lots of paint! I'm also going to need some nails, a hammer, paint brushes, rollers, and maybe some more cleaning supplies," she said, grabbing a small red shopping basket from a stack by the door.

Helen made her way over to the paints while Henry picked up the tools and other items she had asked for. After looking for quite some time, she decided on the colors: frozen white for the outer walls of the cottage and her bedroom, a deep navy for the sitting room, a fern green for the front door and the kitchen, and lastly classic black for the shutters.

After getting all the paint mixed and paying a small fortune, they headed back to the car with one of the store clerks pushing a trolley full of supplies after them. With everything loaded into the car, Helen asked if they could pop back into the grocery shop to get a few things.

Greeting them once again was the scowl of the old woman behind the cash register. Helen made her way to the back of the store where the pet supplies were located.

"Henry, do wolves eat dog food?" she joked, grabbing a bag of value brand dog food and a lead and collar.

"Hard to say, I thought they preferred skinny American girls," Henry joked back.

Helen grabbed a few more supplies: milk, another loaf of bread, an extra jar of instant coffee, and another flashlight. They checked out and headed back to the car when something caught her eye. It was a political poster protesting a large industrial building being built in Inveraray, a small town about an hour from Oban. A large red X was painted over the image of the building on the poster, with the words "Down with Regmata Industries" in deep blood-red ink. Glancing at the poster, Helen had an overwhelming feeling of nausea. She thought she was going to retch right then and there. Henry, seeing Helen turn pale, guided her to a bench to sit down.

"Helen, dear, are you alright?" he asked as he sat down beside her.

"Yes, I think so. I just need to take a moment," she said as she looked down at the ground and tried to steady herself. She had never experienced anything like this before. It was as if the poster had triggered a panic attack, but she didn't know why. Maybe it was just the fact she hadn't eaten much in the past couple of days and she was still fighting jet lag.

"You're not taking care of yourself, give a care. You need to eat something. Let's get this stuff back to the car and then we can grab a sandwich at a delightful little deli just round the corner," Henry suggested, helping her back onto her feet.

Slowly making their way back to the car, they got everything loaded in and grabbed a sandwich from the deli. After eating, Helen began to feel better, and they decided to get back on the road and head home.

The ride back was slow. They encountered sheep on the road twice and had to wait until they crossed over which added an extra fifteen minutes to the drive. It gave Helen plenty of time to think about everything that had happened since she arrived in Scotland. She was starting to think she had gone a little mad with all the unexplainable and mystifying occurrences. It seemed to be the most logical explanation—she had, after all, traveled here under an immense amount of stress. Plus, all the time she had spent in solitude at the cottage must have taken its toll on her. She decided that after Henry dropped her off, she would take the afternoon to decompress and paint.

When they arrived back at Fernbeg, Henry helped unload the car and get everything inside. Storm greeted them with a wag of his bushy tail as they came into the cottage with all their wares. Henry stoked up the fire once more before telling Helen he had to be on his way.

Helen walked him to the front gate and thanked him for all the help and the ride into town.

"I'll call the McKenzies when I get home and see if Connor can come over and check out the things that need fixing. And I'll tell him you need a bit of wood to heat the cottage. He should be able to bring a wee truckload over to get you through the next couple of weeks while you're here."

"Thank you, Henry. You know, they don't make them like you anymore," she said, hugging him.

"Oh, they do, my dear. You just haven't found yours yet." He winked at her, got into his car, and drove off.

As she watched him go, she looked out over the fields. They were calling to her. She yelled for Storm, grabbed her bag of art supplies, and walked out the door to find the perfect place to set up her makeshift easel and paint the foreign landscape that so captivated her.

Art was something that helped fill a void in her that she never could quite reach otherwise. Without it, she didn't feel whole. The only time she felt truly at peace and happy was when she had a paintbrush or a pencil in her hands, creating something. Right now, she was feeling that rush of excitement she always got right before the paint touched the brush, in anticipation of a possible masterpiece.

She and Storm made their way out into the field behind the house where she found a small cluster of rocks to sit on. Looking out over the valley, Fernbeg sat nestled between the hills, and in the far distance was the loch with the sky—gray clouds and patches of sapphire—reflecting off its waters. The clouds cast long shadows across the valley, darkening patches of grass and turning them from bright pine green to dark emerald. There was still a low, lingering fog resting around the shoreline of the loch, giving it a mystical appearance. Altogether, it was the perfect scene for her to paint.

She laid her watercolor paper out over the largest rock then set her paint palette and brush alongside. She had taken a small jar of water with her and unscrewed the lid, letting out a pop that echoed down the valley. As she sketched out the landscape, Storm walked about sniffing the tall grass, then took chase at some small critter. Helen guessed it to be a field mouse. She sketched him as he leaped and jumped like the wild animal he was, adding an element of vitality to the scene, turning it from a normal landscape into a painting that felt alive.

She was still in awe that he was a baby wolf cub. He had adapted to being a house pet so quickly. She figured that he had been orphaned and found his way into the house through the broken floorboard, seeking shelter. When she found him he'd looked as if he had scarcely eaten, probably surviving on mice. He was more than happy to be taken care of by her as he was still so young, not knowing any better yet, and she was happy to have him in her company. She didn't feel so alone in this vast space with him by her side. It just felt right, like they were meant to help each other.

Helen dipped her brush into the water and swirled it into the paint, gently pulling up a drop of green and then letting the drop flow and pool onto the page. She repeated this process with several shades of green until the fields began to take shape. Then she moved to the sky and painted the heavens, echoing them down to the loch. She took her time and slowly the beauty of the scene in front of her also lay on the small pad of paper resting atop the rock. Painting always helped her work through organizing the chaos in her mind. Now that she was able to pour her emotions out onto the paper, she felt a bit better about things. She stopped and let her creation dry, watching her fears and worries soak into the fibers of the paper before closing it up and packing everything away.

Storm was still in the field chasing the critter from left to right and then back again. Helen tried to catch his attention by calling his name—which was no good, since he'd only had it for less than a day. She started to chase after him in hopes he would notice her and come back, but he did not. She was now regretting not using the collar and lead she had gotten for him at the shop. She dropped her bag and took chase after him as he bounded after the mouse up the field and out into another pasture, further and further away from the cottage. Thankfully, he chased the little creature through a break in the stone wall, giving the small animal the perfect place to hide and therefore stopping the long-winded chase. Helen came to a halt at the wall, huffing and puffing, and braced herself against it to catch her breath. Storm came over and gave her hand a gentle lick.

"Ugh, Storm, you naughty little wolf. You just about killed me with all that running. Note to self: get in better shape."

Just then she saw movement out of the corner of her eye. To the far side of the field was a rowan tree growing in front of a small, wooded area. Its red berries gave it an almost pink hue from her vantage point. The tree moved in the breeze, dancing back and forth in the dusty afternoon sky. She looked hard into the undergrowth but couldn't see what had caught her eye. She was sure she had seen something move there but it was too far away to make anything out.

She decided to take a closer look and called Storm to follow her. Even though she didn't think he recognized his name yet, he followed, appearing to want to stick close to her.

As they neared the tree, Storm perked his ears up as if he had heard something. Helen stopped and listened through the persistent wind. She could have sworn she heard small, chiming bells bouncing and echoing off the hills as the wind blew. The more she listened the more it sounded like a familiar tune, something she recognized but couldn't make out fully.

When they reached the base of the tree, Helen looked around but found nothing. The ground was scattered with the red rowan berries. Probably a bird or other woodland animal had been grazing on them and dashed off into the trees when it saw her. Storm, with his nose to the ground, sniffed out a trail and Helen worried she would be on another chase if he caught sight of the animal that made it. She walked around the tree after him and found that he was digging at its base. As he dug, dirt flew out covering the berries on the ground. He had gotten almost a half-foot into the soil when he stopped and pulled something out.

"What do you have there, boy?" Helen said as she bent down. She thought it was a bone at first, but it was darker than the antiqued white of a bone buried in the earth. Wiping off the dirt with her sweatshirt, she studied it. It was a curious-looking stone in the shape of a long, distorted teardrop with a perfect hole right through it on the smaller end. She had never seen anything like it before. It must have been made long ago, maybe an ancient piece of jewelry from the Celts. It wasn't a precious gem or anything special, just a plain gray stone.

As she examined it, the wind picked up and she heard the familiar tune once again. This time it wasn't bells but bagpipes that she heard in the wind. They were coming from the other side of the wooded area. Curious, she tucked the stone in her pocket and skirted the edge of the trees. She found her way to the field on the other side that seemed to go on forever around her.

There, next to a tall oak tree, stood a man in a gray t-shirt with brown work pants and an argyle paperboy hat. With his back to her, he played the bagpipes as still as stone. It was a melody that grabbed at her heartstrings even though she had never heard it before. She could feel sadness in the way he played, yet it was beautiful.

As the stranger finished, she was about to turn away and sneak back down alongside the tree line when Storm let out a loud bark. The man turned and saw them standing there watching him.

As soon as Helen saw his face she felt as if she was staring back at someone she had known forever. A long moment passed between them.

"I am so sorry," she said, feeling quite awkward about the long, drawn-out stare. She stumbled over to him. "I'm Helen Kent, your new neighbor down at Fernbeg cottage. I heard you from the other side of the trees and had to come see who was playing. Oh, and this is my pup, Storm." She stuck out her hand to introduce herself.

"No need to apologize. I'm Connor McKenzie. Henry called me this afternoon to ask if I could bring you down some firewood and take a look at a few odds and ends you need help fixing. I was going to load the firewood into the truck but the pipes were calling and I couldn't neglect them any longer," he said, taking her hand into his and shaking it.

At the moment their hands met, there was a collision of energies so monumental that time seemed to stand still and stardust was created. Caught in each other's eyes, they stood motionless. The intensity of the moment left her feeling a little stunned. Helen gently pulled her hand away and looked down in a desperate attempt to regain her composure. It took a bit more for Connor to break his gaze but he soon followed suit and took a step back, breaking the energy field they had unknowingly created.

Connor's dark green eyes caught the lowering light of the afternoon sun so they were the same shade as the hills in her painting. With chestnut hair and stubble along his sharp jawline, he was ruggedly handsome, his angular features breaking away into a kind smile. Just looking at him gave her an ache deep inside her that made her feel as if she was falling and couldn't catch her breath. It was unlike anything she had ever felt before and something she had fought desperately to avoid. She had to remind herself that this was no time to be getting butterflies for some brawny Scotsman.

"That's no dog you have there," he addressed her as he bent down to look at Storm.

"Yes, I know. He's a Highland wolf pup, Henry said. Pretty amazing, huh? He told me they were thought to be extinct. He'd been living in the cottage under my bed when I arrived and we came to an agreement that we would share the house. I'm not sure why he seems so domesticated. He's a bit of a mystery," she said, ruffling the scruffy fur on Storm's head.

"Oh, you clever little thing," Connor said as he looked down at Storm. "I think I can solve this mystery for you." He smiled. "This pup came from a domesticated wolf named Onora. My grandfather found her abandoned in the woods as a young pup. He was stunned to find a creature long thought extinct. Took her in and cared for her, telling the locals she was a wolf-hound mix. She was his constant companion and protector for years until one day she disappeared. Came back a month later with a swollen belly full of pups. My grandfather was overjoyed that she was home, but it was short-lived. He got a call from Barbara Cowley from the neighboring farm telling him Onora needed to be put down because she had slaughtered a flock of her sheep the night before. He fought and pleaded that it couldn't have been her since she'd been at the farm with him. But it was no use. Barbara sent out the local police to collect her. Before they arrived, my grandfather begged Onora to leave and go back into the wild so she and her pups could live.

She did as she was told and disappeared into the woods. A month later, we came across her body in the woodlands out back of the farm. She looked to have died in childbirth. We thought the pups had been picked off by predators. But it looks like one of her pups survived." Connor patted Storm's head and then scooped him up into his arms.

"Storm, I knew you were special, but I didn't know how much. You are quite the little survivor," Helen said, looking at the wolf in amazement.

"We'll have to bring him back to show my granda. You have no idea the joy this'll bring him. He was broken after Onora died. Do you mind walking with me to the farm? It's only over that knoll."

"Of course, I'd love to," Helen said, her heart catching in her throat.

Connor tucked his pipes under his arm and walked through the tall grass toward the small hill.

It was only a short distance and Storm bounced and ran between them as they strolled up the knoll and down into the farmyard. It was a beautiful place and very well kept. The barn was of modest size and she could see they had a few dozen sheep, herding dogs, and two stout workhorses. A wide driveway separated the barn and the house and wrapped its way up and around the barnyard in a large circle. The house was made of deep gray fieldstone and looked very manly and rugged with its black slate roof and stone wall bordering the garden. The front gate hung open, looking as if it was left that way often.

Connor walked them up to the house and called in through an open window to his grandfather. After a few minutes, an old man opened the front door. He was tall like Connor with a white wiry mustache and a head of snow-white hair. He had kind eyes and Helen could tell right away he was a gentle soul.

"Granda, this is Helen Kent, our new neighbor down at Fernbeg, and this is Storm. Take a close look at him. Helen found him living under the bed in the cottage when she arrived," Connor said with excitement in his voice.

"Well, I'll be! He looks just like Onora. Her lone surviving pup," the old man said, looking down fondly at the little wolf.

He slowly bent as far as his body would allow and stuck his hand out. Storm walked closer to him and sniffed his shoe. Once he had given him a good sniff, his ears lifted up and he jumped and licked the old man, sending him into a fit of laughter.

"I must still smell of his mother," the old man sang out as Storm continued to dance about him.

"He's certainly taken to you," Helen said with a pang of sorrow. She knew that Storm would not be coming back to Fernbeg with her now.

"Where are my manners? Sorry, my dear, I'm Seamus, Connor's grandfather. It's a pleasure to meet you. Would you like to come in for a cup of tea?" He opened the door a little wider, gesturing for her to come in.

"That's kind of you but I need to make my way back. I left my bag in the field and I want to make sure I can find it before the sun sets. I'll take you up on that lovely offer another day," Helen answered. "I'll leave Storm here with you. I believe this is his home."

She ruffled the pup's unruly fur and waved goodbye to them both.

"Let me walk you back to your field," Connor offered.

"No, it's fine. I can find my way. Thank you," she said, feeling as if she may cry and not wanting anyone around to witness it.

"I'll bring you down some wood tomorrow morning and take a look at what needs fixing," Connor called after her as she began the walk back up into the field from the yard.

"That would be wonderful. Thank you, Connor," she called back.

Just as she was about to crest the knoll, she heard something rushing toward her at lightning speed. When she turned around, she saw Storm bounding up the hill after her.

"I think he knows best where home is!" she heard Seamus call out as Storm trotted up next to her.

She smiled and bent down to give the wolf a hug and whispered in his ear, "You don't know how much I needed that. Thank you."

As she stood up, she looked back and gave a big wave over her head to Seamus, who stood in the doorway looking up at her and Storm. Even though she couldn't see him clearly, she knew he was smiling.

They walked up the hill, past the rowan tree, and then out into the wide, open field that overlooked Fernbeg. She found her bag and paused for a second, looking out over the valley as the sun set behind her. The light bounced off the white stone walls of the cottage, giving it a warm, soft glow. There was magic here, she knew that for certain now.

She and Storm made their slow descent down the hill and back to their home.

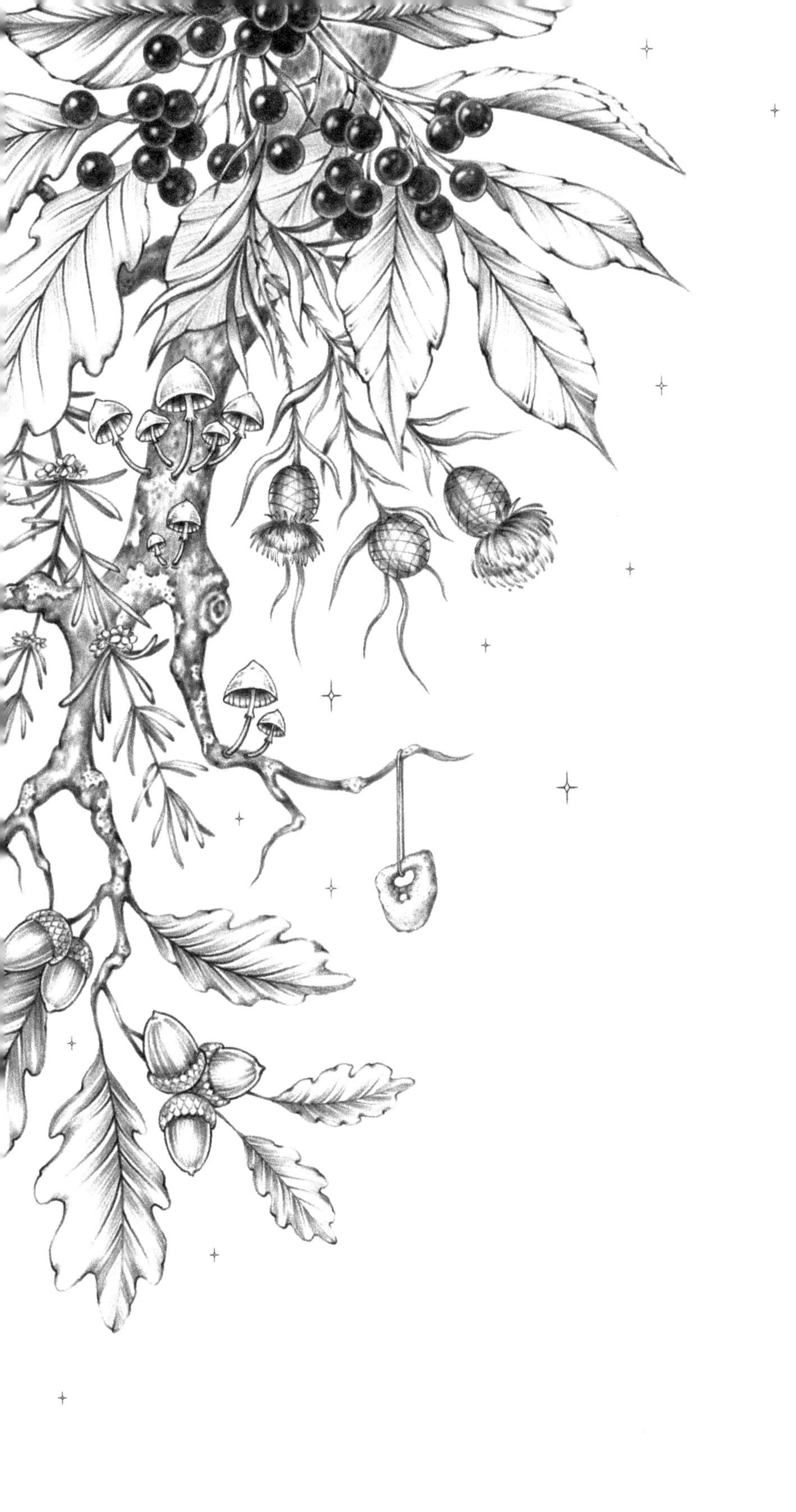

Chapter Ten

CONNOR

Storm got up and stretched lazily before walking into the kitchen where Helen was sitting at the table with a cup of instant coffee in one hand and the little black leather book in the other. She was so enthralled in what she was reading that she didn't even notice him. He gave her leg a gentle but firm nudge, letting her know that he was up and ready for his breakfast.

"Storm, you lazy little wolf. You finally got up to greet the day?" she asked, patting him on the head.

He looked up at her and then proceeded to walk over to his bowl on the floor next to the counter.

"Ah, I see, you're hungry," Helen said as she set down the book, ripped open the bag of dog food, and poured it into his bowl.

The wolf pup looked at it curiously, then sniffed. He seemed hesitant at first as to whether he should or should not eat this weird-looking but fine-smelling food. Then, carefully, he took a kibble in his mouth and crunched it between his teeth. He paused, and then began devouring it.

"Well, that was touch and go there for a minute," Helen said as she watched him happily dig in.

She leaned back in her chair, her gaze fixed on the book. She was still unsure if she had witnessed the candles hovering with flames lit over the table or if it was a figment of her imagination. Maybe she had hoped the magic could be real so much that she'd imagined it all. After all, the wicks on the candles were still intact, and not a bit of wax had melted. However, if it had really happened, if the magic *was* real, then she had performed a spell that actually worked. She decided that the only way to be certain was to try again, but this time she would stay put. There was still plenty of rainwater in the cart out front and she still had half a box of salt left. However, this little test would have to wait until later—at this point she hadn't gotten much done and her "To do" list wasn't getting any smaller. It was time to get going on this renovation.

After Storm had finished his breakfast and the last of her coffee was drunk, she put on her sneakers and grabbed the collar and lead. Her leg was still a bit sore for a run so she decided to walk down to the loch with Storm instead.

"Come here, boy, look what I have for you," she said, holding out the thin leather collar with its shiny silver buckle. Storm came over and gave the collar a sniff and then let her fasten it to his neck. "Well, don't you look handsome," she said, giving him a wide smile. She hooked the lead to the collar and walked with him out the front door.

It was another cool morning. A low mist covered the valley.

The rising sun cast rays of light that caught on the dewdrops hanging from spider webs in the tall grass, causing a prism effect on each woven thread. Even in the brisk air, the birds still sang their cheery songs, echoing back and forth across the valley. The grass's color was muted by the morning dew, but each footprint she made returned it to its natural shade of dark green, leaving a distinct trail where she had been. Storm ran alongside her, becoming matted with the dampness.

They walked down the hill until they came to a trail that was laid out with loose gravel and slowed their pace a bit. Their footsteps were no longer silent as Helen's trainers spit and kicked up the rocky ground. As the loch came closer, Helen could see a small boat drifting a short distance from the shoreline. Fishermen, she guessed. The loch was still with the morning air and the reflection of the hills could barely be seen in its misty water. Down near the water was a small, stony beach that hugged the shoreline.

She drew closer and noticed that the surroundings seemed familiar. Had she seen an image of it on the website when she bid on the cottage? No, that wasn't it. The closer she got, the more familiar it became until she was standing at the water's edge. She looked out over the loch and within a moment it came to her. This was the lake from her dreams, this was the water she had drawn and painted hundreds of times before.

But how? She had never been here before, she'd never seen any pictures of it before last week, yet she had been dreaming of this place for as long as she could remember.

She lowered herself to the ground and rested her hands on the cool earth, looking out, deep into the water, feeling perplexed. There had to be a logical explanation, but she couldn't think of one. It was yet another mystery that lingered in the Scottish air around her. She was starting to think she was completely losing her mind. Maybe this whole thing had been too much for her to handle, and she'd snapped. Yet she felt more at peace than she ever had since arriving in Scotland. Nothing made sense to her anymore, she was a mixed-up mess of emotions.

At that moment, Storm, who had been sniffing around the pebbly beach, broke free of the lead and took off into the water. He jumped and played, splashing Helen as he leaped around. She smiled. Maybe things were completely strange here, but it was a type of strange that felt right to her. She felt like this was where she belonged, here with Storm playing by the water. It was a feeling she had deep within her, something that she had felt since the day she got off the plane, and she knew it now, she was meant to be here for one reason or another. Even if it was for only a short while.

With a loud bark, Storm broke her trance. She turned around to see a figure walking down the hill from the cottage. Even from a distance, she could tell it was Connor by his tall, masculine frame. He waved and Storm took off after him up the hill. Helen got to her feet and began the ascent up the long sloping incline.

Once she was within earshot of him, she called out, "I didn't expect you so early."

"Sorry," he yelled back. "I tried to call but your phone still isn't hooked up. I came to the cottage but you didn't answer the door, then I saw your footprints in the grass and followed them down here."

As they met midway on the hill they stopped and in the short, awkward silence that followed, their eyes met. Helen felt as if she was lost in time when she looked into his eyes, the green of them captivated her. She almost had to force herself to step back and stop looking into them.

He was the first to break the silence.

"I have half a truckload of wood for you. It should get you through the next few weeks while you're here. I also brought along my tools and a few boards we had lying around the farm. Henry said you have some holes in the floor that need fixing," he said, spinning his truck keys on his pointer finger nervously.

"Oh, thank you. But I'm hoping I won't be here for more than another week. I have to do as much as I can to get this place back on the market and then I'm headed back to the States," she said, making a point to touch on the fact she would not be sticking around.

Connor pocketed his keys and began walking up the hill next to her.

"That's too bad, it's a great little place. I've always liked it. When I was a wee boy, I used to walk down and visit Flora, the old woman who lived there. She always had the most amazing tales of adventure."

"Oh really, What sort of tales?" Helen asked.

"You know, the ones with knights, dragons, and beautiful princesses imprisoned in towers. That sort of thing. She was a wonderful woman—despite the things people around here say about her. I was very sorry to hear of her passing."

"Do you know how she died?" Helen inquired.

"I'm not quite sure, old age I think. I never understood why the cottage took so long to sell. It stayed empty for nearly five years until you came along. What drove you to buy a house in Scotland?" he asked.

"Well, it was a bit of a rash decision on my end. When I saw it, it called to me. As crazy as that sounds. But I didn't think it through thoroughly, and I emptied my savings account as a result. That's why I need to repair it and re-list it as soon as possible."

"It doesn't sound crazy, who wouldn't be drawn to that little cottage? Well, it's sad to hear you'll be leaving it so soon, I'm sure it's liked the company," Connor said, taking long strides next to her as they neared Fernbeg.

"You speak as if the house had feelings," she said, amused.

"Well, they do, you know. An abandoned house will become depressed and give up on holding its walls up and its roof steady. But a house full of joy and love will hold fast and strong for the people it keeps dear inside. It starts with the first person to lay a brick into place, putting their love and care into it, then on to the first owners, filling its walls with hopes and dreams and all the generations to come with their loves and losses. How can a house not feel?"

Helen thought long and hard about it as they walked the rest of the way back. It was a very profound thing. She couldn't help but smile thinking about this five-hundred-year-old cottage, a guardian to all who'd slept within its walls for generations.

Back at the cottage, they began carrying wood from the truck up through the garden and stacking it next to the front door. By the time the pile was fully formed and the truck was empty, it was past noon. Helen invited Connor in for something to eat and to have a look at what needed to be fixed.

"Well, let me see what I have to offer you for lunch," Helen said, as she rooted around in the kitchen for something that would resemble a midday meal. "Okay, I have cheese and bread, or cereal? Before you even say anything, yes, I know that is not the best choice for one's nutritional needs but it's what I have," she said with a smile and raised both hands in a gesture of surrender.

"Well, I have to say you have the makings of one of my favor-ite meals," Connor said as he stood up and grabbed one of the cast iron pans off the beam and placed it down on the old cookstove. He struck a match and brought the stove to life with a dancing blue flame that licked the bottom of the iron pan. Then he grabbed the cheese and began cutting thin slices, laying one on top of the other. With a few slices of bread, he headed back to the stove and began to cook.

Helen sat back and watched as he whipped up the perfect grilled cheese sandwiches. She laughed to herself. How had she not thought of that days ago?

"Voila! The best lunch one can have with only two ingredients on hand," Connor said, as he handed Helen a perfectly toasted sandwich.

"Wow, a sheep farmer, handyman, and chef. It's almost too much," Helen joked as she bit into the first real warm meal she had eaten in days. Connor blushed a little as he sat down beside her.

While they ate, they made small talk about the weather. Once they had finished, Helen got up and placed two small crusty edges she had saved for Storm into his bowl, causing a fit of tail wagging from the little wolf.

"Well, even wolves like table scraps," Connor joked as they went into the sitting room. He took in the broken floorboards and cracked windows. "Wow, this place really needs some TLC."

"Yeah, there's more of the same in most of the rooms, unfortunately. Also, the bathroom has some plumbing issues. It's quite a bit of work and I understand if you don't want to take it on," Helen said, secretly praying these were all things in his skill set. An official contractor would be way out of her budget with all the repairs that needed to be done.

"Oh, this is nothing, you should have seen the barn after a massive storm back in 2007. We practically had to rebuild the whole thing. This is just some small stuff. I should be able to fix it all within a couple of days." After examining the broken floorboards a little more, he asked Helen to show him the rest of what needed to be fixed.

She showed him the bathroom and the leaky pipe that had rotted the floorboards under the sink, then the bedroom with its broken window and damaged flooring. The tour of damage continued until they reached the door to the library.

"How is the library? Any damage there?" Connor asked as he opened the door.

"No, for some reason this room is in perfect condition. It's strange but the door was closed when we got here so I'm assuming none of the elements got in because of that."

Connor stood there in amazement. "This room hasn't changed a bit since I was a boy. It still looks just as I remember it. Right down to the emerald-green armchairs. It's amazing! This is where Flora would tell me all her wild tales of adventure. Right there." He pointed to the chairs that faced the fireplace. He walked over and pulled a book off the shelf. It was a book of children's stories with a red cover and worn corners. "She used to read to me from this book and tell me how the Grimm brothers came up with their tales. The stories she told of their quests for stories were more interesting than the stories themselves," Connor said, holding the book and looking deep into its cover as if he was staring through it into another world.

"She sounds like she was a wonderful woman," Helen said, smiling at him. "You should keep that book. It belongs to you and the memories you have of it."

"No, this book belongs to the library, it wouldn't be right to take it from its home," he said, putting the book back in its place on the shelf.

"Well, if you change your mind before I leave, you don't have to ask," Helen said.

Turning around, he gave her a nod, then headed out of the library and back into the broken-down part of the house.

"Okay, first we should get a fire going and then work on those windows. What do you think?" he asked Helen as she stepped out of the library and shut the door.

"I think you're the expert. Let's do it!"

Connor started a fire and got the house back to a comfortable temperature before he took out his measuring tape and began to take measurements for the glass replacements, writing them down on a small notepad he had tucked into his back pocket.

Helen resolved to do some work while Connor went about his business. Deciding to paint the sitting room first, Helen took out the gallon of navy paint and began mixing it up. Then she took out the roller and brushes from the hardware store bag and assembled them on the small coffee table. She made her way around the room and filled in small patches where the plaster was degrading before brandishing her paintbrush.

"Right, I'm going to run into town and get the glass to replace these windows," Connor said as he snapped the tape measure back onto his pocket. "Do you need anything else while I'm there?"

"No, I think I'm okay for now. Thank you. Let me go and get some money for the glass," Helen said, setting down her plaster knife and making her way across the room. She was mentally calculating the cost of the glass, feeling that nervous ache in the pit of her stomach as she considered her finances, when he interrupted her thought.

"No, that's okay, I'll put it on your tab," he said with a smile and a nod, then walked out the front door and got into his truck. As he left, she breathed a sigh of relief. He had lessened her financial worries, even if it was only temporarily.

Helen watched him drive off, thinking about how much she liked his company. He was easy to be around and seemed sincere. It was similar to the way she felt around Kevin, but Kevin did not stir up the same feelings that Connor did in her. Connor gave her an ache deep down in her soul. As if she'd found a missing piece of herself she didn't even know was lost until they met.

But this was not the distraction she was looking for. In fact, it was the opposite of what she needed. She had to keep her head in the game and fix this place up so she could get back to her normal life.

Chapter Eleven

RAINED IN

She grabbed the old sheets Storm used as a bed and threw them down as her drop cloth, deciding on the wall opposite the fireplace as the first one to tackle. Opening the can, she slowly poured the deep blue paint into the tray, watching its thick rolling waves double over on themselves. She glided her roller into the paint and made her first stroke on the wall. It was harsh on the light yellow and she second-guessed her choice of color. But after a few more strokes, the wall started to transform. The navy blue seemed to deepen the look of the room. With each stroke, she felt as if the room was beginning to change.

Once the entire wall was painted, she took a step back and looked at it. It was like gazing into the deep blue of the night sky. She felt a calm come over her, like the room had taken a deep breath, and was happy to be rid of the unnatural, cheery yellow it had been stuck with for years. She kept going until the only wall left was the one that housed the fireplace, hesitating for a moment. She felt as if she needed to preserve something here. There was something that needed to be saved, but what was it? She was unsure until she saw it: carved into the wall just above the fireplace were the initials F+T with a small heart next to them. Helen ran her fingers over the engraving and felt a deep sadness overtake her. It pained her to think of these two people who loved each other, lives that had come and gone, leaving their mark for someone to just paint over and erase.

She decided to paint over the initials first, being careful to not fill in the grooves with the thick paint. Once the roller turned the sunshine yellow into dark midnight, she took a small knife and picked away the wet paint so that the F+T showed through with the yellow underneath, giving a glowing effect. It felt right to have it showcased, preserving a bit of the home's history.

She continued on, painting until the whole room was the color of the deep sea. It suited the room well and even gave new life to the floral sofa, its rose pinks and periwinkle popping like flowers in a night garden. Now, it was time to give the baseboards and window trim a fresh coat of white.

She was finishing the last baseboard when she heard Connor's truck pull in. The door to the cottage opened and he walked in with a nice clean piece of glass for the window.

"Wow, what a transformation. It looks great! You have an eye for color," he said, setting the glass down and inspecting the room.

"Thank you, I guess that's the perk of being an artist," she joked.

Connor smiled, then walked over and began removing the gray grout that held the old broken pane in place.

"Can you give me a hand, Helen? I want to make sure that

the glass doesn't come out while I'm removing this grout. Just put your hand here."

She had to stand in front of him, their bodies almost touching, as he worked around her to remove the last of the grout from the top of the frame. Helen's heart quickened at their close proximity and she bit her lip, trying to remind herself this was not what she was here for.

"Okay, great. Thanks. You can let go now," he said, moving aside so that she could scoot out from under his arm. He slowly let the glass drop into his hands and set it up against the wall. "One step closer to keeping the fire's heat inside this place," he said.

Feeling flushed, Helen decided to take Storm out for a quick walk so she could get some fresh air, while Connor finished the window installation. She hooked the lead onto his collar and walked him out the front gate and down the hill toward the loch.

"Well, boy, it looks like another storm is coming in," she said to the little wolf.

Storm stuck his nose into the air and sniffed out the direction of the rain before bounding down the hill and back, making circles around Helen as she peered into the distance. There were black clouds looming on the horizon, moving at a rather quickening pace. She could hear the distant crack of thunder as rain came down in sheets over the hill across the loch. The storm seemed to be rolling in from the sea; she could smell salt in the wind. The fur along Storm's neck stood up almost like a mohawk as he let out a low growl.

"It's okay, boy, it's only a thunderstorm. Just think, if you were a wild wolf you would be out in the elements facing that thing head on."

It was a funny thought; Storm had become like any other pet dog, eager for his daily meals and walks and days spent lazily sleeping by the fire. Yet he was a wild animal and, if need be, his instincts would kick in and he could survive out here in the open. She looked down at him and smiled. There was a deep connection between the two of them and she was certain by the way he looked back at her that he felt it too.

Small drops of rain hit her forehead as the storm raced inward from the sea. She turned and began to walk with vigor up the hill, Storm close by her side. By the time they arrived back at the cottage, the rain was coming down in buckets and they were both soaked to the bone. Walking in the front door, they looked like a couple of drowned rats.

Helen wrung out her wet hair and unhooked Storm from his leash. After intensely shaking himself off, he went over to the fireplace and laid down on the rug next to the fire, still burning with the cured wood from the McKenzie farm.

Helen took off her wet shoes and looked up to see that Connor had fixed the window. Then she caught a wonderful scent coming from the kitchen. Storm also noticed the smell and headed directly into the hallway. Following behind him, they entered the kitchen to see Connor standing at the old cookstove with a large cast-iron skillet in front of him. He was scraping the pan with a wooden spoon and grabbing a package of what looked to be some kind of fish off the counter next to him.

"Well, I didn't realize I ordered a full-service handyman. Is it customary in Scotland to cook dinner after doing your repairs?" Helen teased as she sat down on one of the long benches at the table.

"Well, from the looks of what you had for us at lunch, I thought you could use a proper meal, or it might be cereal for dinner. So I picked up a few things at the shop when I was out getting the glass." He gestured over toward the sink where a bottle of wine sat with two mugs next to it.

"Is it that obvious?" Helen said, popping the cork and filling the two glasses half full with the rich red wine. Just then, a loud crack of thunder shook the house and the rain began pounding down on the roof.

"Seems the storm has finally made its way to land. My granda said he expected it before nightfall," Connor explained, taking the mug Helen extended to him.

"I've always loved thunderstorms, even as a kid. My mother hated them but my father would bring me out into the garage and we'd sit in these old folding lawn chairs and count the time in between the flash and the bang. But, somehow here it all seems so much more intense," Helen said as she walked over and inspected what was being cooked. "This smells incredible. What is it?"

Connor carefully added the fish fillet to the skillet along with some freshly chopped herbs in what looked like a milky liquid.

"You are being treated to my famous Cullen Skink. Don't let the name fool you. It's delicious and just the thing to warm you up. But I think having those windows fixed will also help," he said, turning the stove down to let the milky soup simmer.

The next half hour was filled with lively conversation as Connor cooked and Helen drank wine. When the chowder was finished, Connor served them both heaping bowls full and large chunks of crusty bread. Storm lay under the table, eagerly anticipating one of them to drop a morsel of food onto the floor.

"I have to admit, I'm not crazy about fish chowder, but this smells tasty. So, let's give it a go!" she said, taking a small spoonful. She was a bit hesitant at first, but she was pleasantly surprised by how much she actually enjoyed it. "Oh, it's absolutely delicious, Connor!" She took another large spoonful, forgetting how good a hot, home-cooked meal could be and throwing etiquette to the wind.

"I'm glad you like it. It was my gran's recipe. I make it every year on my dad's birthday."

"Well, he's one lucky guy to have such an amazing cook for a son. He must thoroughly enjoy it."

"He used to. He's been gone for a little over five years now. That's why I moved back home to help Granda with the farm. My dad was mostly running it when he passed and my granda just couldn't do it alone at his age. So, it was the next logical move for me to come back and take over the family business." As he spoke, he moved the food around in his bowl, not eating any of it.

"I'm so sorry. I didn't know. That must have been a hard decision to make. Is your mother still living?" Helen asked, taking another sip of her wine.

"She left when I was seventeen. She and my dad had a falling out and rather than fight for her he just let her go. She lives in Kent with her new husband now. I haven't seen her much in the last ten years or so. It wasn't a hard decision for me to move back home, I knew it was where I needed to be. I'd just finished university and moved to Glasgow. I was about to start my first job as a geo-environmental engineer for a large company that dealt with surveying coastal erosion when it happened. My granda would have never been able to keep the farm if I hadn't come back. I couldn't let that happen. It's been in our family for generations," Connor said, finally taking a bit of chowder as another large crack of thunder shook the cottage and the storm moved closer.

"I'm sorry, that doesn't sound like an easy situation even if you knew what you had to do. I read an article on your family farm in a local paper, actually. It was in amongst a stack of newspapers in the sitting room when I got here. It must have been written before your father passed because it mentioned him as the person who was running the farm at the time. It was a very interesting article, talking about how your family had owned it for generations and been part of the witch trials. Seems as though you guys were on the right side of the fight."

"That would have been my great-great-great-great-grandfather, William McKenzie. His oldest son, Tomas, was engaged to one of the girls accused of witchcraft before he died. William tried to protect her by letting her stay in his sheep barn. But they found her, and there wasn't much he could do. It's quite a tragic tale."

Connor refilled their wine glasses. A chill ran down the back of Helen's neck as she thought about the story, sipping slowly at her wine.

After finishing their meal and polishing off the rest of the bottle, they headed into the sitting room so Connor could restock the fire and check to see if the grout around the windows had properly sealed. Helen sat on the floral sofa and looked at the room in the fading light. It was almost dark outside now and the storm raged on around them. Sharp flashes of lightning lit up the room as if it was midday, then in its absence, the room turned almost black with its new, dark walls. The lightning became so frequent that it almost caused a strobe light effect in the room, making Helen's head spin after all the wine. The thunder grew louder and soon the storm was raging directly over the cottage.

"Wow, this is quite the storm. I don't think you'll have power much longer if this keeps up," Connor said, just as a loud crack echoed off the hill, sending shock waves of sound raining down on Fernbeg. Within a minute the power flickered, flashed, and then went out.

"Shit!" Helen said as she stood up and fumbled around with only the light of the smoldering fire to guide her.

"Do you have any candles or torches?" Connor asked, grabbing the box of matches off the mantel and striking one, sending the darkness back and briefly lighting up the room.

"Yes, I have some candles in the kitchen and a flashlight on my nightstand in the bedroom."

Helen thought about the candles and the spell. She was grateful that she hadn't used them for any more silliness or she wouldn't have them now when she actually needed them. Pushing all that to the back of her mind, she found her way into the kitchen and gathered the candles. Setting one in an empty cup, she lit it and brought light back into the kitchen.

The room looked different under candlelight, almost as if she had stepped back in time and could see the way it may have looked back in the 1600s. She pictured all the women who'd lived here over the centuries cooking dinner for their families by candlelight and felt a newfound appreciation for modern-day conveniences. It would have been quite a chore to do everything a woman was expected to do in those times in such dim light. But she couldn't deny there was a romantic aspect to it that she did find appealing.

Connor came into the kitchen with the flashlight from the bedroom and Storm at his heels.

"Are there any candle holders in this place?" he asked.

"Yeah, in the library on the mantel."

Helen led the way down the hall to the library door. Upon opening it, the room glowed, just as it had the last time the power had failed. The whole room sparkled as if it was made of some sort of bioluminescence.

"The last time the electricity went out I came down here and it was just as it is now, almost glowing," Helen said as she glided her finger across one of the bookshelves.

"There's certainly something different about it, something

almost magical," Connor said as he grabbed the candle holders off the fireplace and put candles in them. When he struck the match, the sound bounced off the walls, creating a chime-like sound that lasted several seconds. The candlelight only seemed to emphasize the magical glow the room held.

Helen felt a strong sense of longing come over her and heard a very low and light humming sound coming from somewhere in the room. She followed the melody over to the journal she had found the last time the lights had gone out. It was the journal—it was singing to her.

She picked it up and sat down in one of the overstuffed armchairs next to the fireplace. The soft yellow glow of the candle illuminated the pages and made the dark ink on the bone-white paper stand out. The shadows of the flame cast down and danced on the page, urging her to read what was there.

"What's that you've got?" Connor asked as he sat in the other overstuffed chair next to her.

"I think it's a journal. Written back in the late 1500s. I found it here the last time Fernbeg lost power. I don't know why, but somehow I feel it calling to me, as if I'm meant to read it." She flipped through a few pages, not daring to read anything just yet.

"Amazing! I can't believe it's that old, it looks almost perfect. Maybe you should give it a go. It would probably be a fairly interesting thing to read," Connor said. He sat back and stretched his legs out in front of him, settling himself into a comfortable listening position.

"You want me to read it aloud? Now?" Helen asked with a bit of hesitation in her voice.

"Yeah, you've got me intrigued about what might be in this magical journal. Anyway, we've got nothing else to do and I can't go anywhere in this storm, so you're stuck with me a bit longer."

He looked at her with the wide eyes and smile of a curious little child about to be read a bedtime story.

"Okay, but just the first couple of pages. My eyes may give out in this dim light," Helen said, flipping back to the first page and smoothing the paper down with her hands.

Every time she held the book it seemed to awaken something inside her. She felt as if it held answers within its pages, answers to questions she hadn't even thought to ask.

As she began to read the first line, the candle flames dimmed then doubled in size, lighting the room up brighter than any lightbulb could have. Each word rolled off her tongue as if she had spoken them before, as if she knew them from her own heart, and before the first line was even fully read, she knew what the next would be.

Chapter Twelve

JOURNAL ONE

September 5, 1597

Today is the 17th year of my birth. I awoke to Mary at my front door with a plate full of hotcakes in celebration. After filling our bellies to the point of bursting, we walked down to the loch to pick flowers and sit by the water's edge. We spent hours talking while lying in the grass by the loch, soaking up the warm, early autumn sun. It was a small delight to be able to set our duties aside for a few hours and enjoy a bit of freedom.

Tomas came down and greeted us as we were packing up our belongings before walking home. He handed me a gift, wrapped in a rough burlap cloth. Upon opening it I found this beautiful handmade leather journal I am writing in now. It is the most beautiful thing I have ever seen, with its deep brown leather jacket. Wrapping its way around the front cover is a border of thistle with small acorns scattered throughout, tooled into the leather. It must have taken him hours to create such a lovely piece. I have never owned such a wondrous thing of my own before. My heart was overjoyed with such a thoughtful gift.

When Mary was not looking, he stole a kiss from me and whispered he loved me for the first time. I do not think I could have been any happier than at that very moment. Even though he has only been courting me for a few months I feel so deeply for him. We share a connection, unlike anything I have ever felt before. He asked me to meet him at the rowan tree in two days' time. I am not sure I can wait that long, but now that I have this journal I can hold him close to me even when he is not near.

With light,
Freya

September 7, 1597

I took leave today after feeding the animals, telling Father that I was going to the northeast field to pick mullein for Killian's son, Roger, who has come down with an earache. It was only a half lie as I did pick the mullein for the poor boy but not until after I met Tomas at the rowan tree.

When I arrived, he was there waiting for me with a large wool blanket thrown down upon the ground. He'd brought cheese from his farm, a round loaf of crusty bread, and a bottle of mead. He gave my cheek a gentle kiss and tucked a small wildflower behind my ear, making me blush.

We sat under the tree with its glowing red berries and indulged in food and talked for what seemed hours. I lay in his arms looking to the sky through the overgrowth of branches and felt as if life could not be sweeter. I listened to the rhythmic sound of his heartbeat and felt mine in sync, two now beating as one. Louder and stronger while they beat together.

Before I left, he grabbed my hand and pulled me in for a long, soft kiss. That is when he told me that he intended on asking my father for my hand in marriage. At that very moment, my heart no longer belonged to me, for Tomas holds it now and will always. I know my father will approve as Tomas comes from a well-respected farming family, but I am not sure how his family will take to the idea of their son marrying a healer such as myself. I now have to pray to the goddess of love and light to bless our union. May our love be as strong as the sea and withstand any storm that may lie ahead.

With light,
Freya

September 12, 1597

The days are growing colder and everyone is working hard to bring in the final harvests of the season and split the last of the wood for the long winter that lies ahead. My days have been consumed with gathering the late-season herbs and processing them into tinctures and salves. Being one of only five healers within the four bordering towns, the people depend greatly on me for remedies for the sicknesses that will come with the bitter winter months. This summer has been kind to us and Mother Earth has blessed us with ample amounts of herbs, berries, and mushrooms needed for a well-stocked apothecary.

As much as I have been focused on my duties as a healer, I have been stealing away time to be with Tomas when I can. For a day cannot be whole without the sight of his gentle smile. Mostly, our meetings are brief, but we make the most of the time we are given. I sometimes walk with him in the fields, gathering herbs while he attends to the sheep. Often, before returning home, we find a spot on the old stone walls in the backfield and watch the sun as it sets over the loch. In these brief moments when we are alone with only the earth and elements as witnesses, we kiss with such passion I feel as if I may burst at my seams with the love that I have for him.

Once harvest season is over we will marry. Both families are pleased with the idea of our union and have blessed us with a late autumn harvest wedding. What a joyous occasion it will be. I feel so immensely blessed that I am spending my life with a man that I love and who loves me. I can't help but dream of the life that lies ahead. We will build our home in the backfield near the old rowan so that it can stand watch over us as we grow our family upon its roots.

I truly believe that it was Mary who created our unlikely union. She had fashioned a love charm the day that Tomas first took notice of me. We had been at the Aingeal Coille Well, known to the wise women of the area for its magical properties. Mary had gathered a small cup of water from the well and dropped two stones in, one light in color and one dark. Then she recited a love charm passed down from her great-grandmother over the cup, rubbing her thumbs around its edge three times. Then we both drank from it, in hopes of finding our true loves. I had taken the first sip and on the way back from the well we saw Tomas herding his sheep into a field adjacent to the woodland from whence we'd come. He turned and looked at me, and even though we'd seen each other hundreds of times before, his expression was different, as if he was seeing me for the first time. He then tilted his hat and smiled. Not long after that, he began to court me.

So it is Mary I owe thanks to for sending my true love to me. One day it will be my turn to cast love in her favor.

With light,
Freya

September 17, 1597

On this coming sabbath, Mary and I will attend our first quarterly meeting of healers from Connel, Barcaldine, and Duror to trade herbs and recipes. We heard of these meetings as children many times but this will be the first we will attend.

Our mothers taught us the ways of the wise women. It is knowledge that has been passed down from mother to daughter for generations in both our families. We took over their positions in our village when they took ill and both perished last spring. The sickness came suddenly and took many in our small village, leaving us with little more than half of what we once had. Thankfully, Father was spared but Mother was not as lucky, as she had been treating the sick for weeks, trying to save anyone she could.

Tonight, I will prepare the last of the things I will bring with me on our journey. I have already gathered the herbs and poultices and have placed them in a large basket that I acquired at the summer market. I have decided to adorn myself with Mother's cape. She was the seer and leader of their group and was looked upon fondly. I am afraid that I may not be able to fill such shoes as hers. I have not yet been blessed with second sight, but I will do my best and step into my position as a daughter must do when she is required. I only hope that I am strong enough and ready for my newfound duties. I ask the Goddess to bless me with my powers as soon as possible.

With light,
Freya

Helen stopped reading and looked over at Connor, who was staring at her with bright eyes, eagerly awaiting the next page.

"Wow, amazing. I knew the legends of witches from these parts but now we have proof! Keep going, let's see what happens.

I'm on the edge of my seat here!" Connor said as he pushed himself back against the velvet chair.

Somehow it felt wrong reading it aloud to him. Even though it had been written centuries ago, it still felt like a violation to read this girl's personal thoughts, however intriguing they were.

At that very moment, the lights came back on and the house began to hum with the sounds of the modern world.

"I think that's our cue. It's getting a bit late, let's pick this up another day, shall we?" Helen said as she stood up, closing the journal and placing it back on the small end table next to the chair. Connor looked disappointed but agreed.

"You're right, I still have the bedroom window to fix before I head home."

Storm led the way back into the kitchen where Helen began cleaning up after their supper and Connor headed into the bedroom to replace the glass in the window.

It was nice to have another person in the house with her, Helen thought as she washed the pan Connor had used to cook their delicious dinner in. Even though it had only been a handful of days since she arrived, it was the most she had been completely alone in a long time. True, she didn't get into the social scene much back home, but she had work and Kevin to keep her company. The feeling that came with being alone in a country where no one knew her, in a small cottage in the middle of nowhere, was a whole other ballgame. It definitely brought a new perspective into view. She knew she was missing something in her life and reading the journal only heightened the feeling. It was a longing for a connection with someone on a higher level, like Tomas and Freya had, and it scared her. This was not what she had in mind for her "new perspective" on things.

She stopped and listened to Connor humming in the other

room. It was the tune he had been playing on his bagpipes the day they met. Something in the melody made her feel very sad even though it was a cheery tune. She could not explain what it was, but it struck her down to her core.

A moment later, Connor came in with his infectious smile, announcing that he had fixed the window.

"This place should stay much warmer now," he said, placing his tools back into his old metal toolbox.

"Thank you so much, Connor. You've been so helpful and I had a wonderful time with you today. It was nice to talk to another human and not a wolf all day," she said with a laugh.

"My pleasure. I'll come by tomorrow and work on the leak in the bathroom. Let's say around eight?"

"Sounds perfect! I'll be here this time, I promise. No running off to the loch. Hey, before you go, can I ask you what that tune is you were humming?"

"It's an old bagpipe melody one of my great-great-grandfathers wrote for his son. Something all of us McKenzie boys learn to play when we take up the pipes. Why do you ask?"

"It just seems so familiar to me. I thought maybe it was a tune my father might have played on the piano, but I guess not."

"Speaking of your parents, how did they feel about you buying a house in Scotland?" he asked.

"They don't know. I didn't tell them. Don't get me wrong, I love my parents, but they are not the kind of people who would understand a spontaneous house purchase. My mother would completely flip. I plan on telling them when I get home and have successfully sold the cottage and turned a profit. That they will understand. We have a good relationship but it's a bit weird because they're left-brained, science-based people and then there is me, their only daughter, who is totally right-brained. Who apparently buys houses in foreign countries on a whim," she told him, throwing in a little laugh to lighten the subject.

"I get that. It's never easy being yourself in the shadow of strong-willed parents," he said, giving her a knowing smile.

Connor stoked the fire before he left, making sure there was enough wood on it to get Helen through the night. She walked him to the door and when she turned around to say goodnight they stood only inches apart, their eyes fixed on one another. In that moment, she had the overwhelming urge to kiss him, but she pulled back and opened the door for him instead. Keeping herself in check.

"Goodnight," she said as he walked past her and out the door.

"Goodnight, Helen," he echoed back as he walked to his truck.

It must have been the mix of wine and the love story in the journal that had her head spinning and her heart beating erratically. She was glad she hadn't made a rash decision that might make things awkward for him to come back. After all, she needed him to help get Fernbeg back into livable conditions so she could get it back on the market, so she would just have to keep things on a friendly basis, even if she was drawn to him. She needed to pull herself back together and get a move on with the renovation, no more idle distractions.

As she watched his truck pull out of the driveway and head back up the road, she felt an unnatural chill in the room. The fire was ablaze and the windows were intact, so there was no longer a draft. Yet it felt as if it had dropped ten degrees since Connor left just a few minutes ago.

Helen had an eerie feeling come over her—like she was being watched. She looked around the room but it was just her and

Storm, who was now dozing by the fire. She chalked the feeling up to too much wine, spooky stories, and being alone again at night in the cottage, then headed into the bedroom, calling Storm to follow suit. She was ready to bring this day to a close. It had been long and full of emotions she was not used to dealing with. She welcomed the blissfulness of sleep as she laid her head down on the lumpy pillow that smelled of old wood and sea mist.

As her eyelids grew heavy and she drifted off to sleep, the outline of a figure trimmed in shadows stood watch over her.

Chapter Thirteen

1597

It was a crisp autumn morning, and the sun was slow in making its way over the hills to greet the rolling meadows. The rising light gave a candlelit glow to the edges of everything it touched in the wake of the dawn. There was a peacefulness that came with being up as the sun rose. The stillness of the air, the cold, dew-dropped grass, and the silence of a land not yet awake were all so alluring.

The small chicken coop was old and weathered by time but still did its job well. Seven laying hens had nested safely and produced six beautiful, brown speckled eggs. The small wooden hatch proved to be the perfect size for a hand to reach in and pluck the eggs from their resting place. The hens clucked as their newly laid eggs were stolen away, breaking the silence that once filled the air. They would make a fine breakfast and fuel for the day ahead. Tucking them into a large pocket sewn onto the front of her apron, she walked into the garden beside the cottage. Kneeling down, she picked small handfuls of rosemary and sage and placed them in the pocket alongside the eggs.

The sun had finally peeked its head over the hilltop and illuminated the landscape with its warm autumn glow. The picturesque scene called out to her and she needed to capture it. Grabbing a small leather journal out of the other large pocket of her apron, she sat upon the stone wall bordering the garden. The stones were cold and damp to the touch and the moss that filled each crack dripped with dew. With a small piece of charcoal in her hand, she sketched the lines of the landscape. From the rolling field and towering hill, down to the shoreline of the loch and the line where the sea met the sky. Then, setting the book down, she went back into the garden and gathered a handful of flowers in golds and oranges, crushing them in her palms until they made a thick paste. Adding a bit of dew from the grass, she created a loose, light pigment and rubbed it onto the paper in different places. Doing this several times with different vegetation from the garden, she produced a likeness of the scene before her.

With an open palm she waved her hand over the paper, and as she did the pigments fused into a vibrant glow. Fragments of herbs or flowers that lay clumped on the page slowly melted into the paper, becoming one with it, creating a painting that looked as alive and real as what she looked out upon.

Behind her, the sound of the cottage door closing startled her out of her thoughts. She turned to see an old man in a long white shirt and brown work pants peering out at her. She had such love for this man; his kind eyes and half-cocked smile made her feel happy.

"Well, are you going to dilly dally all day in that garden of yours or are you going to come in and make your father a proper breakfast?" he said, patting his belly.

"Yes, Father. We had quite the bounty from the hens today, six eggs! How about I cook you some of your favorite herbed eggs for breakfast?" she said as she closed her journal and tucked it back into her pocket before heading into the cottage.

It was still quite dim in the kitchen as the sun had not risen high enough to cast adequate light through the window. A candle burned by the stove on a small side table, giving just enough light so that she could see.

On the edge of a well-used cast iron pan, she cracked the first egg. It hissed and crackled as it hit the hot metal. Then the next and another until all but two were cooking—she set those aside for another meal. She sprinkled the eggs with the herbs from the garden, lighting the room aloft with the sweet aromas of the wild. She muttered a protection charm as she added the sage, just as she did most mornings. Once the eggs were cooked, she placed them in a small wooden bowl and handed them over to her father. She sat beside him and buttered a small slice of bread for herself.

"When will you and Mary leave for Duror?" the old man asked, as he spooned egg into his mouth.

"We need to leave soon. It's a long journey and we have many miles to cover before dark. I am hoping that we are blessed with dry weather. I looked out to the sea and sensed a storm, but it was too far away to tell which direction it will take."

"Well, you best take your staff then. It might come in useful if you need to change the direction of the storm."

"I wouldn't leave here without it on such a journey. Are you sure you'll be alright here on your own?

"Oh, course I will. Now, don't you go on worrying about me. You have a lot to think about. Being sworn in as a healer is no small thing. It is important that you go into this with the grace and power of your mother."

"I know, but I am not even half the witch Mother was. My powers never matured more than silly charms and protection spells. I do not hold the power of second sight as she did and I am not sure I ever will," she said, looking down at the floor and prodding a small beetle into a crack near the door.

"Freya, from the day you were born your mother could see great power in you. That's why she insisted we named you after the goddess of love and light. You may not have found it yet, but it *is* there." He grabbed her hand and gave it a gentle squeeze.

"Thank you, Father," she said, holding his gaze. "I have to go now, Mary will be waiting for me. I'll see you in three days' time and I will make sure to find you some goat cheese while I'm gone." She smiled at him then leaned down and gave the old man a gentle kiss on the forehead before leaving the room.

Gathering her basket, she threw a lush green velvet cape around her shoulders and fastened the silver clasp. The cape was the color of the rich moss that grew deep in the forest on the roots of the oak and rowan trees. It not only protected against the cold but would provide camouflage if trouble arose on her travels.

Leaving the cottage, she grabbed a tall, twisted branch resting against the outer wall. It had a delicate carving of a thistle, with acorns wrapping around its handle. Her father, being a woodworker, had fashioned it for her out of an old fallen branch of the rowan tree she had brought home one day.

Once it was firmly in her grip, she pressed it down hard into the ground and pushed off, walking up the path toward the large green field. The only sound in the air was that of her shoes pushing the rough gravel beneath her feet. The sun had now risen over the hill and was gracing the land with its warmth and beauty. It seemed the day would be brisk but not cold, which was perfect for the trek that lay ahead.

Cresting the hill, a voice rang out, splitting the silence that still lay heavy in the early morning air.

"Well, it's a good thing I didn't stay at home waiting for you to come and get me or we would be utterly behind," Mary said teasingly as she grabbed her bag off the stone wall and took up a step beside her.

"Ha, you are always two steps ahead of me, Mary. That's why I need you by my side, to keep me in line."

The two girls laughed as they walked down the rough dirt path together.

Two hours into their journey, they arrived at Loch Etive. Mary called out in a Gaelic song across the water. The lingering mist split and moved so that they could see across to the other side.

On the opposite side of the loch was a raft with a smooth gray seal lying on top of it. When it heard Mary's song, it lifted its head up and looked. The girls watched it slip off the raft and into the water. As Mary sang, the seal swam closer, dragging the old raft alongside it. For a brief moment, before it reached the shore, it disappeared into the mist. When it reappeared, it was no longer a seal but a man, glorious and muscular. He handed Mary the rope and gave her a small bow before walking back into the water and disappearing.

They boarded the raft with what little they had with them and made their way across the loch. Once they reached the other side, Mary searched through her baskets and pulled out a small parcel wrapped in paper. Opening it, she placed a fish upon the deep brown earth on the water's edge, as a gesture of gratitude for the help that was given.

"Tapadh leat mo charaid, thank you, my friend," Mary said, turning from the water. As they walked on, they heard a splash and knew that the selkie had retrieved its reward for helping them.

They walked on for another few hours before stopping to rest and eat. They chose a small field scattered with curly dock along its edges that had taken seed. It was a herb they could not pass up gathering the roots of. It had powerful purifying and cleansing properties and could be used for a number of ailments such as digestive problems and blood cleansing. They could never have enough of it in their supplies.

Pulling up half the plants and chopping off the stalks, they piled the roots up and wiped them down with a dry rag so as not to fill their baskets with dirt. They had a rule to only gather half of whatever they harvested, leaving the remaining half for the animals and Mother Nature, to ensure that it would grow again in the coming year. It was something that Freya's mother had taught her. It was a balance with nature, a promise to only take what was needed, no more.

After they finished, Mary pulled out a loaf of crusty bread and a bottle of mead. They took small portions of the bread and only a few sips from the jug, just enough to sustain them until they arrived in Duror. Packing everything up again, they headed back down to the path and out toward the forest. It was the last leg of the journey and the most demanding.

"Do you think we will make it before nightfall?" Freya asked

"We will, as long as we don't slow our pace or stop again," Mary answered back, looking at the dimming light in the sky. Being in the forest at night was not something either of them wanted to experience. If darkness fell while they walked the forest path, they feared they may never come out the other side.

The sun was starting to set as they made it to the forest's

edge. The tall, gangly trees turned to dark silhouettes against a sky that burned with reds and oranges. An opening cut through the immense, ancient forest edge, dark and foreboding. A sense of danger came over them both.

Freya had heard stories of this densely wooded area being inhabited by the fae. Her own mother had often told her tales of this forest as a child and, from what she remembered of them, they weren't happy ones.

"It's true what they say. I can feel them. They dwell here," Mary said with a hint of anxiety in her voice.

Mary's abilities had evolved on her fifteenth birthday. Her mother always said her talents would lie within her huge heart, and they did. She had been blessed and cursed with the powers of an empath, along with the ability to communicate with most beasts. So, when she said that the stories of the fae being in the woods were real, there was a good chance she was right.

The opening to the forest path was flanked by two ancient oaks. Their bark was thick and grooved with age and their leaves had turned the crisp color of autumn. Once the two girls stepped bravely past them into the thick woodland, the light was cut in half by the thick overgrowth of trees. In most places, the trees' roots had broken free of the ground, giving the illusion that they could get up and walk away at any moment. The forest floor was thick with velvety moss, which sprouted mushrooms of various types and colors, the majority of which were poisonous. The path, in contrast, consisted of a very dark, rich earth that sliced through the green moss like a black river. Their soft steps echoed in the tree roots below as they ventured onward.

They had only walked a few hundred yards into the dense woods when they heard a sweet melody chasing through the trees in the wind.

"Block your ears!" Mary commanded, stopping in her tracks and cupping her hands over her ears. "It's the song of the fae."

A sense of foreboding raced through Freya as she held her hands tight over her ears, knowing that the song of the fae had lured many to their deaths. She stood still, her eyes fixed on Mary's as the damp forest air licked their faces.

Standing still as stone, they waited for quite some time before daring to remove their hands to check and see if the song could still be heard. Once they determined it was safe, they continued on, this time with a heightened sense of their surroundings. Picking up their pace, they both agreed that they needed to reach the other side of the woodland before the sun had completely set. It was dangerous there and the stillness of the night would bring out all sorts of other creatures to fear.

They walked for what felt like hours with no signs of the woodland coming to an end, the light growing dimmer by the minute. Fearing they had taken the wrong path, Mary stopped and put her hand to the ground, slowly pushing the tips of her fingers into the rich soil. She waited in silence for a few moments and then stood up.

"We're on the right path. Just a bit further," she said, gesturing onward.

Freya exhaled a sigh of relief, as she was beginning to worry that they wouldn't make it to the other side until after dark.

Soon, there was a patch of light breaking through the trees up ahead, the opening to a field that would take them onto the very last part of their journey. Letting go of the tense feeling they had harbored through their walk in the forest, they both took in a deep breath and let out a long exhale, releasing their fears.

Just then came a low, deep growl from a dense patch of nearby thicket. A few steps ahead, onto the path, stepped a charcoal gray wolf, its hackles as high as the girls' chests. Baring its teeth, it slowly walked toward them, its bright green eyes reflecting what sunlight still broke through the trees. Mary took two steps forward and lifted her hand towards the wolf.

At that very moment, the wolf lunged forward and Mary let out a blood-curdling scream.

Helen sat bolt upright in bed, sweat pouring off her brow. Storm, startled by her abruptness, let out a loud bark that scared Helen into a scream, echoing off the stark bedroom walls.

"My God, Storm, you scared the shit out of me," she said as the wolf pup jumped up and gave her cheek a wet lick. Patting him on the head, she pushed off the covers and made her way out of bed.

Disturbed by her vivid dream, she headed into the kitchen to put the kettle on. It took two strong cups of coffee to bring her back to reality. She had never in her life had a dream so real. Even her dreams about the lake weren't as lucid as this one.

Filling up her third cup of coffee, she walked into the sitting room and added a small log to the coals resting snug in the bed of ashes from the fire the night before. She knew that the journal must have played some sort of role in evoking the dream. It was as if it had opened a door in her mind that she couldn't close or turn away from, even in sleep. Pacing back and forth and still feeling shaken, she decided to go into the library and get the journal. She needed to know if it was all just her crazy imagination playing out the events from the night before in her head, coupled with too much wine and a full stomach.

Setting her mug down on the side table in the library, she picked up the journal from where she had left it the night before. Flipping through the pages, she stopped. There on the page, as plain as day, was the picture of the sunrise she had seen being painted with magic in her dream.

"Holy shit!" She began picking her way through the pages, reading the words of the dream that had played out in her head.

She read of Mary and the song she had sung to bring the seal to her on the loch, the forest where the fairies lived, and the wolf. It was all there in the journal. Freya's words raced through her mind and her head spun. She set the book down and sat in one of the large, overstuffed armchairs.

What was happening to her? There was no doubt about it, there was something magical happening here in this place. She could feel it. It was as if every day spent in the cottage opened up a glimpse of a new reality that she had never even considered before.

She needed to find out everything she could. About this cottage, this journal, and the girl who wrote it.

Chapter Fourteen

TRIQUETRA

It was almost eight o'clock and Connor was due to arrive any minute. Helen got up and left the library with her cup of coffee in hand and headed into the bedroom to change out of her PJs. She pulled on a pair of loose-fit jeans and a white t-shirt, then went into the bathroom and pulled her hair up into a messy bun. She dabbed on a bit of mascara and penciled her lower eyelids with a thin black border; the effect made her green eyes stand out like gems. She realized as she looked at herself in the mirror, even as shaken as she was, she cared how she looked in front of Connor. This realization made her feel a bit queasy. She hadn't had butterflies like this since she was in high school.

"Okay Helen, get a grip. You're not sixteen," she told herself, shaking it off as she went to the kitchen to fix a quick bite to eat.

Looking at what she had on hand, she decided on a simple

slice of toast to soak up some of the caffeine in her stomach. She filled Storm's bowl with the dry dog food and sat and waited to hear the sound of Connor's truck coming down the gravel road.

It was a quarter till nine when Helen began to worry. Connor had not arrived yet, and from what she could tell, he seemed to be a punctual person. Something was wrong, she could feel it in her bones.

Nine-thirty came and she decided that she couldn't sit idly by any longer. She would walk to the farm to make sure everything was okay. Pulling on her trainers, she grabbed Storm's lead and her raincoat and walked out the front door. It was cold and rainy, and the visibility was so poor that she couldn't see the loch or even the road leading down to the cottage. She stepped carefully as she made her way up the hill and into the backfield, Storm at her heels. The grass, being almost knee height, soaked her jeans in a matter of minutes and Storm became half the wolf he was, fur slicked down on his skinny frame.

The trek up the hill was slow and slippery and more than once Helen lost her footing and fell into the wet grass. The wind picked up and blew fiercely through the fields. There was an ominous feeling in the way the sky darkened and the rain began to beat down hard. Then all at once, the sky lit up as if it was a bright summer's day, and a crack of thunder rang out so loudly that it shook the very ground she stood on. The storm had come in so fast and with such force, it frightened her. She was out in the middle of a field in a raging thunderstorm like a lightning rod waiting for the strike.

"Come on, boy, stay close," she called out to Storm. Panicking, she ran as fast as she was able into the dense woodland that bordered Connor's land, Storm keeping near to her. She knew it was risky going into the woods during the storm, but she liked her chances there much better.

Slipping and sliding on the thick moss that covered everything in the woodland, she decided to rest against a large stone sitting snug beside an old oak tree. The storm raged on and she cowered each time the thunder rang out, echoing off the hills. She felt so weak, so vulnerable out in the elements. The sheer force of the storm was unlike any she had experienced—then again, she had never been out in one unprotected. The lightning flashed, lighting up the sky and casting everything else into dark silhouettes. *One one thousand, two one thousand, three one…* A loud crack followed by a deep rumble cut her short of her next mark. *Almost three miles away* she told herself in an attempt to calm her mind.

Storm rested by her side and didn't seem concerned at all with the storm raging around them when all of a sudden he lifted his nose straight up to the heavens and began to sniff the air. He caught the scent of something in the wind and stood up. In an instant, he had taken off at a full run and was out of eyesight before Helen even made it to her feet.

"Storm, NO! Come back, boy!" she called out to him as she went deeper into the woods in the direction he had gone.

The storm seemed to be getting closer, the thunder and lightning becoming more and more violent. Amongst the chaos, her mind kept slipping back to the little black spell book in the kitchen. She knew she had seen a spell in the book for casting off a storm, but she couldn't think of the words with the storm raging around her.

Deeper and deeper into the forest she went, calling out to Storm as she searched for him, but he was nowhere to be found. All that lay before her was more dense brush and trees. The rain was coming down so hard now that pools of water gathered around her feet as she stepped through the underbrush.

She had almost given up when Storm came running out from behind a large tree with a twisted branch in his teeth and dropped it at her feet.

"Don't tell me you had me chase you halfway into the bloody woods because you wanted to play fetch!" she said, crossly picking up the stick.

The lightning branched out across the sky, and before she could even begin to count, the next crack of lightning struck so near that she could smell the scorched air. Fear now held her tightly in its grip. The rain came down harder, striking like tiny pins with the force of the wind behind it. When the thunder rang out, it was so loud that Helen cupped her hands over her ears and screamed, "STOP!"

She slammed the point of the large branch down on the ground. When the stump end of the branch touched the earth, it sent energy surging through her. Her back arched, head tilted to the sky. Her hair twisted and whirled about her in the wind as her body held itself in an unnatural pose, almost suspended in the air.

Then the storm broke.

All at once, the thunder and lightning stopped, the rain ceased, and the clouds began to lighten and dissipate. As Helen came out of the trance she had been thrust into, the clouds broke apart and the sun pushed through, sending beams of golden light down onto the wet and ravaged landscape.

Helen swayed back and forth before falling to her knees in exhaustion. She felt different, every cell in her body pulsating with raw and untapped energy. She could feel the force of every living being in the forest. She could sense the trees loosening their grip on the earth as the storm passed, the aquifer deep within the earth taking in deep breaths, the grass reaching for the sun again. It felt as if she was the earth, with the power of all the elements pulsating through her.

And then she let the branch fall from her hands. It didn't make a sound as it hit the forest floor, but as soon as it left her hands, the feeling of enlightenment vanished. Blinking her eyes several times as if trying to wake from a dream, she looked around, unaware of what had just happened.

It was at that point that she realized she had no idea where she was. In the midst of the storm, she had chased Storm into the woods so far that she had gotten turned around and didn't know which way was home.

She went to stand up, slipping several times on the wet, velvety moss before grabbing the branch and using it to prop herself up.

"Okay, boy, here's your chance to prove to me what a clever little wolf you are. Can you find our way out of here?" she said, looking down at the little wolf who was not so little anymore. He looked like he had grown quite a bit bigger in the past few days.

Storm sniffed the air, moving his head from right to left and back again. After deciding on a scent to the right, he started off with his nose to the ground. Helen followed, her wet clothing clinging to every inch of her, weighing down each step. They walked for quite some time, weaving in and out of the thicket, when a break of bright light silhouetted the trees ahead. *It must be a field*, she thought as a chill chased the length of her body.

Just a few yards ahead, the tree line gave way to a stone wall bordering a field. As they stepped out of the shade of the forest and into the sunlight, Helen heard some sort of motorized vehicle coming up the hill toward them.

"Good boy, Storm," she said, patting the sopping wet wolf on his head.

As the vehicle came closer, she could make out the driver. It was Connor on a quad bike. She recognized the field now as the one she'd found Connor in, playing the bagpipes. A huge feeling of relief hit her. Not only was Connor okay, but he could not have come at a better time to rescue her. She was exhausted and cold from walking in her rain-drenched clothing.

Connor pulled up next to them and shut off the motor.

"Oh my God, Helen. What were you thinking walking out into the field during a bloody thunderstorm?" he said in a scolding tone, an edge of concern to his voice.

"I was worried about *you*. It was after nine and you still hadn't shown up. You said eight last night and I was worried something had happened. It's not like I have a phone or car, what other choice did I have? It was only sprinkling when we left the cottage. I had no idea it was going to turn into such a huge storm," she said.

"We had a herd of sheep break free last night and didn't realize it until this morning. Granda and I took out the quad bikes to see if we could find them and get them back safely before the weather got any worse. I would have called you but your phone still isn't working."

"Did you find them?" she asked, shivering.

"Yes, before the thunder and lightning started. Granda thought he heard a woman's voice when he was up this way so I told him I'd have a look. Never would have guessed I'd find you out here looking like a drowned rat in a water pail," Connor teased. "Now let's get you back to the farm and warm you up, shall we?"

"Yes, please. That sounds wonderful," Helen said.

Connor gestured for her to join him on the back of the bike, but she hesitated. The thought of being so close to him left her feeling a little reluctant.

"It's fine, don't worry, I'll take it slow," he said, patting the seat.

Thinking about the warm fire and a hot cup of tea pushed her on. She climbed up and rested the stick across the seat between her and Connor, then wrapped her arms around him.

"Are you bringing that branch back with you?" he asked.

"I think I will, it came in quite handy getting me around on this wet terrain. I might need it again."

Connor started up the motor and drove off down the field, spinning up mud as he went, Storm chasing behind them.

Soon, they were at the farmhouse. Connor pulled up next to the front door and shut the quad bike's engine down, then stood and held out a hand for Helen to hold as she dismounted. They walked into the old stone farmhouse with Storm at their heels.

"Have a seat by the fire while I get you some dry clothes," Connor said, gesturing her into the sitting room. Storm immediately walked over and laid down directly in front of the fire.

The room was very masculine and didn't seem to hold much of a woman's touch, other than a very delicately crocheted doily on a small side table and a hand-knit, cream-colored blanket hanging over the plaid couch. The walls on three sides of the room were the dark gray fieldstone the house was made of. The fourth wall separating the sitting room from the kitchen was a newer addition, constructed out of sheetrock. The couch rested against this wall and faced two leather armchairs on each side of the fireplace. An old shotgun hung off a set of brass hangers that had been jammed between the stones. Atop the mantel were four pictures in various antique frames. Helen walked over and picked one up. The image was of a young man pushing a beautiful woman on a swing under a large oak tree. The man looked just like Connor, but it couldn't have been, as this image looked as if it was taken back in the 1950s.

"That was me and my sweet Katherine, back when we first fell in love," said a voice, cutting through the silence.

Helen turned to see Connor's grandfather standing there. He walked over and sat himself down slowly in one of the armchairs.

"Connor looks so much like you," Helen said, setting the picture back down.

"Look at the one to the right of that."

Helen picked up the picture to the right. It was a wedding photo of a man and woman holding up champagne flutes in cheers. Once again, the man in the photo looked just like Connor, though this picture appeared to be from the mid-eighties.

"That's Connor's father and mother," the old man said with a sad smile.

"Wow, the men in your family have very strong genetics."

Just then, Connor walked in with a set of dry clothing and handed it over to Helen.

"Why don't you go ahead into the bathroom and clean up and get these dry clothes on. Just down this hallway to your right."

"Thank you, that would be wonderful." She took the clothes and walked down the hallway.

As she shut the bathroom door, she could overhear the men talking in low whispers about the house being too messy and unkempt. Helen got a good chuckle out of it. To be fair, they did live a bachelor's lifestyle and the house didn't look as bad as she might have expected.

After washing the mud off her face and brushing out the tangles in her hair, she slipped into the large university t-shirt and baggy flannel pajama bottoms Connor had given her. She looked at herself in the mirror and laughed.

Back in the sitting room, Connor had tea and a plate with sweetbreads on it. Helen sat in one of the leather chairs by the fire in hopes that it would help her kick the chill she still felt.

"Tell me, my dear, how did you come to find yourself out in such awful weather?" Seamus asked.

"It was kind of foolish of me; I was walking to check on you both when Connor didn't show up this morning. I was worried something was wrong. I didn't realize how quickly the weather could shift here. Where I live, the storms don't sweep in quite so fast."

"It's the sea, the weather can change quite quickly out here on the west coast."

"Of course, I hadn't thought of that," Helen said, as she blew into her teacup.

"How are you finding yourself at Fernbeg? It's such a beautiful little cottage."

"Quite well. Connor was a huge help yesterday, he managed to fix the broken windows. It's much more comfortable in there now without the breeze sneaking its way inside."

"I told Granda about the journal we found last night. He was quite intrigued," Connor said, sitting himself down on the couch.

"Yes, very interesting. I do believe it's the diary of Tomas McKenzie's fiancée, Freya. She's part of a family legend passed down from generation to generation," Connor's grandfather said as he filled his teacup and sat back, resting it in his lap.

A pang of excitement raced through her. "I would love to hear the story if you're willing to share it with me," she said.

Maybe if she knew more of the story then she could figure out why all of these strange things kept happening to her. They seemed connected in some way or another.

She took a long sip of the hot tea and felt it slide deep inside her belly, warming her from the inside out. The chill of the storm and the events of the morning still held her in their grip. She was ready to shake the unease and get down to the bottom of this, and who better to enlighten her than someone with ancestral knowledge of it all?

"It all started back in the late fifteen hundreds, right before the witch hysteria corrupted the land. Tomas fell in love with a local girl who was the daughter of a woodworker and a local healer. Her mother died before Freya turned sixteen and she took over her role as healer for the village. They were to be wed during the harvest. The story goes that one late afternoon, Tomas went to the seashore to collect a beach pebble to be fashioned into a ring for his beloved when somehow he drowned during the rising of the tide. Freya found his body on the beach the next morning. She cried out that foul play had been at hand but no one listened to the ravings of a grieving girl. No more than a week later she was hunted down and hung as a witch. Tomas's father tried to protect her, but it was of little use. She'd been betrayed by another healer, who gave her up to save herself. Soon after, the witch trials swept across Scotland. It's a very sad tale."

Helen was speechless. The story didn't sadden her as much as it made her burn inside with rage. Her heart raced inside her chest and she felt as if she was about to spontaneously combust when all of a sudden the lamp on the side table bulb popped and then shattered into pieces. The sound of the breaking glass snapped her back to reality and her blood cooled.

"Good God, what happened?" Connor's grandfather asked, looking around to see what had broken.

"It's okay, Granda, it's just a burst bulb in the table lamp. I'll clean it up." Connor got up and headed for the kitchen.

"Let me help you," Helen said, following after him.

Connor grabbed an old broom from the corner of the kitchen.

"Do you have a trash bin we can put the broken pieces in?" she asked.

"Under the sink," he said, picking up the dustpan and heading back into the sitting room to clean up.

Helen opened the cupboard door under the sink. It was a dank space with little light, but she found the trash bin quickly. As she pulled it out, she noticed a symbol carved into the back wall. It was the same symbol as the one on the key to Fernbeg and on the mantel in the library. It looked to have been etched into the stone. It was a circle with a three-pointed knot in the center. One of the points faced the heavens and the other two faced the east and west. She had seen the symbol before in some New Age shop near Kevin's apartment. They had gone into it once, just to look around and poke fun at all the wacky witchy stuff inside. Now it didn't seem so weird to her, and she wished she had actually paid attention when the woman was telling them about it.

She decided to search in the library when she got home to see if there might be any books about symbols. There were hundreds of books in there—surely there would be one that could help her.

Walking back into the sitting room, she handed Connor the bin and sat back down next to the fire. His grandfather had a frightened look on his face, as if something had startled him.

"Are you alright?" Helen asked as he sat staring off into space.

"He's fine, this happens sometimes," Connor said quietly, sweeping up fragments of smashed glass and tipping them into the bin. "It's one of the reasons I needed to come back home. He has these episodes. It's as if he floats away to another universe for a few minutes then snaps out of it. The doctor says it's the beginnings of dementia."

"Oh, Connor, I'm sorry. Does he know?" she said in a light whisper.

"He does but denies there's anything wrong. He just says it's part of getting old."

Helen had a feeling deep inside her that it wasn't dementia that had Seamus in a trance-like state either. He looked as if he was listening to something, or someone.

Connor finished cleaning the last of the broken glass and walked back into the kitchen. As soon as he had left the room, Seamus snapped free of his trance and looked straight at Helen.

"She is still here and very much alive. Stay vigilant and on guard. It won't be long until she senses you are here," he said, looking deep into Helen's eyes.

"Who? Who knows I'm here? Why should I be on guard?" she said, shaken by his abruptness.

He looked at her then put his finger to his lips in a gesture of silence.

Just then Connor came back into the room. "So, are you warming up yet?" he asked Helen.

Totally thrown off by the bizarre interaction with his grandfather, she nodded her head yes, in a bit of a daze herself.

"Good! Now, shall we head back to Fernbeg and have a look at the leaky sink?"

"Yes, I suppose we should," she said, getting up and setting her teacup on the tray. "Thank you so much for letting me warm myself up by your fire and for telling me the story. I'd love to come over and talk more about it all with you."

"You're more than welcome, my dear. Why don't you come for dinner tomorrow night?" Seamus said, giving her a tilt of his head.

"Sounds lovely," she replied, trying to be as polite as possible after such an awkward moment.

On the ride back to Fernbeg she couldn't shake the image of the old man's eyes when his trance broke and he spoke to her. It was as if he'd had a vision and was waking up from it. Was it the ravings of an old man who was suffering from dementia, or was it a warning?

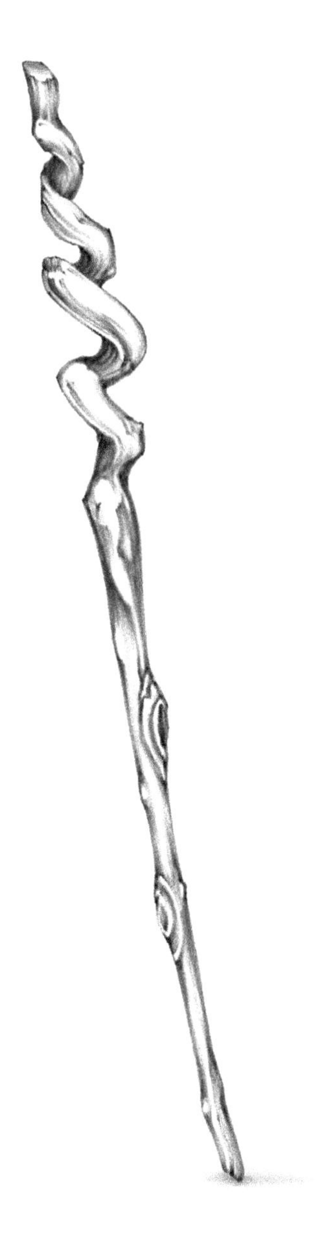

Chapter Fifteen

HOLD YOUR TONGUE

When they arrived back at Fernbeg, it was past noon and the fire in the sitting room had completely gone out. The house had cooled a little too much for Helen's comfort, especially after being chilled to the bone. She feared it would take her days to fully warm up again.

Connor got right to building a new fire while she went to the kitchen and put the kettle on, Storm at her heels, eager for a bit of kibble.

Helen stared down at the list on the kitchen table, but couldn't concentrate on anything other than the bizarre things that had happened over the past couple of days.

Forcing herself back on task, she looked at the list and picked out something she could do—fixing the hinges on the kitchen cupboards and giving the hutch a fresh coat of paint. Two small tasks she could set to and finish while Connor worked on the plumbing.

They had a quick cup of instant coffee before setting off to work. Helen borrowed a screwdriver from Connor and got to fixing the cupboards while he worked on the leaky pipes. She could hear him humming along to a Billy Idol tune playing on his phone in the other room. It made her smile. It was comforting having Connor around, even if they were set off on their own tasks. Just hearing him moving about in the cottage helped fill a void somehow.

The day went by quickly and before they knew it the light outside was dimming and the temperature was dropping further. She had successfully fixed the four cupboard doors and painted the hutch with fresh white paint. It lightened up the room considerably and Helen thought that she might get ambitious and paint all the cupboards that color as well.

"Well, I think I fixed the problem," Connor announced. "I dare say there's a leak no more! But we're going to have to do something about the floor in there, along with your room and the sitting room. Can't have you falling through one of the floorboards and breaking your ankle. Let's plan on that task for tomorrow. We'll need to go into town to get what we need. The boards I brought down are a wee bit too narrow," he said, lifting his shirt up and wiping sweat off his forehead, exposing his stomach and bare chest.

Helen's heart began to beat faster. He had a body like a Greek god. She turned herself away so that he couldn't see how she had blushed and stopped herself from indulging in the glory of this man she was fighting so hard not to think of in that way.

"Do you want to stay for dinner? My treat this time," she said, unable to stop herself.

"Sure, why not. I'm sure Granda is loving all this time alone. He's always complaining about me being underfoot all the time," he said, giving her a charming smile.

"Okay, well, you go check the fire and relax and I'll start cooking. I think there might be a little wine left from last night over by the sink if you'd like."

Connor headed into the other room and Helen took out the box of pasta and jar of sauce she had gotten in town. *Such an American dinner*, she thought, *I need to spice it up a bit*.

She started to look through the spice cupboard. There was no basil or oregano, and most of the other herbs she had never heard of before: vervain, henbane, and aconite just to name a few. She decided on a pinch of lemongrass, a dash of mint, a bit of ginger, and some rosemary, the only spices in the cupboard she recognized. Truth be told, she was no cook, so this was a long shot.

As she stirred the sauce, she thought about how Connor was unearthing feelings in her she had kept dormant. Her time here was now running short. It wouldn't be much longer before they had the cottage in a salable condition and then she would be heading back home. Maybe a fling with Connor wouldn't be so bad, maybe it was just what she needed to get out of her own head for a while. It wasn't like it could get serious, she was leaving in just a few weeks. She wished she knew how he felt about her. She didn't want to make a fool of herself by making a move on him if he just thought of them as friends. Truth be told, it was probably a good thing if he thought of her that way. It would make things a whole lot easier and then maybe she could shake this crush she was developing and move on.

Soon the kitchen was full of a delicious smell that wafted throughout the house. Feeling that she may have pulled it off, she called Connor in for dinner. She served him a large helping and the last of the crusty bread from the shop.

"It smells amazing," he said, taking a bite. "Tastes amazing too."

He spun the pasta up and onto his fork, taking another large mouthful.

"Thank you, nothing special," she said as she took her own bite. It *was* good—hell, it was great. It might have been the best thing she had ever had. *Wow*, she thought, *those spices really did the trick*. She took another large bite while she watched Connor do the same.

"It's actually really tasty," Connor said. "I was a bit scared when you said you wanted to cook. I had a feeling you might not be a wiz in the kitchen. I just wanted to stay so I could be around you. You're quite nice to look at, you know."

He looked immediately shocked at what had just come out of his mouth and took a big gulp of wine.

Helen could feel her cheeks redden as she blushed. "Well, you're not wrong. I'm not a good cook and this is about the only thing I can make, so you're lucky I had pasta at hand. I could have cared less if we ate or not, I just wanted you to stay later, especially after seeing your chest earlier. My God, you look like something Michelangelo carved from stone."

Cupping her hand to her mouth, she looked at him with wide eyes, her cheeks now redder than ripe tomatoes.

"Oh, I did that on purpose. I wanted to see your reaction at the sight of my bare skin. You didn't disappoint me. Your blushing cheeks said it all," he said without missing a beat. Again, he looked shocked at what had just come out of his mouth. He stopped eating and stood up, pushing in his chair. "Sorry, I'm not feeling well. No, that's a lie. I'm fine. I just can't be here right now or I might tell you how much I really like you. I'll come by tomorrow to fix the floors."

He grabbed his jacket and keys off the table and practically ran out the door. But before his truck door shut, Helen managed to yell out, "But wait, I wanted you to kiss me!"

Stunned at her outburst, she walked back inside, slamming the door, then returned to the kitchen.

She sat at the table, completely confused. What the hell just happened? It was like they'd had no control over themselves. Was it the wine? But they really hadn't had that much. Or maybe it was the paint fumes and they were experiencing some sort of high. But it was latex paint so that was highly unlikely. She had said every thought that had come to the forefront of her mind, no holds barred.

Then it hit her. The herbs!

"Oh my God!"

She went quickly to the cupboard to find the little black spell book.

She hadn't thought of the herbs as anything other than ingredients for cooking, but they weren't, were they? They were herbs for potions and spells. She looked into the book, flipping page after page until she saw it—a spell called "Speak the Truth and Tell No Lie". It called for none other than rosemary, ginger, mint, and lemongrass and instructed the user to cook with the intention of the truth said over the potion as they stirred.

She had done just that. She had been thinking how much she wanted to know if Connor felt the same way about her as she did him.

Holy shit! I just cooked and served up two giant plates of a truth spell for dinner. How am I going to explain this to him tomorrow?

She was completely mortified, but she had to admit she was also a bit impressed. She had recreated a spell without even seeing it before. It was as if she knew somewhere deep down inside her what to do and she just did it. A lot of things like this had been happening to her lately. It must have been the influence of Fernbeg, its history of wise women. Maybe there was some special magic here within its walls.

She cleared the table off, throwing away the truth pasta. No one needed to have that as leftovers, she thought. Storm, disappointed to see all the lovely food going into the trash, retreated into the sitting room, leaving Helen alone to clean. As she washed the dirty dishes, she kept replaying the day's events over in her head. She wasn't sure if things could have been any odder.

Her mind returned again and again to that symbol she saw under the sink at Connor's. It was a very odd place for something like that to be. Why would it be hidden there?

After cleaning everything up, she went into the library in search of a book that might help her explain the symbol. There were so many books she had no idea where to even start. She wondered if they were arranged in a particular order. The main wall was mostly novels with a few historical books mixed in. There was a rather large section of poetry with Burns, Frost, and Shakespeare taking up most of the shelf, but nothing that pertained to Celtic symbols. She moved over to the bookcases on each side of the fireplace. The bookcase to the right was mostly books about war, all sorts of historical texts dating back centuries. The one on the left was full of books on folklore and myths from a variety of cultures. Bingo! There it was, an entire row devoted to Celtic mythology. The symbol she was looking for had to be in one of these books.

The first one she chose was called *Celtic Mythology and Legends*. She ran her fingers over the embossed text on the front cover. It was velvety green with gold lettering and gilded edges. Flipping it open, she thumbed through the pages, but it was nothing but text, no illustrations or images. The second book she picked was called *The World of the Druids*. It was full of interesting information but didn't have the symbol she was searching for.

She returned the book to the shelf and stepped back. An idea formed in her head. She closed her eyes and envisioned the symbol, then took two steps with her hand outstretched, running her fingers across the spines, one by one. Her fingers stopped and she felt a pulsing in her hand. When she opened her eyes, she had tipped out a book called *Celtic Myth and Magick*. Grabbing it, she sat in one of the overstuffed armchairs by the fireplace and flipped it open. The book was heavier than it should have been. It was as if the book's knowledge was the weight she was feeling, not the actual volume of pages.

As she flicked through, she came across many symbols but not the one she had seen in the cupboard or on the key. She was about to give up when she noticed a page with a dogtooth on it. She flipped to the page and there it was, the symbol etched into the stone at Connor's home. Above the symbol was the name: The triquetra or trinity knot. Underneath it read:

The triquetra symbolizes eternal spiritual life, one with no beginning and no end. The Christians adopted it as a symbol for the holy trinity but the symbol is much, much older, dating back to the eleventh century. It is considered one of the oldest symbols of spirituality. The three-pointed knot represents Life, Death, and Rebirth. The circle around it creates the unity of the three parts.

Helen sat back in her chair and closed the book. Knowing the meaning behind the symbol only brought up more questions. Why would that symbol be hidden there, and why etched into the stone? Why was it also here at Fernbeg? She had a feeling deep within her that whatever it was, it was important for her to find out.

Chapter Sixteen

HIDDEN SPACES

It was 7 a.m. and Helen was up with a pencil in her hand and her sketchbook laid out in front of her on the kitchen table with the key to the cottage next to it. She had been drawing the triquetra symbol for over an hour now, and the book had received three new pages of the design. There was something to it, she could feel it deep in her bones. She thought if she drew it, she might start to understand the mystery behind it better, but it only brought more questions. She was sure she'd seen the symbol somewhere else before, and it wasn't at the New Age shop back home. It was right in the forefront of her mind, but she just couldn't retrieve the memory.

Frustrated, she slammed her sketchbook shut and got up to make her second cup of instant coffee. She would have killed for a cup of brewed coffee today but she choked down the bitter black sorry excuse of a cup and headed into the sitting room. Once she added a few small logs to the bed of hot coals, the fire lit back up quickly, casting its warm glow across the room.

She decided that she would test out Connor's handiwork and take a shower. The sponge baths were getting old and her hair was in desperate need of a wash after yesterday's tumble in the storm. She was still picking dry pieces of mud and leaves from it. She went into the rustic bathroom and turned on the water in the old clawfoot tub. The pipes groaned and rattled and then out of the tap came a bubbling burst of rusty water. She let it run for a few minutes until it slowly became a crystal-clear stream and steam rose over the tub.

"Hallelujah!" she said, pulling up the knob and watching the hot water surge through the showerhead.

Stripping off her clothing, she jumped in and felt the hot water begin to loosen every muscle in her body. She hadn't realized how much she needed this. Tilting her head back, she let the water smooth down her dark hair, resting it flat on her back. There was something almost religious about a good shower, she thought. The way it could make you feel whole again, clean, and ready to start anew.

As she let the hot water run over her, she began thinking about Connor. How was she ever going to explain what happened last night? Things were destined to be awkward today when he arrived. He was going to think she was crazy—if he didn't already. The thought ended her enjoyment of the hot shower and she turned off the tap.

Stepping out of the tub and into the steamy bathroom, she walked over and wiped the mirror free of its fog, when she noticed something strange. The right edge of the wall by the mirror was not wet with steam. Instead, the steam in the air moved next to the space, blowing away from the edge of the mirror as if a draft was there. Wrapping her fingers around the side of the mirror, she could feel cold air moving out from behind it. She tried to pull it back but it must have been screwed onto the wall. It would not budge. She grabbed her makeup bag and pulled out a pair of fingernail clippers. Extending the nail file out, she wedged it behind the mirror and slid it up. About a third of the way to the top it hit something, and then she heard a click as if a latch had been lifted. She grabbed ahold of the mirror's edge and tried to pull it again. This time it swung open like a door.

Deep inside the opening was a room. It was no larger than a small closet recessed into the wall.

It was dark and hard to see so Helen went into the bedroom, threw on some clothes, and grabbed her flashlight off the nightstand then came back in for a better look. The light, being almost too bright at first, lit up layers of spiderwebs and dust particles. Once she had cut through the thick curtain of cobwebs, she gasped.

In the narrow little space was an altar. On the floor stood a thin wooden table with a hand-embroidered cloth adorned with leaves, acorns, and thistles arranged in a delicately stitched circle. Within the circle were two candles, a small cast-iron cauldron, a mortar and pestle, and five glass jars. On the walls to each side hung bundles of dried herbs and in the center above the altar was the triquetra, carved into the wooden wall. A feeling of déjà vu coursed through her as she peered into the hidden space. She had to go in there.

Carefully, Helen lifted herself up onto the sink and climbed in through the square opening. It was just big enough for a small adult woman to fit through. The cloth at the base of the altar was in poor shape and looked to be rapidly decaying around the edges, but in the center of the circle it was intact and the colors of the thread were still vibrant and strong. The cast-iron cauldron smelled of spices and there was a black residue lingering at the bottom. One by one, Helen examined the glass jars around the edge of the circle. Each contained something different. The first looked to be filled with soil, the second water, the third ash, the fourth was filled with what appeared to be some sort of crystal, and the fifth was empty.

"The elements," she murmured to herself, setting the last jar back down in its place. "Earth, water, fire, air, and spirit."

The altar was set as if someone was calling on the elements of nature. Behind one of the candles was a small skull—some sort of small animal, a rabbit perhaps. There was also a delicately carved wooden spoon beside the cast iron cauldron. The handle was carved with vines that worked their way to the mouth of the spoon, ending in tiny leaves to each side. Everything seemed to be picked not only for functionality but for its beauty as well, all paying homage to Mother Nature.

Even in the darkness of the space, there was a radiant light that seemed to seep out of the objects, just as the journals in the library had. As she stood there looking with amazement upon this newfound treasure, she began to wonder how long this had been here. Had Freya carved out this space or was it another inhabitant of the cottage?

She carefully climbed back out and shut the mirror passageway. No longer looking into the hidden sacred place, she now gazed at her own reflection. The woman who stared back looked different than she remembered. Something had changed in her, not only emotionally but physically in her looks. Her hair seemed a little more auburn than before and she had developed freckles across the bridge of her nose. It wasn't just those subtle differences she noticed; along the outline of her body was a shimmer, a radiant glow she now recognized as the essence of magic.

She smiled. She'd felt it evolving slowly with each strange thing that had happened since she arrived. The magic of this place was changing her.

She brushed her hair and fixed it into a long braid that she let slip over her left shoulder and down her chest. Then she put a bit of makeup on and wrapped herself up in a giant wool cardigan. It had gotten noticeably colder in the past few days, so she pulled out the thick wool socks she had packed. Today she would need more than just the fire in the sitting room to keep this place warm.

She went into the kitchen and built a fire in the large fireplace next to the old cookstove. Within a few minutes, she had a nice fire going and Storm was happy with the warm place to rest by his food. She sat down and looked over the list of things to do. They had gotten quite a bit done over the past couple of days but there was still the large task of painting the outside of the house to do. She feared with the cold weather setting in that this might be one of the last chances she would get to accomplish it. She decided this was the task she would take on for the next couple of days.

In the hallway, she looked down at the buckets and picked up the white outdoor paint. Shaking it well, she popped the lid and stirred it, watching the milky waves swirl and circle in on themselves. It was mesmerizing to her. She loved the smell of paint, whether it was oil, acrylic, or watercolor. Each one of their distinct smells brought her joy.

She grabbed the paint and walked out the front door. As soon as she had stepped out into the garden, she knew it was too cold. The air was still heavy with morning mist, leaving a coat of dew on everything, including the stone walls of the cottage. Scotland's weather was temperamental at best, she thought.

"Well, I guess that will have to wait until later," she said to herself as she set the paint can back down in the hall and fastened its lid.

Just then she heard the familiar sound of tires on gravel. Looking out the window, she saw Connor's truck speeding down the hill toward the cottage. A pang of nervousness rang through her as she thought about the way they had left things last night. She knew she would have to explain everything to him but still wasn't sure how he would take it.

The truck came to a slow stop in the driveway. Helen looked out the window and watched Connor hesitate. He sat there for a few minutes before gathering the courage to get out and come in. Helen was waiting at the door in nervous anticipation when he knocked. She counted to ten in her head, not wanting to seem too eager. When she opened the door to greet him, he stood there, toolbox in hand and a forced smile on his face.

"Good morning, Helen," he said, stepping in past her and walking into the sitting room without making eye contact. Storm came running in from the other room to greet him with a wet lick across his hand before finding a cozy spot in front of the fire.

"Hey, Connor, I wanted—" But before she could even get out the next word, he cut her off.

"Helen, I am so sorry about last night. I don't know what got into me. I wish I could blame it on the wine but I can't. I was a total arse," he said, running his fingers through his dark hair.

"No, you weren't, and it wasn't your fault at all. It was mine."

"No, don't be daft."

"Really, it was my fault. You won't believe me if I tell you, it's that crazy."

"It can't be any crazier than how I felt driving home last night," he said, looking at her for the first time since he came in.

Helen sat down on the couch to brace herself while he stood next to the fire. She picked at a loose thread on the cushion, trying to work up the courage to speak.

"I found a small black leather book in the spice cupboard the second day I was here. At first, I thought it was just a recipe book but the more I read the more apparent it became that I was reading a handwritten book of spells. I should have known that they weren't normal herbs and spices for cooking. My cooking skills are … let's say mediocre at best. After your amazing dinner the other night, I felt a bit insecure. So, I tried to spice up the pasta by adding a few to the sauce. It just so happens the spices I chose were a perfect match for a truth spell in the book. So, yes, it was my fault. I served us both spelled pasta for dinner." She shook her head and rolled her eyes.

There was a lingering moment of silence that threatened to break her. *That's it, he thinks I'm crazy*, she thought.

"Ha! You're kidding me on, right? Are you sure the herbs and spices weren't out of date or something?" he said in a playful tone, trying to lighten the mood.

"I'm pretty sure that's not the case," she said reluctantly.

"I kinda thought it was something stranger than being a bit tipsy from the wine. When I got home, I blurted out the night's events to Granda. Then proceeded to lock myself in my room before I told him where I hid the whiskey from him. It was as if I couldn't keep a single thought from spilling out of my mouth. I might have thought you were crazy a week ago but after everything we've seen and read, I guess that makes the most sense. At least I know I'm not going crazy or developing late-stage Tourette's," he said with a bit of relief in his voice.

"No, you're not going crazy. I'm so sorry. I swear it's just my luck to do something stupid like that," she said, giving him a smile and hoping he might bring up what they had said to each other last night, as she was too nervous to do so herself.

"Well, now that we've got that out of the way, I can blame my behavior on the supernatural. You ready to head to town?"

She stood up and headed out of the room, a little disappointed that he was avoiding the fact that they had both openly admitted to liking each other last night. It seemed as if he wanted to keep pretending they were just friends. Or perhaps that was the issue, perhaps that was all he wanted them to be.

"Oh, that's right. I forgot we needed to go there today. Let me go grab my hat and wallet," she said, taking off into the other room.

She grabbed her wallet off the bedside table and pulled on a green knitted cap. She looked at her reflection in the mirror and reminded herself that this was not something to get hurt feelings over. He was probably feeling just as much inner turmoil over the situation as she was. She glanced at herself one final time, making sure she was presentable. Setting her frustration aside, she walked back into the sitting room.

"All ready to go," she said, giving Storm a pat on the head. "Be back in a bit, boy."

Connor added a few logs to the fire and then set out the door for their trip to town.

Chapter Seventeen

LORE

The autumn day proved to be a beautiful one. A glow of orange and red was painted across the tops of most of the trees and shrubs now. The underbrush had started turning to burnt umber and gave a sharp transition from the edge of the woodlands to the fields. The grass was tall and fading to a golden brown. The nip in the air was significantly colder than days prior, causing the animals to scuttle and scurry faster than normal in preparation for winter.

Helen glanced over at Connor, his fingers nervously tapping the steering wheel of the truck as he drove. There was still a bit of tension between them and she began to fear the trip into town was going to be unbearable if one of them didn't break the silence.

"Are the winters quite cold here?" Helen asked, fracturing the awkwardness that lay heavy in the air between them.

"It depends. They can be, and the cold that comes off the sea can be quite bitter," Connor answered, happy to be rid of the uncomfortable silence.

"I love this time of year. The colors, the smells, getting all cozy by a fire and reading a book. Hot cups of coffee or tea that warm you from the inside out. It feels so magical."

"I agree. There's a certain magic that comes with this time of year. I think you proved that with your dinner last night," he said jokingly as the mood lightened.

"Haha, not funny," she said, swatting his shoulder with the back of her hand. She was grateful for his easygoing personality and that the awkwardness between them had vanished quicker than she expected.

Soon, they reached Oban. Connor navigated the streets until they were close to the hardware store, then pulled into a parking spot. Inside the store, the clerk recognized Helen from the time she had come in with Henry.

"Hello, miss, how can I help you today?" he said with a wide smile.

"Hello! I'm in need of some light bulbs and … I think Connor can handle the rest."

"Of course, right this way, miss," the clerk said, walking her down an aisle with tools and home goods scattered throughout. He showed her the small selection of light bulbs they carried and walked back to the front of the store. She grabbed a set and headed back to the front. Connor had taken off into the building section, leaving her to roam around by herself.

She walked over to the paint palettes and was browsing the colors on the thin strips of paper when all of a sudden the temperature seemed to drop ten degrees. She looked around to see if anyone had entered the store, leaving the door open to cause a draft, but the only people in the store were Connor, herself, and the clerk. She remembered feeling this same kind of cold at the cottage a few nights ago. It was a different kind of cold, not so much a temperature change but a sense of dread and darkness. Almost as though she was being watched.

She looked around, sweeping her eyes the length of the store, but no one was there. Then, as she turned back to the shelf of paint strips, she caught a glimpse of someone out of the corner of her eye looking into the storefront window.

When she turned around, they were gone. So was the cold.

Feeling a bit shaken, she headed over to find Connor. She was ready to leave and get back to the coziness of the cottage, but Connor was still in the process of having some boards cut. Helen decided to step outside and turn her cell phone on to see if she could get a good enough signal to call Kevin.

As soon as her phone found two bars, it lit up like a Christmas tree with notifications. She had seventeen missed calls and eight voice messages. Wow, she didn't think she would be so missed. It had only been about a week since she left, though that felt like a lifetime ago now.

The first missed call was from her parents, wanting to know if they should come up for Thanksgiving this year or if she wanted to come down to visit them. She felt a pang of guilt for not letting them know she was in another country. But still, they were completely oblivious to her situation and she wanted to keep it that way. She would never hear the end of it if her mother found out.

The next five messages were from Kevin. Each one expressing how worried about her he was and that she must call him back immediately. The last even threatened to call the American embassy. Ha, she laughed at this.

The next was William letting her know that all the paperwork had been filed and that she would be receiving the final papers in the mail within the week.

The last message was from a woman at the bank letting her know that she had been denied a charge on her card for $500 in Istanbul. She needed to call them back before her card could be used again as it was set on fraud alert and frozen. *Crap* she thought. This was the last thing she wanted to be dealing with.

Well, it was a good thing she had decided to check these before they got ready to check out. It could have proved to be an embarrassing moment when her bank card got denied in front of Connor. She called the bank back and got the card free, then set off to call Kevin. Her parents would have to wait a few more days. Thanksgiving was still a month away, and she wasn't quite ready to face reality and the responsibilities that awaited her in her life back home.

The phone rang only once before Kevin picked up.

"For Christ's sake, Helen. I've been so worried about you."

"Well, hello to you too."

"What the hell have you been doing? I've been calling you twice every day. I was worried you'd been killed and buried in some rutty Scottish barnyard."

"Sorry, Kev, there's no service where the cottage is and this is the first time I've been in cell range for a while. I still have no landline but I'm told it should be on in the next few days."

"Thank God. How are the renovations going?"

"They're coming along. I hired a neighbor to help with fixing some stuff in the house. I'm in town with him now getting replacement floorboards for a few of the rooms."

"The old farmer is helping you out? Well, that's nice of him."

"No, it's his grandson, Connor. He's a local handyman here."

"Well, I'm glad you found someone to help you out. Does that mean you're going to be able to wrap things up sooner and get back here?"

"I'm hoping I can be finished up in a week. So, how are things back home? You surviving without me?"

"Things here are the same as always. *However*, Jenny ended up getting that promotion. Can you believe Tom? What an ass."

"Crap Kev, I've gotta run. We're headed back to the cottage now. I promise I'll call you as soon as my landline is in. Miss you, bye!" she said, cutting him short as Connor approached her with boards in hand.

"Miss you too. Stay safe," she heard Kevin say as she ended the call.

"Connor, I'm so sorry I stepped outside to check my messages. I can give you some cash when we get back."

"No worries at all. I got it," he said, handing her a bag with the light bulbs in it. They walked back to the truck where Connor secured the boards in the back before opening the door for her. "I have to go grab a few things. I'll be right back," he said. He flashed her a mischievous smile and took off down the street.

While she waited in the truck, she checked her emails. Nothing too important stood out, just a lot of junk mail and a few bills. She decided she would use the time she had with the internet at her fingertips to look up a few things. She wanted to know more about Fernbeg and why the locals seemed so wary of the place.

She pulled up a search engine page and typed in the query: *Oban Scotland Fernbeg Cottage*. Only a few articles referenced the cottage, mostly advertisements for the sale of it. But one piqued her interest, a local newspaper story about fairy legends in the area. It read:

There are many local legends or fairy tales in our land, but the one that stands out from all the rest is the tale of the two sisters. The legend goes that once upon a time there was a farmer who had two daughters. One was born with hair the color of silver and the other was born with hair as black as the night sky. Lucian, the silver-haired sister, was sweet and kind and as she grew, she showed great promise as a healer. Kiera, the dark-haired sister, was always in the shadow of her beautiful silver-haired sister and became bitter and jealous.

One day Kiera was walking the woodland near their home when she heard a sweet melody being played near the base of an old oak tree. She slowly walked toward it and found a small woodland fairy playing a tiny flute.

The fairy stopped playing upon seeing the girl and asked her who caused her heart to turn black and bitter, for only the cold-hearted could hear her melody. Kiera responded, "My sister. She glows like the sun and I stay hidden in her shadow." The fairy told her that if she wished to be the sun then she could grant her that one wish but for a price that she would collect when she pleased. Kiera agreed and the fairy told her to go home and place one golden feather under her pillow and a black feather under her sister's. She did as she was told, and the next morning Lucian woke with a horrible sickness. Within only a few days, she lay dying in the dark-haired sister's arms. "What have I done?" Kiera lamented.

That night, the fairy appeared to collect her debt. Kiera explained that she had not asked for her sister to fall ill and that no light was cast in her favor. "Oh, but it will be," the fairy said, "for you will trade your life for your sister's and she will know it." Perplexed, Kiera told the fairy she did not understand. The fairy touched Lucian's forehead and she awoke, free of her illness. The fairy then took Kiera's hand and walked her out of the house and into the woodland, never to be seen again.

The following day, Lucian told her father how her sister had saved her life by making a deal with a fairy. That day the father and the rest of the town threw a celebration in honor of Kiera's fearlessness and did so for many years after.

Kiera was never seen again but her sister Lucian lived out her days here in Oban in a little cottage by the sea we know as Fernbeg.

Was this the tale that caused people to be afraid of the cottage? Helen wondered. She decided to ask Connor about it when he came back. She sat and browsed through a few more articles, coming across more local lore and legends surrounding the area and the witch trials. It was unsettling to think of all the deaths that had transpired here, and it left her with a feeling of unease.

Chapter Eighteen

PASSING SHADOWS

With a bag in each hand, Connor returned to the truck. He slid them into the rear of the vehicle and climbed inside.

"You ready to go?"

"As I'll ever be," Helen replied with a smile, trying to shake off the creeping feeling that was lingering around her from the articles she had read.

Connor drove slowly on the way back. She wasn't sure if it was because he was enjoying the autumn day or her company but either way, she was happy.

The sun was well overhead at this point and the farmers were out in full force, harvesting. The low rumble of tractors could be heard from miles around in the crisp air. It was a picturesque sight as they rounded the top of the hill and started their descent toward the cottage. The sun cast a golden glow onto the loch that bounced off its waters and sprayed the landscape with soft amber light. Everything was a wash of oranges, reds, golds, browns, and fading greens.

Once they arrived at the cottage, they carried all the purchases from town into the kitchen. Connor pulled open one of the bags he had brought back.

"Close your eyes," he said.

"What? Come on now."

"No, you've got to or I won't show you what I have, and believe me you'll want to see it."

"Okay, I'm intrigued," she said, placing her hands over her eyes. She heard what sounded to be plastic hitting metal and then whatever it was being placed on the table.

"Okay, open your eyes."

Helen took her hands off her face. There on the kitchen table was a coffee maker and a large bag of coffee.

"Oh my God, I could kiss you," she said, walking over and inspecting the machine.

"Well, if you must," he said, jokingly sticking his cheek out as if waiting. "It might have been a selfish purchase—I wasn't sure I could handle another cup of that God-awful instant coffee of yours."

"You sure know how to get on a woman's good side, or at least this woman. You up for a cup?"

"Yeah, why do you think I bought it? We're going to need fuel to finish these floors before nightfall. Make it strong, I'm going to go and start pulling up the old boards in the sitting room." With that, he grabbed his toolbox and headed into the other room.

Helen wondered if this was his way of smoothing things over a bit more from last night or if it really was just because he couldn't stand any more of the instant crap. While chasing the thought around in her mind, she brought the slim black coffee pot over to the counter by the sink and plugged it in. She got it brewing and soon the house filled with the rich delightful aroma of fresh coffee. This brought a smile to her face. It had been far too long since she'd had a proper cup.

While she waited for the machine to complete its brewing cycle, she went into the bathroom and shut the door. She wanted to have another look at the hidden room before deciding whether or not to share this secret with Connor.

She thumbed behind the mirror with her nail file until she triggered the latch and pulled the passageway door open. The smell of damp wood and mildew made its escape, filling the air in the bathroom with a wet earthy scent, and then the room turned cold.

Helen grabbed her flashlight off the sink and lit up the tiny room. She focused on the dried herbs hanging from the left wall, scanning them over with her light. As she moved the thin light beam from one wall to the next, she caught a glimpse of a shadowy figure facing the altar.

She let out a startled scream and dropped the flashlight. It clattered into the room and sat there, as still as stone with its beam pointed directly at the triquetra. Helen quickly looked back into the space but there was no one there.

Connor came bursting in and Helen shot around to face him.

"Are you alright?" he said, sounding winded.

"Yes, I'm fine. I just thought I saw something," she said, knowing there was no getting around telling him about the hidden room now.

"What is that?" He walked over, looking into the black hole in the wall.

When Helen turned to face the opening, she saw Connor holding the flashlight, the same one that had fallen into the room.

"Where did you get that?" she asked, pointing at the light.

"It was right here on the edge of the sink," he said, giving her a questioning look.

A jolt of something crept along her spine, but before she could say anything else, Connor shone the light into the little room.

"Oh my God, this is incredible. It's some sort of shrine," he said, sticking his head into the opening to get a better look.

Helen had a sinking feeling come over her. She'd seen someone or something, and perhaps whatever it was had returned the flashlight to the sink while she had turned away. How else could she explain it? She'd felt it drop from her hand, heard it clatter on the floor, saw it light up the triquetra... And there was that cold again, the kind she had felt before in the cottage. It wasn't the same kind of cold she had experienced in the hardware store, which had felt menacing. This was something else. She knew deep down that whatever spirit she had just encountered was not out to harm her.

"Did you see this?" Connor said, pointing the light at the triquetra. "Don't you think it's a bit strange that both our houses have this symbol carved into the wall in hidden places?"

"Yes! I do. It seems to be that our houses have a shared secret, but I haven't quite figured out what it is yet. I did a bit of research into the symbol but it only led to more questions."

"When did you find this?" he asked.

"This morning. I was debating whether or not to tell you. Didn't want to freak you out any more than I had to in one day. First, the truth spell fiasco, and then this. I must seem like a magnet for weirdness right about now," she said, laughing a little in spite of the situation.

He smiled. "Well, you certainly keep it interesting."

Helen reached over his shoulder and shut the mirror. She didn't want him catching a glimpse of her guest if they decided to reappear or he might never come back.

"Let's go see if that coffee is done yet," she said, going for the door and beckoning him to follow her. He did, but not before turning around and giving the bathroom one last glance, as if he was hoping to see a glimpse of something magical.

Connor took a short break and enjoyed a fresh cup of hot coffee with her before setting back to work on the floors. Helen decided that she wasn't up for painting today and took her cup into the library for a little light reading.

When she opened the door, the room glowed in the afternoon sunlight, illuminating the particles of dust that floated and hovered in the still air. It was her favorite room in the house—she really ought to spend more time in it. She was gazing around at all the knowledge and adventures that sat nestled on the shelves when the three journals on the top shelf caught her eye. The radiance emanating from them was much brighter than before. She wasn't sure if it was because she understood that it was magic now or if they were calling out to her. She decided to climb up and retrieve them.

She placed the three leather-bound journals next to the first that rested peacefully on the side table next to the large green velvet chairs. Helen picked up the second journal. Upon opening it she was surprised to see that it was not another journal belonging to Freya. This journal belonged to a woman named Clara and was dated in the 1700s. She picked up the next, flipping it open and finding it had belonged to a woman named Elizabeth and was dated 1839. She placed that book down and picked up the last. It had been signed by a woman named Abigail in the 1940s.

She didn't understand. The journals looked to be a set and she would have guessed they were all made around the same time, yet they spanned over four hundred years. How did these get to be together when they were clearly owned by women from various centuries? Maybe the person who had started this library had found them on their hunt for books and created this collection, but that seemed highly unlikely.

She decided to go back to the first book belonging to Freya and read a bit more about the life of this witch who had a connection to Connor's family. Maybe it would shed some light on the triquetra carvings in both their houses. She felt there had to be more to the tale than what Seamus had told her, and she suspected the answers would be in the diary. Helen took a large sip of coffee before sitting down and turning the page to the next chapter of Freya's life.

The pages started to violently flip, as if a gust of wind had burst through the library. Then as quickly as it had started, it stopped, landing on a page dated September 20, 1597.

Chapter Nineteen

COVEN

September 20, 1597

Mary and I made our way safely to Duror with only a few stumbles along the way. Thankfully, due to Mary's ability to communicate with the animals and her quick wit, we made it out of the forest unharmed. We even acquired a guardian wolf. He tried to attack us in the forest but Mary convinced him to stay guard on our journey, promising him safe passage back to his homeland in Oban. Wolves have been hunted mercilessly, and he needed our protection just as much as we needed his. He has taken quite a liking to me, and I to him. He reminds me of the dogs on Tomas's farm but much larger and more rugged, with wiry gray fur. The thought made me miss my sweet love all the more.

When we arrived in Duror the townsfolk looked upon us in awe as this large Highland wolf walked alongside us, appearing to be domesticated. They are so rare these days that most people have never seen one in person, only heard tales of them. I fear it frightened a few people but also kept the rustlers at bay.

The meeting was to take place in a large barn on the back end of town and we arrived a few hours early. Mary wanted to go to the farm right away, saying she had a feeling we needed to be there before the others arrived. She has been having visions for over a month now and most of these have come to be. Trusting her intuition, we made haste to the barn. Here, Mary sent the wolf off to the wooded area for his safety while we waited for the others to arrive.

Fran, an older woman in her late years with silvery-white hair and wise eyes, was the first to greet us. She is the owner of the farm and a friend of both our mothers and was happy to be our guide through our first meeting. The second to arrive was a younger woman named Fionna, who looked to me in her late twenties with hair the color of an autumn sunset and a peppered face. She had a glow of silvery-white light that beamed off her and matched her cheery disposition. We greeted each other and went into the barn for the first meeting as the new Coven of the Highlands. We each took out our items for trade and placed them upon a long wooden bench spanning the short side of the barn.

Fionna brought several tins of a herbal paste consisting of lanolin, meadowsweet, and sphagnum moss, a mixture for treating wounds and the anguish that accompanies them. She also brought five small jars of a rheumatism tonic prepared from willow bark and thyme. Fran had bundles of dried yarrow, lavender, lemon balm, elfwort, and betony, along with preserved carrageenan and elderberries for teas and tonics. Mary and I added our herbs and tinctures to the bench alongside the others.

There were five old wooden milking stools set in a circle amongst the hay in the barn. Fran was the first to take her seat and then Fionna and Mary and I followed suit. Each of us took turns telling tales of new remedies that have worked on the sick and wounded or of magical creatures we have worked with to acquire new knowledge. Fran told us of a kelpie off the shores of Iona that nearly drowned five little boys. One escaped to tell the tale and the kelpie is now being pursued by the locals. "They'll never find it," Fran said. "They're cunning creatures who know when to flee." She said she was afraid it will go north and that any waterways we cross are now unsafe. It was intriguing to us, but it also left us anxious about our return journey.

Fionna tried to lighten the mood by telling us a lively story of how she helped deliver twins during the summer to a poor girl at the age of sixteen, when all of a sudden the barn door swung open. The light of the setting sun along with a cold autumn breeze entered through the large wooden door as the silhouetted figure of a woman walked in. She looked to be in her forties. Her long black hair was fashioned in a large braid that wove its way around her head. Her eyes sat sunken like pools of darkness resting in her hollowed face. With dirty, tattered clothing she walked over to the stools and took her place. There was a staleness that lingered in the air as she stepped into the barn and the mood abruptly changed.

Fran introduced the woman to us as Margaret Aitken and she bowed her head in a gesture of greeting to us.

She had only sat but a minute before she began to speak. As she did it was as if she brought darkness into the room with every word. She told us a story of a priest new to her village who came talking of the Queen's God—a god of all gods—and scolded the old pagan ways, saying they were the workings of the devil. She spoke of how the townsfolk had turned away and shunned her. They had come to her home only a few days prior, in an angry mob, and drove her from her house with only the clothing on her back and a small sack of items she was able to grab on her way out. She was bitter and angry, full of a dark rage. She gave up her youth to help keep the people of her village healthy, not marrying or having children, and then they turned on her on the word of a stranger. It was a heartbreaking story, and we all felt badly for her. Fear filled the barn, as we have all heard of the hangings of women such as ourselves. We all know what kinds of things happen when people start to fear one another.

Seeing the look of concern on our faces, Fran assured us that it was only due to the new priest setting up residence in the towns to the north and that we have nothing to fear from it here. She then offered Margaret a place to stay at the farm while she figured out what her next steps would be.

After Fran brought the mood back from the edge of darkness, we exchanged herbs, poultices, and spells. We were excited to procure vervain for cleansing our altars, poppy seedpods for pain, and silphium for stopping the bearing of a child. These are all necessary things for any healer's apothecary but not easy to come by. Then we packed up our new bounties and headed out of the barn and toward the old farmhouse. Fran, who lives there, offered us a warm meal and a place to sleep for the night.

Together we prepared a rabbit stew and enjoyed lively conversation around the fire that night. Fran had many stories to tell about our mothers that we happily listened to. I told them of how my sweet Tomas asked me for my hand and how we are to be married in the coming weeks. Fionna entertained us with funny tales of her children. Margaret sat mostly in silence and retired to bed before the rest of us. Fran assured Mary and I that she was just in one of her moods and that her story had been grossly exaggerated. She is known for having a flair for the dramatic. I could tell she is not like the others; her magic is from a dark place and is tainted with a kind of evil that makes my soul uneasy to even be around.

That night while everyone slept, I lay awake with a feeling of dread. I looked over at Margaret. I could tell she lay awake as well, as she was chanting an incantation in a low whisper while she held what looked to be a small talisman made of twigs and hair. It was dark magic, and such a talisman is designed only to cause harm towards someone. Margaret had mentioned working with fairies, who in turn work for the devil. I couldn't sleep in her presence. I longed to be in Tomas's arms, away from all the darkness that lay around me.

I did not sleep much that night as I whispered incantations of protection to combat whatever evil Margaret was spilling forth into the world. However, as much as I had fought sleep off, it eventually overtook me in the wee hours of the morning until the sun came up.

Mary and I greeted Fran and Fionna in the small farmhouse kitchen. Fran informed us that Margaret had left in the early dawn before anyone woke. We enjoyed a hearty morning meal of eggs with bread and goat cheese while listening to Fionna's humorous tales of being the mother of five. The tone was cheerful, in stark contrast to the oppressive darkness brought on by Margaret's presence, yet I still sensed a lingering malice in the air. We said our goodbyes and left the farm as the sun was beginning to illuminate the world with its soft rays of morning light. As soon as we made it away from the farm and back onto the path, we were reunited with our wolf companion.

We walked with haste to make up the time we had spent enjoying breakfast at the farm. The path quickly led us to a small grouping of trees between Fran's farm and the village, not enough to be called a forest but just enough for danger to lurk. Upon entering the wooded area, my senses became heightened and our guardian wolf let out a low growl in warning. I could almost taste the thick musk of dark magic in the air. I kept vigilant of my surroundings and noticed a small talisman made of small twigs and hair hanging from a tree a little way off the path. I swallowed hard, knowing exactly who had placed it there.

It was early morning and the sun had not yet risen high enough to cast proper light into the dense patch of trees. Through the thicket was a tiny flicker of light, dancing off the edges of the branches. The light came from a small fire in the woods, the sparks giving it away as they floated their way to the heavens. Mary silently warned me not to walk any further but to stay still and silent. I did as she bid and we listened. The voice of Margaret Aitken broke through the thick morning air, chanting in an ancient language that we could not understand, all but one word, "Fend-inn"—devil. A melody of small pipes played and then another voice broke through, dark and low. The woods grew cold and became filled with dense, dark magic like nothing I have ever felt before. The two talked in the foreign language briefly and then the light of the fire went out and the woods became dark and silent once more.

We stayed quiet and still until we were certain she had gone, then made haste out of the wood, staying silent as we went. Once we had broken the border of the town, Mary finally spoke. She told me of a vision she had before we left on our journey. At the time it hadn't made much sense to her but now she understood. The vision was of the king's crown, a storm, and the death of many, many wise women and men. Margaret stood in the center of this storm in her vision, a dark force to be feared. After what we witnessed in the woods, we both knew it was a warning to stay clear of that woman. We stopped and dug a small hole off the path and buried the few things we had acquired from Margaret's herbal stores, not wanting to take them home with us for fear they were tainted with her dark magic.

It became dreary and overcast on our walk home and the rain fell hard. I pointed my staff to the sky and chanted a charm my mother once taught me to ward off bad weather. The rain slowed to a drizzle and we were able to press onward toward home in fairer conditions.

The trip back was spent mostly in silence, both of us thinking about what we had seen in the woods. An uneasy feeling in our stomachs pushed us onward, needing to put as much distance between us and the ominous darkness as we could. We made good time and arrived home before the sun set. The wolf stalked off into the woods before Mary and I parted ways. Mary took off her hag stone necklace and slipped it over my head. She told me I would need it and that it was time to wake up the magic that lies within me.

"Anything good happen in there while I was working on the floors?"

Helen was startled out of her reading trance by Connor, who had come in as she was deep into reading the journal.

"Lots—journeys, evil witches, spells with the devil. That kind of stuff."

"No! Really?"

"Well, kind of," Helen replied, closing the journal and setting it on top of the others. "Want to hear something odd? The other journals aren't Freya's. They're written by three entirely separate women, spanning over four hundred years. Isn't that weird?"

"How could that even happen?" Connor asked, looking puzzled. "They look like they're all part of a set."

"I don't know. Shit around here just keeps getting weirder and weirder."

Wanting to stretch her legs after sitting for a while, Helen got up and walked past Connor out into the sitting room.

"The floor looks great!" she said, looking down at the newly laid boards.

"Thanks. I haven't gotten a chance to replace the ones in the bathroom yet but this room and your bedroom are finished. You're going to want to throw a bit of varnish on them to seal them up. I can bring a can down from the farm the next time I come."

"Thanks. I'll add it to the list!"

"Are you ready to go?" Connor asked, picking up his tools.

"Go?"

"Yeah, dinner with my granda, remember? I'm sure he's been making a fuss and cooking all day."

"Oh, I completely forgot. Yes, just give me a few minutes and I'll be ready."

Helen went into her bedroom and dug through her clothes, looking for something that would be appropriate for a dinner out. She had packed one long-sleeved, floor-length dress. It was made of simple cotton the color of fresh moss. She slipped it on and dressed it up with a floral scarf she had tucked away in her bag. Then she went into the bathroom and pulled her hair up into a bun, pinning it and leaving a few loose strands to hang around her face. Lastly, she touched up her makeup and added a little plum lipstick to her lips. After giving herself a final once-over in the mirror, she went back into the sitting room.

Connor was stoking the fire when she entered. Turning around, he couldn't seem to hide his expression.

"Wow, you look beautiful," he said, staring at her.

"Why thank you, sir," she said, with a tiny curtsy and a laugh.

Connor smiled.

"Well, shall we?" he said, holding out his hand to her. She took it and gave Storm a gentle pat on his head goodbye as they walked out into the brisk evening air.

Chapter Twenty

THE SHATTERING

They arrived at the farm just as the sun was setting. The stone farmhouse was aglow with the last light of the day dripping down upon the hills. The windows were lit from within, making it feel alive and welcoming.

Inside, they greeted Connor's grandfather, who was busy pulling a tray of fresh rolls out of the oven. The house smelled of earthy vegetables, burned butter, and sweet homemade bread. It was delightful and reminded Helen of dinners at her grandparents' house back in Vermont.

Connor poured them both tall glasses of red wine that tasted of honey, rose, and wild berries.

"Do you need any help?" Helen asked Seamus as he moved about in the kitchen.

"No, no, I'm fine. You kids go and enjoy your wine. Dinner will be ready in just a few minutes."

They sat by the fire while Seamus finished off the last bit of cooking. The night was cold and the warm fire was inviting. The crackle of logs created an almost rhythmic sound that bounced off the stone walls, mingling with the shadows cast by the flickering flames. They both moved in an ancient dance; flame, shadow, light, and darkness.

"Okay you two, dinner is ready," Connor's grandfather called out from the kitchen.

They walked in with eager anticipation, their noses causing their stomachs to moan out in hunger for the tasty food.

"It smells wonderful," Helen said, as she sat at the modest kitchen table, covered in plates of food. She gave Seamus a wide smile, surprised at the bounty laid out before them. "You must have been cooking all day. This all looks marvelous."

"I do love to cook. It's one of the few things I can still do as well if not better than in my youth," he said, sitting down and tucking a napkin into the top of his shirt.

On the table was an oblong platter with a large pheasant on it. Surrounding it were potatoes, turnips, carrots, and beets with sprigs of rosemary and a few bay leaves. There was a small bowl of brown gravy and a basket of fresh hot rolls that were still steaming from the oven. Alongside that was a plate with sliced cheese and what looked to be some mint jelly.

"It looks and smells amazing, Granda," Connor said.

"It really does," Helen echoed.

"This was something my wife and I created many years ago. We called it the poor man's harvest. Every autumn, on the twenty-second of September, we would gather up the last of the harvest and throw whatever we had together. Some years were different from others but the one thing that always remained the same was that it was all food grown or hunted on our own land," Seamus said, cutting into the bird and laying a small slice of the breast on Helen's plate.

Over the next hour, they all enjoyed the food and company, with lively conversation and second helpings. Once everyone had filled themselves to bursting, Connor and Helen picked up and started to wash the dishes while Seamus went out into the night air to enjoy a smoke of his pipe.

"I miss having a dishwasher," Helen said as she dipped a plate into the soapy water of the sink basin.

"Oh really, you were one of those kids growing up? Not having to actually wash a dish, ya lucky bastard," Connor said, blowing a clump of soapy bubbles off his hand and onto Helen's shoulder.

"Hey! I'll have you know I did my fair share of handwashing as a kid at my grandparents' house." She shot him a mischievous grin before blowing a handful of bubbles onto his cheek. She burst out in laughter as his eyes widened in surprise.

"Oh, it's on!" he said as a large cluster of shiny little bubbles flew up in the air and landed on her head.

They both laughed and he stepped up and gently wiped them off her hair. They were left standing only inches apart and holding each other's gaze until Seamus stepped back inside and the moment ended.

Upon his return, Seamus pulled a pie out of the oven, kept warm in there while they ate. Its golden top was split with three small crosshatches that the fruit peeked through, and it rested in a beautiful handmade ceramic pie dish.

"Who's up for a slice of hot rhubarb pie? We can take it into the living room by the fire with a glass of whiskey, what do you say?" Seamus asked.

"How could anyone refuse such an amazing pie by a fire,

and whiskey to boot?" Helen teased, grabbing a small plate and handing it over to Seamus for a slice.

Pleased with Helen's response, Seamus dished out large slices of pie while Connor poured them each a short glass of whiskey and brought everything into the living room on a large tea tray. They each found their own cozy place to sit.

"Seamus, can I ask you a question?"

"Oh, course my dear, anything you like."

"Do you know anything about the symbol carved under your sink? How long has it been there?" Helen asked, taking a large bite of pie and sitting back in anticipation of a story.

Seamus took a sip of his whiskey and began.

"It's been there for as long as I can remember. I found it when I was a boy playing hide and seek with my brothers. I asked my father about it and he told me it had been there since he was a little boy as well and that his father had told him the story of its origins. It actually has a little bit to do with the story of the girl who wrote that journal you found at the cottage—Freya. As the story goes, back when Tomas's father tried to save poor Freya from the witch hunters, he hid her away here at the farm. Hid her in the cupboard under the sink, thinking it was an unlikely place for them to search, and it worked. The patrons of the church came in search of her more than once without success. But the final time they came, they brought a woman who claimed she could tell a witch by the mark of the devil in her eyes. She was the one who found her, cowering in the cupboard like a frightened rabbit. After they took her away, Tomas's father found the etching in the stone and left it in remembrance of her. He was later tried on counts of harboring a witch, but it did not stick, as he was a very prominent landowner and supplied most of the area with food."

"It's such a sad and heart-wrenching story. Why do you think she left the symbol there?" Helen asked.

"The triquetra is a fairly common symbol these days, but it meant something different to the people of Freya's time," Seamus said. "Some say it was part of a spell she was casting, others say she was praying to the old gods for help. Either way, it didn't work. She was hung the following day."

"That's terrible. She died at such a young age, and for what? The ravings of the insane religious world. From her journal, she seemed to be a kind and caring person. It's all so tragic. Do you have anything in the house that belonged to Tomas? Maybe a journal of his own?" Helen asked.

"No, I believe the only thing we have left from that time is the house and the old stone walls, sadly."

They sat eating the last of the pie off their plates and finishing the few drops of whiskey left in their glasses. The mood had turned somber and Helen was deep in thought about Freya and the terrible turn of events that had befallen her. It was hard to wrap her mind around, since the beginning of the journal was so carefree and full of hope.

Soon, Connor stood up and piled the plates and cups onto the tray and took them into the kitchen. When he left the room, Seamus leaned forward and spoke to Helen in a low whisper.

"If the stories are correct, the woman who pointed the finger at Freya was a witch herself and betrayed her own kind. Souls that are taken in such a horrific manner tend not to cross over but stay in our realm until justice is paid in full. Be careful how much you dig up, you don't want to awaken the spirits. Fernbeg has its own secrets, be wise about uncovering them," he said, resting back against the chair and gazing into the fire.

Just as Helen was about to question him, Connor came back

into the room with her jacket.

"Are you ready to go?" he said, handing it over to her.

She glanced at Seamus, who looked as if he was not about to speak any further in front of Connor. She was curious as to why he didn't want his grandson involved in their conversation. But she decided now was not the time to question him about it.

"It was a lovely evening, and I very much enjoyed your delicious cooking and wonderful stories. Thank you, Seamus," Helen said, pulling her coat on.

"You're more than welcome, my dear. Come back and visit anytime—and remember what I said." He winked and smiled, though something about it seemed worried.

The drive back to Fernbeg was dark and cold as Connor's truck had a poor heating system and one blown headlight. Helen didn't speak much as they drove. Seamus's words kept echoing back at her. *Be careful how much you dig up.* By the time they made it back to the cottage, it was near 10 p.m. and poor Storm was in desperate need of being let out.

Connor and Helen walked the little wolf out into the yard. The moon was full, and its silvery light illuminated the loch below.

"Do you want to take a walk down to the water?" Helen asked Connor.

"Love to."

They walked down the stony dirt path, the moon's light casting long shadows across the valley. Storm ran ahead of them to the water's edge. He dipped his nose in and took a long, deep drink of the cold lake. By the time they had made it down to where he was, he had found himself a spot on the shoreline and sat looking up at the moon overhead. The loch was so still that it mirrored the moon's reflection perfectly. It was cold out and Connor took off his wool jacket and placed it around Helen's shoulders when he saw her shivering.

"Thank you," she said. His jacket was heavy and still warm from the heat of his body. The smell of him lingered on the fabric and she breathed it in like the fresh, cool air. Looking at him in the pale light made her heart race. She forced herself to look away out over the glassy waters. "It's so beautiful here."

"Even more so with you in the picture," Connor said.

She turned and looked at him. His kind eyes stared back, reflecting the moon off the water like small silver coins. There was no denying it—as hard as she had tried to fight it, she was falling for this man. This was not her intention, she wasn't planning on staying in Scotland. She needed to fix the cottage up and sell it as soon as possible so she could get back to her old life. But what was waiting for her there? Work, the repetitive day-in, day-out grind that never seemed to end? For all the things she wasn't even sure she wanted anymore—the job, the condo, her life back in the city.

"Helen," Connor said, her name from his lips thrusting her back into the moment.

Her mind raced as Connor stepped forward. He bent down and softly kissed her under the light of the full harvest moon.

Lost in the kiss, they couldn't tell that the magic they felt between them was visible, that it burst forth in a blue pulse of energy from where their bodies met and went surging through the world, like ripples in water.

The wind blew through the trees, playing a smooth melody as the water lapped the shoreline. The faint hooting of an owl could be heard far off in the distance, the beating of Connor's heart and the sound of Storm's panting. As they broke their kiss she looked up. The stars in the sky shone brighter than before and then started to spin into a blurry circle of light as she fell into nothingness. A deafening silence, accompanied by darkness, was the last thing she felt before her world shattered.

Chapter Twenty-One

THE AWAKENING

All Helen could remember was waking up in the cottage in her bed with a splitting headache, worse than the ones she had gotten from nights of overdrinking in college. Her head spun so badly when she tried to sit up that she retched toward the bedroom floor. Falling short of throwing up, she laid back on the pillow and clutched the sides of her head as it pounded. There was the hum of electricity buzzing, along with an immense mix of sounds. The crackling of the fire, the rhythmic sounds of hearts beating, water running through the soil outside the cottage walls, and millions of bugs and birds across the valley. It was as if she could clearly hear every little sound in the world around her. This sensory overload proved to be more than her body could handle.

Then, as if the floodgates had opened, a surge of memories rushed back, causing her to pass in and out of consciousness.

The second time she woke, Connor was sitting next to her on the bed. He was wiping her forehead with a cold, damp cloth. She wanted to speak to him, but before she could say anything, another wave struck her and she faded back into the darkness.

Freya crested the top of the hill. In the valley below lay her tiny stone cottage with puffs of milky white smoke billowing out of the chimney. She raced down the hill, eager to be back in the safety and comfort of her home. Upon opening the door, Tomas stood there, waiting. She ran into his arms. He embraced her with such love it was as if they hadn't seen each other in a year, not just three days.

They sat and enjoyed a hearty vegetable stew her father had cooked and she told them stories of her journey and showed them all the new things she had acquired for the village's winter stores. She then took out a round of goat cheese folded in a linen cloth. Her father's smile lit up the room. Her mother had always brought him back a round of cheese from Fran's farm when she journeyed there. Carrying on that tradition just seemed right; it kept her mother's memory alive and present.

Night came quickly and Tomas retired back to his farm, knowing Freya was tired and weary from her long journey. She drifted off into a dreamless sleep, only to be woken in the middle of the night by the incessant hooting of an owl outside. She sat up and went over to her window. The full moon scattered shadows across the landscape. A sudden impulse compelled her to press her hand flat against the windowsill. Her vision changed as soon as she did.

She was frightened as her vision blurred in and out of focus. When she reopened her eyes, she was taken aback by the light and found herself inside Tomas's barn where a ewe was giving birth. Tomas was next to the poor creature, petting it gently on its back, trying to comfort it. Finally, after a long and grueling labor, one of the babies slipped out and landed in the straw below. There, lying in harsh contrast with the golden straw was a tiny lamb, black as the night. It was followed quickly by another who was white as snow. Tomas tenderly cleaned the lambs with an old cloth and then rested them next to their mother. Then, as quickly as it had come, the vision ended and she was back in her room looking out into the smoky darkness.

The vision left her feeling shaken and dizzy. In the moments it took afterward to ground herself she thought of her mother. A single tear trailed down her face. It was the first vision she had ever experienced, something she had thought would never occur. It foretold a dark omen; a black sheep born on a farm was a sign of bad things to come. There was a darkness about to fall upon the McKenzies.

She lay back down but could not sleep. She could feel an evil lurking in the air. The faint hooting of the owl could still be heard but was now off in the distance. The air was still and silent until an unsettling sound pierced the lull. A low howl drifted down from the woods that rimmed the hilltop. She knew without a doubt that it was her guardian wolf, and he was warning her of the danger he sensed, but she was already well aware of it.

The next day she was up before the sun and took to her morning duties before her father had even risen. By the time he was awake, breakfast was waiting for him on the table and she was kissing his forehead and walking out the door to the McKenzie farm.

The day was cold and the colors of autumn washed the landscape in a glow of amber as the sun rose. By the time she had arrived at the farm, her long skirts were thoroughly wet from the dew and the braid in her hair hung loose and disheveled. She had made good time, arriving at the farm before Tomas took the sheep into the backfield. As she entered the barn, Tomas was leaning over a ewe that was giving birth. The animal kicked and moaned as the lamb made its way into the cold new world, landing at Tomas's feet. It was an ebony-black lamb, just as she had seen in her vision. Tomas looked up at her with worry on his face, for he knew the significance of such a thing. Soon after, another lamb arrived in harsh contrast to her brother, being the shade of ivory.

After Tomas had found a secure place in the barn for the mother and her new lambs, he walked Freya out into the barnyard. A small, rusty-colored dog named Braun walked the line of the outer fence, checking for any predators that might be lurking in the early morning light. On the surface, it looked to be any ordinary day, but the birth of a black lamb meant things were about to take a turn for the worse.

They walked together, bringing the sheep into the upper pasture.

"Tomas, I saw this all coming to pass in a vision I had last night."

"You received your first vision?" Tomas said. "So you've inherited your mother's special ability. You must be relieved. I know you were concerned it wouldn't come." He held her hand tightly in his.

"Yes. If it hadn't prophesied a warning to your family, I would be. I'm now questioning whether such an ability is a blessing or a curse."

"Oh, Freya my love, it is a blessing, but one you must be careful with." He stopped to look at her. "With the talk of witches and the awful stories coming from the south, you must be careful who you trust with your new gifts."

"I will. No one knows of my skills apart from you, Mary, and

Father. I will be safe. But I am more worried about you. A black lamb is an omen of bad tidings. You must also be diligent. Promise me," she said, looking deep into his eyes.

He pulled her into an embrace and whispered, "I will, my sweet love. You have nothing to worry about. I will be fine."

"Tomas, do not brush this warning off. These types of premonitions are not to be taken lightly," she said crossly, pulling herself away in hopes that it would make him take her a bit more seriously.

They walked back to the farmhouse in silence, the tension between them holding fast until Tomas reached for her hand and held it once more.

"I promise you I will stay vigilant. Now please, must we quarrel on such a fine morning?"

She smiled. His tenderness had won her over.

Freya decided to stay at the farm and help Tomas's mother, Sibeal. She was in the process of making cheese and could use the extra set of hands. This gave Freya the excuse to stick around and make sure things were alright. Tomas kissed her gently on the forehead and then went back to tending the sheep and fixing up a stall in the barn for the new mother and her babies.

"Freya dear, can you go into the pantry and grab me another bundle of muslin?" Sibeal asked.

Freya walked past the kitchen and into the small room that was shut off from the rest of the house. The space had been designed to stay cooler than the other rooms in order to ensure the food stayed preserved longer. She searched the shelves for the cloth, finding it tucked behind some canned beetroots. When she reached in and touched it, her vision blurred and she started to feel light-headed. She shut her eyes tight to stop the sensation of spinning. When she opened them again, she was no longer in the pantry.

She was now looking at a small black cauldron over an open fire in the woods. A silver-white stream of smoke rose from its mouth and drifted up into the dark night sky. She heard chanting in a language she had heard only once before—when she was with Mary in the woods of Duror. She knew right then she was seeing through the eyes of Margaret Aitken.

The outlines of the large trees were the only things visible until a figure stepped out of the darkness and into the dim-lit area of the fire. The firelight was not enough to illuminate its face or any clear details, but it was clearly a masculine figure that stood before her. Freya felt the dark magic pouring from this creature. It was not human; its heart did not beat. Margaret's right arm reached out over the cauldron as, with her left, she dragged a silver dagger across it. A steady stream of blood dripped down her fingertips and into the potion below. It looked to be a mixture of hemlock and belmony, two herbs that were often used in curses. As Margaret chanted, the cadence of the words sent chills down Freya's spine. Despite her inability to understand them, she knew they were fundamentally evil. The creature's eyes shone bright yellow in the glowing light of the fire, cutting through the darkness. He looked straight at Freya, not at Margaret, as his gaze pushed through Margret's eyes and directly into her psyche. He knew she was there, seeing through the eyes of this other witch. Frightened, Freya flipped back into reality with a sudden crash to the ground.

Cailean, Tomas's younger brother, came rushing in to find Freya on the floor with broken glass and beetroot all around her.

"Are you okay, Freya?" the boy asked with a frightened look across his face.

"I'm fine, Cailean. Just a bit clumsy, that's all. It's not blood, just beetroot juice," she reassured him.

Cailean reached out his hand and helped Freya back to her feet. She thanked him and sent him to his mother with the cloth, while she cleaned the broken jar of beetroot off the floor. As she soaked up the red liquid, a flash of Margaret's fingers, dripping with blood, raced through her mind. She didn't know the spell she had been casting but she knew it was dark magic unlike any she had ever seen. Visions, her mother had told her once, are not given unless needed or sent as warnings. She needed to see Mary right away.

But the broken glass lay around her like a fence keeping her at bay from making a quick departure. Freya bent down and began picking the shards up. Not paying close attention, she cut her hand, leaving a thin red line across her palm. After gathering all the glass up, she apologized to Sibeal about the broken jar and left for home. She gathered her large wool shawl and headed out the door. Before she even made it into the field above the cottage, Mary was there waiting for her on the moss-covered stone wall.

"Mary, I had my first vision," Freya said, as soon as she was close enough to her friend not to be overheard.

"Did you see it too?" Mary asked.

"If you mean Margaret Aitken muttering incantations for a blood ritual with a creature in the woods, then yes, I did see it," Freya replied.

"Well, well. So, your second sight has finally come. I didn't see Margaret last night. I dreamed about the birth of a black sheep at Tomas's farm."

"So did I. I went to warn him about it this morning but as I arrived, the lamb was already being born. And while I was there, another vision came to me. Mary, I saw through the eyes of Margaret in my vision. She was making a blood sacrifice in the presence of some sort of creature. It looked human but its eyes glowed yellow and its heart did not beat. He must have sensed my presence, because he turned and looked right at me. Not at Margaret, at me. He saw me there behind her eyes, I'm sure of it. It frightened me and then the vision ended," she said, clutching Mary's arm.

Mary went still, as she could see the fear in Freya's eyes. "It sounds like she summoned a demon, but for what purpose? I knew she was evil from the moment I heard her voice in the woods that day. It was dark magic she was chanting, ancient and black, and we heard her call out to the devil that day. It seems she has found one."

"Mary, something is happening, a shift of energy. Ever since we came back from Duror, there has been darkness following us."

As they walked on there was rustling in the woods off to the right of the stone wall. They looked over in surprise to see their large, gray Highland wolf come walking through the thicket. He padded over to Freya and placed his head under her hand, then turned to greet Mary.

"Why, hello again, my friend," Mary said to the wolf.

"He warned me last night. After I slipped back from my vision, I heard him howling off in the distance," Freya said.

"I believe now that he was sent to protect us by the Goddess," Mary said.

"Did he tell you that?"

"Yes, in his own way on our way home from Duror," Mary replied, giving Freya a smile.

"What are we going to do? I warned Tomas of the danger but he does not know the true darkness out there. We must protect him and his family."

"It's time to gather herbs and make a protection spell for Tomas's home," Mary said.

The two took off down the hill to the cottage, leaving the wolf at the edge of the woods to wait for their return.

They set off to prepare protection charms to place in the four corners of her, Mary's, and Tomas's homes. Once the herbs were mixed and the incantations said, they sealed the jars with wax and placed them in the north, south, east, and west corners of the house. Packing up the remaining jars, they headed out the front door. Tomas stood there in the front garden.

"What are you doing here, Tomas?" Freya asked, looking at the sack he had slung over his shoulder.

"I'm in need of more nails for the new stall and thought I would ask your father before heading to Hamish in the village. Mother sent me with a loaf of fresh bread she baked this morning to give your father. Where are you going?"

"Mary and I were coming to give you protection jars for your house." She gently took the four small jars out of her pocket. "Put these in the four corners of your house as soon as you get home. They will protect your home and anyone inside of it."

Tomas reached out and took the jars from Freya, tucking them into the large front pockets of his coat.

"Thank you, my love," he said, bending forward and kissing her softly on the forehead.

Freya led Mary and Tomas through the cottage to the backyard, where her father was planning a bench he was making for the church in town.

"Father, Tomas has come to ask for nails. Do you have any to spare?"

The old man stopped what he was doing and looked up. Even though the weather was brisk, a bead of sweat rolled down his brow and onto his cheek. It was hard work for a man of his age but he was never one to complain, as long as he was able to feed his family. Plus, keeping his hands and his mind busy helped with the grief of losing his wife.

"I'm sorry, son, but I have none. Ran out a while ago. Have mostly been using pegs these days. Hamish always has a few spare he'll be willing to part with."

"Thank you, sir, I'll make my way to the village then." Tomas turned and handed the loaf of bread to Freya from out of his sack, and they walked out of the garden. Mary stayed back to give them privacy and made small talk with Freya's father.

"Promise me you'll be safe and as soon as you are home, put those jars in the four corners of the house," Freya said, standing on her tippy toes and wrapping her arms around Tomas's neck.

"I promise! Please stop worrying about me. That is my job as your soon-to-be husband," he said, bending down to kiss her.

As their lips met, a sweet, gentle breeze broke free and twirled around them. A whirlwind of leaves spun up from the ground and encircled them, all burnt oranges and deep reds. Then, the moment their lips parted, the wind ceased, causing the leaves to rain down around them. The clouds covered the sun once again and all became normal.

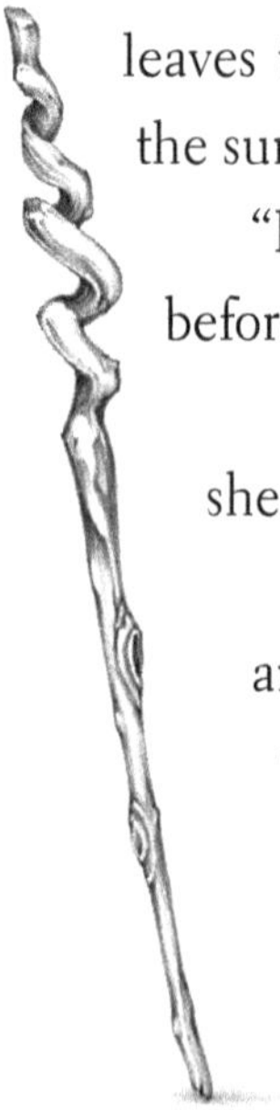

"I love you, Freya," Tomas said softly in her ear before he pulled away.

"I love you with all my heart, Tomas McKenzie," she echoed back.

She watched him walk off up the dirt path with an ache in her stomach. Despite his reassurances, there was still an uneasy feeling in the air that made her fear for him.

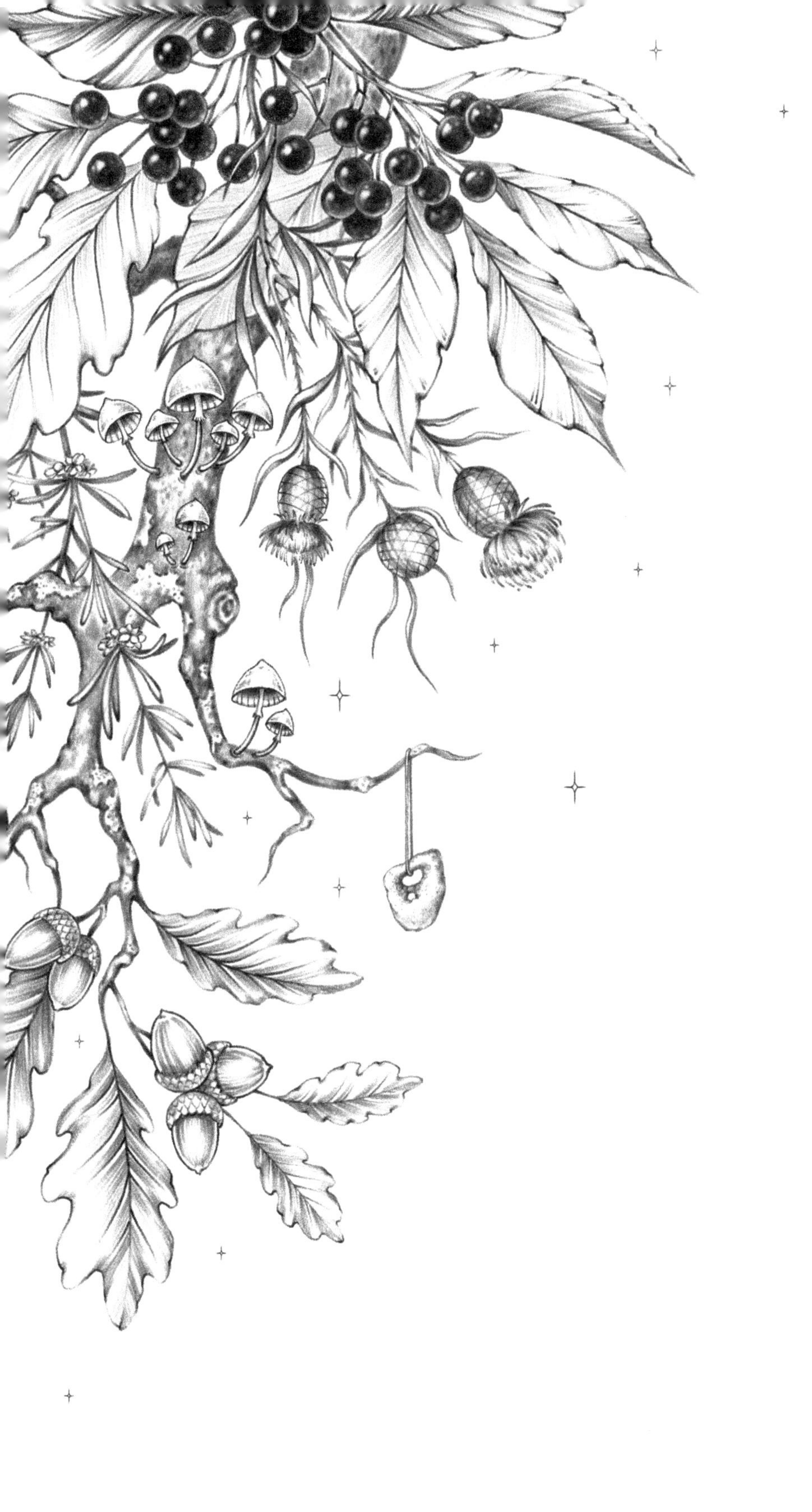

Chapter Twenty-Two

BLACK TIDE

That night Freya was restless, her sleep broken by nightmares.

She dreamed of a stormy sea. Violent waves crashed, dragging pieces of the shoreline out into the water, leaving it jagged and thrashing. In the center of the storm, unfazed by the elements, she saw a naked woman with long black hair dancing around a fire. The flames burned black with tips of green that licked the air. A dark and ominous laughter cut through the raging wind. It had come from the demon from Freya's vision who stood on the outside of the circle and looked upon the spectacle with an evil smile across his distorted face. A human sacrifice lay dead, face down in the center of a six-pointed star drawn into the sand. Black candles burned at the tips of each point. As the woman continued to dance and chant, the storm grew in its fury, threatening to capsize a ship that was being thrashed in the raging waves of the sea. The last part of her dream was of a golden crown resting in a nest of red velvet. It was almost perfect, except for a missing jewel on one of its many tines of gold.

Freya woke to a crack of thunder. A storm was raging outside her window. There was a stale taste in the air as if the salt from the sea had permeated it. She sensed a shift. The scales had tipped. The darkness in the air now outweighed the light, and she knew from an ache deep down inside of her that something was terribly wrong.

She went out into the garden and looked out toward the water. The rain was coming down with such vigor that it was almost impossible to see the loch in the distance.

"Freya! Come inside. What are you doing out there?" her father called out to her, struggling to be heard above the rage of the storm.

Slowly, she walked back to the cottage. Her father made a fuss about her catching a cold, stoking up the kitchen fire so hot that she thought it might cook them both.

"What were you doing, my child?" he asked her.

"Father, I have received my second sight. The other night, my first vision came to me, a black lamb born to a sheep on Tomas's farm. The next day that very sheep gave birth to a set of twins, one of which was black as coal. An omen of bad luck. Then last night I dreamed of this storm. Something terrible is about to happen," Freya said, as she paced back and forth in the blazing hot kitchen, twisting her skirt in her hands.

"Oh, my dear. I wish your mother was here to walk you through all of this. She used to have terrible visions but not all of them came to pass. Not all visions are as they seem, they are meant to be interpreted," he said, trying to soothe her.

"Father, something is very wrong. Mary has even been having visions of descending darkness."

Just then, there was a knock on the cottage door. Freya's father answered it. Standing there in the pouring rain was Cailean.

"Come in, boy!" said Freya's father, ushering him inside and away from the storm.

"Freya, have you seen Tomas? Is he here with you? He never came back home last night," the boy said, dripping wet with rain.

Freya's heart sank, for as soon as he spoke, she knew what that terrible feeling she had woken with was. Something had happened to Tomas.

"No, he is not here. He came to visit us yesterday afternoon but left for the village," Freya said, biting her lip as the anxious feeling built inside her.

"Father has gone into the village to look for him and I was told to come here. Maybe he stayed with Hamish because of the storm?" Cailean said, trying to reassure Freya as he watched a tiny tear fall silently off her chin and onto the floor.

"Don't you worry, my boy, we'll find him," Freya's father said.

Freya walked out of the house with her staff in hand and raised it to the sky. She let her voice echo out across the mountains, loud with purpose.

"Tha mi ag àithneadh dhut stad, I command you to stop!" she said, slamming her staff into the ground. As soon as it struck the earth, a white pulse of energy broke free from its point and raced across the landscape. Soon, the rain slowed and became nothing more than a drizzle. In the distance, she could see the wolf standing guard on the hill, looking down at her. He let out a howl of warning and pointed his nose toward the loch.

At this, Freya dropped her staff and ran as fast as her feet would take her down to the shore. She stood there with the tips of her boots in the cold water and looked out to where the loch melted into the sea. It looked as it always had and with the storm receding, the waters had become calm. The cloud cover was still thick, casting gray reflections across the water's surface, bringing a dullness to everything around.

But even though nothing looked out of place, something unsettled her. She stood there, looking out to the edge of the water where the sky met the sea, when something knocked against her boot. She looked down and saw a small glass jar lying by her feet.

As soon as she realized what it was, she ran into the water, frantically searching for Tomas, screaming out his name into the unforgiving waters. After feverishly searching the water and discovering nothing, she collapsed on the shoreline, tears streaming down her cheeks. It was one of the four protection jars she had given to Tomas. She had seen him place them in his jacket pocket yesterday.

She could hear soft footsteps as someone approached slowly from behind. She turned to see the wolf, standing there with a look of sorrow in his eyes. He came over and sat next to Freya and she rested herself against him and cried. Her tears flowed down her cheeks and dripped off her chin, falling silently to the ground. As each tear hit the earth, it let out a spark of blue light that the earth drank up.

After a while, she dried her tears and looked up. She was amazed to see that a circle of wildflowers had grown around them as she wept. She stood up. The flowers were a mix of lavender, yarrow, sage, and foxglove. All flowers of protection. She had grown a protection circle around herself without even knowing it. Her magic was beginning to emerge and was more powerful than she had expected.

In that moment a thought struck her, and she knew what she

needed to find Tomas. The hag stone Mary had given her. She steadied herself and then raced back up the hill to the cottage, with the wolf following close by.

She arrived to find her father and Cailean gone. Mary was there, standing in the doorway, a look of distress on her face. She was no good at concealing her emotions, especially from Freya.

"Something is terribly wrong. I could feel the shift as the storm came in last night. There is a real danger here and now," Mary said.

Freya stood, a look of shock still plaguing her face, and in her hand she held the jar. Mary looked down at the small protection charm and then up at her friend.

"I found this down at the loch. It washed up on the shore at my feet," Freya said, a tear breaking free once again and streaking her face.

"Oh Freya, it might be nothing. Maybe he lost one yesterday. It doesn't mean—"

"I dreamed again last night of Margaret and this storm," Freya said, cutting her off.

"Was there a golden crown missing a gem?" Mary asked.

"Yes! Did you also have this vision?"

"I have been having that same vision since we went to Duror," Mary said. She grabbed hold of Freya's hands and took the jar from them, placing it on the table.

"I fear something terrible has happened to him, Mary. But I won't give up. I may know how to find him. The hag stone."

"Yes, that could work. You can dowse for him like water. You've always been gifted with that," Mary said.

Freya went straight to her bedroom and grabbed the necklace from the wooden stool beside her bed. She tied it around her neck and went back out to Mary. Together, they bundled up and walked out the front door, where their loyal guardian wolf was waiting to escort them on their hunt for Tomas.

Walking up the muddy path to the top of the hill, Freya slipped off the necklace and held it up in front of her. It wasn't much to look at, just a simple gray stone that had been smoothed by the hands of time and ancient waters. The thing that made it unlike other stones was the perfectly round hole that went all the way through its center, created by centuries of water flowing over it. These stones were rare and held great powers of protection. Wise women often used them for visions, invoked by a glance through the hole.

Freya pinched the twine between her thumb and forefinger and let the hag stone dangle. Her left hand floated under it and she closed her eyes.

"Goddess, guide me to my love. Make our footsteps swift and bring us to him quickly," she uttered to the stone. She waited until she felt movement and then opened her eyes again. The stone swung persuasively to the right, toward the village. This gave her a grain of hope that Cailean was right and Tomas had been stranded there due to the storm.

They stopped at each crossroad to check the pendulum on their way to town. They had almost arrived at the village when the pendulum changed directions and sent them back toward the coast. It was a road that crossed the trail they had traveled but led down to the harbor where the ships were moored.

The walk was long and the day grew cold. Dark clouds gathered overhead and threatened rain. The road to the port was much rockier than the paths Freya was used to walking and her feet began to ache with each step on the gravelly ground. The soles of her shoes were not thick enough to pad her feet well, but she pushed the pain to the back of her mind.

When they reached the port, the pendulum swung to the left of where the ships sat, tied up in their watery resting places. A large beach broke away to a small cove beyond a grouping of sizable rocks. This seemed to be where the pendulum was taking them.

Freya had been here before with her mother when she was little. They would come to collect a special type of algae that washed ashore during the autumn months. It was something her mother said would bring them good luck, and Freya always thought of it as a treasure hunt to find the lucky weed.

The wolf went forward to scout things out and disappeared behind the first large rock just before a wave crashed upon it. Mary and Freya waited for the water to recede and then made their way around the rock, leaving shoeprints in the wet sand. As they rounded the rock's edge, the cove came into view and it was there they saw the wolf standing over a body, smashed up against the rocks.

Mary, in the lead, was the first to see the body and came to a halt. Freya took a tentative step around her. The only thing visible from where she stood was a pair of boots, but that was all Freya needed to know it was Tomas.

She lunged forward, screaming out his name as Mary grabbed her and tried to hold her back. But it was no use. She broke free and ran to him, throwing herself on top of his cold, lifeless body. She let out a scream so loud it stopped all life. Her tears flowed like the rivers after a hard rain, flooding the earth with magic. Mary looked on in disbelief, with heartache for her dear friend. The wolf took a step back and sat next to Mary, both looking on, as part of Freya died.

Tomas had drowned. His body was blue with death, his clothing soaked and covered in tendrils of seaweed and sand. Why was he here? What had he come down to the shoreline in a raging storm? Nothing made sense.

"Freya," Mary said after a while, putting her hand on her friend's shoulder, "we need to find Tomas's father."

Freya looked up with tear-soaked eyes, her arms still embracing her lost love.

"I can't leave him, Mary."

But as Freya spoke, her gaze was caught by something bobbing up and down in the water a few feet from the shore. Slowly, she rose to her feet, letting go of Tomas's body, and waded out into the water. There, floating in the waves, was a black candle, its wick burned down to nothing more than an ashy stub. She plucked it from the water's surface, a white-hot rage blazing so deep within her that she believed the candle would melt in her hands as she held it.

With a feeling of total despair, she walked back to Mary.

"Freya, what…?"

"It was her! He was her sacrifice," Freya said, gripping the candle with an iron fist, fingernails etching crescent moons into its soft, waxy surface.

"Who?" Mary asked.

"Margaret. Last night's dream was a vision. It was Tomas I saw lifeless in the sand, it was always him. I was just too distracted to see it. She made a deal with the devil and sacrificed him. I'm certain of it. She won't get away with this. I'll hunt her down if it's the last thing I do," Freya cried out, throwing the candle onto the damp sand and began to walk back to Tomas's body.

Mary stood and watched in shock as Freya walked back to him, entirely oblivious to the fact that she was releasing bright white sparks from the tips of her fingers. As the white-hot magic hit the sand it caused small glass balls to form. Freya's magic had come in full force within a matter of days and with her heightened emotions, she was not in control. Mary feared for her friend. These were unstable times for people like them and if someone saw her in this state, she would be persecuted as a witch. The hysteria was swiftly spreading from the south, and many individuals in these parts were infected with radical ideas. She walked over and placed her hand lightly on Freya's shoulder.

"Freya, I know your heart is breaking but you must try and calm yourself. I have to go to the docks and find someone who can help us. They cannot see your magic, you must ground yourself and hide it. Do as we were taught, push your fingers into the ground and draw from its energy."

Freya looked up at her friend with tear-soaked eyes and then down at the ground. Around her were the small glass spheres she'd unknowingly created, peppering the ground. In a confused state, she shook her head yes and wedged her fingers deep into the sand, closing her eyes.

Mary patted the small glass orbs down into the sand and then left Freya there to calm down while she searched for help.

Freya did not move until she felt her magic soften. As soon as she did, she threw her arms around Tomas's lifeless body once more, placing her head on him. Her ear pressed into his chest in search of a beat that would not come. How had such an awful thing fallen upon him? How had he found his way into the hands of Margaret Aitken?

The wolf came over and pushed his nose under Freya's arm to lift it. She looked up into his yellow eyes, his stare transfixing her. She moved her hand over his warm, silky fur. It was a harsh contrast from Tomas's body and made everything all the more real. But with her gaze locked on the wolf's, her pain eased a little. She moved her other hand from Tomas's body and wrapped both arms around the wolf. He sat there, as still as stone, allowing her to nestle into his warm fur and sob.

Mary was gone only a few minutes and returned with two large men following her. With somber looks, they carried a wide plank down towards the shore. Both men froze upon seeing the wolf but Mary soon eased their minds by informing them it was tame.

Gingerly, the men hoisted Tomas's body onto the board and knotted a rope around him to ensure he remained securely on the frame. Freya stood up, but could not bear to watch them walk away with him. Instead, she stared out into the endlessness of the ocean, wishing for the tide to come in and carry her out to sea, to a place away from all the pain and sorrow.

Chapter Twenty-Three

THE BEGINNING OF THE END

It took all of Freya's strength to go to the farm the following day. When she entered, Tomas's body was displayed in the front room awaiting the sin eater's arrival. Tomas was dressed in his finest clothing, the same outfit he would have worn to their wedding. Bundles of fragrant lavender had been scattered around him, encircling his body like a wreath. A small loaf of bread lay on his chest above where his arms had been crossed, and a glass of wine sat on a small milking stool next to him. He looked peaceful with his eyes closed, she thought, as she looked down where he lay, waiting for his journey to the Summerlands.

Tomas's mother came over and they embraced each other, tears freely flowing from their eyes. Cailean sat with his father, both silent in their mourning, staring down at hot cups of mead held tightly in their hands.

A sharp knock at the door brought everyone to attention and Sibeal broke away from Freya to answer. There, in the stone doorway, was a tall slender man in his later years dressed in a dark woolen coat that touched the tops of his knees. He had an odd appearance, with high cheekbones that caused his light gray eyes to look sunken into his skull. This was Hector Murray, the local sin eater. Freya knew the man well and had seen him perform the ritual many times in their community, the last time for her mother. The custom started in their small village after the tragic loss of so many people due to the plague that had come the past winter. Hector began offering his service of absolving the sins of those who had been too weak to attend church or had died suddenly before giving a proper confession.

Sibeal greeted him. In turn, he took off his hat and gave her a small bow before entering the house. She escorted him over to where Tomas's body lay in its everlasting slumber. Hector took off his jacket and set it on a chair next to the body. He hovered over Tomas for a few moments before sitting and bowing his head. In a whisper Freya could not quite decipher, he recited a passage, then picked up the bread and began eating it. After the bread was consumed, he drank the wine, then stood and bent down towards Tomas's body. In a low gentle voice, he said, "You are free to go now, my young friend. Your sins have been absolved."

When Hector stepped back from Tomas's body he looked to Freya, then nodded back toward Tomas. As she followed his gaze, she saw a blue mist rise from his body and condense into a small blue ball of light. It traveled over its earthly vessel and toward Freya, hovering next to her briefly before disappearing into the veil. The only people to witness his spirit depart his body were Hector and Freya. Tears fell from her eyes and landed softly on the old wooden floorboards. He was gone, she felt it. His soul no longer inhabited this space. He was free.

Freya wanted to fade away into the earth, just as her tears had faded into the old porous wood floor. How could she go on without him?

As if Hector knew just what she was thinking, he placed his hand on her shoulder and gave it a squeeze.

"It will get easier, miss, as you know. It's not goodbye forever."

Freya looked up and gave him a fleeting smile, and Hector moved off to give his condolences to the McKenzie family. William thanked him kindly and handed him a shilling, which he placed in the pocket of his coat. Hector gave a nod of gratitude, then pulled on his hat, before walking out into the cold autumn evening.

Freya, in turn, said her goodbyes to the family and hastily left in hopes of catching up with Hector before he was out of sight. She lifted her long, thick wool skirt and ran up the hill to where he was making his slow progress. When she reached him, he was out of breath and had stopped for a brief rest to catch it.

"Freya, dear, are you alright?" he asked her in a long-winded voice.

"Mr. Murray, sir, can I ask you a question?" Freya said, letting go of her skirt so it could once again shield her ankles from the cold.

"Of course, you may ask me anything you like," he said to her with a sad smile.

Freya felt bad for the man. He had stepped up to help the community when all felt lost and was repaid by being shunned and cast out by the people of the village. It was the price that many cunning folk paid these days. People believed the more sins he ate from the dead, the eviler of a person he became.

Soon, no one in the village would even look at him, unless to acquire his services. She couldn't imagine how lonely he must be.

"Did you see it? Did you see his soul leave his body?" she asked.

"Yes, I always do. It's different each time, each soul being unique. I knew you would be able to see it. You are more your mother's daughter than you know."

"I do not believe he drowned. He fell into the hands of an evil woman and was used as some kind of sacrifice," Freya said, rage building inside her with each word.

"I know. If a man dies of natural causes or an accident, his soul lays peacefully in his body waiting for the time to leave. Souls of those who have been killed by the hand of another are restless and are not easily convinced they can go. Tomas's soul was not waiting peacefully when I arrived. That is why I spoke the incantation before I started. To help settle him so that he could let go and ascend."

"There is a magic that hovers over our village like a cloak of darkness," Freya said. "I think Tomas's murder is just the beginning of the evil we must face. Prepare yourself." She took his hand.

"They will not look kindly on people like us. You must protect yourself as well, young one," Hector said, a look of distress on his lined face.

Freya let go of his hand and said goodbye. She watched him slowly walk down into the field and then out of sight. As soon as he was gone, the wolf came out from his hiding place in the thick undergrowth of the woods. They took the long way back to the cottage, stopping several times just to look at where the earth and sky met, wondering if Tomas was now part of that beauty. She liked to think so. It gave her comfort to think he was still there, somewhere in the beauty of nature, waiting for her in the Summerlands.

She sat on her bed looking out the window at the moon. It was now waning, no longer full. There was a piece missing, the piece that would make it whole again. Thinking it was the perfect symbolism for her life at the present, she sat there with her companion moon and longed for something she would never have again.

Just as she was about to close her eyes and try to sleep, she heard the hooting of an owl. Another omen of death, she thought. She sat up and listened as the hooting became louder and more intense. She got out of bed and wrapped herself in a thick wool blanket, then walked out into the garden.

There, on the small tree growing next to the cottage gate, was a large barn owl, its ghostly pale face looking down at her. With its head cocked to one side and staring right at her, it let out a long screech. The noise cut through the night, sending a chill running down the length of her spine. With that, the owl flapped its wings harshly and flew into the night sky. It was an omen foretelling danger, but she had no need of its warning—she was already well aware of the threat that lurked in the shadows.

Freya did not sleep that night. She lay awake, her eyes sore from tears and too little rest. Her father found her the next morning in the kitchen, looking out of the window at the loch. He knew all too well the pain she was going through, and there was nothing he could do to ease it. Boiling water, he fixed them both steaming mugs of tea and cooked up the last of the eggs for breakfast. But she couldn't eat, and she couldn't think of a single thing to say, so they sat there in silence.

Midday, there was a knock on the door. Mary came in completely out of breath, as if she had run all the way from her home in town to the cottage. She waited a moment to catch it before she spoke.

Freya looked up at her friend, knowing whatever news she brought with her would not be good.

"Freya, old man Murray has been accused of witchcraft. They have him tied up and someone said they used the pilliwinks on him. The whole town is out for blood. They want to see him hanged."

"No! This can't be! When did they begin the talk of witches?" Freya's father asked Mary, with panic in his eyes.

"We heard that in Barcaldine someone accused one of their wise women of being a witch and she was run out of town, only a few weeks ago," Mary explained

"Poor Hector, of course he'd be the first to be pursued," Freya said. Sorrow poured off her like a rain cloud.

"You both need to go. Pack up your warmest clothes and I will get you enough bread and cheese to last you a week. You must go and hide until this hysteria passes or you will be next on the stake," Freya's father said, gathering a large cloth and beginning to fill it with bread and cheese.

Mary looked at Freya. They both knew her father was right. They had heard the stories coming from the south and knew the townspeople would turn on them next. Freya dressed in her thickest woolen skirt and overcoat and loaded her basket with the food her father collected for them.

"There's no time to waste. Whatever you hear, do *not* come back here. You must stay hidden until this passes. Go to the McKenzie farm for the night then go into the woods under the cover of darkness before the dawn, and hide there. Keep yourselves alert and watch out for one another." He pulled Freya in and hugged her so tightly that she could not breathe. "I love you, my sweet daughter—go and live."

"I love you, Father. Do not fear, we will see each other again, Mary and I will stay hidden and all will be well once this passes," she said. But there was apprehension in her voice, and she did not want to break their embrace for fear it may be the last.

The wolf was waiting for them next to the large rowan tree halfway between Freya's cottage and the McKenzie farm.

"He is your familiar, Freya. Only the most powerful of witches have one. Your mother was right, the magic was in there all along. It just needed its time to finally emerge," Mary said, patting the wolf on the head.

"But it was you that tamed him in the forest."

"I was simply his guide in his journey to you."

Freya smiled down at the wolf in silent acknowledgment. "Poor Hector. He is such a kind man. Why can't people see that? He has only been there to help," she said. The thought of him being imprisoned and tortured made her stomach churn.

"People are scared of things they don't understand. Things they can't see with their own eyes. Things that are different," Mary said, sorrow shadowing her face.

"Do you think they'll stop after they're done with him or do you believe they will come for us?" Freya asked.

"They will come for us. I have seen it."

"Why did you not tell me before now?" Freya's heart sank into her stomach and she began to feel sick with worry.

"You were grieving the loss of Tomas. I could not bring that to you while you were so broken."

The day slowly faded into night and the girls made their way to the McKenzie farm under the cloak of darkness. When they arrived, Cailean was waiting for them in the field above the barnyard with a small lantern. He led them down the hill and into the barn, taking them to a dark corner where the grain was kept. They had crafted a small nook between boards and bags for the two girls to sleep. It was fashioned in such a way that the boards could be slid over the top to create a perfect hiding space. Freya gave Cailean a hug and thanked him, then sent him back to the house.

Both girls rested little that night, with fear as their constant companion, keeping them from sleep.

When the sun began to rise the next morning, they gathered the few things they had and headed out of the barn. Tomas's father greeted them as they emerged, with fresh milk and sweet bread. He warned them not to go toward the woodland where they had spent the previous day, but to head south to the patch of woods below their southern field. He thought it prudent for them to not occupy the same place twice until things blew over—though how long that would be, no one was quite sure of. They thanked him and made haste before the sun had broken free of the hills.

The wolf caught sight of them halfway to their destination and quickly caught up. They spent most of the day gathering what little herbs they could and creating protection charms. Mary found a large group of mushrooms that were good for poison and thought they may come in handy at some point. Freya found dried heather and a few large stalks of mugwort, which she broke down and rolled in her fingers until she produced a coarse dust. Around themselves, they spread a circle of pinecones, sticks, and rocks on the forest floor. Freya walked around its edge, sprinkling the mugwort dust upon the earth, chanting.

"A circle formed from sticks and stones. The seeds of life in the form of cones, the rocks for strength, the sticks for kin, protect whoever may step within."

On her third pass around the circle, the ground began to tremble and sprigs of rosemary and thistles slowly pushed their way through the thick forest soil. The ground where they sprouted glowed with a dazzling white light that faded back into the soil as the plants took root and formed a perfect circle.

"The Goddess has answered your prayers, Freya," Mary said, bending down and running her fingertips over the plants.

Rosemary was Freya's mother's favorite herb. She always said it was one of the best to have on hand at any given time. Good for cooking, healing, and for protection. Freya couldn't help but wonder if maybe it was her mother and not the Goddess who had answered her call. She plucked a sprig and breathed in its rich aroma. It smelled of her mother. She rubbed the leaves together between her fingers, releasing the smell into the air around them. As she did this, a gentle wind blew through the tops of the trees, and she felt a new strength build inside her.

As they waited for nightfall, Mary carefully prepared the mushrooms she had found into a mash and added it to one of the empty jars she had brought with them for spells.

"This will come in handy if we find ourselves in the company of Margaret. It will only take a little to subdue her," she said, pushing a cork tightly into place.

"Will we encounter her? Your vision of the witch hunters, what did you see?" Freya asked.

"I am not certain. The vision was shattered. The only piece that stood out was of you. You resisted those who were attempting to persecute you and showed no fear; you were strong and fearless."

Freya held Mary's gaze and then spoke. "Will we survive this?" she asked.

Mary broke her eyes away and looked toward the ground. "I do not know," she admitted in a somber voice.

They sat in silence for what seemed to be hours after that. The weight of their situation weighed heavy on each of their thoughts.

Chapter Twenty-Four

WHITE-HOT RAGE

As the sun finally began to set, Freya worried they would have a harder time finding their way back to the farm, with the cloudy sky and no moon to guide them. Peering out from the clearing on the edge of the woods, they decided it was safe to leave before the sun had fully set. Halfway to the barn, it became dark, and they could scarcely see a foot in front of their faces. At that point, the wolf became their guide and safely led them back to the McKenzies'.

They had taken longer to arrive this time and Cailean was not waiting for them. However, they could see a lit candle in the farmhouse window, a sign from Sibeal that it was safe to approach. As they crept towards the barn, they heard men's voices coming from within.

"I should hope not for your sake. Harboring a witch is a crime," one of the men said.

A wave of panic flooded them and they were both frozen with fear. By the grace of the Goddess, Sibeal saw them and ran out, quietly ushering them into the house.

"Freya, I am sorry. They came so quickly I didn't have the time to blow out the candle. They have already searched the house so it is unlikely they will return, but we must still hide you," Sibeal said, opening the door to a large cupboard under the counter. Freya was the smaller of the two girls and fit well into the hiding spot. Mary was taken into the pantry room and tucked behind two large sacks of flour.

Cailean came rushing into the kitchen.

"Mother, they are coming back this way," he said in an urgent whisper.

Sibeal stationed herself in front of the cupboard where Freya hid, peeling apples. Cailean stood next to her, chopping the apples and depositing them into a ceramic bowl.

The front door swung open and two large men stood in the doorway, along with William, protesting as he followed them in.

"She is not here. I have told you both several times. If you must come in and look, then do so," he said in a tone that suggested he had nothing to hide.

"You know what the penalty for harboring a witch is, William," said the taller of the two men as he stepped into the house and began walking toward the kitchen.

Upon hearing the man's voice, who she recognized as one of the local constables, Freya's heart began to beat so heavily she feared the men would hear it and find her.

"Now, if I were you, I would avoid that devil. I know you hold feelings for the creature since she was supposed to be your daughter-in-law, but she was just playing you and your family for fools. William, she deceived all of us. We should have realized that her healing talents went deeper than her understanding of nature and herbs. She obviously conspired with the devil and the sin eater. God only knows how many curses she has brought upon our town," the man spat as he looked around the room and then walked back to the door.

Freya, crammed in the small dark space, shook with fear and anger as she listened to the man talk about her in such a way, and she muttered an incantation under her breath to send them away.

"Of course," William said as the two men approached the door to leave.

At the last moment, one of the men turned and gave the room one more glance before grabbing the door behind him and slamming it shut.

Freya's heart sank at the thought of any harm coming to this family on account of her or Mary. They had all gone through so much with the loss of Tomas that she could not bear for any other ill to befall them.

Sibeal opened the cupboard door once they were sure the men were gone and let Freya out, while Cailean freed Mary.

"I am so sorry. I will not have any harm come to you on my account. We will go and make camp in the woods tonight," Freya said.

"You will do no such thing," William stated.

He looked at her with a mix of sadness and pity that unsettled her. She initially mistook it for grief over Tomas's death, but something wasn't quite right. Freya looked over to Sibeal, who was busy preparing a kettle, but she could see the unease on her face as well. Something wasn't right, and she could feel tension filling the little room.

"I am afraid that I must be the bearer of bad tidings to you, sweet Freya," William said, guiding her to sit on one of the kitchen chairs.

A tightness gripped her chest and her breathing stilled as she looked into his sorrow-filled eyes.

"Your father was taken into town after refusing to tell them of your whereabouts," William said softly.

Freya felt as if her heart had stopped, or perhaps she was refusing to let it beat, trying to stop time from moving forward since she knew what his next words would be.

"He fought valiantly for you, but he suffered from a weak heart and he did not survive. I am so sorry, my dear." William drew her up onto her feet and held her. She stood stunned in his embrace. Inside her, a storm was brewing, churning the magical waters that moved through her veins, and her powers surged as each tear burst free.

Once they had calmed her, the McKenzies insisted that Freya and Mary eat with them before heading back to the barn for the night. The dinner was solemn with few words spoken and even less food eaten on Freya's part.

When they settled themselves into the small space in the back corner of the barn, Freya's rage let loose.

"I will go and find the men who killed my father and make them pay. He never hurt a soul. He was only being a good father," she yelled with fists clenched, startling the sheep in the stalls beside them. Her thoughts turned dark; if she could get her hands on the men who carried her father into town, she would set them ablaze with witch fire and watch as they burned to ash. She teetered on the edge of darkness as her fury and grief built.

As her temper heightened, she stood to leave, her eyes glowing like embers pulled from a hot fire and the tips of her fingers glowing white hot. Mary grabbed ahold of her hands before she could set the barn ablaze with witch fire.

"No Freya, you will not. Do as your father wished and stay safe or his death will be in vain."

She knew Mary was right, and her anger faded into defeat and despair.

Then came the tears, and as they broke free, it began to rain outside. The harder she cried, the fiercer the rain became. Mary looked on in shock at the powers that Freya held within. Powers such as these were far beyond the normal abilities of a novice witch. Even the most experienced witches didn't hold the kind of powers that Freya displayed, which bordered on godlike. It took Mary several hours to calm Freya down and only after expelling all that power and emotion did she finally succumb to sleep. Her head lay on Mary's lap, resting upon a tear-stained skirt. Freya welcomed the blissful nothingness of sleep, but she was not blessed with a dreamless slumber that night.

Black candles burned, and the rain poured down. On the sand, a circle was drawn in blood, with a six-pointed star in the center. Margaret was at the center of it all once more. She was naked, the markings on her body drawn from the blood in a silver chalice that rested in her hands. She began chanting in a dark voice, her eyes tightly shut. The silhouette of a tall, dark man appeared within the circle. The light seemed to reflect off him as if he were made of obsidian, plunging him into shadow no matter where the light touched him. It was the demon, with his bright eyes piercing through the storm like stars in a cloudless sky. Margaret knelt before him, and he took her head in his hands. She trembled at the overwhelming power he radiated as he touched her. She yearned for power like this, for the kind of influence and authority it bestowed, and she would go to any length to have it.

"My master has agreed to your proposal and will grant you eternal life—*if* you can bring him the souls of a thousand men," he uttered in a dark, menacing tone that sounded nothing like a human man's voice.

"My lord, I cannot collect that many. It's impossible," Margaret said.

The demon touched her forehead and her eyes glowed yellow. "There are many ways to gather souls," he said.

"I understand."

Her eyes transformed back to their normal brown color, and then the demon vanished.

She clothed herself and walked toward town. There, she came across a young man. She noticed a small jar poking its way out of his pocket.

"What is that you have there in the jar?" she asked.

"Oh, my soon-to-be wife brewed these up for me. A bit of a worrier, she is," he said, a kind smile gracing his handsome face.

"Can I ask you for a favor? You seem like a nice boy and I need to get down to where the ships are. Could you escort me?" Margaret asked, with a smile only a viper could carry.

Tomas looked back toward town and then up at the darkening sky with hesitation before he spoke.

"Yes, miss. I can take you down but then I must go. There looks to be a storm coming in from the sea and I have a bit of a journey back to my farm before dark."

"That's very kind of you," she said, with hidden malice in her voice.

She knew from the moment the charm jar was revealed that it was Freya who had made it. The protection jars had been part of an array of items Freya had brought for trade to Fran's farm on the day of the coven meeting. The Goddess gave that little twit everything: beauty, power, respect, and love. *Why?* Margaret's thoughts roiled with simmering fury. *Why should she possess all of this when I had to give up my chances at a happy life to keep my community safe? No one saw me as a treasure to be obtained or a friend to be had. I was simply "The Healer," nothing more. People only came to my home if they needed healing. True, I may have demanded a bit more for my tinctures and remedies than most, but it was a tiny price to pay for everything I sacrificed for the betterment of the community. I dedicated my life to curing their illnesses and helping aid them in the birthing of their children, and for what? To be cast out on the word of a stranger? Curse them and their children's futures. And what made Freya so special? Why should she have everything? Yes, this boy will be the ideal sacrifice. He will not only aid me in my ritual, but his death will deprive Freya of the love that was not granted to me by the Goddess.*

Margaret made easy conversation with the young man while they walked to where the ships kept port. When they arrived, she told him that beyond the large rock there was a cove with a beautiful array of sea stones that would be perfect to fashion into a ring for his beloved. He hesitated once again, looking to the sky, then turned back and walked beyond the rock. Once they were beyond sight in the cove, she stepped up behind him and in one fell swoop, hit him on the head with a heavy stone. When his body fell to the ground, she checked to make sure he was dead, and then promptly began her ritual. She chanted as she stripped off her clothing, and lit the candle once again, dancing around the six-pointed star she had drawn in the sand.

When the demon appeared this time, it looked on with delight.

Chapter Twenty-Five

CAPTURE

Freya was yelling in her sleep when Mary woke her with a forceful shaking. She was initially disoriented, but she soon realized she was still in the McKenzies' barn.

"Freya, wake up! It's okay. It's only a dream."

Freya's eyes blinked away sleep and she sat up slowly, trying not to forget even a moment of her vision. "But it was not. It was a nightmare of reality." Seeing the events through Margaret's eyes had left her sickened and full of despair. She had lost nearly everyone she loved, and her own fate remained uncertain. "Mary, can I ask you a question? Have you seen my future? Will I survive this?"

A conflicted look came over Mary's face. Her eyes welled with tears that broke away and trailed down her pink cheeks.

"I see. Mary, there is something I must do and something that you must promise me."

"Anything, Freya," Mary said, reaching out and embracing her friend.

"You must leave me. You heard those men last night. They are only looking for me, not you. Promise me that you will take care of the cottage and make sure it is waiting for me when I return, however long that may be. This as well." Freya reached into the large pocket in the front of her wool coat and pulled out the journal and hag stone.

"No, I cannot leave. I'm not going to abandon you to fight this on your own."

"Mary, my sweet friend. This is not your battle. This, I must do on my own," Freya declared, lifting her head and setting her shoulders.

"What is it that you plan to do?" Mary asked, looking at her friend with wide, frightened eyes.

"I plan to stop Margaret and her evil intentions. If I do not succeed, I will come back until I do. She is in league with the devil and many lives will be lost if she succeeds. Promise me you will do those things for me, Mary."

"Of course I will," she said, taking the journal and hag stone from Freya and tucking them safely into her bag.

"Make haste to the circle in the woods and do not leave it until the Goddess commands. The wolf will guide and protect you. Now go," Freya said, pulling Mary in and hugging her fiercely. "I love you, my sweet Mary, you have been and always will be my sister."

Mary held her tightly, not wanting to let go. "I love you as well," she whispered.

She gathered her bags and made her way quietly toward the front of the barn, turning back to glance at her friend one last time.

Freya waited for what she thought was an hour before

gathering the last of the few belongings she had and departing the barn. She was greeted outside by Cailean, who grabbed her hand and ran her into the house.

"The two men are back and coming down from the upper field with Father and a woman. You must hide!"

Freya's stomach twisted but she pushed the feeling down as Cailean ushered her into the kitchen and quickly opened the doors to the cupboard. This time she was not frightened. She had a plan and knew what needed to be done.

Once inside the cupboard, she opened a small bag and pulled out a knife. She held it tightly in her hands and whispered an incantation, then began to carve into the stone of the farmhouse wall. The spell she cast on the blade helped it carve into the stone like butter, leaving smooth, deep lines. As she etched, she softly repeated the verse.

"Life, death, rebirth, I bind all three, past, present, future as earth, sky, and sea. If taken by unearthly sin, let my soul be reborn again. Every time my soul is awoken, I will not stop till her spell is broken."

Once the symbol was complete and she had spoken her spell three times, Freya took the blade and slashed the soft flesh of her palm that had just begun to heal from her encounter with the broken beetroot jar. Taking her blood-stained hand, she placed it over the symbol and said, "As above, so below. Mote it be."

As soon as the words were spoken, a blue light glowed behind the symbol on the stone. She smiled; the Goddess had blessed her spell. There was no way she was about to let Margaret go through with the destruction she planned to inflict on the people of Oban. This was for Tomas, her father, and herself, and she would fight with everything she had. If that meant she would sacrifice her soul being earthbound until Margaret was defeated, then so be it.

It wasn't long before she heard the men enter the house. There was another voice that accompanied them, a woman's voice. The voice of Margaret Aitken. Fury built up in Freya's blood and it took all her willpower not to burst out from the cupboard and tackle the woman to the ground. Instead, she waited and listened.

"Where is she?" asked one of the men who had been there the night before.

"She is not here. We told you this last night," Tomas's father said in an uneasy voice.

"She is here. Check the kitchen," Margaret said, her voice cutting through the air like a knife.

Freya began quietly moving pails and loose odds and ends in front of the symbol so that it would not be seen.

Footsteps grew closer until there were five people standing in the small farmhouse kitchen. The men walked into the pantry room while the distinct sound of a woman's light footsteps walked right over to stand in front of the door Freya crouched behind.

"As my husband said, we are hiding no one. Now, if you don't mind, I need to get back to my duties," Sibeal said, stepping up in front of the cupboard as if she was about to tend to the dishes.

Margaret placed both of her hands on Sibeal's shoulders and forcefully moved her out of the way.

When the door opened, the light flowed in, blinding Freya for a brief moment before seeing the face of the one person she hated most in the world.

"She is here," Margaret said.

One of the men walked over and pulled Freya free of her hiding place.

"NO!" Cailean cried, bounding forward and wrapping his

arms around Freya. "She has done nothing wrong," he said, tears streaming down his cheeks.

"The Magistrate will be the judge of that, boy. Take her out of here," the man cried as he pulled Cailean free and the other man dragged Freya toward the door. She did not resist, she let the man take her willingly.

"Do not worry. All will be right," she called out to Tomas's family, giving them a forced smile of reassurance as the man dragged her out of the house.

Outside, a horse with a cart waited in the cold autumn day. The men threw Freya into the back and climbed up to man the horse. Margaret stepped up and sat beside Freya as the cart shook and shuddered off toward town. Freya's blood seemed to boil in the close proximity.

"Why are you doing this? I saw you make that deal with a demon the night you killed Tomas," Freya said, looking straight into the darkness of Margaret's eyes. "Why would you want to live forever when you are totally alone and unliked by so many?"

"You, my dear, are young and naïve," Margaret hissed, looking down her nose at Freya as she spoke. "You know nothing of the cruel ways of mankind. I gave my life to the people of my village and how did they repay me? By shunning me and running me out of my home with only a handful of my belongings. They will never take another thing from me again, with the power that I will wield. They will fear me and I will have more power than kings and queens could dream of. I do not need such petty things as love and friendship when I hold the force of a thousand seas inside me."

"*You* are the evil you speak of, no one else. You took my love, my father, and now you intend to take my life along with thousands of others. How are you any better than the people you speak of?"

"Oh, I am far superior. It's a shame that with the power you hold that you did not take my offerings. We could have worked well together, you and I. But alas, you are just like your mother, righteous to a fault."

"Offerings?" Freya questioned her.

"Those potions you took from me at the farm then buried on your way out of town. Had you opened them, you would have seen things my way and found yourself on the other side of this problem that you now find yourself in."

"I would rather die," Freya said with contempt in her voice.

"Well, you won't have to wait much longer then."

Freya grabbed Margaret's wrist with her right hand and dug her fingernails deep into her skin until they drew blood. Margaret screamed out in pain and struck Freya across the face, leaving a swollen red welt.

"You little wench. I should have killed you when I had the chance," she scoffed, holding her arm where Freya had left perfect crescent moon-shaped cuts in a jagged line.

Freya looked down at the three small red spots on her skirt and smiled as they rode on.

They traveled in silence for some time until the cart suddenly came to a halt and Freya lunged forward. The taller of the two men jumped down and pulled Freya out and onto her feet. He dragged her at a quick pace down the small walkway to a one-room holding cell. The bulkier of the two men opened the door and Freya was flung into the room. It was a dark and damp space. The only light came from a small window above the door. The floor was covered in a thick layer of straw that stank of urine and feces.

"Who's there?" a man's voice called out into the darkness.

"Hector, is that you?" Freya called back.

"Freya? Oh, my stars. Not you, my sweet child." His voice was thick with sorrow.

"Yes, but do not fear. I will get us out of this once we have been brought in front of the Magistrate."

"My poor girl. There is only one way we get out of this and it is not alive, I am afraid. I am old and do not fear death, but you are young and do not deserve this fate."

"None of us deserve this fate, Hector," Freya said.

They sat there in silence for a long time, Freya pulling strings loose on the hem of her skirt and winding them around the crease of her thumb. Once her eyes began to adjust to the darkness, she was able to make out the shape of Hector's body. His face was battered and deformed with swelling. The sight made her feel ill. How could the people of their town have done such a cruel thing to him? He was old and frail and she knew that his body would not survive much more.

This knowledge made her work faster and she began to rip her skirt where the three drops of Margaret's blood had soaked in. Once the piece was free, she folded it three times and began to wind the thread from her thumb around the fabric.

I bind you, Margaret Aitken, from causing harm. Your magic is now bound with this charm.

She chanted it in her head, over and over, until the entire length of the thread was wrapped around the cloth and tied with a knot. Then she prayed to the Goddess that her binding charm would work and that she could find a way to free herself.

"Goddess, bless this charm. Make it steadfast and unwavering."

The day turned to night and she listened to the rats as they scuttled in and out of the room, looking for food. At one point, a rat crawled up her leg and she thrashed it off so hard, it hit the wall on the opposite side of the room. She wiggled her fingers through the straw until the tips touched the cool, gritty earth below. She closed her eyes and sent a shock down into the ground. This scared the rats away for the rest of the night, giving Hector and herself a few minutes of peace while they rested their eyes.

Chapter Twenty-Six

SPELLS SET IN MOTION

Two days later, Hector and Freya were pulled from their cell and dragged into the Magistrate's office. They were both filthy and smelled of the foul odor that permeated every inch of the cell where they had been kept. The courthouse was full of villagers who spit and swore at them as they were led in. Hector, weak from lack of food and water, could hardly stand and put up no fight when he was brought before the assembly.

"Hector Murray, you stand accused of two counts of witchcraft. Ellen Byers accuses you of casting a spell upon her son who took ill after you visited their home this past winter. Jim Mclean accuses you of hexing his crops. He says after acquiring your services for his deceased wife, his fields were no longer fertile. How do you plea?" the Magistrate boomed, his voice casting the crowd into silence.

"Not guilty, sir," Hector said in a weak voice, clasping his hands together as if in prayer.

It only took but a few minutes for the court to decide his fate: guilty on several counts of witchcraft. The Magistrate sentenced him to be hanged that afternoon in the town square. The crowd in the courtroom let out cheers of "Burn the witch!" and "God have mercy on his soul!" as he was led back to the bench where he would remain for his final hours on this earth.

The room fell silent as Freya was brought up before the court. Looking around, she saw many faces of people she knew. The McKenzies sat in the front row, with somber expressions. Margaret was also there, sitting next to some of the council members. She looked straight at Freya. A small piece of deadly nightshade hovered above her lap, a dark glow of magic surrounding it. Despite the fact that the crowd was on high alert for anyone practicing magic, no one appeared to notice Margaret as she sat there weaving hers. Freya's heart sank; the binding spell had not worked. Margaret's magic was already too strong, and it was obvious that she was using it to sway the town officials.

"Freya Lorin, you stand accused of three counts of witchcraft. Ben Kinney accuses you of placing a hex on old man Peterson's well. A week after seeing you there, he came down with a sickness that has left him bedridden. Blair Adamson accuses you of bewitching her fiancé, Billy Duncan. Margaret Aitken has accused you of using your ungodly powers to lure Tomas McKenzie to his death. How do you plead?" the Magistrate boomed once again.

"Not guilty, sir. I am only but a healer, I have not done any of the things I am accused of," Freya answered. Margaret accusing her of Tomas's death made her seethe inside with anger but she held it down, in an attempt to keep her composure.

"Is there anyone in this court that will stand for this woman?"

"I will," William said, standing up in front of the court. "Freya has never done anything other than make herbal remedies to help the sick and wounded in this town, and she in no way had anything to do with Tomas's death," he said with conviction in his voice. Freya's heart sank, what was he doing? This type of action might land him in jail, or worse—destroy his family's reputation permanently.

"Sir, please. I have done nothing wrong. These accusations are false!" Freya interrupted William, in an effort to stop him from saying anything else that might jeopardize his family.

Freya looked over at Margaret, who stared back with a wicked smile plaguing her face. The room went into an uproar again. The Magistrate slammed his hand down on the table, demanding quiet.

"I see nothing to disprove these claims, therefore you are sentenced to be hung alongside Mr. Murray this afternoon."

"NO!" Sibeal cried out, pulling Cailean to her and sobbing. William put his hand on her shoulder and looked over at Freya, grief stricken.

There was nothing anyone could do for her now. She hadn't held much hope of escaping this fate but she did not fear what was to come next. She knew this was not the last she would see of this earth if her spell held fast.

Freya and Hector were dragged out of the courthouse that afternoon toward the town square where a set of gallows had been erected. The streets were lined with people, eagerly awaiting the spectacle. Margaret was in the center of the front row, as close as she could be. They were prodded up three large steps and onto two makeshift boxes to await their fate. Above them was a thick wooden beam with two rough sailor's riggings attached, slung down into nooses.

Freya looked over at Hector, fear beginning to work its way into her.

"Do not be scared," he whispered. "There is nothing to fear in death. You will be reunited with Tomas soon and you will live forever in the Summerlands." He smiled at her and she, in turn, smiled back. One last attempt at comforting each other.

The hangmen slipped the nooses over their heads. The cold, rough rope rested heavy on her shoulders.

Freya looked up. It was a beautiful autumn day and the sun had reached the highest point in the sky. She thought of her mother and father, of Tomas and Mary, and felt blessed that she was able to have the time she did with them, however brief it was. She felt the cool breeze pass through her hair and caress her cheek as if to say *All will be well.* It was the Goddess, reassuring her that her plan was still in motion.

A man's voice echoed out across the crowd, but before Freya could register what he had said, the box below her feet was kicked out and her neck snapped.

Helen woke bolt upright, her hair soaking with sweat. She looked around the bedroom, her vision coming in and out of focus. It took a minute for her head to stop spinning and her vision to fully return. She opened her mouth and called out to Storm in a dry, hoarse voice.

Connor came running in from the kitchen when he heard her.

"She's awake!" he cried out.

His grandfather and Henry quickly appeared behind him.

Helen's vision was still a bit blurry. Her head swam with a mix of memories. Hearing Connor's voice brought her back to reality. There he was standing over her, worry pulling at his face, looking just as handsome as he did the night at the loch.

"Helen, how are you feeling?" Connor asked as he walked over to her and rested the back of his hand on her forehead, checking for a fever.

"I feel fine, a little thirsty I guess," she said, shivering slightly at Connor's touch.

"You gave us quite a scare, young lady," Henry said. A look of relief moved across his face as he stood there, hands on his hips like a worried parent.

"You've been out of it for almost two days," said Seamus. "The doctor came to look at you but she seemed to think it was just the flu because of your fever, and you had no other physical symptoms. We were just discussing whether or not to call her back or just take you to the hospital." He walked almost all the way around the bed, regarding her cautiously as if she might spontaneously combust.

Helen sat up, her head feeling as if it weighed a thousand pounds, and promptly rested against the headboard. Storm jumped up and started licking her face, obviously happy to see her awake. She stroked his wiry fur and he laid down next to her.

"He didn't leave your side the entire time. Not even to eat, and you know how much he loves food," Connor told her, petting the wolf on the head.

"Of course, he didn't," she uttered, smiling down at the little wolf and pulling him in for a hug.

"Can I get you something? You must be hungry," Connor said, stepping away from her bedside and walking toward the door.

"I could use a glass of water." *And some time alone*, she thought. Her mind was trying desperately to heal but it kept catching on the broken shards of memories as she tried to piece everything back together.

"You need to take it slow for a couple of days. Get your

bearings back," Henry said. "Connor is going to stay here and look after you. Make sure you take full advantage of having your very own personal servant." With a smile and a cheerful laugh, Henry created a much-needed break in the intensity of the room.

"Sounds lovely. I've always wanted my very own butler," Helen said, poking fun.

"Haha, very funny. You know I can hear you. I'm just in the kitchen, not Norway," Connor scoffed. He came back into the room a moment later.

"Well, us old men are going to leave you be. If you need anything, you just ask. We're all so relieved you're okay," Seamus said, patting Helen on the shoulder.

The two men said their farewells and left the cottage, leaving Helen and Connor alone together.

"Here you go," Connor said, handing her a tall glass of water. He was staring at her as if she were a beautiful porcelain doll that might fall and break at any moment. If only he knew how close he was to the truth right now. She was doing her best to keep her composure, despite feeling like her mind was about to burst with everything going on inside it.

"Ah, thank you. I'm completely parched," she said and took a long drink. "But I'm fine really. Just a little dizzy still."

"Well, I can see why. You ran a very high fever and you were thrashing around in your sleep like you were having fits. I wanted to take you to the hospital but Granda insisted you were fine and would come out of it before long, and that if things got worse he'd call the doctor back."

"I was?" she said, a bit alarmed that her body had processed things so aggressively; it had clearly not been a smooth transition.

"Yeah, it was scary as hell. Never seen a sickness like it," Connor said. When he spoke, she detected a flicker of fear pass over his face. Whatever had occurred had left an impression on him, and not in a good way.

"This is going to sound strange, but that's because it wasn't a sickness. Your grandfather was right," she said, sitting up a bit and looking Connor in the eyes, anticipating the barrage of questions that were about to come.

"What do you mean? I watched you spike a fever higher than I've ever seen. Your skin was burning hot." He shook his head in disagreement as he spoke.

"It wasn't an illness, there was nothing wrong with me medically. My body reacted to the shift in a different way than I anticipated. This wasn't a sickness, Connor, it was my body breaking free from a binding spell. All the memories that surged back drove my body into a type of shock." She looked at him and hoped that he wasn't about to go running for the hills.

"Binding spell? Was it the pasta? That was some strong shit."

"No. It wasn't the pasta," she said with an amused smile. "This is going to be really hard to explain and even more difficult for you to understand. You may walk away thinking I am entirely crazy after hearing it. But please, let me attempt to explain everything to you."

"Try me," Connor said, taking a seat on the edge of the bed next to her, settling himself in for a long conversation.

She looked at him. There was a mix of emotions playing across his face—curiosity, worry, and a little bit of unease. She knew he was nervous. He was picking at a small hole in the sheets and she could almost hear his heart beating from where she sat. *This all must seem so crazy to him* she thought. *Now, it's time to help him understand.*

Chapter Twenty-Seven

TALES TO BE TOLD

Helen regained her composure before continuing. All of her memories flooding back had left her feeling exhausted and weak. She shook off the weariness that was setting in. It would take days before she would feel comfortable in her own skin again.

Then gave Connor a reassuring smile, and began.

"A long time ago, there was a girl who was accused of witchcraft by a fellow witch and was put to death. The witch who accused her, Margaret Aitken, was wicked and had crafted an ungodly pact with the devil for everlasting life. But in order to achieve her reward, she needed to acquire a thousand souls. The first soul to be taken in trade was that of your ancestor, Tomas McKenzie." She paused briefly and glanced at Connor; he reminded her so much of Tomas, which brought a feeling of sorrow to the surface that she had kept hidden away for so long. She looked away from him, holding back tears she wished to let go of.

"Not being able to defeat her, the accused witch placed a reincarnation spell on herself before she was hung. This ensured she would come back lifetime after lifetime until the evil woman could be defeated. You have already read a little bit about this story in the journals in the library. Those journals are mine." Again, Helen stopped, letting Connor absorb everything she had just said.

"Wait, what do you mean, the journals are yours? I thought they belonged to Freya and a handful of other women? That's what you told me the last time you were in the library," Connor said, a look of utter confusion plaguing his face as he ran his fingers through his hair.

"They are one and the same. The journals were all written by me. It was a way for me to keep track of things from one lifetime to the next, and the library is where they always have stayed for safekeeping. Fernbeg always drew me back, no matter how far away I was born," she explained carefully as a look of disbelief passed over Connor's face and he began to fidget with the keys in his pocket. *Is this where he's going to go running for the hills thinking I'm a crazy woman?* she thought. But he stayed put, so she went on.

"You see, the memories of my past lives only surfaced after my seventeenth birthday. However, in this life that didn't happen."

"Why not?" Connor interrupted, eager to fully understand things.

"Well, my last death was at the hands of a friend and before I died, he cast a binding spell on me so that I would no longer remember my past lives until the right moment. The night we had dinner with your grandfather was on Mabon, the twenty-second of September. Do you remember the moon that night? It was full. A full moon only comes around on Mabon every so many years. When you kissed me under that moon, it unraveled the last of the threads that bound the spell to me. They had slowly been coming undone since I arrived back in Scotland, but I think that with you being a direct descendent of Tomas, the final strand was broken." Helen waited nervously to see what his reply would be. She hoped he'd seen enough strange things in the last several weeks with her to believe she wasn't a total nutjob.

"Let me get this straight. So, you're telling me that you're Freya?" Connor asked, looking at her with a calmness she had not expected.

"Yes. Also Clara, Elizabeth, Abigail, and now Helen. I am still the person you know, nothing has changed in that way. It's just that now I have all my memories back." She spoke smoothly, but her heart was racing in her chest.

"Well, that ties a lot of loose ends together and explains all the weird things we've been experiencing over the past two weeks. I knew there was something magical about you from the moment we met. You had this ever-so-soft glow always around you. I think Granda knew as well. He was always rambling on about how you were meant to be here and that the homeland had called you back. I just thought he was nuts," Connor said.

Helen's heart rate slowed as relief overtook her worry. She had hoped he would understand, but after hearing the words come out of her own mouth, she was more than a little uncertain how he might react.

She swung her legs over the edge of the bed and stood up. She was a bit wobbly on her feet after not using them for a few days.

"Steady now, you've got your sea legs on," Connor said, holding out his arm for her to take.

"I want to show you something," she said, taking his hand in hers tightly and pulling him out of the bedroom, toward the library.

The door was shut as it always was, and when she opened it the room glowed with the iridescence of magic. The light came from the four corners of the room, where she had blessed it during her second life when she had the library built. It was where her father's room had been. The top shelf of the longest bookcase where her journals were kept had also been spelled. To the ordinary eye, it appeared empty, but she could see the journals.

Through Connor's eyes, it looked just like a normal room full of books, even though he knew deep down there was something special about the place. Helen stepped over next to him and placed her right hand on his shoulder. She let out a pulse of magic through her hand and into Connor. At that moment, he was able to see the room as she could, aglow with the white-blue light of magic. He gasped as he looked around with new eyes.

"Now you will be able to see magic where it hides," Helen said to him.

He turned and looked at her. He had been right; she did glow with magic, now stronger than ever. There was a white-blue halo of shimmery light encircling her whole body. She looked like an angel, he thought, as he stared at this magical being before him.

"You are the most beautiful thing I have ever seen," he said, looking longingly into her light green eyes.

His hands moved around her waist and up the length of her back as he softly brought her closer to him. She looked up into his deep emerald eyes, then rose to her tiptoes. He bent down to meet her and their lips met in an all-encompassing kiss. The passion of a thousand Shakespeare sonnets could not contend with the energy that filled the room. Helen let go of the world around her and fell deep into his embrace, causing her to glow even brighter than before.

She pulled away, breathless, and looked deep into his eyes. He had Tomas's eyes, she thought. A twinge of sadness, along with a lingering feeling of betrayal, overtook her and she pulled away slowly.

"There is something I want to show you. It's something I have been working on for centuries."

Helen walked over to the largest wall, running her finger across the hundreds of books held there.

"It wasn't until my second life that I began to understand the full scope of what Margaret bargained for. She was part of a much bigger plan than she even knew at the time. Each time the Goddess sent me back, it was in the midst of a great time of peril. The first time I was reborn, the plague had begun to spread by the time I turned seventeen. I heard the stories when I was younger about the witches who were killed over the years, but it wasn't until I turned seventeen that I realized just how far Margaret had taken things. Thousands of women and men had been accused of witchcraft and put to their deaths in the time that I was gone."

From the shelf, Helen pulled out a book bound in pale gray. It looked very old by the condition of the cover and the yellowing of its pages. She opened it, flipping to a page marked by a long strand of purple silk. She pointed her finger down at the text and read:

"'Margaret Aitken advised King James during the Great Scottish Witch Hunt. She was said to be able to identify a witch by the mark between their eyes, given to them by the devil. She was solely responsible for 2,300 women and men being brought before the gallows.'"

Connor looked on in disbelief and shook his head solemnly.

"This right here, this was the beginning," Helen said.

She closed the book and then pulled another large-looking history book from the shelf. Opening it and flipping to a page marked with a green piece of twine this time, she pointed her finger down at the page where a bold line had been placed under a sentence that read:

"'The Great Storm of 1703. A hurricane wracked its way across southern England and the English Channel, resulting in 8,000 deaths. Most of the deaths took place at sea; over 1,083 navy ships perished in the malevolent storm. It was described as a storm like nothing that had ever been witnessed before on the English seas.' This was also her doing. It was the same kind of storm that kept King James from his bride in Denmark back in the autumn of 1597, an ungodly storm. Margaret summoned it by stealing one of the gems from his crown. It was the beginning of the witch hysteria."

Once more, she closed that book and pulled another out, flipping to another marked page with a picture of Hitler. Standing behind him was a tall, dark-haired woman who looked to be in her fifties. Below the picture in fine print was a caption: *Adolf Hitler gives a speech in Stuttgart in Schwaben Hall 1939, accompanied by an unknown female adviser.*

"This is Margaret herself. She has been part of every single major catastrophe caused by mankind since 1598. I have dozens of history books marked with tragedy after tragedy that I believe she took part in. Everything from The Great Famine of 1695 in Scotland to the Spanish flu outbreak in 1918. I was not reincarnated for all of these events, the Goddess only sent me back as she saw fit. I made sure to keep a close record of each one with the books here in the library."

Connor plucked the book from Helen's hands and inspected the page she had read from. "It's truly unbelievable, and sickening," he said, closing it and handing it back to her.

"Yes, it is," Helen said, placing the book back on its resting place alongside the others.

She walked over and sat in one of the overstuffed chairs, running her fingers across the smooth green velvet, leaving trace lines where her fingers had been.

"It wasn't until my last life that I figured out what it was all about. When I was Freya, I witnessed her making a pact with the devil. A thousand souls in return for everlasting life. She achieved that with the Scottish witch trials. So why was she still killing? Then it dawned on me. As children, we were always warned about making deals with fairies. They were sneaky and always took more from the arrangement than spoken of in the contract. Why would it be any different with the devil? The fairies were his minions after all, and learned all they knew from him."

"Those are only stories told to scare children into behaving," Connor said.

"Oh, fairies are very real. Or they were, anyway. They began to die out years ago when the famine hit Scotland in the late 1690s. It wasn't just the Scots that died, plenty of animals and creatures did as well. There were only a few fairies left when I was on Earth last in the early 1900s. I wouldn't be surprised if they are all but extinct by now."

"So, if that's true, then what hand did the devil play with Margaret?"

"That's what I've been trying to determine all these years. I was told stories of her being involved with powerful and evil people such as the Duke of Cumberland, Maximilien Robespierre, King Leopold, and even Jack the Ripper. Mary's descendants kept good records of all the evil acts that stood out in the periods of time when I wasn't around. It wasn't until I saw her with Hitler back in Nazi Germany that I understood what was going on. I had found my way over to Berlin after seeing an image of her standing behind him on stage in a newspaper. I attended a rally where she appeared with him. When she walked up onto the stage, I saw that murky brown aura pulsating around her body. Then as she rested her hand on Hitler's shoulder, her aura expanded threefold and glowed dark and black. The power that came from her at that moment was stronger than anything I had ever seen before. It was then that I realized that she was not the owner of this power. She was merely the vessel for it."

Connor sat down in the chair next to her. His eyes were wide, like a child eagerly awaiting the next chapter of a story.

"I believe that she signed a contract with the devil that allowed her to live forever, unknowingly giving him a vessel to inhabit whenever he liked. He used her to wreak havoc on mankind as he saw fit. Margaret was bitter and hateful, but she never possessed the power or the ambition for such endless devastation."

"Well, that is scary as hell!" Connor said. He shook off a chill that ran down his spine.

"You're right about that. I've taken bits and pieces from all different religions to try and find a common thread on how to break the spell that binds the two, but so far I've been unsuccessful."

Helen pointed to the bookshelves on the far right wall. One shelf was full of all different kinds of religious books. The Bible sat next to the Quran which sat alongside the Dao De Jing and the Tankah. There was also a Book of Shadows, The Tipitaka, and many other sacred texts of different origins.

"How were you able to keep all the books secure here in the library?" Connor asked. "Weren't you afraid that the house would be sold and the books burned or thrown out?"

"I had faith in Mary. She followed through on her promise and took care of the cottage, along with the books, until I returned.

It was passed down to her children and her children's children to take care of over many years. Each generation was told the story and each awaited my return. The woman you knew, who owned Fernbeg, was Mary's great-great-great-great-granddaughter. Sadly, she was the last of Mary's descendants. Thankfully, she was quite cunning and cast a spell on the house so that it was undesirable to anyone other than me, knowing it would remain unsold until I purchased it once again, even though it did take me five years to come across it after her passing."

"Well, I feel like I should be in shock or denial but deep down I think I knew that magic was real and the stories I was told as a boy were true," Connor said, a vague expression on his face breaking away into a smile of validation as he went on. "My father was a skeptic and hated it when my grandfather would tell me stories of magic and the fairies that roamed the Highlands. But the look in his eyes when he told me the tales was the look of a person who had seen the tales he told. Those stories stuck with me my whole life. Even when I was in the city away from this place, there was an unexplainable feeling that would come over me when I thought about it. I guess it was my grandfather who made me a true believer."

"You're right. He has seen magic before," Helen said. "He knew who I was before I did. He tried to warn me not to push too hard while the binding spell was being unbound. As soon as I woke up and regained all my memories, I recognized him. We met when he was young, in my last life. He knew me then as Abigail."

"Really? Are you sure it was my granda? Seems this would have been a tale he would have told me." Connor leaned forward in his seat, awaiting her response.

"It was late September when I found my way back from Berlin, tired and defeated. It was my goal to make it back to the cottage and regain my strength before setting out to seek the help of an old wise woman who lived on the mountain of Slioch near Kinlochewe. Finally understanding what I was dealing with and why I had not been able to defeat Margaret, I needed guidance to move forward. The day I arrived home I had a visitor—your great-grandmother. She was also a seer and came to warn me of a vision she'd had. A little scruffy-haired boy accompanied her. He couldn't have been more than five years old at the time. Once she had delivered her message and set out to leave, little Seamus walked over to me and grabbed my hand. He looked up at me with those deep blue eyes and asked me if I was the good witch from the fairytales. I knelt down and grabbed a handful of earth and squeezed it tight in my hands. When I opened them, the earth had been transformed into a silver arrowhead. I handed it over to him and told him to keep it close for good luck."

"Ha! It was you! He always told me a witch gave it to him when he was little. But I thought he was just pulling my leg. He never went anywhere without it. My grandmother had it fashioned into a necklace for him the Christmas before she passed. I don't think he's taken it off ever since."

Helen smiled, but the thought of him made her heart ache a little. This was the first time that one of her past lives and her present life had a living reminder of what had been.

She stood and stretched her arms over her head. Her body was stiff and sore from not moving the past couple of days.

"Hey, let's go make some coffee and take a walk down to the loch. What do you say?"

"And there it is! I was starting to think you were still ill, not asking for coffee. You practically run on the stuff," Connor said with a mischievous grin. He stood up and came over to her.

"Ha! Very funny," she said, giving him a bit of a shove with her hips.

Chapter Twenty-Eight

BOOKWORMS

It was almost three days since she had woken with all her memories intact, but her brain still felt scrambled. It was hard to keep track of things—one life seemed to always get jumbled up with another. That was why she had always kept journals. It was a way for her to keep track of people, places, and events in each life. Today she planned to start her journal as Helen Kent.

She went into the library looking for her next journal but the place on the shelf where it should have sat lay unoccupied. She stood there confused for a moment. Then it dawned on her: she already had it. The little bookstore back home in Massachusetts—the old woman had handed her a journal made here in Oban. Her fifth journal.

She scrambled into the bedroom and dug through her bag until she found it, resting snugly under an old Cambridge

University sweatshirt. Sure enough, it was the same as the other journals, leatherbound with acorns and thistles that worked their way around its cover. It amused her that the Goddess had been throwing her breadcrumbs the whole time, trying to help her break free of the spell that bound her. It wasn't until now that she could see all the things that led her back home to Fernbeg.

She went into the kitchen and put on a fresh pot of coffee. Storm was in there, already lazing by the fire. His head perked up and he looked at her as she walked in, then rested back down into his cozy spot.

The days were growing shorter, and she realized that it had been almost two weeks since she had arrived in Scotland. A sudden wave of worry passed through her. That meant it was at least a week since she had called or texted Kevin. He might very well be on a plane over here right now looking for her. At that, she walked over and checked to see if her landline had been properly turned on yet.

She lifted the blue-corded phone to her ear. Nothing. She decided that when Connor came down today she would have him drive her into town so that she could call the phone company herself and find out what the holdup was. But for now, she would drink her coffee and make the first entries into her new journal. Book five, "The Life and Times" of Helen Kent.

As the pen neatly trailed her words across the paper, she hoped this would be the last journal she would ever write. Being reborn so many times had begun to take a toll on her emotions. So many feelings from past lives had come bubbling up to the surface since she regained her memories, and sorting through them all was painstaking. But this was the price that she was willing to pay if it meant finally stopping Margaret.

It wasn't until the afternoon that Connor's truck came rumbling down the road to the cottage. He gave a respectful knock on the door before opening it when he heard her call for him to come in.

Helen was sitting on the overly cheerful floral sofa with a steaming hot cup of coffee clutched between her hands. She wore a pair of black leggings and a dark-green knit shirt. A large wool blanket hung over her shoulders like a cape. Even with the two fireplaces going, the cottage was still damp and chilly.

It was the end of September and the warm autumn days were now turning bitter and cold. It seemed that for the last week the sky had carried a thick, gray blanket of clouds around with it and the only sign of the sun was the occasional break, either in the late afternoon or early morning. However, this morning was dark with clouds and there was a high likelihood it was going to rain, judging by the dampness that hung in the air.

Connor came in, letting a cold gust of wind and a few stray leaves in with him.

"It's a blustery one out there today," he said, sweeping the leaves to the side of the rug next to the door.

Helen stood up and offered him a cup of coffee. They made their way into the kitchen and she started another pot. The fire in the kitchen had all but burned out and Connor started building a new one while she pulled him out a clean mug and put in a few slices of toast.

"Are the matches in the sitting room?" Connor asked, looking around for means to light the fire.

"No need," Helen said, looking over at the fireplace and giving a quick snap of her fingers. White-hot sparks burst out around the bottom of the wood, setting the logs ablaze. She looked over at Connor and gave him a wink and a devilish smile. Not only had all her memories come back, but so had the use of her magic and she was having a bit of fun showing off in front of him.

"Now, that's a handy bit of magic right there," he said, raising one eyebrow and giving her his cute, off-centered smirk.

Helen felt a flutter in her stomach that wasn't magic, or at least not her magic. She smiled back at him and set about buttering their toast.

"Do you think we can swing into town today? I need to call the phone company and see what the holdup is on my landline. It's time I get in touch with my parents as well. I've been avoiding their texts about Thanksgiving long enough. Plus, I want to pick up a new light fixture for the hallway."

"Aye, sure, I just need to be back to the farm by dark to help get the sheep from the upper fields. With the days getting shorter, I don't like Granda out on the quad bike at dusk by himself," Connor said, taking a long sip of his coffee.

They sat at the kitchen table and enjoyed their poor man's breakfast and each other's company.

"Can I ask you a question?" Connor said after a while. "Now that I know this place has been yours all along, what's the hidden altar room all about?"

"It was built during the years I was gone, before my first rebirth. Mary had it constructed out of an old closet and had it hidden into the wall, sealing off its original door. Those were trying times and if you were caught with pagan items, it would have been a death sentence. It was the only way Mary could continue to practice the craft safely. I discovered it in my second life, when I was eighteen. It was the only time I used it. Things were still uneasy for pagans and it was best to practice in secret. It's where I kept the things I didn't want others to find while I waited for my next life," Helen said, spinning the ring on her middle finger.

"That makes sense. Now, what about this binding spell? You

didn't get much into that, with everything else you needed to explain to me."

He was still struggling with everything, she could see that, but he was trying his best to understand. She hoped that if she was completely honest with him, he would stay and not think her completely mad. She answered his question in the most uncomplicated way she could.

"It's not an easy thing to explain. You see, in each lifetime, when I turned seventeen and regained my memories, I would search out a new teacher, some kind of sage to help me gain knowledge and a better understanding of magic and the powers I held. When I died as Freya, my magic was just beginning to bloom. I didn't fully understand it yet, or how to use it. If I had, my life surely wouldn't have ended there on the gallows that day. I've had many wonderful teachers over my lifetimes, but the one who pushed me the farthest was a Ukrainian witch called Artemas Rogowski. I went to him for help after I saw Margaret with Hitler. We spent hundreds of hours researching and reading ancient texts to try and find a way to stop her. She was untouchable, somehow always one step ahead of me in each life."

She explained, as she stood up and began to pace the length of the kitchen, following the worn grooves in the wood with each step.

"You see, each time I was reborn, my magic was like a beacon for her. All true witches have their own unique magical pulse, which only a highly skilled witch can sense. Artemas came to the conclusion that she was always one step ahead of me because she could detect my beacon from the moment I was reincarnated. Then she had seventeen years to gain knowledge of my strengths and weaknesses in each life. In order to defeat her, she couldn't know who I was in my next lifetime. The only way to accomplish this was to bind my magic and the memories of my past lives. With my magic bound so was my beacon— it was as if I hadn't been reborn yet."

She stopped pacing, went to the sink, and stared out the window toward the loch. Thinking about everything past, present, and future was raising her anxiety level but she knew that if Connor was going to stick around then he needed to truly understand it all.

"Well, now that your binding has been broken, won't she be able to find you?" Connor asked, a bit of nervousness playing around in his voice.

"Yes, she knows I'm here now, but to her, I've just been reborn. I'm an infant in her mind and she won't be coming to look for me until I'm about eight years old. Artemas made sure that the binding spell would come unraveled slowly once I was where I needed to be."

"Here at Fernbeg?"

"Yes. In order to break the binding spell, I needed to find my four tethers to the magical world. My staff, the hag stone, all four journals, and my familiar. On top of that, I needed to be at Fernbeg during Mabon on a full moon. However, I believe it was your kiss that broke the final thread of the binding spell. Artemas would have also wanted to make sure that I had someone on my side that I could fully trust." As she said this last part, she turned around and looked at him. His brows were slightly raised and a trace of a smile flashed across his face at the mention of their kiss and him being her breaking point.

"Well, I'm glad I could assist you in breaking your binding spell, but I'm not sure how much help I'll be. It's not like I have any magical abilities or even knowledge of the supernatural that might help."

Helen's heart sank. This was the moment she had been dreading, the moment that he decided it was way beyond what he could handle and he would leave.

Instead, he walked over to her and clasped her hands in his and said, "But I will be here for you no matter what may come, magical or not. So, what's the next move?" With that, he pulled her into an embrace. A feeling of relief washed over her and she nestled into his huge arms. It was exactly what she needed to hear.

"Well," she said, stepping back from his embrace and getting down to business again, "the first thing we need to do is go get my phone turned on so we can get some internet access in this cottage. We're going to need it, with all the research that needs to be done to find Margaret."

"Well, what are we waiting for then? Let's head into town. You need to get some food anyway. You can't live on toast and coffee."

"I beg to differ," Helen said with a laugh, eating the last crust of toast and washing it down with coffee for good measure.

Chapter Twenty-Nine

THE SMELL OF 1947

It was close to two o'clock when they rolled into town. By then, the lunch crowds had dissipated, leaving the streets vacant except for a few locals and the occasional tourist down by the loch taking photos. They still had a few hours before Connor needed to get back to the farm so they decided to take their time and walk the cobblestone streets for a while.

"It always amazes me how things change so much in such short spans of time. That place over there," Helen said, pointing at a long building where a few boutique shops had taken up residence, "that building used to be a boot factory. They were making boots for the war in the early forties the last time I saw it. Not all things change though, there are still many things that have stayed the same."

"Such as?" Connor asked, looking at her with amazement in his eyes.

"Well, for one, the docks and slips are all still in the same place they were back in the late seventeen hundreds. The inn is just the same, except for a coat of white paint and some black shutters."

"So, cool," he said, smiling at her as they continued down toward the inlet.

She walked up to the railed boardwalk that led down to the loch and looked out over the water. The cold, dark clouds cast their reflection onto the water, turning the world around them into a dull shade of gray. It somehow suited the town and her mood, melting into the gray stone buildings and streets.

It was always hard the first few days after regaining her memories. All the love and loss felt fresh, and it took all her strength to hold herself back from crying at times. It was something she had grown accustomed to, but it really never got any easier. However, she knew it would pass within a few days and she could move forward with her plan.

Connor must have sensed something was wrong by the look Helen had in her eyes. He swooped his arm around her waist and pulled her tight against him. She looked up at him and smiled. It was just what she had needed and she was glad Connor was so observant.

They found an empty bench and sat down so Helen could make the calls she needed to. She decided to call the phone company first and get things straightened out. It took a total of forty-five minutes, forty of which were spent on hold and five talking with an ill-tempered Indian man. He was finally able to figure out why the phone lines had not yet been turned on and reassured her that she would hear a dial tone before the day was up.

The next phone call was to Kevin. This one went about as well as the first. She spent the majority of her time listening to him rant, first about how concerned he was that she still didn't have a phone in the cottage, and then about the awful temp they had hired to fill in for her while she was away. She reassured him that she would have a working phone by the end of the day and that he could call and complain about work whenever he wanted. Then he asked her the hard question: when was she coming home? This, she answered with a vague "Soon," not knowing how to tell him that there was a good chance she was never going back.

The third and final call was to her parents. Parents were a funny thing. In each life, she had a set and they all had one thing in common: they worried about her endlessly and she loved them for it. Even if some worried more than others.

Her mother picked up on the second ring.

"Helen, where have you been? Your father and I have been trying to get a hold of you for weeks now. We even called your work to check on you. They told us you'd gone on vacation."

"Hi, Mom. I'm sorry. It's been a crazy couple of weeks and I didn't want you worrying about me. I took a trip to Scotland."

"What on God's green earth could have possessed you to go to Scotland this time of year? Is it a man? Don't tell me you met a man on one of those online dating sites and flew over to meet him. You know that's how women get abducted and sold—"

Helen cut her mother off. "Mom, God no. That isn't it at all."

"Oh, thank God. Your father and I were thinking about coming up for a visit next week. What do you think? You up for having us around for a little bit?"

"That sounds great, Mom, but I'm kinda still in Scotland."

"WHAT? Why?"

Here came the hard part, explaining to her parents she had bought a house and was here to fix it up. She would leave out the part about finding out she was a sixteenth-century witch who had been reincarnated lifetime after lifetime.

The rest of the conversation went as expected. Her mother had a complete bird because she spent her life savings on some derelict cottage in another country, and both she and her father were sorely disappointed that Helen had not consulted them before making such a life-changing decision. They left on a semi-okay note though, with Helen promising to send pictures of the cottage and to make sure she called with weekly updates. It was just enough to keep her mother happy and leave an open-ended timeframe for her not to worry.

After almost an hour and a half spent on the phone, she needed a drink and some food. Connor walked back over to her when he saw she had put her phone away and they decided to have an early dinner at one of the local cafés on the shorefront—a posh little place called BAAB. They served a variety of food but most of the menu was inspired by Greek and Italian cuisine, Helen's favorite. Connor indulged in sea bass and prawns while Helen had falafel with sumac onions and salmon filet. The food was good and the wine was even better.

By the time they were done, it was almost 4:30 and the sun was setting behind the buildings in town. Connor promptly took the bill off the table, not giving her even the slightest chance to reach for it herself, and paid.

They walked out into the brisk evening air, the streets set aglow with old-fashioned streetlamps, casting a yellow light on the cobbled streets. They stopped into the small grocery store and grabbed a few items of food, a bottle of wine, and a newspaper before leaving.

The ride home was uneventful and with the wine and a belly of carbs, Helen almost fell asleep. Something by Modern English played on the radio, reminding them that "Things were getting better all the time". She hummed along with the song. It had been one of her favorites when she was younger. She looked over at Connor who was mouthing the words "I'll stop the world and melt with you," obviously one of his favorites as well. She smiled. He was everything she had ever looked for in a man. She guessed that her ideals had all stemmed from Tomas and very few men of the modern age held up to them.

But every time her heart drew closer to Connor, she also harbored feelings of guilt and felt as if she was betraying Tomas. She was unaccustomed to these emotions. She had never let herself fall in love in any of her past lives and she was torn inside. She wanted to be happy but also knew she had a very important task to accomplish, and she couldn't lose sight of that.

Connor looked over at her as her expression grew solemn.

"Are you okay?" he asked, turning down the music.

"Yeah, I'm fine," she answered, turning the music back up and giving him a forced smile.

The rest of the car ride they sat there tapping to the rhythm of the music and enjoying the blissful moment of just being a guy and girl in an old pick-up truck listening to some '90s jams.

When they arrived back at the cottage, the sun had fully set, leaving the world dark under a moonless, starless sky. The temperature was dropping rapidly at night now and they felt the threat of a frost when they exited the truck.

The cottage didn't feel much warmer than the chilly night air when they entered. Connor walked over and stoked the fire, but it was burning brightly and had a nice bed of hot coals.

"The other fires must have gone out," he said, picking up the iron rod that rested against the stone fireplace and giving the coals a good poke.

Storm came running in to greet them and did circles around Helen until she bent down and gave his ears a good scratch.

All three of them walked into the kitchen to check on the fire in the kitchen's hearth. Just as the sitting room had been: a bed of hot coals and plenty of logs burning. It didn't make sense, both fires were burning hot and should have been heating the house, but it felt as cold in the cottage as the air outside.

"That's odd," Helen said, looking at the fire as it crackled and spit.

"Let's go and start one in the library," Connor suggested.

They walked down the hall and opened the door to the library. A burst of hot air bellowed out. The room was at a cozy temperature, as if a fire had been burning all day in the room with the door shut. But the fireplace was barren; no logs or embers graced its cold, black center.

"Okay, is this another one of your magic tricks? Are you trying to get me to snuggle down and read books with you all night?" he teased her with a mischievous grin.

"No, something isn't right. The house wants us in here," she said in a serious tone.

She glanced around the room, looking for something that might be out of place. Everything seemed to be untouched, nothing out of the ordinary. But as they stepped into the room, the fireplace burst to life. A faint smell of wood smoke traveled across the room, along with a lovely mix of cinnamon, cloves, and allspice. It was as if the herbs had been steaming in a bowl by the fire, but no cauldron or cooking pot was anywhere in sight. It reminded her of the smell of Christmas.

Helen sat down in one of the overstuffed velvet chairs and tried to understand what the magic in the house was trying to tell her.

Connor was standing by the large windows in the back of the library while Storm lay cozy by the fireplace. Helen picked up journal number three from the top of the stack and started thumbing through the pages, but nothing stood out. She set it down and began looking into the fourth journal. It only took her a few minutes to find what she was looking for. Her fingers lay on one of the last entries from her previous life.

December 24th, 1947

It's Yule, or what is now called Christmas Eve here in England. Artemas and I have rented a small room in the city of London above a butcher shop called The Ginger Pig. We traveled here from Artemas's home in Ukraine in search of a manuscript that is said to contain rituals for exorcising a demon. We believe it is being held in the crypt of Southwark Cathedral by Father McMillan, who takes care of the artifacts. We plan on going to Midnight Mass and seeking counsel with Father McMillan after.

As for now, I am enjoying a lovely fire and a fine cup of Yule tea. The tingle of cinnamon on my tongue and the sweetness of allspice reminds me of the mulled cider and ginger cookies my mother made every Yule in my first life. Father always said that it warmed the body and soothed the mind.

It's bitterly cold outside and the snow has been coming down for hours now. Artemas is quite the humbug and has buried himself in his work instead of enjoying the evening by the fire and listening to holiday concerts over the radio. I think we are both secretly wishing for a Christmas miracle this year. Maybe, just maybe, this manuscript will be what we have been searching for.

With light,

Abigail

And just like that, she remembered.

Chapter Thirty

THE BINDING

It was a bitterly cold Christmas Eve in 1947, one of the coldest Britain had ever seen. The snowdrifts had made it difficult to maneuver around the city by motor vehicle so most of their traveling was done on foot. She remembered being thankful for the modern clothing of the time, but wished for a long wool cape to protect her from the wind.

The walk to the church was two city blocks from their flat but with the freezing cold and harsh winds, they arrived at Midnight Mass late. Gathering attention as they entered, the cold winter night breeze slithering through the giant doors, they slipped themselves into a pew toward the back and waited out the service. When it was over, the other churchgoers rushed home to tuck themselves into their warm beds. Abigail and Artemas made their way to the front of the large nave, where Father McMillan stood, gathering his belongings.

The priest was reluctant at first to talk to them but once Abigail told him the story of Margaret, he began to listen. He invited them back into the small room off to the side of the sanctuary and made them tea, while Abigail explained what they were looking for. After what seemed to be hours of talking, they finally convinced the priest that the threat was very real. He disappeared into another room and came back with a small worn-looking book. It was bound in black leather with a golden cross embossed on the front and looked to be a very well-used, very old bible. When he opened it, Abigail and Artemas saw that the pages had been carved out in the center to make a small concealed compartment. There, in the carved-out hollow of the old parchment, was a rolled-up piece of paper, tied with a fine crimson silk ribbon.

Father McMillan crossed himself before lifting the scroll from the book's hidden compartment. It couldn't have been more than three inches wide and six long. Frail and yellowing with age, he took care as he unrolled it. It looked as if it might crack and crumble into a thousand pieces at the wrong touch.

He explained the origins of the paper to them as they encircled it. Legend said that it had been snuck out of the library of Pergamum before Mark Anthony had seized the vast collection of scrolls to give as a gift to his wife Cleopatra. The manuscript resurfaced in Rome in 1785 during the Age of Enlightenment and was found by a scholar and gifted to the Vatican in 1793. In the autumn of 1896, it was sent to the crypt of Southwark Cathedral and had been sitting in there, unmoved, for as long as Father McMillan could remember. Said to have been written by the archangel Michael himself, the manuscript formed a manual on how to cast a demon back to hell if one was ever to take possession of a human. As Father McMillan translated the ancient text, Artemas transcribed it word for word on the back of an old bomb shelter flyer that had been mixed in with a stack of papers on the priest's desk.

As Father McMillan spoke, a power could be felt by all three in the room, pouring from the words to sit heavily in the air. Abigail could sense the immense power in this spell—for that was what it was, a spell. Ancient and otherworldly. She had never come across anything like it in all her lifetimes. It was clear why this tiny piece of paper was being kept hidden away.

At that moment, she was hopeful they had finally found what they were looking for. Artemas looked over with hope in his eyes as well.

Then Father McMillan began explaining the seriousness of doing such rituals. If they did not perform the ritual correctly it would most likely end in both of their deaths, or worse—it would open them up to be possessed by the very demon they were trying to exorcise. They were well aware of what they were going up against, but it was the first time they had a fighting chance at being a step ahead of Margaret and they were going to take it, even if it was risky.

They thanked Father McMillan for his help and he blessed them both before they left, waving them off with a "God be with you."

The storm had gotten worse while they were in the church and they emerged to snow drifts covering the cars on the street. The wind was cold and fierce and had them fighting against it the whole way back to their tiny flat.

They spent Christmas Day snowed in and decided to set all things "Margaret" aside for the day so that they could enjoy a bit of the normal festive cheer around them. Artemas read while Abigail cooked a large meal of two Cornish hens, roast potatoes, parsnips, carrots, Yorkshire pudding, and buckwheat, a traditional

Ukrainian Christmas dish. After they had filled themselves up to almost bursting, they sat by the fire and enjoyed homemade blackcurrant wine as Christmas music played over the transistor radio. Artemas, being almost thirty years her senior, had ample stories to tell of Christmases past, and she sat and listened happily to tales from his homeland until the wee hours. It was one of the best Christmases she remembered having.

After several days, the city streets were cleared of the massive amount of snow that had fallen over the holiday and she and Artemas made their way back to Scotland. When they arrived back at Fernbeg, they began devising a plan to effectively use the translation of the manual. Artemas had copied it down onto proper paper and burned the old bomb shelter flyer it had been previously written on.

It took months before they tracked Margaret down, when finally there was a sighting of her in Wales, near Neath. She was trying to keep herself under the radar as she made her trek back up to Scotland. Artemas worked tirelessly to find a way they might be able to defeat her in the present. However, their time was growing short and after debating and discussing what the next step should be, Artemas concluded that what needed to be done could not take place in this lifetime. They needed Margaret to be totally caught off guard, unsuspecting of the trap she was to be lured into. Now was not that time. They had been playing a game of cat and mouse and she would be anticipating the next move. Abigail needed to have the upper hand and the only way of gaining that was to make sure Margaret couldn't find her when she was born. For that, she would need her magic to be bound.

By mid-March, they had come up with a spell to carry this out. Artemas worked day and night for months to get the wording right. Abigail's magic was old and strong and not just any old binding spell would work on her. He believed he had perfected it but the only way to know for sure was to try and complete the binding. They only had one shot at it and time was running short. They needed to perform the ritual on Ostara, the spring solstice, before Margaret struck first.

When the day finally arrived, Abigail prepared the items that would not be taking the journey with her. Before the sun had fully risen, she walked into the backfield to the rowan tree. It had been there with its strong roots in each of her lives. This was where she decided she would leave Mary's hag stone. She had always placed it in the care of one of Mary's descendants, but this time was different. Flora was the final surviving daughter and Abigail had known from the moment they met she was barren and therefore the last of Mary's bloodline. So, she entrusted the mighty rowan to look after her protection stone and buried it between the roots of the tree.

Next, she walked to the bordering stone wall of the McKenzie farm. The place where Tomas would sneak kisses from her when she was Freya. She followed the wall into the thickening woods that had slowly been taking over the back pasture for decades now. There, she rested her staff against the large oak that stood taller than all the other trees around it, entrusting it to Mother Nature until she could return.

Now, the final things to prepare were her journal and the translated manuscript page. She headed back down the field as the sun rose over the hills and cast its light off the last of the snow, scattered over the field in patches. The new green grass was just starting to poke its head out from the thick, dried wheat stocks. Spring was starting to show her beautiful face. The days were warmer than normal for this time of year, feeling more like early autumn than early spring.

Abigail took her time as she walked back to the cottage, making sure to take in all the beauty and magic that surrounded her. She felt the weight of all her past lives, the loves and losses slowing each progressive step forward. The next time she was born she would not remember it. It saddened her but she knew it was the only way to bring this to a close and be able to finally go to the Summerlands, and to Tomas.

When she arrived back at the cottage, she found Artemas in the library going over their plan for what must have been the hundredth time. She reassured him that things would be fine and that she had done all that needed to be done. One of the only things left to do now was find the proper hiding place for the manuscript page. They decided to hide it in the book *Demonology*. It seemed fitting in more ways than one.

The final piece was her last entry in her journal. She needed to leave her future self some clues for where to find the page. She scripted it carefully, then placed it back upon the shelf, running her fingers down the spine one last time.

She wasn't afraid of dying, she had gotten past that fear lifetimes ago, and she was ready to leave this life behind. She had grown accustomed to living her short lives alone and with very few personal attachments. It made it easier for her to know that her death would not cause grief to others. It was a lonely way to live through the centuries, but she knew it was the only way. However, this time she was unable to avoid the connection she shared with Artemas. It saddened her to leave him. He reminded her so much of her father in her first life and she would miss his loyalty and support in her next.

When they had everything in perfect alignment, they waited for the sun to begin setting and then headed to the cliff face that hung over the loch.

Abigail was clothed in a long shift dress, sheer white. Her long, brown hair flowed down her back and caught the wind as it blew strong along the cliff's edge. Artemas lit a fire and Abigail knelt before it, her arms outstretched, palms to the sky. Sage was thrown into the fire, filling the air with a thick, white aromatic smoke. Artemas laid an athame in her hand and she cut a large lock of her hair off and threw it into the fire while chanting the binding incantation. They repeated this part of the ritual three times before Artemas grabbed Abigail by the hands and pulled her to her feet. There was a stillness in the air, an unnatural silence broken only by the distant cry of a Highland wolf. It was time.

Abigail approached the cliff's edge and looked out over the vast loch, reaching to the sea, reflecting the last bit of the day's light off the edges of the water and giving it the illusion of a golden rim. Looking into the mirror-like reflection, she saw Artemas step up behind her and before she could say goodbye, he pushed her.

As she fell to her death, she heard him call out, "Good luck, my friend."

Helen quickly flipped through the pages to the last entry in the journal. It took her but a second to realize the clue she had left herself. She rushed over to the wall full of history books, searching for *Demonology*. She scanned each shelf and couldn't find it. Frantic, she raced over to the other side of the room and scanned the shelves alongside the fireplace. Nothing.

"Are you alright? You have me a bit worried. Zoning out like that and then racing around the library like a chicken with its head cut off," Connor said, looking on as she searched.

"I'm fine, I just remembered something really important. Help me look for the book *Demonology*. It must be here somewhere. It has to be."

"It's not on any of the shelves. It's over here," Connor said.

He walked over to the small wooden barrel next to the windows in the back of the room. A small pot of dead ivy sat on top of a book being used as a makeshift tabletop to the barrel.

"I noticed it the night we started to read the journals. At the time, I didn't think much of it, but I did remember the title because it was part of a study we did in history class on King James when I was in uni."

Helen smiled to herself and walked over to the book, sliding it out from underneath the pot. The book was worn and yellowed with age and now sported a stain where the pot had sat for many years, leaving a dark half-moon shape on its leather cover. She opened the book and flipped through its pages, casting a large plume of dust into the air that hovered in the beams of light. She stopped when her fingers came across a rough piece of paper that had been slipped between the pages, hidden away for many years. When she pulled it out, she saw Artemas's meticulous handwriting sprawled out across the parchment. At the top was a small note clipped to the edge. It read:

To the "you" that is reading this now, you were my most prized student and cherished friend. I hope that you are able to end this and find the peace you have been searching for in this lifetime and all the others. ~A

Chapter Thirty-One

MOBY DICK

Helen let out a sigh of relief when she had the transcription of the spell to exorcise a demon in her hands. Everything hinged on that one delicate piece of paper and she was determined to transcribe it again as soon as possible. It was too risky to only have one hundred-year-old copy lying around. She carefully removed it from the book and inspected it to make sure that it was intact and no damage had been done to it over time. None had; Mary's descendants had always come through for her. She looked up to the heavens and whispered a silent thank you.

Connor came over to inspect what it was that Helen had been in such an uproar to find. When he saw what she was holding, he grew confused.

"What is that?" he asked in a worried tone.

"This here is my ticket out of this reincarnation hell. This little piece of paper is the only weapon I have against Margaret and whatever devil is possessing her," she said, as she carefully placed the paper back into the book and closed it, setting it back down.

"What's your next move, now that you have it?" Connor asked.

"Finding Margaret. But that will have to wait until tomorrow. It's been a long day and I'm ready to throw on my sweatpants and jump into bed," she said wearily, thinking of the danger lurking somewhere unknown.

"That sounds like a plan, *but* ... I don't believe I have any sweatpants here," he said, one eyebrow raised and a smirk on his face.

Helen gave him a playful push and walked out of the library and along the hall into the sitting room. She was too distracted at the moment to flirt with Connor, even though she knew he was working hard at it.

The house was back to a cozy temperature now and she flopped herself down on the couch in front of the fireplace. Storm jumped up onto her feet and tried to find a comfortable position. This was a hard thing to do at this point as he was almost a full-grown Highland wolf and took up more than half the couch on his own.

"Oh boy, you're getting way too big to lay on me," Helen said with a breathy laugh, pushing Storm off her.

"He's gotten so much bigger in the past week. I didn't know wolves grew at this rate," Connor said, sitting down next to her.

"They don't. The Goddess has decided to speed things up a bit so he'll be fully grown and ready to help me when the time comes. He is my guardian, after all."

Storm looked up at her with his wide eyes and licked her hand. He knew what he was there for and was ready and willing to step up to the plate.

"I kind of figured that," Connor said, as he stroked the wolf's ears. "Well, it's getting late. I guess I should be heading back. Now that you seem to be okay, I mean."

"Do you think you could stay just one last night? I really don't want to get up and deal with the fires in the morning," she said. With a snap of her fingers, the smoldering fire in the stone hearth flared up into a fully roaring fire again. She let out a chuckle and smiled at Connor. He looked back at her and laughed.

"I think you have it under control. I need to go help my granda and it's been two days too long sleeping on this lumpy sofa. I think I'm ready for a night in my own bed. Plus, I won't have to get up at four to head back for barn duties. Once I'm done, though, I'll come back in the morning and we can get started on figuring out where Margaret might be."

"Sounds good. Bring over your laptop. The phone lines should be working by then and we can try and get the Wi-Fi hooked up."

Connor left for the night to help Seamus, and even though part of Helen wanted him to stay, she was happy to have the time to herself. There were things she needed to do in preparation for the exorcism spell to work correctly. They only had one shot at getting this right. If they failed, they would never get close enough to Margaret to try it again.

It was imperative that Helen stay masked. As far as Margaret knew, Helen had just been born. When her binding spell broke and her magic became visible again, it was as if she had just come into the world. Margaret would not have missed it and it was only a matter of time before curiosity got the better of her and she came looking. It had only taken her a little over a year to find her back in 1947 and with the advances in technology, it would be much quicker now. This meant they only had a short span of time to get everything ready.

Helen went into the kitchen and opened the spice cupboard, pulling down several small jars. She then proceeded into the bathroom to where the hidden altar room lay. There, she gathered two of the herb bushels from the back wall, along with the brass bowl and athame off the old wooden table. Back in the kitchen, she cleared off the table and laid out the herbs. She grabbed a large mortar and pestle off the windowsill and began grinding them down into a fine powder.

First, she blew the dust off a small bunch of Angelica and began to crush it. This was not only good for protection but would also destroy any residual parts of the binding spell. Next, she added in a pinch of basil and dried chrysanthemum petals for warding off evil. Once the herbs were mixed, she added bits of cherry bark for invisibility and put the mixture inside a black walnut shell. She added a thin layer of camphor oil around the rim to strengthen it. The final touch was a pinch of ash from the fireplace for luck. There was no need to read the spell, she knew it all by heart; it flowed through her entire being. Raising the athame in her right hand, she pointed it at the sky and then to the ground, as she spoke:

"Cloak my magic, hearth, and home. Cloak this flesh down to bone. Let no eyes see that wish me harm, protect me with this ancient charm. With the power of three, so mote it be."

With that, she lit the herbs, creating a white aromatic smoke. She walked all four corners of each of the rooms of the house, crossing them with the smoke of the spell. Before the last of it burned out, she set it on the floor and stood above it. As the smoke rose, she guided it up and over her body, springing and twisting it around her like a thin wisp of rope, enveloping herself with the magic.

Once the herbs had burned out and little was left of the shell, she swept up the ash and placed it into a small cotton bag that she slipped under her pillow. She couldn't risk dream-walking into Margaret's mind, and the ashes of the spell would keep that from happening. The bed looked inviting after such a long day, and she finally gave in to the temptation of sleep. Before her eyes closed, she saw Storm standing guard by her bedroom door. Between the warding spell and her guardian, she fell asleep with ease.

Helen was up before the sun rose the next day, hunting through the library for her spell books. With all the memories she needed to keep track of as her lifetimes multiplied, she had forgotten where she'd tucked them away in the library. In each lifetime she would hide the spells she had collected in plain sight by disguising them as popular books from whatever particular time she was in, the logic being that people were less likely to pick the book up if it was readily available in any bookshop.

The first she found was *Moby Dick*. She had hated the book and for that very reason, she had no shame in destroying it to tuck her spell book into. The second to come off the shelves was *Robinson Crusoe*. This one she hadn't minded as much but still had no issue defacing it to house her spells. The third and final book was George Orwell's *Animal Farm*. This book was the hardest for her to ruin; she quite enjoyed the story but knew that there would be many copies available in modern times.

Once all three books were in her possession, she headed back to the kitchen and laid them out across the table. While the coffee brewed, she sifted through them, looking for a locator spell. She knew she had one in one of the books but couldn't remember which. She'd only ever used it once, back in her original life as Freya, and it completely failed her. However, she was inexperienced with such things at that time. Now, she was more than a seasoned witch, she was a master with over four centuries of knowledge to guide her. The spell should be easy for her to use now—once she found it.

She had written down every spell or charm she'd ever come across in all her lifetimes. She had spells from covens all across Europe and even as far away as Africa. As she searched for a way to rid the world of Margaret, she was introduced to different forms of magic from different witches she'd come across in her travels. She had made it as far as India once, where she'd lived with an older Indian witch named Deepti for over a year. Deepti had shared with her a book of spells collected over many centuries by her own family. These spells were unlike any Helen had ever seen, full of rich spices contained in special metal boxes to protect their vitality. The entirety of *Robinson Crusoe* was full of these spells, transcribed from Deepti's family grimoire.

It became important for Helen to write and preserve the spells she came across as the old ways were practiced and taught less and less with each subsequent generation. Many spells were being lost to the hands of time. Between the three books, she believed she had over a thousand spells. Magic was required to find the spell she needed, or she would be sitting here all day.

She closed her eyes and let her hand hover above the books. An unnatural calm filled the room when she began to speak.

"A search for something I must find, open up the space of time. Bring the pages unto me, by powers of the wind and sea."

The calm of the room broke and a gust of wind blew through the kitchen. *Moby Dick*'s pages began to turn, flipping rapidly, and then as quick as the wind came, it stopped, leaving the book spread wide in the center of the table. There, on the open page, was the locator spell. Helen peered down at her old familiar handwriting and ran her fingers across the cool, black ink.

The top of the page was bordered by small drawings of the

herbs used in the spell, while the center contained the incantation. She had always been intrigued by alchemy and took it upon herself to practice drawing images of the important plants needed in her craft. This was helpful in two ways: one, she would know what the herb looked like so that she didn't pick the wrong plant, and two, if for some reason the words of the spell were unreadable, she would be able to still decipher the plants needed for it.

Tucked into the far left-hand corner of the page was a drawing of Mary's hag stone. The sight of it brought back a twinge of sadness and longing for her friend. The last time she had seen the hag stone was the day before her last death when she had buried it by the rowan tree. It was something she was going to need to find to complete the spell.

At that moment, Storm let out a loud bark from the other room that startled her out of her thoughts. Of course, she already had it: the first time she had explored the backfield, Storm had dug it up under the rowan tree and she had taken it and tucked it into the pocket of her jacket.

She rushed into the sitting room and pulled her jacket off the old pegboard near the door. Stuffing her hands into the pockets and rooting around for a few seconds, she pulled out the stone, still dusted with earth. It was as simple and beautiful as she remembered, even more so now with a thin layer of green moss gracing the center of the hole. Tucking it into the pocket of her jeans, she went back into the kitchen to continue her reading.

The spell was one of the oldest in the book and, like many things, age had not treated it well. Some of the words had faded and others were worn off the page entirely, but she was still able to make out most of what she needed.

It was a simple spell, with only a few items required. The first was an undyed piece of cotton cloth, muslin if possible. Helen went into the pantry and ripped off a piece of an old grain sack that lay on the floor. She placed the cloth in a pot of boiling water alongside a large slice of ginger root; this would help aid in the success of the spell. The room filled with the aroma of the ginger, making her stomach growl from neglect. She removed the cloth and set it on the edge of the sink to cool down. While it cooled, she found a slender piece of hemp rope to tie through the hole of the hag stone, turning it into a pendulum. Glancing one last time at the spell, she rang out the cloth and went outside into the garden, grabbing her staff as she went. Near the south end of the lawn was a large patch of raw, exposed earth. She pushed the point of the staff into the semi-frozen dirt and worked it until she had a hole the size of a fist. Stretching the cloth out, she tied a large knot in its center and placed the knot into the hole. Covering the knot over with the dirt, she left the two ends of the fabric reaching out of the hole so that it resembled a plant pushing its way up to the spring sunshine.

Finally, holding the hag stone out in front of her, she spoke the incantation.

"Back to the earth, back to the ground. I won't untie you until you are found. From earth, sea, and mountain peak, bring forth the visions that I seek."

Holding the hag stone to the sky, she waited for a sign that the Goddess had heard her plea. A gentle breeze blew down the valley and whistled through the hole of the hag stone. Helen smiled and thanked the Goddess as she tied the rope around her neck and tucked the stone into her shirt. Now, she would just need to wait and hope that the spell pointed her in Margaret's direction.

In the far distance was the rumble of a motor vehicle. She turned to see Connor's truck coming into view. As promised, he was headed to help her.

For the first time since Tomas, she felt something other than plain lust for a man. Connor was the first thing she thought of each morning and the last thing each night. He was her second chance. But she was scared to dream about a life with him. If she had learned anything in all her past lives, it was that things rarely went as planned. This time, though, she had more than just memories of love to fight for.

It was time to finish this never-ending nightmare so she could finally have her chance at a proper life. She had never made it to this age in any of her lives, which meant that some part of the awful cycle was already broken. Now, it was time to finish it off.

Chapter Thirty-Two

REGMATA

Helen greeted Connor outside in the garden, the cold pushing them quickly inside to the warmth of the kitchen. Connor sat at the table, throwing his bag onto the chair next to him. He smelled of cedar and gasoline and sported a small grease spot over his right eyebrow.

"Working on the tractor today?" she asked as she walked over and took his head in her hands, slowly wiping off the oil from his brow and smiling at him. He looked up at her, his dark green eyes sparkling with anticipation of a kiss. She bent down and landed one softly on the top of his head, then walked back across the room, smiling to herself. She caught him smirk out of the corner of her eye. She was getting quite good at this game of flirting that they were playing. At this point, she was one move ahead and now had him in checkmate, and he knew it.

"Do you want a cup of coffee?" Helen asked, turning back toward him and flashing another teasing smile.

"Do you not know me at all?" he joked, raising his eyebrows in response. "The fire looks like it's about to go out. I'm going to go and grab some wood to stock it back up."

Before he could even push his chair in, Helen gave a quick glance over to the fireplace and a slight wave of her hand. At that, a roaring fire was in place of the old smoldering one.

"You do know that my masculinity takes a hit each time you do that, right? I need to be useful in some way," Connor said, half-seriously, as he sat back down.

"Oh, come on. You know as well as I do that you have much more to offer," she said with a smirk, pushing the flirtation to the next level and causing him to blush.

She carried two large mugs of coffee to the table and set one down in front of Connor, who immediately took a sip. She raised her eyebrows and smiled.

"Bit eager today?"

"Well, only after staying up until eleven last night listening to Granda going on about some company constructing a corporate building and how it takes away from the scenic beauty of the area. Then getting up at five to a broken fence and a tractor that wouldn't start. All that with zero coffee in the house. So I'd have to say yes. Very much so, yes."

Helen smiled and spun her spell book around to Connor. The book was still open to the locator spell. She pointed down at the picture of the hag stone.

"This is how we're going to find Margaret. I've already completed the first part of the spell and charged the stone." She pulled the hag stone out of her shirt. It was warm to the touch, full of the heat and magic from her body. She took it from around her neck and handed it to Connor. "This was given to me many lifetimes ago by Mary. It's not only a protection charm but also has the ability to find missing objects or people. Now, all we need is a map."

"I have one in the truck. Give me a second."

Connor walked out and came back a few minutes later, spreading the map over the table. Helen moved the books aside to make room; it was so big it took up half the surface area. Connor ran his hand over it, smoothing it out, and then began to trace his finger down the border between land and sea. He stopped and tapped the map.

"Here, this is us. The map is a bit outdated. I think my granda has had it in the truck since before my father was born, but it should do."

"Okay, let me see if I can get us in the general area of where she might be."

Helen pinched the hemp twine between her fingers and let the hag stone slip down to hang above the map. Closing her eyes, she focused on Margaret, calling upon the Goddess to guide her. The stone was mostly still, only swaying a bit side to side. Then all of a sudden, it began to create large sweeping circles over the map. Helen opened her eyes and let the stone guide her, the circles tightening. Soon, it hovered over a small town on the map—Inveraray—and then stopped.

"Inveraray, that's about fifty minutes from here," Connor said, with worry in his voice. "I was hoping it wasn't even going to show her on this map. I was hoping maybe she was somewhere else in the world."

"I knew she was close. I could feel her dark magic when we took our trips to town. There was always something off-putting while we were there that I couldn't quite put my finger on. What's in Inveraray these days?"

"Not much. About the same as Oban but smaller with fewer tourists."

"Let's see if I have internet yet. Did you bring your laptop?"

Connor reached down and grabbed his bag from the chair, pulling out a small black router and well-used laptop covered with stickers. One announced "Men who wear kilts are never caught with their pants down". Helen made sure to point it out with a smile and a laugh.

"Oh God, don't mind the garish display of manhood on the top. I bought it off a friend from uni."

"Well, I'm glad to know I won't catch you with your pants down then," Helen joked.

Connor got up and took the router into the living room. He fiddled around for a bit and then finally announced they now had Wi-Fi. Helen walked in carrying the laptop under her arm and coffees in each hand.

"Let's do our research here. It's a bit more comfortable."

Connor dragged the coffee table closer to the couch and they sat down to begin their search.

"Look for any news articles in the past few years having to do with anything major going on in Inveraray," Helen said as she sipped her coffee.

Connor tapped away at the keyboard and scrolled for only a few minutes before he stopped and began reading an article from that past week.

"Holy shit! I should have thought of this already. Remember me telling you about Granda keeping me up half the night bitching about the new commercial building that's going up? Well, guess where it's going?"

"Inveraray?"

"You got it! It says here, 'Despite local pushback, Regmata

Industries, a bioengineering company, was able to acquire building permits last April and has nearly completed the five-story facility. When interviewed, Jannet Combs, CEO of Regmata Industries, said, "Regmata Industries is looking forward to this new opportunity for growth and hopes to bring significant job opportunities to the area." Regmata Industries plans on opening its laboratory this coming January.' Okay, let's look into this Jannet Combs."

Connor's fingers moved quickly over the keyboard again, pulling up Regmata Industries' website. It only took a minute to find the board's information, along with a full bio on Jannet Combs. As the page loaded, Helen held her breath in anticipation of seeing Margaret's face, but instead she saw the image of a young black woman who appeared to be in her mid-thirties. Surprised, she looked at Connor and shook her head. Maybe it was just a coincidence, and the two things—Margaret and Regmata—were completely unrelated. Yet something inside her told her not to move forward.

"Go back to the main page," Helen said.

Connor clicked on the "Home" button and began to scroll down. There were numerous links to different types of research the company was doing. Everything from vaccines to genetic testing for diseases, even cancer research, but they were most well known for their leading advances in DNA research. One of the articles seemed to catch Connor's eye but before he could even begin scrolling down, Helen reached out and stopped him. At the top of the page was a picture of a group of scientists. There in the background was Margaret Aitken.

"There she is. In the background, like she always is," Helen said, pointing to the pale-faced woman in the back of the image.

Connor leaned forward and peered into the screen. "You were

right. She is up to something and whatever it is, it's not good." He pointed to the title of the article on the screen, which read: *Regmata Industries signs five-year contract with U.S. on biowarfare research*.

"That doesn't sound promising. Listen to this," he continued. "'Regmata Industries has signed a five-year contract with the United States government to lead the world in biowarfare research. The contract was signed in January 2019 and there are plans to build a facility entirely dedicated to the project in April 2019. Regmata hopes to shed light on safer strategies when it comes to the housing and creation of bioweapons.'"

As they sifted through the background of the company, it took them only a few minutes to find Margaret's alias. She was now going by the name Irma Bathory and was the founder and owner of Regmata. She had started the company in 1978 under the name Kentia and had originally been based out of London. The company specialized in recombinant DNA and had previously worked on various initiatives to preserve the DNA of prominent international leaders, both alive and dead. A web search pulled up an old newspaper article from 1980 in which an ex-lab assistant gave an exposé claiming the company was doing illegal experiments on humans. Specifically, fusing strands of DNA from snakes with human embryos in an attempt to create a hybrid. The company went under a large-scale investigation by the British government and its lab was shut down the following year. However, five years later they were back up and running under a new name, Regmata Industries. They started up in a shiny new facility in Lichfield and were apparently now working in the field of cancer research, specializing in DNA rebuilding. Irma Bathory was referenced in numerous scientific articles and papers, seeming to have her nose in anything that had to do with manipulating human genomes.

"I can't believe it's a bioweapons lab," Helen said, feeling cold dread welling up within her. "This must have been her end-game all along. With her company's leading research in human DNA manipulation she was a shoe-in for any government contract on biowarfare research. It was just a waiting game for her in the end, all she needed to do was sit it out and wait for one powerful government or another to come knocking at her door. If she gets her hands on the actual biological warfare materials, we're all screwed."

"She must have chosen Inverary because it's rural and out of the way," Connor said. "If there was a 'leak' into the local community it would be weeks if not months before anyone took notice and came to investigate. Giving it just enough time to spread out and infect the other small communities in the area and once it reached that point, it would be too late to stop it. Within months the entire world would be affected."

"Oh God, Connor. This is not good. We have to stop her before that laboratory is finished," Helen said, her eyes growing wide with worry.

Connor closed the laptop and grabbed hold of Helen's hands. "It's going to be okay. Now that we know her identity and what she's up to, we're more than a few steps ahead of her. Plus, she thinks you've just been born. She has no idea you're here. She won't be looking for you quite yet."

"I can only conceal my magic for so long, Connor. It's nothing to hide these small charms and spells from her but when I create the spell that will finally stop her, she's going to know it's me. I can't hide that kind of power. We need a solid plan in place. I need to hold off using my magic right up until the moment before I start the final spell. I can't risk her finding out that I'm an adult."

"So, what's the next move?"

"Well, first I need to gather all the items needed for the spell, then it's a waiting game. The spell only works on the final hour of the winter solstice. It will take some strategic planning to get her where we need her on that day and time. We have a month and a few weeks to get things in order. Let's hope the lab isn't completed by then and we still have some time," Helen said, as she rested back against the overstuffed cushion of the sofa and took a long sip from her coffee.

The task was daunting, and she was unsure of how she would even accomplish it by herself. In the past, she had been surrounded by others who were versed in magic and could provide a sort of backup if things went awry. And even then, it had never been enough. This time it was just her, and it would take every ounce of magic that flowed through her veins to complete the task ahead.

She wasn't afraid of dying—she had lived through that many times. The fear that had set into her bones was the fear that this might not end things, even if her life did. This was the closest she had been thus far to any hope of this never-ending nightmare coming to a close. If it didn't work, she was back to square one. Plus, she had Connor to think about. He was the only man she had fallen in love with since Tomas. What bad timing, she really didn't need this kind of distraction at the moment but there were no two ways around it: he was her driving force. He was the reason she wanted a normal life so badly this time around. She was looking forward to a long, amazingly boring life together. Spending evenings reading by the fire, long walks in the fields with Storm, holidays and vacations, and growing old together. Those were the simple things she longed for.

Then it dawned on her: her life as Helen Kent needed to be tied up. She needed to finalize things so that there was no one coming around looking for her. She couldn't deal with such distractions and maintain the level of focus she needed while up against Margaret.

"I think it's time I contact my parents and Kevin and let them know that I won't be coming home this year," she said.

Connor tried not to show his happiness, but there was no doubt that his eyes lit up at the prospect that she would be staying longer. "So, does that mean you're going to keep the place?"

"Of course I am, this is my home. Fernbeg has been part of me for lifetimes now. I could never let her go."

"I'm glad to hear it. I knew from the moment I saw you there in that doorway it was yours all along," he said, leaning in to kiss her.

As their lips touched, a spark of magic bounced between them. It was a mixture of blue and gold, the luminescence of which lit their faces for a brief moment before fading into the space between them.

Helen felt herself getting lost in the kiss when the moment was cut short by the ringing of the telephone.

Chapter Thirty-Three

PENTIMENTO

Helen picked up the old, corded phone to hear Henry's upbeat voice greet her on the other end.

"Hello there, darling. I see you finally have the phone lines working. Seamus said you're back to your old self again."

The way the line came out of his mouth seemed to have more behind it than just a simple friendly statement.

"Yes, feeling much better. Thank you."

"Well, in that case, I have something for you. Will you be home this afternoon? I can drop it off on my way into town."

"Sure. Connor and I planned to stay in today. The weather is a bit nasty and I don't think I want to let that cold set into my bones just yet."

"Well, I'll be over around four then."

She hung the phone up onto the wall mount and headed back to the sofa where Connor lay outstretched.

"Scoot," she said, nudging his shoulder with her knee.

He sat up and grabbed her, swinging her body down onto his in one fell swoop. As their bodies landed on the cushion, a large puff of dust sprang up and floated into the air, then hung there in the light from the table lamp as they kissed.

"I swear, even the dust in this house looks magical," he said, after breaking away from their kiss and waving the dust away with his hand.

She laughed. They sat back up and Connor placed his arm around her as she nestled snugly into his embrace.

"Who was on the phone?"

"Henry. He's coming over to drop something off later. He was vague, not sure what it is."

"Well, I don't know about you, but I'm starving. How about I make us a bit of brunch, what do ya say?"

"Sounds perfect. I'll do a bit more digging into Regmata and see just what role Margaret is playing here."

Connor headed into the kitchen and Helen went to work on research. There was plenty of information to read about the company and quite a few local news articles on the new facility in Inveraray. Most of these voiced the opinions of the locals, none of whom wanted it in their town. But somehow the permits had passed and it was built regardless. There was an uproar in the community and even a Facebook page had been started to organize protests.

One of the protests was being held at the Regmata building tomorrow.

Helen knew she couldn't go and risk running into Margaret, but maybe she could convince Connor to go and do a bit of scouting for her.

When Connor came in with a plate of egg sandwiches, Helen

closed the laptop. They ate in silence, both lost in thought and too distracted for common conversation.

"Hey, do you feel that?" Connor asked, breaking the silence. "The room feels like it dropped ten degrees in an instant."

"Yes, I feel it too," she said, standing up.

She took a step forward and closed her eyes, taking in a deep breath and focusing on the energy in the room. She could feel Connor's energy, pulsating with strong masculinity. Then there were the earthly elements like the fire and the stone walls, moving in a rhythmic manner with one another. Beneath that were the small bits of energy that reverberated off ordinary objects. Together, they made a whirlwind of currents that danced around her. However, there was something off about this dance. The energies in the room seemed to be gravitating toward something. Following her mind's eye, she turned and faced the back wall of the sitting room. When she opened her eyes, she was looking at a painting hanging on the back wall. The room grew colder as she walked toward it.

The painting was one she had decided to keep when she redesigned the room. It was a scene of a forest; large oak trees broke away to a small opening where the sun beamed down and illuminated a tiny gray rabbit sitting among a circle of stones and thistles.

She lifted it off its hook and held it, but it was large and not easy to hold.

"Let me get that," Connor said, stepping up and grabbing the painting with ease.

Helen looked at it. There was something to this painting that she hadn't noticed before. Rabbits represented witches in Celtic folklore. The circle of stones with thistles, the woods. Then it dawned on her: it was a depiction of the protection circle that she and Mary had built in her first life as Freya.

"Can you turn it around so the back is facing me?" she asked.

Connor did as she asked and Helen pulled back the brown paper backing. Nothing. She had expected to see a note or something hidden in the back of the painting, but it lay empty.

"Huh. I thought maybe there was something in it," she said, motioning for him to place it back onto the wall.

But as Connor spun around, the light from the window showed through the back of the canvas, illuminating another hidden image under the one that was visible.

There, on the backside of the canvas, was the same rabbit. This time around her lay three objects: a large, twisted oak staff, a deep gray hag stone, and a leather book. In the background, looking at the rabbit, was a wolf resting in a bed of green velvet on the forest floor. The look in the wolf's eyes was not that of a predator but a protector. Painted in fine print at the bottom were the words "Helen, Tha a h-uile càil a dh 'fheumas tu". The translation came to her instantly: *Helen, you have all that you need* in Gaelic. She recognized the writing as Mary's. Each object in the painting was a reminder of the elements needed in order to fully achieve her powers in this life. She had all but one: her mother's green velvet cape. It was the one item that never appeared to her in any of her lives but the first. She didn't have a clue where to even start looking for it.

"Wow, that's incredible," Connor said, looking down at the backside of the painting.

"It's called a pentimento. Many painters used other artists' paintings for their canvases or added to the already painted images. In the seventeenth century, canvas was hard to come by and pentimentos were commonly found on paintings from that time period. This one, however, was not done only with paint but also with magic. It was the handiwork of Mary."

Helen ran her fingers down the gold-flecked frame, remembering back to past lives. It had always hung on this very spot in the sitting room, yet she never took more than a brief glance at it as she passed it by. It wasn't super eye-catching, but she supposed Mary wanted it that way. It was meant for her now as Helen, not as any of her former selves.

She motioned for Connor to hang it back onto the wall and explained to him what the significance of the image was.

"The cloak, do you have it?" he asked.

"No, and not a clue on where to even begin looking for it. The last time I saw it was in the late fifteen hundreds." Her mood immediately turned melancholy at the thought of her mother's cloak lost to time.

Connor, noticing her change in spirit, spun her around and pulled her into a hug. "Why don't we get out of here for a bit and take Storm out for a walk?" he suggested.

"Yes, I could use a bit of fresh air right now," she agreed.

As soon as they opened the front door, an icy gust of wind pushed its way past them into the cottage, cooling the room down almost instantly. It had grown cold in the past week and there was the threat of snow in the air. They both pulled on knitted hats and zipped their jackets fully up. Even though it was mid-afternoon, there was still a crunchy layer of frost coating each blade of grass.

Storm was more than excited to be out in nature. He had been cooped up in the cottage far too long and needed a good run. He raced down the hill to the edge of the water and back up to meet Connor and Helen, doing loops around them as they slowly made their way down the hill. He spotted a rabbit by the edge of the field near a small bush of bramble. He stopped and stared at it, slowly crouching down, getting himself ready to give chase. At this, the rabbit hopped into the bush, and Storm bolted forward.

Connor and Helen chased after him as he raced around the bush with his nose to the ground.

"Storm, NO, leave the bunny alone!" Helen called out.

"Oh God, I hope he doesn't kill it," Connor said.

By now, Storm had his whole head and upper body inside the bush, only his tail and back legs visible. There had been nowhere else for the rabbit to run and it was surely trapped. But when they arrived, Storm was wagging his tail, body still chest deep in the bush.

Helen reached over and pulled Storm out, then pulled back the thicket to peer inside. The center of the shrub was hollow, having grown up like a fence around a smaller bush that lay inside. The bush had teardrop-shaped red berries hanging off its small stems. Right away, Helen knew just what it was; barberry, a powerful magical herb, and this bush was perfectly preserved and full of the berries.

"Do you see the rabbit? Is she hurt?" Connor asked.

Taken off guard by the oddness of the plant inside the bush, Helen hadn't realized there was no rabbit to be found. It must have broken its way to freedom while she pulled Storm back.

"No bunny in here. Just a barberry bush full to the rim with berries. Can I see your hat?"

Connor removed his hat and Helen began to fill it with the berries.

"Why do you need them?" Connor asked.

"Barberries are a particularly good ingredient to add to spells that break bonds or curses, and also spells to do with controlling others. What luck to find a bush with berries still on it this time of year. Normally the animals would have stripped it by now," she said, loading the last of the berries into the hat and standing up.

Storm looked at her, panting and wagging his tail. He had a look of satisfaction on his face, like he had just successfully completed a task. She smiled at him and ruffled the fur between his ears.

"Did you want me to find this, you silly little wolf?"

He gave her hand a lick and took off running back toward the cottage.

"I'm going to take that as a yes," she said, smiling at Connor and turning back toward Fernbeg.

They spent the rest of the afternoon doing research in the sitting room by the fire. Connor scrolled the internet while Helen searched in her spell books for ideas on the spells she might need along the way. At one point Helen took over the laptop, deciding it was time to write to her boss and let him know that she wouldn't be coming back. The letter of resignation was the first of three emails she had to write that day. The other two would go to her parents and to Kevin, but those would take a bit more finesse and time.

The letter to her boss was short and to the point. She thanked him for the opportunities he had given her and let him know that she would miss working for him. She offered up some suggestions for her replacement in the office and ended it by saying she would have Kevin clean out her desk in the coming week.

Letter number two was to her parents. She played the "I've fallen in love" card and explained that she really enjoyed the slower-paced life in Scotland and wanted to give this new lifestyle a chance. Her mother had been dying for her to show some sort of long-term love interest in hopes of grandbabies someday, so she was hoping this might just play on those emotions, smoothing over the conversation a bit. She knew her father would be more skeptical about the whole thing, but she sent them her phone number so that they could reach out when they wanted.

Kevin's letter was the hardest to write. He knew her better than anyone else and this was totally uncharacteristic of her. She was going to have to convince him that she was staying in Scotland for some big opportunity. Something that she just couldn't pass up. She decided to tell him that after fixing up the cottage and pouring all her life savings into the project, she wanted to stay for a while and was offered an online marketing job from a company in Edinburgh. She asked him if he could clean out her office and drop off the boxes at her apartment. She finished off the letter by telling him how much she would miss their daily talks in the office kitchen and hoped that he would come and visit her in the spring.

Her apartment was another thing that needed to be tied up. She decided the best route was to sublet it and ask Kevin to put the word out in the office. If there were any takers, she would hire a moving company to bring her things down to her parents' house and deal with the rest later.

After hitting send on the last of the emails, a sadness overtook her. This could be the last contact she had with them. As much as she was trying to stay optimistic about her future life with Connor, she still feared that things may not go as planned.

"Are you okay?" Connor asked. Her mood had shifted since she had written the letters and Connor had picked up on it.

"I think so. Just a bit worried, that's all. It's hard to write these kinds of letters. I never know if it will be a final goodbye," she said, looking down.

A look of realization came over Connor's face, accompanied by worry. "What do you mean, final goodbye?"

"Connor, there is no guarantee that this spell will work. It hasn't been used for hundreds of years. If something goes wrong or the spell doesn't hold, there's always a chance I may not survive."

She looked at him as she spoke. It was as if someone had taken the wind completely out of his sails. He was deflated and somber.

"I'll put everything I have into this. I don't plan on letting her win this time," she said, trying to boost his mood.

He gave her a forced smile, but she knew that this worry would plague him until things came to a close. She knew, though, that it was better for him to be prepared for any outcome. Nothing was written in stone.

Chapter Thirty-Four

VELVET SHIELD

It was a strange thing, being so many different people yet still being the same person as a whole. If Helen had learned anything from her past lives, it was that times changed and trends and fads came and went, but the one thing that stayed constant was nature. No matter what, nature was there, willing and ready to provide what she needed. A friend through the ages. A prime example was the barberries. After spending the afternoon going through her spell books, all three spells she settled on included barberry as an ingredient. Thanks to Storm and the rabbit, she now had more than she needed.

At that moment, Storm came bursting into the room at top speed, barking and looking towards the window facing the road.

"Looks like Henry is here," Connor announced.

"Is it four already? The day flew by."

Helen walked to the door and held it open for Henry as he struggled against the wind that lashed the walls of the cottage.

"It's a fierce one out there today," he said. "The winds off the sea have brought a new kind of cold in. I do believe that winter is settling its roots into the land. The fields are at least an inch frozen at this point."

"Come in, let me take your coat," Helen said, removing the old man's jacket and hanging it on a peg.

He was carrying a wooden trunk the size of a milk crate, which he set down by his boots on the floor.

"Can I get you a hot cup of coffee or tea?" Connor asked.

"No, but a dram of whiskey would warm the soul if you've got it."

Connor smiled and walked into the kitchen, reappearing with a tray containing three cups and a bottle of whiskey. Pouring out generous amounts into the cups, he passed them out.

"So, what is it that brought you out in this cold?" Helen asked, eagerly waiting for his reply. She couldn't help but keep staring at the wooden trunk by the door. Whatever had brought him out in the cold was in there and she wanted to find out what it was.

He crouched down and picked up the trunk, holding it by two little metal handles on either end.

"This has been passed down from generation to generation in my family. It was given to my ancestor Fionna O'Brien by a powerful wise woman in the early sixteen hundreds," he said, sitting down and resting the wooden chest on his lap. "It was said that someday one of our bloodline would come across the person it belonged to and reunite it with its original owner. My grandfather used to tell us stories of how this box survived some of the most horrific circumstances. His great-great-grandfather's house burned down and the only thing that survived the fire was this trunk. The house lay in ashes around it but not a lick of fire ever touched it. There were other things too. The village suffered a major flood and my great-grandfather's house, with all its belongings, was washed away. The only thing that remained, other than the stones the house sat upon, was the chest. My father told me it was a family legend that it was blessed by a powerful witch and those who kept it safe would be blessed with a long-lasting bloodline. It was passed down to me upon my father's death and now I believe I have found its rightful owner. You."

"Why?" Helen asked.

Henry held the chest out toward her. "See for yourself."

As soon as Helen grabbed hold of it, a rush of energy passed through her. She looked down at the lid and there on the top, carved into the wood in delicate script, was the name *Helen*. She looked up at Henry and gave him a confused smile before unclasping the lock and flipping the lid open. Inside lay a thick green velvet cloak. Her heart began to race as she pulled it out. It was her mother's cloak and it looked as new as it had the day it was given to her. The box had been spelled to protect and preserve the cloak for centuries until she needed it again.

"Is that your mother's cloak?" Connor asked.

"It is," she said, as tears ran down her cheeks.

She pulled the fabric up to her nose and took in its smell. The scent of rosemary and fennel still clung to the fabric along with the earthy smell of moss and the salty sting of the sea. It smelled just like her mother. After all this time, after so many lifetimes, it was as if her mother—her first mother, the woman who had taught her everything—was there with her in the room.

"I knew from the moment I picked you up at the airport it was meant for you," Henry said. "It was just a matter of waiting until you realized who you really were."

"How did you know?" she asked.

"It was part of the story that was passed down from my ancestors. A very powerful witch named Freya cast a spell on herself many centuries ago to avenge the death of her beloved. She swore she would come back lifetime after lifetime until she defeated the malevolent demon who took her love away from her. You are Freya reincarnated, aren't you?"

Helen just smiled at the old man and raised her glass in thanks, drinking down all the whiskey in one go. She closed the chest and set it on the coffee table.

"I knew your ancestor, Fionna. She was part of our coven. A wonderful woman with a kind heart. Now, I know where you get it from. Thank you, Henry, for keeping this safe for me. You have no idea how much I needed this," Helen said, getting up and hugging the old man.

"Of course. I hope it helps you in whatever you have planned," he replied, sporting a proud smile.

"It certainly will. It's the most effective form of defense I could have. It'll function as a sort of magical shield when I need it. You really are a lifesaver, Henry."

She carried a kind of confidence now that she hadn't before, a sense of power that came from the fact that she had all of her magical tethers.

The conversation petered out as their glasses emptied and the sun dipped behind the hills, casting long shadows and darkening the skies. Eventually, Henry left, and Connor followed suit, leaving Helen alone in the cottage with Storm. Once the house was quiet and the darkness set in, she opened the trunk once again, pulling the cloak up to her chest in an embrace. She swung it around her shoulders and clipped the large brass clasp together. Twirling around, the cape plumed out around her in a swirling mix of green and gold. She could feel the magic in the cape and it was strong, much stronger than she remembered.

As she went to take it off, she noticed that a pocket had been sewn into the inside lining. In the pocket was a small piece of folded parchment. As she unfolded it, she saw the same recognizable handwriting as in the painting. It was a note from Mary.

Dear Freya,

My dear friend. I know that you have lived many lives and gone by many names and that you will find this as Helen Kent. I have kept your mother's cloak safe and over the years have added many layers of protection to it. I want you to know that I was able to lead a long and wonderful life because of your sacrifice. I married a wonderful man and we had three sons and four daughters. I am at the end of my days now and all of my children have heard the many stories of our adventures together. They know of the sacrifices you made and I have made them swear unto me that they will care for Fernbeg and your belongings as long as our bloodline lasts. I do not know how your journey will end. I only hope that this cloak will provide you with what you need to finally put an end to the battle you have fought for so many centuries. Good luck my friend, and may the Goddess ever be on your side.

Your faithful friend through time,

~Mary

Helen held the note to her heart and looked to the skies, uttering the words "Thank you" up to the heavens. She was certain that whatever lay ahead, it was a pivotal point in this journey of hers. After centuries, she finally had the cloak, and Mary had known that this was the point in time she needed to have it. Now, it was up to her to get the next part right.

Chapter Thirty-Five

THE ART OF WAR

Before they knew it, December had come. Connor had attended every single protest he could at the Regmata building, hoping to gain information other than idle gossip from the townsfolk. But at each event, Margaret was nowhere in sight, and they began to believe that she was running things from afar. They decided, in order to ensure that she was in Scotland at the time, they needed to create some sort of issue at the lab.

Connor devised a plan that was sure to create a big enough problem so that all of the board members, including Margaret, would need to be at the site in Inveraray. While scouting the place during the protests, he observed that the loading dock was only covered by guards during the hours the lab was being worked on. They were still having two to three daily deliveries of lab equipment as they stocked the facility. It was the perfect place to break into during the night. The security cameras were the only real issue, but Helen assured him that she had that part under control.

The idea was to sneak into the loading dock around eleven and place a few cherry bombs in the toilets and flush them. The damage to the lab would be minor, but it would create enough of a commotion to summon the owner and members of the boards for an inspection.

In addition, because it was vandalism, Margaret would have to deal with a police investigation.

Helen worried about Connor being the one to carry out the task, but he assured her that it would be fulfilling a boyhood dream of his. After seeing some '80s movie as a kid, he had always wanted to try it, but she feared he might be caught and end up in jail, or worse, be hurt by one of the nightguards. To put it mildly, she felt apprehensive about the plan.

The phone rang, breaking her free of the worries that were racing around her head.

"Hello?"

"Hey you, I need to take a trip down to Glasgow. I have a mate who's going to hook me up with some of the stuff we're going to need. Do you fancy a trip out of town with me?" Connor asked.

"That sounds fun. I need to stop by an apothecary and pick up the last of the ingredients for my spell anyways. It calls for a few rare herbs that I can't pick up in just any shop and I think I know of a place where I can get them on the way to Glasgow."

"It's a plan then. I'll be over after I help Granda with the chores. Say around twelve?"

"Perfect, gives me time to get ready and pack us lunch. See you soon."

Helen hung up the phone and made her way to the bathroom.

She turned on the shower and undressed. The bathroom filled with thick white steam as she stepped in and let the hot water temporarily wash away all the tension she'd been carrying. The bathroom was always ten degrees colder than all the other rooms in the cottage. Helen figured it was because of the altar room causing a draft. However, today she couldn't help but pick up on something else. It wasn't just cold; the energy felt off.

As she rinsed her hair and shut off the tap, she heard a noise. Carefully, she stepped out of the shower. The room was heavy with steam, and the haziness of the atmosphere made it hard to see. As she reached for her towel, she glimpsed something from the corner of her eye. There, by the sink, stood a figure.

Before she could even let out a startled scream, it vanished. Wrapping the towel around herself, she went to the sink and flipped on the light. The glow illuminated words scrawled on the mirror in steam.

The power to defeat evil lies within the lines.

She was shaken but not scared. She had sensed a presence in the house before, a few different times, including once or twice there in the bathroom. Whatever spirit walked within the walls of the cottage did not mean her harm. It would stand to reason that it could be one of Mary's descendants. This was a message not to be ignored; the spirit realm could often see a much larger and broader view than the human world could. But she wasn't quite sure what to make of the message. *The power to defeat evil lies within the lines of what?* she thought. *A spell perhaps, maybe the lines of a book?*

Helen went into her bedroom and retrieved her cell phone, something she had barely touched since she arrived at Fernbeg. It was funny—back home she had felt as if it was her lifeline and never went anywhere without it. But here, she could care less about the stupid device. It was handy for situations like this though. She wanted to snap a photo of the message to show Connor, but by the time she had taken it, there was little to nothing left. Just a few faded streaks on the mirror.

"Well, I guess good old-fashioned pen and paper will have to suffice," she said to herself.

Twelve o'clock came quickly and Connor showed up in the truck with a full tank of gas. Helen let Storm out quickly before they left, but on a leash this time. She didn't want to go chasing after him if the rabbit decided to show back up.

Once they were on their way, she told Connor all about the message in the bathroom and that she believed it must be from one of Mary's descendants.

"Wow, I'm not sure how you kept your calm. I would have shit my pants if that kind of thing happened to me," he joked.

"Well, it kind of comes with the territory—witches, reincarnations, demons, ghosts. Ya know, all that stuff," she replied playfully.

"So, do you have any clue what the message means? Are you even sure that this spirit is on your side?" he asked.

"I didn't get any threatening vibes from whoever was there. So, I don't think that's something I need to worry about. I have no idea what it means. I was thinking maybe it was something about reading between the lines in a book or a spell but that doesn't seem quite right."

"Well, maybe you should have a look back into the last journal again and see if there's something you might have missed."

"That's a good idea. I hadn't thought of the journal."

It was a beautiful day in Scotland, not a cloud in the sky for miles. The colors of fall had faded now, leaving the landscape a rich brown with dabs of gray. A fine layer of snow coated the ground but not enough to completely cover the tall grass in the fields. Tufts of golden wheat stuck up through the snow, giving it a majestic feel. The land was quiet and devoid of movement, as most of the farmers had their animals tucked away inside the barns, away from the frigid temperatures. Somehow, no matter the season, Scotland's beauty shined through. It made Helen long for her paintbrush and pad.

"Know of any good art supply shops in the city?" she asked, dreaming of the pigments she would be mixing up to achieve the shades of the early winter landscape.

"Sure, I know just the place. I think you'll love it."

"Fantastic, I'm out of most of the supplies I brought with me. I did a lot of sketching and painting when I first arrived and if I'm sticking around, I'm going to need a restock."

As they came upon a road sign that stated they would soon be arriving at Luss, she told Connor that they needed to make a pit stop—she needed to see if the local herb shop had the remaining ingredients needed for the exorcism spell. Some of the herbs were rare and not just any shop would carry them, but she had a feeling the one in Luss would have just what she needed.

They pulled down to the quaint little eatery that Henry had taken her to on her first day in Scotland.

"Let's stop here for a quick bite to eat. I didn't have time to pack anything for lunch. Their sandwiches are quite good here."

"I'm well aware of that. This is one of Granda's and Henry's favorite Sunday lunch spots." Connor raised his eyebrows with a toothy smile.

After they ate, she told Connor of the small shop she had seen when she passed through with Henry. She remembered it being on the street that led down to the loch. It was a small, stone house with a green door and a sign out front written in Gaelic.

It had caught her eye the first time she had seen it and now that she was standing in front of it for the second time, she knew why. Below the words "Luibh-eòlaiche" on the sign was a very fine print that read "Luchd-slànachaidh o shean," meaning "healers of old". In many areas, a healer was another name for a witch. This sign had been designed so that any witch who read it knew it was a safe space.

The thick wooden door to the shop was stained a weathered, moss-green color and sported large, black iron hinges. Decorating the entryway was a beautiful yule wreath made of juniper and cedar and adorned with dried oranges, cinnamon sticks, and star anise.

As they entered, the sound of tiny chimes rang out, letting the shopkeeper know that visitors had arrived. The smell of the room was enchanting, a robust mix of sage, rosemary, allspice, cedar, and hints of citrus. The sides of the shop had floor-to-ceiling shelving that was full of all sorts of herbs and spices. Bundles of dried herbs hung from the overhead beams and old oil lamps lit the space with the warm glow of times past. At the back of the store was a large old oak desk that served as the counter. Behind it was a woman who looked to be older than time. Her moon-white hair flowed down her back in large waves almost to her waist. She was clothed in an old smock-like dress with a utility apron over it. She was tinkering away at some sort of tincture when they walked in.

Helen went over to the large array of herbs and began collecting jars. Betel nut and boneset were on the list of things to find, along with clear camphor and chrysanthemum oils. The shop was so well organized that she found everything she needed pretty quickly and walked to the back of the shop to pay while Connor puttered around the front.

As she approached the desk, the old woman took one look at

her, her old, drooping eyes opening wide, and said, "Neach-coise-achd ùine," which was Gaelic for Time Walker.

"Yes," Helen answered. An almost instant connection was made between the two, one powerful witch to another.

"You have lived many lives throughout time. Are you bana-bhuidseach neach-gleidhidh? The guardian of witches?"

"Yes, I have been called that before."

The old woman bent her head down into the lowest bow that her crooked back would allow.

"It is an honor to assist you. Is there anything else I can get for you?" she asked as she carefully filled a paper bag up with the herbs Helen had brought to the desk.

Helen considered for a second whether or not this woman was old enough to recall the magic of wishing wells. It would significantly boost the strength of her magic and keep her protection charm fully bound to her if she had water from one.

"Your shop is wonderful, the best I've seen. You wouldn't happen to have any water bottled from the old Clootie well in Inverness, would you?"

The old woman hobbled away, disappearing into a small room in the back. She reappeared with a small leather bag which she placed on the counter and untied. The leather fell down around a small tear-shaped bottle fashioned with an old cork top.

"I believe you require a powerful protection charm. Your current cloaking spell is not completely functional. It has fissures in it that can be seen through with a skilled eye. Have you been using old herbs in your spellcraft?"

"Yes, there aren't many fresh herbs at this time of year to forage. I'm glad you warned me, it's imperative that I stay hidden for the time being."

"I thought so. I have something better than the Clootie well water." The old woman picked up the tear-shaped bottle and placed it in Helen's hands. "This is water from an island on Loch Lomond in which a very powerful energy line exists. The ley line runs right through a stream that stands at the intersection of two extremely powerful energy points. This water will boost any spell a hundredfold."

"Ley lines? My friend Artemas told me about them a long time ago. He would sometimes take months out of the year to journey to the connecting points to do energy work or charge objects."

"Yes, they are very powerful. In fact, many of us believe they are the roots of magic. The midpoints are like charging stations for us. Many healers choose to live close to or within the lines for that very reason."

Helen flashed back to the bathroom and the cryptic message on the mirror. *The power to defeat evil lies within the lines.* The ley lines.

At that, she knew just who the ghost was in the cottage—it was Artemas. She couldn't help but smile. He was still there guiding her through this whole thing.

"You're absolutely right. Would you be willing to sell me the water?" Helen asked.

"I'm sorry, but this is not for sale. It is a gift from me to you," the old woman said. "Now, take a sip of this before you leave the shop. My wards are up and you are unseen here, but as soon as you leave you will be visible again to whoever you are hiding from."

"You have no idea how much this has helped me already. I hope to live up to the name Bana-bhuidseach neach-gleidhidh," Helen said, reaching out and taking the old woman's hands. Closing her eyes, she sent a soft glow of magic drifting outwards and into the woman's body. When she let go, the woman seemed to have aged in reverse ten years.

The woman looked up at her with her pale blue eyes and uttered the words, "Thank you."

Helen smiled and then paid the old woman for her herbs.

Before she left the shop, Helen turned back to see the old woman going back to her daily tasks as if their conversation had never happened. She pulled the cork out of the bottle and took a tiny sip of the ley line water. As she swallowed it, she could feel its power moving into each of her cells, rejuvenating them with magic. She capped it and stuck it back into the inside of her jacket.

Connor gave her a look of confusion, to which she just smiled and said, "Fill you in later."

Chapter Thirty-Six

GLASGOW

The traffic was heavy going into the city and what should have taken only forty-five minutes took upwards of an hour and a half. Helen didn't mind as it gave her the opportunity to fill Connor in on everything that happened in the shop.

Once the traffic let up, Connor was able to find a parking spot and they decided to walk the rest of the way to visit his friend.

Being late in the autumn, the days grew dark early and by three o'clock the sun was making its way to bed. The city was a harsh contrast to the open fields and forests surrounding Fernbeg; the gray of all the buildings, roads, and sidewalks mixed in with the sky left an altogether depressing feel. The last time she had been to the city was back in the 1940s. At that point in time, Glasgow was dealing with overpopulation due to the industrial revolution and the streets were a complete mess. Thankfully, it was much cleaner now and no longer tarnished by slums and poverty as it had been decades ago. However, she still did not enjoy the smells of the city—between the exhaust and variety of food odors, the air left her feeling sick.

How had she come to this? Only a few short months ago, she was a city girl, thriving on the sounds and smells of the busy life the city held. Now all she wanted to do was get the hell out of here.

Connor's friend lived in a shared flat on Argyle Street above a small pizzeria. They buzzed him from the downstairs intercom and waited for the door to open. A broken elevator sign greeted them as they entered the building, so they had to walk up three flights of stairs. The third-floor hallway was stained with an array of colors and a foul smell of stale urine and vomit hung in the air. Helen gave Connor a raised eyebrow.

"Well, he isn't a friend so much as an acquaintance," he said, as he knocked on the door.

Helen felt like she was doing some sort of shady drug deal, standing in the open hallway, waiting on this stranger to let them in and give them illegal fireworks. It took only a minute for the door to swing open. There in the doorway stood an overly thin man with skin the color of paper, covered in light brown freckles, and hair as orange as a carrot. His face broke away into a wide, toothy grin upon seeing Connor and he pulled him in for a bro hug. They patted each other on the back before breaking free and the man glanced over at Helen.

"Eh, Connor, and who might this beauty be?"

"Ewan, meet Helen. Helen, Ewan."

"Hi, nice to meet you, Ewan," Helen said with a forced smile.

"Oh, come in and get out of that nasty hallway. Our neighbor is a complete alchy, he's pissed and puked more times in that bloody hallway than we can count. Nasty bastard," Ewan said, waving them through the door.

The flat was quite substantial and consisted of a large kitchen common room area with three doorways off the far ends of the room. A large, worn red couch sat centerfold in the common room alongside two black leather armchairs. '90s movie posters in thin, black metal frames adorned the walls, 100% bachelor pad. Helen and Connor sat on the couch and Ewan sat opposite them in one of the chairs.

"Can I get ye some tea?" Ewan asked.

"No, we're good, thanks, Ewan. We actually can't stay long, I'll need to get back to the farm so I can help Granda with the sheep."

"Ah, that's right. I forgot you're a country boy these days. Let me just get your stuff."

He went through one of the doors at the far end of the room. When he came back out, he was carrying a small black duffle bag.

Oh good God, Helen thought. It was like something out of a movie from one of the posters that hung on the wall. Ewan walked over and unzipped the bag to show Connor. His eyes lit up and a boyish grin broke across his face at the sight of all the fireworks in the bag.

"So, you're sure all you want are the cherry bombs? I have bottle rockets, Roman candles, and even some flying fish in here. I'll give ye a good price on the lot."

Helen looked over at Connor as he started to open his mouth and shot him a *Don't you dare* look.

"No, just the cherry bombs will do, but give me all you've got of them," Connor said.

Ewan took out a small container the size of a box of chocolates and handed it to him.

"Forty quid, mate."

Connor dug into the back pocket of his jeans and handed the small wad of cash to Ewan.

"Thanks a lot, Ewan, I owe ye one. I wish we could catch up and have a pint but we have to be going," Connor said as he stood up and tucked the box into the front part of his jacket.

"Next time you're in town, ring me up and we can go down to the pub," Ewan said.

As they exited the flat back into the rancid hallway, Helen turned and said thank you to Ewan.

"My pleasure. Nice to meet you, Helen. You guys have fun blowing stuff up now," he called back.

Once the door closed, Helen slugged Connor in the shoulder. "What did you tell him?"

"Owww! Nothing. What did you think he would think we were doing with these, lighting birthday candles?" he said, rubbing his shoulder.

It was getting late, but they had one last stop to hit before they headed back to Oban. Connor flagged down a cab and took her to one of the nicest art supply shops she had ever been in, Cass Art. It was small but delightful and had everything she needed. It didn't take her long to fill her basket up with paints, a few brushes, and a new watercolor pad. She could have spent the rest of her day there but that would probably have resulted in also spending the rest of the money she had in the bank, which wasn't much. So she decided to just get the essentials and promised herself to come back and browse the shop some more one of these days when the fate of the world wasn't hanging on her shoulders.

As they were leaving the shop, Helen had an odd feeling come over her, as if someone was standing right in front of her looking her dead in the eyes. The feeling moved and glided around her like a predator circling its prey.

Then she saw them, just for a split second—a set of black eyes. A feeling of utter dread hit her full-on when she realized that her cloaking spell had broken for a brief moment and she was seen.

She had completely lost track of time and hadn't drunk any more of the ley line water since they got to the city. She quickly reached into her jacket pocket and grabbed the bottle, taking a larger sip than she had in Luss. Then she took hold of Connor's arm and started walking as fast as her legs would carry her, away from the spot they had just been.

"What's going on?" Connor asked, as he tried to keep up with Helen's pace.

"I was spotted. My cloaking spell broke for a second and I was spotted," she said breathlessly.

"By who, Margaret? Is she here in the city?"

"No, much worse, it was a demon that spotted me."

"Holy shit! How could you tell?"

"Well, the black eyes burning a hole in my soul was a pretty good giveaway. The ley line water patched the break in the cloaking spell for now, but I can't be sure how long it will last. We need to get out of the city—now!"

Connor grabbed a taxi and they got back to the truck quickly. They were able to get out of the city much faster than they'd gotten in, and before Helen knew it they had broken free of the paved landscape and were back in the crisp countryside, but the darkening skies outside the truck's windows felt watchful and menacing.

"This changes everything," she said. "There's no doubt Margaret will know I'm not a child by the end of the day. It's imperative that my cloaking spell does not break again until the solstice. That's still eight days from now and she'll be looking for me."

"Is there a chance the demon you came across won't know her or you?"

"Unlikely. From everything I've gathered over the years, she is second in command. It's possible that most of the demons go to her for orders. Finding me would be major brownie points for the demon and it's doubtful they would pass up on the opportunity to impress her."

"Well then, from this point on, it's defensive actions only for you. You stay hidden and I'll try my best to get everything done on my end without drawing any attention."

They drove back the rest of the way in silence, late afternoon now stepping into the darkness of night. Helen's heart raced, thinking of all the what ifs. What if they hadn't stopped at the apothecary first? What if they had skipped going to the art store? What if she hadn't used the old herbs for her cloaking spell? Her thoughts piled up into a head full of doubt and worry. If she had misstepped this early in the game, was she really up for taking Margaret and the demon on? She needed to get back to the cottage as quickly as possible to find a way to talk to Artemas.

Chapter Thirty-Seven

THE RABBIT

Two days had passed since the trip to Glasgow and Helen had zero luck contacting Artemas. She tried to communicate through a candle-lit circle on the floor of the bathroom, Tarot cards, and even an old Ouija board Connor found at the farm, but nothing worked. She tried to pick up on his energy, but it was as if he wasn't there anymore. She feared he had completed his task and ascended to the Summerlands.

She hadn't left the cottage since they got back. Each day, she took small sips of the ley line water to keep her cloaking spell strong. It was best to stay out of the public eye for the time being, just in case. She hoped Margaret wouldn't believe the demon since she wouldn't be able to sense her any more than she already had, now that the spell had been patched. But she didn't want to push how long it would be before curiosity got the best of Margaret and she came looking.

With such little time left, she decided she needed to change her priorities and start researching the ley lines. If Artemas reached out to tell her about them, they must be a vital part of something he discovered after her death as Abigail. She remembered Artemas briefly telling her about them back in London, so she must have written about them in her spell book at some point during their time there. She went into the library and pulled down *Animal Farm* and ran her fingers down the pages, gently fanning them out. Closing her eyes, she thought of the time and place where Artemas had first told her about the ley lines. When she opened her eyes, her fingers lay on a page with a drawing of Scotland. Running the length and width were lines that crossed each other, creating a polygon. A set of numbers was written below with a note that said *The center of the sacred pentagram of Scotland*. Under the picture she had written:

Ley lines are straight alignments of earth energy that connect ancient sites. The most potent energy source for magic is here within the center of the connecting lines. At this point, magic can be increased and spells can be amplified. In order to obtain the energy from these points, you must go to them at dawn, as the sun begins to rise. Create an outdoor altar and ask for permission to use the lines' energy before performing the ritual you intend to execute. Once you have completed your spell, leave an offering to the Goddess. There have been tales of wise people who have visited the lines and left with powers like the gods. Beware: only those of adequate magical training can withstand the direct energy from these lines and hold it within them. Trying to hold the energy without the proper knowledge can result in instant death.

This was what Artemas was trying to tell her. Not only did she have the ability to amplify her spell using ley lines, but if she used her training she would be able to increase her own magical abilities as well. She was going to need to figure out just where that pentagram of Scotland was. The drawing was old and it was hard to tell just where the line actually lay on a modern map as there were no names or landmarks clearly identified. The only writing on the drawing was a string of random numbers scrolled down the side of the paper. Maybe Connor could help—with his background in geology it was likely he would recognize the area. However, this would need to wait until morning.

She pulled the copy of *Demonology* out from under the planter and carefully removed the weathered parchment. She laid it out over the top of the book and read the ritual for demon exorcism for what must have been the twentieth time. There was no space for even the tiniest mistake. As she read it, she recited it line by line.

"In charcoal, draw a circle on the ground and cross in the center, then repeat with salt. Lure the intended into the center of the circle. Once they have entered they will not be able to leave. Then place four bowls on each of the points of the cross. In the bowl to the north, burn boneset; in the bowl to the south, burn clove; to the east, burn betelnut; and to the west, burn chrysanthemum. Walk the circle, starting from the north and moving to the east and around. Circle three times repeating the incantation in Latin: *Exardescat e tenebris lumen, neque rursus malum eiiciatur. Per ipsum dei potentiam ad infernum redeas.* Amen."

The incantation, translated to English, read: Let the light burn out of darkness, and let no evil be cast out again. By the power of God you may return to hell. Amen.

"Once the words are spoken three times," she continued, "turn and walk the circle backward, smothering the smoke from each bowl as you go. Once the last bowl has been smothered, make the sign of the cross in the air in front of the intended."

She had all the ingredients she needed. The hardest part of this was going to be not only tricking Margaret but also tricking the demon. She needed him to show himself just long enough to get him into the circle. Once she performed the exorcism, there would still be Margaret herself to deal with and she was a worthy foe, even without the demon in her corner. Defeating her required a spell powerful enough to break her eternal life bond. For this, Helen needed three very specific things: a compass made of silver, a timepiece from the decade when Margaret was born, and a mirror.

Artemas had found the spell in an old book written in Copenhagen before the 1500s. He transcribed it for her into the Orwell book on the back of the ley line drawing. She already possessed two of these things but was lacking the timepiece. A watch from the 1500s was a rarity—at that time they had just been invented and were primarily made in Italy. The ones that had survived were mostly in museums, private collections, or sold at prices that would be too far out of her reach. This was definitely an obstacle, but not one she couldn't figure a way around. It was going to require a bit of sneaky magic that was surely unethical, but for a good cause.

Her thoughts were interrupted by Storm, who came into the library looking almost double the size he'd been a week ago. It was like having a small pony in the cottage. Thankfully, he was a gentle giant, maneuvering his way around the place without knocking things over. He was now the spitting image of his ancestor from her time as Freya. His eyes looked back at her with not only protective instinct, but love. He had been her pup and she'd raised him into this giant he was now, and she loved him fiercely. She knew that when it came down to it, he would protect her at all cost, and it made her feel safe at the cottage.

Storm stood beside her, looking up, tail wagging. He seemed to know just when he needed to interrupt her deep thoughts and bring her back to reality.

"Oh alright, I guess we can go for a quick walk. Let me get my coat."

It had snowed the night before, covering everything in a thin layer of white. As they stepped out into the cold air, Helen pulled her knitted hat down over her ears and tugged the zipper to the very top of her jacket. At that, Storm took off running and jumping about in the freshly fallen snow. It had been cold enough in the night to freeze the top layer, leaving a nice crunch to each step they took.

Storm ran up the backfield toward the rowan tree and Helen followed a little way behind. As they rounded the top of the field, things began to look more like the tundra with its frost-covered plants and bushes. Even the tree branches were covered in a fine layer of ice, making the edge of the woods near the rowan look more magical. The rowan stood tall with its branches umbrellaed out, leaving a small patch of earth exposed, void of snow. As Helen stepped beneath the branches, a small rabbit that looked like the one from the loch hopped out from behind the tree. Storm immediately ran up to the rabbit, who stood still, not even moving a whisker. Storm turned back to look at Helen, as if asking her for permission, and then did the oddest thing: he sat down next to the rabbit under the tree.

Helen stood there and stared, the scene that lay before her mimicking the painting in the cottage. Then she noticed something—the eyes of the rabbit looked familiar to her. She knew those eyes.

The wind blew and small bits of icy snow rained down from the tree branches like tiny crystals in the air. As they landed on the ground around the wolf and the rabbit, the rabbit moved and twisted in an unnatural way, bending with the light around it until it had transformed into a beautiful woman in a deep-red, velvet cloak. It was Mary, her long red hair flowing down her shoulders just as Helen remembered it.

Tears formed in Helen's eyes as she stared at her best friend. Even after all this time, she hadn't forgotten a single detail about her.

"Mary, how are you here?" Helen asked.

"My beautiful friend, I wish I was truly here with you, this is but an echo of myself."

"Was it you down at the loch that led me to the berries?"

"Yes, I was going to show myself to you that day, but you had a friend with you," Mary said with a smile.

"Yes, that was Connor."

"I know, he is what we have been waiting for all these years."

"What do you mean?"

"You would not truly be able to break this loop without someone to break it for."

Helen smiled. She knew what Mary meant. Out of all the lifetimes she had lived, she'd never let herself love again until now. She wanted more in this life other than just revenge.

"Yes, you're right. This is the first time I truly wanted more than just retribution. I'm ready to love again. But I only have a few more days until the solstice and still have so much I need to figure out. I can't fail this time around, Mary."

"You must have faith in yourself. You have everything you require. All you have to do now is gather your strength and courage."

Mary's specter began to fade, flickering like an old motion picture.

"Wait, no, don't go," Helen said, reaching out for her friend. "There are so many things I want to know about your life. I have so much to ask you."

"I cannot stay. Everything you need will find its way to you. There are much greater forces at work than you know, trust in that. I love you, my sweet friend." Mary smiled one last time, looked down at Storm, and said, "Good boy," then vanished into the crystalized ice floating in the stillness of the air.

It took Helen a few moments to gain her composure as she stood there staring at the spot where her friend had just been. Storm came over and gave her arm a nudge. She bent down and grabbed the wolf around the neck, hugging him.

"Thank you," she said, kissing the top of his head. After a minute, she stood and they made their way back toward the cottage in the cold winter's afternoon sun, casting long shadows across the land as they walked. Helen only gazed back once to see if her friend was still there, then turned back and kept moving forward.

Chapter Thirty-Eight

DREAMWALKING

She spent the remainder of the day reading and checking emails. She had put it off for two weeks now and decided it was now time to plunge in and see what everyone had to say. Her mother was the first to respond back. She was over the moon that Helen had finally found someone but wished it wasn't in another country. She promised to send over her Christmas gift and said they would come to visit her in the spring when the weather was nicer.

Kevin was next. He bawled her out on more than one account, but finished off the email with an "I love you" and advice to drop the farm boy and come back home because he missed her.

The last person she heard back from was her boss. He was sorry to hear she was leaving and thanked her for her years of dedicated work. He even told her they would send her a check for the last few sick days she had left over for the year. It was short, sweet, and to the point.

Now that that bandage was ripped off, she didn't need to worry about her life back in America—for now at least.

Connor called that night to check in and tell her that everything was set for tomorrow night. They had planned out every detail, right down to what Connor was going to wear.

"Everything is a go for Operation Chocolate-Covered Cherry," he said with a chuckle.

This was their little joke. Operation Chocolate-Covered Cherry was Connor's idea for a code name and Helen couldn't disappoint him. This whole thing was really bringing out the boy in him. She thought it was kinda cute.

Before she went to bed, she brewed herself a strong cup of tea composed of mugwort, valerian root, and mullein. The mugwort and valerian root was to aid in dreaming and the mullein was to protect her from unwanted evil that may try and work its way into the dream world to find her. She also added in a few pieces of cherry bark for invisibility, to keep her hidden while she was dreaming.

Her plan was to try and break into the ethereal realm in one last attempt at contacting Artemas. Ever since she was seen by the demon in Glasgow, she had made sure she kept herself from dreaming by drinking a special tonic each night. The dream world was one of the easiest ways into someone's mind and she had made sure that hers was locked tight. Breaking through the dream realm and into the ethereal world was extremely risky. She was hoping that with the aid of the mullein and cherry bark, she would be able to slip through, unseen.

After finishing her tea, she went into her bedroom and tied the hag stone around her neck for a bit of extra protection. Then she called Storm up onto the bed, as she wanted him standing guard over her body while she dreamwalked. She laid her head down on her pillow and pulled the old worn quilt up to her chin. The blanket smelled of lavender and wet dog, a combination that would not be pleasing to most, but to her it smelt like home. Soon she began to drift off, her eyes closing and her body and mind giving in to the tea's potent mix.

The sky was cloudless and the rush of running water was so loud that Helen could hardly hear herself think. As she looked around, she saw a vast loch with a large stream running reverse into it. There was a footbridge over the stream leading to a path that went into a wooded area on the far side of the loch. As she walked over the bridge, she looked down at the water lapping over rocks and logs, the strength and power of it not being stopped by anything thrown in its way.

On the other side of the bridge, there was a large patch of heather growing. Its bright purple flowers reached for the sky, for the energy of the sun. She examined the forest path before entering. It was packed down and looked well-traveled. A thin layer of moss coated the ground, giving a soft squish to each step. The forest was thick with mighty oaks, standing tall above the forest floor.

As she journeyed down the path, she spotted a clearing. At the end was a little wooden cabin with a thin stream of white smoke trailing its way out of the chimney. There was a beautiful garden to the side full of flowering herbs. The smells brought her back to when she was Freya as a little girl. Her mother had a garden just like it, a live-growing apothecary.

She walked up and knocked on the small oak door. Beyond, she heard footsteps, and then the door swung open. There in the doorway stood a handsome man, rugged looking but not large, standing just a few inches taller than her. It only took a moment looking into his eyes to recognize him—it was Artemas.

"Well, it took you long enough. I expected you days ago. What held you up?" he asked.

"Artemas?" she asked, staring at a younger version of her old friend.

"Yup, you guessed it, but it's me at my peak. One of the many benefits of being dead—you get to return to the self you loved most," he said, patting his chest.

She stepped forward and pulled him into a fierce hug. "Oh, how I have missed you, my friend," she said, letting him go and stepping back to look at him once again.

"Now, tell me what the holdup was," he said.

Swinging the door wide, he gestured for her to enter the little one-room cabin. They walked over to a small table that faced a fireplace and sat down.

"It's a long story. I tried to contact you via candlelight circle, Tarot, even through a Hasbro Ouija board that Connor found in the barn. I was holding off dreamwalking as my last option. I was seen briefly by a demon a few days back. My cloaking spell was compromised by old herbs and it cracked. Thank goodness I went to the apothecary in Luss right before and the old woman there gave me a bottle of ley line water. It was then that I figured out your cryptic message. Next time, just spell it out, okay?"

"Oh, that's not good. Do you think the demon knew who you were?"

"I have no idea, and I didn't stick around long enough to find out. I took another swig of the water and booked it back to Fernbeg. I've been keeping my spell juiced with the water to make sure I stay hidden."

"It's only a matter of time before she goes looking for you

there. She knows it's your go-to homebase. You need to leave as soon as possible. Stay with the McKenzies, there's a better vantage point there and you will have others to keep watch."

"You're right. It's time to switch things up a bit. I need to stay under the radar for three more days. I looked back at my journal from our time in the forties and read a little that you taught me about ley lines, but I still don't quite understand. Should I go there first, charge myself and my spells, or should I get Margaret to go there and complete the ritual at the spot?"

"Loch Moy is where you will go to charge yourself and the spells. The energy is at its peak during the hours of dawn. You must perform the ritual to increase your power at the very moment the sun begins to break the surface of the sky. If you miss that moment, the transfer of power will not be complete. After that, you can charge your spells and any objects you might need for protection. The power you drain from the lines will only stay with you until the next dawn so you must go on the morning of the solstice. This is going to be your biggest advantage, other than her not knowing you're an adult. She knows that you are a powerful witch, but she won't expect the god-like powers you will have."

"I'm so worried that something will go wrong and this whole thing will have been for nothing. I almost blew it using those aged herbs for my cloaking spell. I can only pray that the demon who saw me didn't realize who I was."

"Don't look back, you've learned from your mistakes. It would have been much worse if you had used the old herbs at the ritual and they only half worked. You made the right mistake at the right time."

"I know. I wish we'd been able to defeat her together in forty-seven. It's just me this time, magic has been almost forgotten in the modern world, and I have no one with powers to help me in this battle," she told him, worry breaking through her words.

"I understand. But keep in mind that while the people you do have on your side may not have magic, they do have love for you, and that, my friend, is just as powerful," Artemas said, resting his hand on her shoulder.

At that moment, the light outside started to flicker and the sky grew crimson. The wind began blowing fiercely, toppling trees like dominoes. Artemas looked at Helen with wide eyes.

"They found you. It's time to go. Wake up!"

Helen quickly closed her eyes and tried to close off her mind from the dream. When she opened her eyes again, she was still there, stuck in the dream realm. The cabin walls began to pull apart and darkness started to creep its way in.

"Be the water, push through, you make your own path, you are powerful, you are strong! WAKE UP!" Artemas yelled.

She squeezed her eyes shut once again and attempted to find her way back. Back to what? Back to Connor! And with that, she opened her eyes and sat bolt upright in bed, Storm standing over her with a look of concern in his eyes. She noticed her face was soaking wet and surmised that he had been licking her in an attempt to wake her up.

Shaken, she looked around her bedroom. Everything seemed fine, none of her wards were down and the cottage was still. She glanced at the clock, which showed 5:24 a.m. She wasn't about to go back to bed so she got up to brew a strong pot of coffee.

Connor had planned to be there at 8:00 a.m. to go over the plan one more time before they executed it that night. His arrival couldn't come soon enough. Helen decided to pass the time by taking a shower and packing up all the things that would be going with her to the farm.

After emerging from the shower, she walked to the mirror, half expecting to see a message from Artemas, but only a thin, untouched layer of steam clung to the mirror.

She went room by room, gathering her things, erasing herself from the premises. By the time she made it to the library, she had filled her bag and was now carrying a cardboard box. All the journals found their way inside, along with the book about demonology and all of her disguised spell books. She tossed a few random books on the top of the box, just to make it look a little less suspect in case anyone peeked inside. From the view above, it looked to be an ordinary box full of unextraordinary books. Nothing that anyone would look twice at.

She walked out of the library, then turned back around. These four walls lined with books were her sanctuary, the one place in the world she loved most. She looked on as if for the last time, bowed her head, and whispered a thank you to the room before closing the door.

As she walked away down the hall and into the sitting room, she felt a sadness fall down around her like light snow on a winter's day. It was subtle at first but gradually built up and weighed on her. She wasn't quite sure if it was because she was leaving Fernbeg or because after this it might never be quite the same for her again. This had been her home in every one of her lives, and each time she'd returned, she'd added little things here and there. It was like her journals, a part of her story. There was always a chance she would complete her mission and also die at the same time, ending the cycle and never returning again.

A tear slipped down her cheek and hit the hardwood floor, leaving a dark spot on the wood. It spread out, darkening a larger spot than the tear could have possibly made. It began to twist, turn, and loop, moving like an invisible paintbrush, laying wide strokes out upon the woodgrain. Helen looked on in wonder as her tear transformed the grains of wood into a beautiful silhouette of a woman with long flowing hair. Standing next to her was a wolf. It looked to be a story older than time, told in the workings of nature. It was the cottage's way of letting her know that she would always be here, no matter what may come.

Chapter Thirty-Nine

TIMEPIECE

Connor arrived a little before eight and Helen greeted him in the doorway, eager to show him the drawing in the journal and get his opinion on where the location might be. She needed to figure out where the ley lines met in order to gauge the power the final spell required.

"I can't quite tell where this is," she said, pointing down at the hand-drawn map in the book. "I thought you might recognize the shapes of the geographical layout in it."

Connor pulled the book closer and looked at it, turning it almost completely upside down. Then he stopped and looked up at her.

"Sorry, I have no idea where this would be just by the drawing, but see these two strings of numbers right here?" He pointed below the picture. She had noticed the numbers the night before but hadn't a clue what they meant. "These numbers right here are geographic coordinates. The first number in the set is the latitude and the second is the longitude. We should be able to figure out exactly where this is. Just give me a minute."

He ran outside to his truck and came back in with his laptop bag in hand. Setting it up on the coffee table, he typed the numbers into a web browser and in a few clicks, they had the exact location Artemas had wanted her to go to—the south side of Loch Moy.

"Looks like the place these lines cross is at the edge of the south end of Loch Moy," he said, an accomplished smile on his face.

"This was a huge help, Connor, thank you."

"Happy to help. I'm glad I could put my degree to a bit of good use," he said with a smile. His expression quickly changed as he noticed her bags packed up and resting against the wall by the door. "Were you planning on leaving?" he asked, a hurt look crossing his face.

"Yes, actually. I wanted to talk to you about that. Would it be okay with you and your grandfather if I came and stayed at the farm for a few days? I don't think it's a good idea for me to stay here any longer. If Margaret gets suspicious this will be the first place she'll look. With all of us there I stand a better chance of knowing if she's coming. It'll only be until after the solstice," she reassured him.

"Of course, you're always welcome. Anytime." A wave of relief washed over his face and he let out a breath as if he had been holding it, waiting for her answer.

Helen stood up on her tippytoes and kissed him. She had seen the worry in his eyes when he thought that she might be leaving and she wanted to reassure him that his arms were the only place she wanted to be. He swept her up off the floor and spun her around as they kissed, softly landing her feet back on the ground as their lips parted.

Connor helped bring her belongings to the truck as she called Storm to follow them out. Closing the door, she grabbed her staff from where it rested against the cold stone wall, erasing the final trace of her at Fernbeg.

When they arrived at the farm, Storm jumped out of the truck and went chasing chickens around the barnyard. This, in turn, caused Connor to chase after him, which was an amusing few minutes for Helen and Seamus, but left Connor tired out and a little pissed off.

Once they had Storm inside and away from the farm animals, they all sat down for a lovely breakfast of sausage and eggs Seamus had cooked up for them. With everything going on, it was a few days since Helen had eaten a proper meal and just having the warm food in her belly was lifting her spirits.

"I have to head up to the backfield and nail down a few new posts. I'll be back in an hour and then we can go over our plans for the night," Connor said, giving her a wink then grabbing his coat and heading off. They hadn't told Seamus about their plans because they didn't want him to worry, plus Connor was afraid he'd want to join them if he found out what they were doing. After all, he was adamantly opposed to the facility going up.

"So, it looks like it's just us here for a bit. Shall we go and sit by the fire and have some tea?" Seamus asked.

"That sounds lovely. Let me get the tea and you go warm up the fire."

While Helen waited for the kettle to boil, she opened the cupboard under the sink and reached her hand in, running her fingers across the triquetra carved into the stone. This was where it all began, where the cycle of reincarnation started when she had cast that spell so many centuries ago.

"Do you wish you never cast that spell?" Seamus said, startling her. He was standing there in the kitchen doorway, looking in. Helen stood up and smiled at him. She knew his family must have kept her and Tomas's tale alive in stories told to children in the family. It had become a legend but stayed true to its original tale.

"No, I've never regretted it. My soul would never have been at rest and I would have walked this earth for millennia."

"You know, I knew who you were from the moment Connor brought you down to the farm. I remembered you from when I was a little boy. I was a bit confused about why you didn't seem to know yourself though."

"It's a long story, but trust me, it was the only way I could break into this life with the chance of it being the last."

The loud whistling of the kettle interrupted their conversation. Helen filled up the tea tray and carried it into the living room. By now, the fire was roaring and the pop and crackle of burning wood filled the air. The cozy space was warm and smelled of wood smoke, cedar, and stale pipe tobacco. Helen set the tray down on the coffee table and took a seat on the couch while Seamus sat in his armchair by the fire. Pouring out the tea, she asked him if he knew of any antique dealers in the area.

"There's a couple in Rothesay on Bute and one or two on Iona that are worth looking at. What are you in search of?" he asked.

"I'm looking for a type of pocket watch, one of the earliest made, sometime between fifteen sixty and sixteen hundred. The watch is most likely held by collectors or museums, but I figured I would give a few antique markets a go, just in case one had been overlooked."

"I think I may be able to help you in that department," Seamus said. "The local museum has a timepiece said to belong to one of the magistrates from back in the early fifteen hundreds. It's kept in a glass case in the back room along with the artifacts that were found at McCaig's Tower. My friend, Susan, runs the afternoon tours there. I can have her show it to you if you like."

"Really? That would be fantastic, but I'm not sure involving your friend is the best option because I'll need to borrow it for the night. I'm not sure she'd agree with that."

"Ahh, I see. So is this something you need for a spell?"

"Yes, and it's a very important part. If I don't have a timepiece from that era, I won't be able to complete the spell without it. It's quite an essential part for ridding this world of Margaret and the evil that follows her."

"Well, in that case, it just so happens that I run a bi-monthly lecture there and have a key to the facility, which may or may not be on my keychain by the door," he said, looking at her and winking.

"Oh, I see. That is a very interesting fact. Thank you for the information," she said, flashing him a conspiratorial smile.

It wasn't long before Connor was back from his afternoon chores and they began going over the plans for the night. They set all the papers up on the kitchen table and worked out their plan in hushed voices so that Seamus didn't hear. Connor had gotten blueprints of the Regmata building from a friend who worked in public zoning. He laid them out on the other papers on the table and circled his route with a red pen.

"Here's where the cameras are. I'll hit them with spray paint as I pass each one." He pointed at three red circles, indicating a camera positioned over the door into the facility and two in the hallways between the door and the bathroom. "This is the closest bathroom to the exit, so I decided on this one. It should only take me eight minutes in and out, tops." He ran his finger from the bathroom down the red line to the exit. "Once the cherry bombs are lit, I'll only have about a minute to get out of the building before they go off. It's going to be cutting it close, but if I run fast, I think I can do it," he said, a grin spanning from ear to ear.

"You're really loving all of this, aren't you?" Helen said, giving him a smile.

"Duh! This is like every guy's dream come true. Sneak into the evil science lab and blow it up, or at least blow up its toilets. Be the hero and then get the girl."

"You already have the girl," she said as she leaned in and kissed him.

"And that's why I'm doing it!" he said, after breaking their kiss.

Even though Connor was doing his best to make the situation light, Helen couldn't help but worry. He wasn't James Bond, after all, and had never done anything like this outside of a video game, but she knew he would give it his all.

Chapter Forty

CHOCOLATE-COVERED CHERRY BOMB

It was 4:45 and the sun had set behind the hills, leaving a thin orange outline along the ridge. Connor had the truck packed up and came in to get Helen. He was dressed head to toe in black.

"Are you two kids going to rob a bank or something?" Seamus joked.

"No, Granda. I'm taking Helen out to eat at that cool new pub in Inveraray tonight. This is me trying to be stylish."

"I'm sorry to say, son, you're doing a terrible job."

Helen laughed, then said goodnight to Seamus and followed Connor out to the truck.

They had only been driving for about fifteen minutes when Connor began to get the jitters.

"Can you double check that I grabbed both cans of spray

paint and make sure the box with the cherry bombs is in the bag?" Connor asked. His voice filled the car with an anxious energy.

Helen sat with the bag containing all the items he needed on her lap. They'd gone through it twice before leaving to make sure they hadn't overlooked anything. He knew everything was there, but his nerves were getting the best of him.

"Are you sure you're up for this? It's okay if you want to wait and plan out something different. I don't want you doing anything you're not sure of."

"No, I've got this. Don't you worry," he said with false optimism in his voice.

"Well, if it makes you feel any better, your wingman's a badass witch who can whip up a storm in a jiff if things get out of hand," she said, trying to help smooth his nerves.

He smiled back and seemed to calm down, but rest of the drive was spent in complete silence.

They parked a block away from the building and walked in the shadows of the trees to the back entrance. It had been an overcast day and the night sky still hung onto the thick layer of clouds, not allowing any light from the moon to guide them. They avoided the two lights that lit up the back parking lot and found a spot to hide in the bushes near the edge of the property.

"I completely forgot about the car park being lit," Connor said with nervousness in his voice.

Helen looked up at him with a sweet smile and snapped her fingers. As she did, the sound of two bulbs popping echoed through the empty parking lot and everything went dark.

"And that's why you're my girl," he said.

"Oh really, I'm your girl, huh?"

He kissed her cheek, pulled down his hat over his hair, and slipped out of the bushes into the dark lot. She could make out his figure running into the loading dock area and then he was out of sight. Helen wished she could do more to help, but it was too dangerous to use any of her magic at this point. Her cloaking spell was growing weaker as the solstice approached, and any spell larger than a basic charm was risky. One false move and Margaret would be alerted.

As Connor entered the loading dock, he pulled the spray paint can out of his jacket and laid a thick line of blue over the lens of the camera facing the door. Once he was sure the camera's view was blocked, he slipped out a credit card and a jackknife. He wedged the card into the crack of the door and slid it down until he hit the lock. Then he used the point of the knife to pry open the door just enough to slide the card in past the lock and *pop*! Just like that, it was unlocked and he slipped inside.

Staying close to the wall, he made his way down the hallway to where the second camera was. Pulling his hat down to cover his face, he got on his tiptoes and put another thick line of paint over the lens of the second camera. He repeated the same thing in the next hallway and then scooted himself into the bathroom.

The bathroom looked like any ordinary, stark industrial bathroom, with white walls, gray floors, and black stalls, separating the room into six pieces. A row of white porcelain sinks lined the far wall with a long mirror backsplash. It had the smell of industrial cleaner and stale shit masked by some sort of floral air freshener.

Reaching into his jacket, Connor pulled out six cherry bombs along with a lighter. Just as he was about to light the first bomb, he heard whistling coming from outside the bathroom door.

"Shit." He backed into the closest stall, jumped onto the toilet, and closed the door slowly shut, without making a sound.

The door to the bathroom swung open and he saw two black boots walk into the stall next to him. A long and loud stream of urine sounded while the man continued to whistle his tune. The toilet flushed and the man walked out, just as Connor's foot slipped into the toilet with a splash.

The whistling stopped.

Connor, heart pounding, peered out of the stall crack. The man was fiddling with something on his hip. *Holy shit, it's an armed guard*, Connor thought.

The man turned around as if to walk toward him and pulled a cell phone out of his pocket. A long cord ran up the arm of his jacket and into a pair of headphones. Then he walked right past the stall Connor occupied and to the sink to wash his hands. He went back to whistling as he dried his hands, then left the bathroom.

Connor waited a few minutes before coming out of the stall, listening to make sure the janitor was gone. Feeling his heart beating rapidly in his chest, he tried to calm himself down, then proceeded with his mission. He began lighting the cherry bombs one after another and flushing them down each of the six toilets. Once the last one was lit and flushed, he took off running as fast as he could, straight down the hallway and out the back door.

Just as his feet hit the pavement, the first explosion went off and by the time he reached Helen in the bushes, all six had exploded. They didn't stick around to see what happened next. They jumped in the truck and Connor started the engine, slowly pulling out onto the roadway like any normal car on the road, fighting the urge to step on it and peel away.

"What took you so long? I thought it was only going to be eight minutes tops? You were in there for almost fifteen. I was just about to come in after you when I saw you come running out," Helen said as she tried to catch her breath.

"Holy shit! You wouldn't believe it. I was in the bathroom

getting ready to light the first bomb when a janitor came in to use the loo. I panicked and jumped up on the toilet and my foot slipped in. I thought at first he was an armed guard and I was caught but it turned out he was just a night janitor with his headphones cranked. Never even heard a thing. I almost had a heart attack though, I swear. What a rush!"

"Oh my God, was that the squishy sound I heard when you were running back to the truck? Gross!" Helen said, looking down at Connor's shoes.

"Yeah, looks like I'm going to need a new pair of trainers."

The rest of the journey passed quietly, both of them lost in thought and trying to calm down from the adrenaline rush. Eventually, they were back at the farm, Connor pulling into the space in front of the barnyard.

"I have no doubt Margaret will be headed there before morning," he said, as they sat in the truck with the engine idling. "That had to have caused major damage to the whole plumbing system and with all the protests she won't suspect anything other than radicals trying to shut the place down."

"I hope you're right. I need her nearby on the twenty-first and that's the day after tomorrow. Let's hope this is something she'll stick around to see through," Helen said.

She wiped the steam off the inside window of the truck and looked down on the farmhouse. The soft glow of the light coming through the house's windows left a nostalgic ache in her for times past. Those four walls held many memories and stories for her, and even now, she was still here making them. She could only hope that things, this time, would turn out different.

Connor turned the engine off and reached his arm around her. He could see the sorrow in her eyes and knew that the burden she was carrying was greater than he would ever understand.

He pulled her in and she rested her head on his shoulder. They sat there in the quiet stillness of the night, looking down on the farm from the cab of the truck for a long while before heading back down to the house.

Chapter Forty-One

PEARL & PEPPER

When they entered the house, Seamus was up reading one of his treasured Sherlock Holmes books by the fire. He offered them both a cup of whiskey as a nightcap and they spent the rest of the evening having quiet conversation about the upcoming holidays and plans for the holiday market they attended each year to sell off their wool. However, worry kept Helen and Connor's minds at a distance from the conversation. They hoped the cherry bombs had done their job effectively and caused a large enough problem to summon Margaret, but they'd have to wait until the morning to find out.

When it was time for them to go to bed, Connor walked her up the stairs to the second floor. There was a large room to the right containing a queen bed, a smaller dresser, and a rocking chair by the window, overlooking the view of the mountains. An old handmade star quilt, with bright, beautiful colors, covered the bed, giving a feeling of comfort to the room. Helen's bags were sitting next to the bed, as if they had always been there.

"This will be your room. Has the best view in the house.," Connor said, looking at her for approval.

"It's lovely," she replied, as she walked in and looked around.

"My room is just down the stairs to your left, if you need me." There was a long, awkward pause before he said goodnight and turned to leave.

"Wait. Would you stay with me tonight?" she asked, catching him a bit off guard.

After this evening, her feelings for him had grown twofold. He was everything she had loved in Tomas and more. Sharing a bed tonight felt like finally giving into what she had been holding herself back from for so long—love.

"Yes, of course," he said, giving her a sweet smile. "I'm going to go back down and put some more wood on the fires and make sure the gates are all locked. A farmer's duties are never done," he said, tipping his head down as if he had a hat on, like an old cowboy. "I'll be back soon."

When he was gone, Helen paced the floor, from one side of the room and back. Each time, she looked out the window to see where he was in the barnyard. When she noticed he was coming back toward the house, she quickly undressed and threw on an old t-shirt. She looked at herself in the mirror and ran her fingers through her long hair. In the reflection behind her, she noticed there was a white candle in a pewter holder on the window-sill. With a pang, she recognized it; it had belonged to Tomas's mother. Sibeal had used it to let her know when it was safe to travel into the house while she and Mary were in hiding.

Helen picked it up and held it, admiring its simple beauty

and marveling at how well it still did its job. She searched her bag for a lighter and lit the candle. Its flame burned bright and cast flickering shadows that danced on the sloped walls of the room. She placed the holder on the dresser and sat back down on the bed. Now that she was only in a t-shirt, the room felt much colder, and she slipped herself under the thick quilt to warm up.

From downstairs, she heard the front door close and a shared goodnight between Seamus and Connor before he appeared back in the bedroom. Nervousness took over and she closed her eyes to fake being asleep but kept them open just enough to see Connor slip out of his black pants and sweater. There he stood in his boxers and t-shirt, the candlelight illuminating the hard lines of his body.

Her heart raced as he slipped into the bed next to her and rested his arm above her head. He slowly moved the hair away from her face so that he could look down upon her. She opened her eyes and looked into his, silently urging him to kiss her. A wave of lust and desire raced through her as he bent down and their lips touched. She pulled off his shirt and ran her fingers across his bare chest. He did the same in return and as their bodies met, a new chapter began, the start of a love story that was as old as time itself, pre-written in the stars. It was in that moment that everything came together, all her lives, her trials and tribulations had all been for this, to take her to this very moment in time. The moment where all her past lives and her present collided, forming a whole. They made an endless loop, intertwining their bodies and souls together.

"You're everything to me," he whispered into her ear as they made love.

"And you, to me," she whispered back.

As they spent the night in each other's arms, all thoughts of the world outside their walls melted away. For that night, it was just about them.

The next morning Helen woke to an empty bed and the smell of fresh coffee. As she made her way downstairs, she found Connor in the kitchen cooking breakfast. Storm was eagerly perched next to Connor, waiting for him to drop even a small piece of the wonderful-smelling food he was cooking. As she sat down, a steaming cup of coffee waited for her at the table next to the morning newspaper.

"Good morning, sunshine! You slept in."

Helen looked at the clock above the stove, it read 10:15 a.m.

"I guess I wore you out last night, needed that little bit of extra sleep to refuel, I suppose," he said with a laugh and a double raise of his eyebrows.

"Oh shut up," she said, throwing a piece of toast crust at him from across the room. Storm ran across the floor to retrieve the treat with a look of satisfaction beaming from his eyes as he gobbled it up. "Why did you let me sleep in so long?"

"I figured you needed it. It's been a crazy couple of days and you have a lot to do in the next twenty-four hours. You need all the energy you can get."

"You're probably right. Where's your grandfather?"

"Oh, he went into town this morning. Said he had some errands to run. It's the first time he's left the house this early in months. I think maybe he wanted to give us the morning alone," Connor said, handing Helen a plate with fried eggs and two large sausages.

He sat down with a plate of his own and began to eat.

"Did you see the paper?" he said, flipping it over.

A headline read: *Protests gone postal. Regmata industries took a hit last night after vandals blew up the east wing lavatories. Pro-*

testers have picketed every week at the facility since the large corporate company made its home in the small country town of Inveraray this April.

"Can you believe that? We made the front page!" Connor said, a wide grin on his face as he bit into a slice of toast.

"Yeah, that's great, but we need to know if it was enough to get her here."

"I know, I'm going to make a few calls. I have a friend who works for the local police. I'll see if he has any info he can share. I planned to make a drive-by later on just to check things out."

"Bad idea. If anyone saw the truck last night, and then you drive by today, they may get suspicious. We can't risk that right now."

"You're right. It's going to have to be all recon from here then," Connor said, looking slightly disappointed.

After they finished eating, Connor handed Helen an old pair of jeans and a large barn jacket and requested she meet him in the barn in ten minutes. She did as he asked and bundled herself in layers before putting on the oversized jacket and heading out of the house. But before she left, she reached into her bag and took a small sip of the ley line water. Keeping her wards up now was the most important thing she had to do.

As she stepped out into the frosty yard, the cold air burned her nostrils and her breath created little clouds of steam as she walked to the barn. She looked back at the house before she entered and saw Storm sitting at the window with a look of sadness in his eyes at not being taken along on this adventure. She felt bad, but he was quite naughty around the chickens and she didn't know what Connor had in store for her. So, today he would just have to wait inside.

The inside of the barn wasn't much warmer than the outside but there was plenty of warm bedding for the sheep, none of which had gone into the field today because of the cold front that was moving in. Helen found Connor down toward the end of the barn where the younger of the lambs were under a heat lamp. There were two lambs in total, one pure white and one as black as a moonless sky.

"This is Pearl and Pepper. These two were born quite late in the year so we have to make sure they're kept warm. Their mother will come back in the pen with them after she eats and has some time alone. Twins can be a handful. I try to check in on them at least a few times during the day. Pearl is quite strong, but Pepper worries me," he said, petting the little black lamb.

The sight of the twin lambs brought a rushing wave of fear through Helen. This was almost an identical set to the ones that had foretold Tomas's death.

"This isn't good," she warned.

"Why? Is there something wrong with her? Can you sense it?" There was genuine concern in Connor's voice. He obviously cared for the helpless little creature.

"This is a bad omen. A black sheep born before winter, and a twin at that. It's not a good sign."

"You're joking, right? We have between three and six pure black lambs born here every year. That's surely an old wives' tale."

"I think it might be a good idea for you and Seamus to go and stay with Ewan in the city for a few days while I finish this whole thing up. I can't risk you getting hurt," she said, turning away from him.

"Hey, I'm not going anywhere, and this set of twins is no omen foretelling my death. We have this kind of thing happen all the time," he reassured her, reaching out and pulling her in for an embrace.

She pushed him back. "I don't think you understand. I might

not be strong enough to protect you and I can't risk you getting hurt, or worse. If you won't go, then I will." She turned and started for the barn door.

Connor followed her, quickly stepping in front of the door before she was able to walk out.

"Listen, I understand that you want to make sure I'm safe but pushing me away or running away yourself isn't going to help. We have a plan, trust in that. Trust in yourself. I do."

"Connor, I can't lose you. If you stay, there's no guarantee of how things will end. If I die, I'll be reincarnated. If you die, you're gone forever. I can't risk that. It's not a chance I'm willing to take," she said. Looking at him was too hard; she glanced away into the cold, wintery barnyard.

"You're right, it's not a chance you're taking. It's a chance I'm taking. I'm not going anywhere. But if it makes you feel better, I can send Granda to his cousin Betty's for a few days. I'll make up some reason for him to go," he said, grabbing her and pulling her into his arms.

As the warmth from his embrace radiated through her, she let go of the fight and gave into the fact that he would not let her go this alone.

"Now that's settled, want to know why I have you out here to freeze your arse off in the barn?" he asked, letting her go and spinning her around.

Helen looked over at a very large, very stinky pile of sheep shit.

"And…?"

"And … that is why I needed you out here. We have to get that pile out of the barn today. Many hands make light work, my grandma always said." He handed her a shovel and set a wheelbarrow up near the pile.

"You have got to be kidding me?" She laughed. "And here I thought you were going to have some romantic picnic planned in the hayloft."

"Ha, maybe next time. Today, we work," Connor said as a large scoop of sheep shit flew over her head and into the wheelbarrow next to her.

Chapter Forty-Two

A PIECE OF TIME

They spent most of the afternoon cleaning up the barn and making sure all the animals were fed and watered. When Connor stepped outside to make his phone calls, Helen decided to stay in the barn a bit longer and check on the twins again.

When she walked up to the pen, the twins were bedded down, snuggled in tightly next to their mother. They still had their mother watching over and protecting them. This was different from the twins born the day before Tomas's death, whose mother had died after giving birth. Another difference that struck her was they were both females. The other set of twins had been a male and a female.

Pepper got up and walked over to where Helen stood on the other side of the fence and looked up at her. As Helen bent down and stroked the soft lambswool, a surge of energy came from the lamb and straight through Helen like a bolt of lightning. Surprised, she looked down at the lamb, its eyes glowing with a kind of iridescent blue for a brief moment. As they faded back to their normal color, the magic she felt was gone as well. It was inside of her now, she could feel it. A raw, animalistic kind of energy that flowed smooth and strong in her veins. The lamb looked up at her lovingly and then went back to lay down with its mother and sister.

Helen walked out of the barn with a bit more confidence in her stride. Whatever spirit magic she'd just been granted by the Goddess had her feeling a sense of calm. All the self-doubt had been replaced with calm assurance that everything might work out okay.

Connor was just getting off the phone when she came inside from the barn. The cold wind followed her in, bringing a fine dusting of snow with it. She kicked off her boots and went to the fire to warm up.

"That was Brian, my friend at the police station," Connor said. "I just got the scoop on the 'bombing'. He said they were called there around seven by the night janitor after the toilets were blown up. They waited until the manager of the building arrived and then left. The owner of the company was coming by this afternoon to assess damages and talk with the insurance adjuster. Mission accomplished! She's in town."

Hearing that their plan had worked and that Margaret was in town brought a wave of relief over Helen.

"Perfect! Now, I need you to do me one more favor that is *slightly* breaking the law again. I have to get into the historical building in town to steal a sixteenth-century watch."

"Bring it on! I'll go get my black sweater," Connor said with that childlike grin on his face.

"That won't be necessary," came a voice from the kitchen.

Seamus walked into the sitting room with a small pewter box and handed it over to Helen. Upon opening it, she saw a beautiful antique watch. She looked up at Seamus and gave him a delighted look.

"Now, that needs to be back in my hands as good as new in twenty-four hours," he said.

"Of course. But how did you get it?"

"It's not one of the popular pieces on display and no one would be the wiser seeing my old one in its place for a day or two." He looked at her with a mischievous smile.

"Hmm, so that's where this one gets it from?" Helen said, pointing at Connor.

"Afraid so," he laughed.

"Thank you," she said, giving him a peck on the cheek. She was relieved he had helped her in crossing that task off her list so she could focus on the final spell preparations, which would require all of her attention.

She brought the box with the watch in it up to the bedroom. She had cleaned out her carry-on bag and placed all the ritual items and herbs in there for safekeeping. The watch was the last of the things she needed. Now that she had it, the only thing left to do was go to the ley lines the next morning. Once she did that, her wards would be broken and her magic would be visible. There would be no turning back.

She decided to go over the spells one last time before bed, after an evening spent enjoying the company of Connor and Seamus, along with some whiskey and a spectacular meal that Seamus had been cooking while they were in the barn.

The evening came to a close with a cold starry walk in the garden with Connor. The moon was peeking out from behind the clouds, wreathed in hazy white light. They didn't go far, a quick stroll in the yard and then to the barn for one last check on the twins. They found Pepper and Pearl curled up, resting peacefully with their mother. Helen still harbored an uneasy feeling about the twin birth, but tried her best to ignore it.

When they finally ventured back inside, she kissed Connor and told him she needed a little time to herself before he came up.

She spent the better part of an hour reading and rereading everything she needed to memorize before she fell asleep. When Connor came up, he found her propped up on the bed, fast asleep with books and papers covering her. He stacked the books and papers onto the dresser and crawled into bed next to her.

He sat there awake for most of the night, just watching her. Taking in every last sight and smell. He knew she had to do the next part of her journey alone but he was afraid that if she didn't succeed, it would be the last time he would look upon her.

He refused to close his eyes, but eventually sleep overtook him, and when he woke the next day, she was gone.

Chapter Forty-Three

LEY LINES

Helen was up and gone from the McKenzie farm by 4:30 that morning. She gathered her bag, jacket, and Storm and left quietly without waking anyone. It was bitterly cold out and the truck turned over three times before the engine finally started. She drove for almost twenty minutes before the truck's heater finally kicked in and started working. Her fingers felt frozen and she berated herself for not remembering her gloves.

The sky was thick with clouds, blocking out any light from the moon or stars and leaving a black void in front of her. The truck's headlights cut through the dark, but it still felt like she was driving down a never-ending tunnel. Turning on the radio, she scanned through the stations, but nothing came in clear, and she gave up after a few minutes.

"Well, it looks like it's just you and me again, boy," she said to Storm. "When we get there, I'm going to need you to have my back and keep a close lookout. No running off chasing foxes, okay?"

Storm looked at her and then moved in and gave her cheek a long, wet lick.

"I'm going to take that as an okay!"

The coordinates Artemas had written down and which Connor had helped translate brought her three hours east of Oban to a small, wooded lot near Loch Moy. She eased the truck down a one-way road that was unpaved and unkempt. She was thankful at that moment that they hadn't gotten much snow yet and the road was still drivable. She drove until Connor's GPS alerted her that she had arrived at 57.382783; -4.037737, her destination. Putting the truck in park, she shut off the engine and grabbed everything she needed.

Around her the trees spread out into a circular clearing. A small stream sliced the clearing in half, one side heading back into the woodland and the other down to the loch. Helen could feel the energy radiating from the stream—it must be part of the ley line, she thought. She checked her watch; she still had ten minutes to set up everything she needed before the sunrise.

Finding an even spot near the stream, she pulled out an old wool blanket and laid it upon the ground. On top of it, she placed a candle, a copper bowl of salt, a satchel full of herbs for the exorcism, and the three items needed to banish Margaret. She whistled to catch Storm's attention, and then pointed to the spot she wanted him to be. The wolf obeyed and stood guard. Then she sat down on the blanket and sprinkled salt around herself in a clockwise circle. Sitting cross-legged, she placed the mirror, compass, and watch out in front of her, along with the bag of herbs.

Closing her eyes, she tilted her head toward the sky and

raised her arms up, and as the sun began to break the edge of the world, she spoke.

"Goddess of the earth, wind, fire, and sea. Help fuel my magic, hear my plea. To defeat the evil that plagues this land, lend me your powers and guide my hand. Charge these objects, break through the veil, so light may fight darkness and prevail. I am a vessel for your powers, help guide me till my final hours."

As the last word was spoken and the first rays of light breached the land, a line of pure white energy broke free of the stream and shot through her like a bolt of lightning. Another line sprang up from the water and began to encircle her, weaving with the other and creating a braided knot that wrapped around and through her at the same time. It stayed there, held in the first rays of sunlight until the light outweighed the dark and it became day. It took every ounce of her being to hold onto the massive volume of energy that was entering her body.

When the energy lines vanished, Helen fell to the ground in a heap. She didn't move, she didn't breathe, her heart did not beat, and at that moment she was gone. She hovered above her body, looking down at the world below. She could hear the sweet lullaby sung by the stars and she wanted to go to them. As she reached up and began to ascend, a loud sound jolted her back down to her earthly body.

She opened her eyes.

Storm stood over her, legs spread wide in a fighting stance. It was his bark that had brought her back from the brink of death. Once she gathered her strength, she wrapped her arms around him and cried.

It had taken all her strength to perform the spell and now she was like an overcharged battery. The Goddess had granted her wish—she was now housing the pure white energy of a goddess.

She was afraid that her human body was not strong enough to hold onto such powers. She could feel it buzzing inside her, racing up and down her body like it was looking for a way to escape.

She looked at the items placed around her. Each one was letting off a low hum. It was the same sound she could hear inside of herself, the power of divine magic.

As she gathered up the items and put them back into the bag, Storm's ears stood straight up and he let out a growl. Helen stopped what she was doing to listen. The sounds of people talking came from down near where the truck was parked. She quickly grabbed the bag, threw the blanket up over her shoulder, and skirted the edge of the woods, back to the truck.

A small group of what looked to be college students came walking up the path, past the truck, just as she had gotten in and closed the door. They waved a friendly hello and continued passing. They must have been curious about this mystical place. Helen put the truck in reverse and backed down the road, heading back toward Oban.

She arrived back at the farm around one in the afternoon and before she could even park, Connor was outside opening the driver's side door.

"How did it go? I've been sitting on pins and needles all morning waiting for you to get back here," he said as he helped her down from the truck.

"It went well. I only died for a moment."

"DIED?"

"Yes, but Storm brought me back. Didn't you, boy?" she said, rustling the fur on top of the wolf's head. He looked up at her with the eyes of a protector and then took off after the chickens in the garden.

"See, that's why I didn't want you to go alone."

"I'm fine. Plus, it wouldn't have worked if you had come. I needed to perform the spell alone, with only the Goddess as my witness."

They made their way into the house after convincing Storm there was a large bowl of food awaiting him in the kitchen. Not only did Storm have food waiting for him but Connor had stress-cooked all morning long and had a large meal laid out on the table. A pot of beef stew with fresh bread and an apple pie greeted her. The smells delighted her in a way like never before. It was like each specific scent carried its own energy mark, like fingerprints. Coriander, bay leaves, thyme, and basil, she could smell every last spice he had used along with each vegetable without even looking at the stew. Something in her shifted and she noticed she could see energy fields around objects. Even the steam coming off the stew radiated a bright orange hue.

She was sensing things she had never noticed before; everything had its own aura and a unique energy sound imprint as well. The world through the eyes of a goddess was overwhelming, to say the least. If she was going to be able to use these powers, she would have to first figure out how to control this aspect. She stood there and closed her eyes. At first, the sounds of all the things in the house were humming so loudly, she thought her brain would explode. She decided to pick one of the sounds and concentrate only on that one. As she did this, the other sounds began to fade into the background. When she opened her eyes and looked around, the auras had also faded away. All but one, the source of the sound she had focused on, a necklace.

It hung off the hinge of the kitchen window, its energy a brilliant blue, and hummed with a sweet melody. She walked over and unhooked it from its resting place. It was a small silver amulet with a Celtic knot that worked its way around a tiny moonstone. Even though the stone was small, when turned in the light, it showed bright streaks of blue.

"Whose necklace is this?" she asked as she spun the thin silver chain through her fingers.

"Yours," Connor said, taking it from her and placing it around her neck. As he fastened the clasp, she felt an instant sense of calmness surrounding her.

"What do you mean, mine? Where did it come from?"

"I bought it for you from that little apothecary shop in Luss."

"But I didn't see you buy anything when we were there."

"That's because the old woman showed it to me when you were busy picking out the herbs you needed. She said that this necklace was meant for you and that it would give you a little extra protection. I thought it couldn't hurt. Plus, it reminded me of you. The way you shine," he said, running his fingers through her hair and caressing her cheek.

She leaned in and kissed him long and hard.

"I take it that means you like it?" he teased when they'd parted.

She put her hand over the necklace where it lay against her skin. "I love it! Thank you."

After they ate, Helen went up to their bedroom and took out her spell book. There was no doubt that at this point Margaret knew something was up. The spell she needed to lure her was the easy part—it was tricking the demon that was going to be hard. She needed to make them both think they had caught her and that she was the one in the wrong place at the wrong time. The only thing she needed was any old spell done in the place where she was going to do the ritual.

After much debate in the forties, she and Artemas decided

that the best place to perform the spell would be on holy grounds. The ruins of Dunstaffnage Chapel were just the place. It was quiet and out of the way, plus the history proved useful. With the array of specters there, she would have a little backup if need be.

Her plan was to go to the ruins around 10:00 p.m. to set up what she needed and make sure the sigils were in place but well hidden. Once that was done, she would wait until 11:30 to cast the spell that would lure Margaret. If all went well, by the time the solstice came to a close, the demon would be cast back to where it had come from, and Margaret would no longer be a threat.

She went over the spells one last time and then lit a candle. She recited a luck charm her mother had taught her many centuries ago when she was Freya. As she spoke the incantation, she lit a small bundle of dried rosemary and knit the smoke around herself in a large spiral.

"From fairy glen to wishing well, let luck pour on me from this spell. Bless me with good fortune free, from earth and sky so mote it be."

As she finished, she looked at herself in the mirror and pulled out the necklace that hid in the folds of her sweater. Its glow was so intense she squinted a bit looking at it. It felt right, like it was meant to be with her, giving her a little bit of extra protection to fill in the cracks. It was the littlest things that held mighty power, Mary used to say. She always thought that people tended to look past the smaller things, even if they contained the most power. As Helen looked down upon the necklace, she agreed wholeheartedly.

Chapter Forty-Four

COLD NIGHT IN HELL

The sun set quickly and by 4:00 p.m. it was completely dark outside. It had turned bitterly cold when the sun went down so Connor and Helen decided to go and check on the twins in the barn to make sure they had plenty of hay in their stall to keep them warm through the night.

They found the lambs snuggled close to their mother, who was shivering from the cold. Connor turned the heat lamp on in an attempt to get the temperature up a bit in their stall. Helen fetched some extra hay and laid it down around the mother like a protective nest for her to sleep in for the night. Under her breath, she uttered a simple spell to help trap the heat in their space. The mother's body began to relax as the heat lamp warmed the area and Helen's spell kept the heat from escaping the pen. The lambs moved in their sleep as if their dreams had just been changed from cold winter days to warm summer frolics in fields full of heather.

She and Connor went about feeding the rest of the herd as well, making sure there was proper bedding for them to get them through the cold night. Helen enjoyed the kind of peace that came from watching and tending to the animals.

After their chores were done, they braved the cold and headed back into the house for dinner. Seamus had spent the afternoon making haggis and fresh bread and the house was full of the pungent smell of sage, thyme, and rosemary. They all went about setting the table and filling their plates with the warm, homecooked meal. Helen had eaten better in the last three days than she had in the past year. She could easily get used to this kind of life. She passed on a glass of wine as she was not to alter herself in any way while inhabiting the energy of the Goddess. Nevertheless, the warm food and good company calmed her nerves enough.

She took it upon herself to do the night cleanup in the kitchen while Connor and Seamus watched a football match on the television. As she mindlessly washed the dishes, she noticed headlights coming down the drive toward the farm. She called out to Connor.

"Are you guys expecting someone?"

"No, why? Is someone here?"

He got up and walked over to the window and saw the lights of the vehicle pull up, parking next to the barn.

"Hold on, I'm going to go out and see who it is. Probably the McCraig boys messing about again," he said as he bundled himself up and headed out the door.

As soon as the door opened, a cold gust of wind burst into the house. along with a feeling of unease. Storm stood up, hair raised on the back of his neck. He came over to Helen and jammed his cold, wet nose into her leg, almost knocking her off balance, and let out a growl that was deep and low.

"What is it, Storm?" she asked, looking out the window.

She dropped the glass she was cleaning into the sink when she saw Margaret step out of the car. The glass hit the porcelain sink and smashed silently under the water, leaving Helen cut and bleeding. Shocked, she stood there still as stone until the wolf nudged her again.

There was no time to think. She grabbed her jacket and slipped out the side door and into the frigid night air, Storm at her heels. Quietly, she made her way to the truck and opened the passenger door, grabbed her bag off the front seat, then headed toward the barn. She could hear Connor explaining to Margaret that it was just him and his grandfather who lived at the farm and that no woman had lived here since his grandmother had passed.

She made her way into the barn, unseen through the back entrance, and tucked into one of the unused stalls to rummage through her bag. Storm stood guard by the stall door, on high alert.

How the hell did she find me? she thought, pulling out a large piece of drawing charcoal from her tote. Then it dawned on her—the heat-trapping spell she had performed on the twins' pen. She had messed up. Her wards were down and even a small spell like that was a beacon. But there was no time for getting down on herself—now that her plan had changed completely she needed to bend things to fit the new situation.

She quickly scooted out of the stall and down toward the barn doors. Sweeping off the floor, she began to draw with her charcoal on the old barn boards. Once she had finished, she swept the hay shaft back over the floor, covering her markings, then added a thick layer of salt around the circle. She tucked her bag behind a grain sack along with her staff and motioned for Storm to come to her.

"Stay here and wait for me," she said, giving him a stroke across the top of his head before exiting.

She made her way swiftly out of the barn and down to the house, being careful not to be seen. Slipping in the back door, she almost made it to the sitting room to warn Seamus when she heard the front door burst open. Helen witnessed everything through a crack in the hallway door as Connor let out a strangled scream and dropped to the ground. Primal fear surged through her as she listened to the man she loved cry out in pain.

Then Margaret's voice rang out through the house. "Freya, I know you're here. Come out. You don't want me to have to hurt this handsome young man here, do you? I know you aren't one for watching people suffer."

She lifted up her right hand and with the twist of her wrist, there was a loud snap and Connor's left arm bent out at an odd angle. His screams of agony followed. Before Helen could even act, Margaret had raised her other hand and with the swish of her wrist, Connor's left ankle snapped. His body lay crippled on the cold floor as he writhed in pain.

Helen burst into the room.

"Enough!" she shouted, sweeping her arm out in front of her and sending out a pulse of energy that knocked Margaret off balance. It gave Seamus just enough time to gather Connor up and pull him from the center of the room to behind a chair near the fireplace.

As Margaret steadied herself, they stood face to face for the first time in almost a century. The darkness in her eyes was just as deep and menacing as it had been all those years ago, if not more.

"Oh, how cute. I see you haven't learned any new tricks since

I saw you last. Except for that one where you kept yourself hidden from me, that is. Well, at least until tonight. I would have thought by now you had learned your lesson—you'll never have the upper hand. In this life or the next or the one after that," Margaret said, slowly walking the edge of the room. She brushed off her jacket in a smug way, as if tainted by Helen's magic.

"It took you long enough to find me. Seems as if maybe your age is showing," Helen replied, as she watched the woman prowl the room like a predator stalking its prey.

"I am getting quite tired of this. After I kill you this time, I think I'll spare myself the trouble of this tedious dance and just end your life as a child next time you're reborn."

"You won't have the chance," Helen said, twisting her wrist and pointing her index finger to the heavens. A vortex of wind picked up and coiled itself around Margaret, knocking picture frames off the mantel and tipping over chairs as it trapped her in its grip. She could feel the power of the Goddess as the spell held strong. "Seamus, get him out of here!" Helen belted out over the deafening sound of the wind. She tried to shield him as he helped Connor onto his good foot and across the floor toward the hallway door.

Margaret began to laugh loudly, sounding less like a woman and more like some kind of beast. As her hair whipped upward into the spinning vortex, her eyes flashed black and with a snap of her fingers, the wind ceased. At that moment Helen knew she was no longer dealing with just Margaret. The demon in her was awakened at the threat of his host being in peril.

Helen looked over toward the hallway door where Seamus had just managed to get Connor through, but before she could even let out a warning to run, Seamus's neck snapped and he fell limp to the floor.

"NO!" she cried out, spinning around toward what now was a much stronger and more dangerous Margaret, the force of her magic being amplified by the demon inside her.

She pulled out the hag stone from beneath her shirt. As she did, the moonstone necklace that Connor had given her wedged itself inside the hole of the hag stone. As the two necklaces became one, they created a large, blue orb around her. Without pausing to think, she raced through the front door and toward the barn.

"You don't really think you can run or hide from me, do you?" Margaret said, stepping out of the house and into the freezing winter night's air, taking slow, methodical strides towards the barn.

It was as dark as it was cold. No stars, no moon. Nothing to illuminate the darkness except for a large floodlight positioned at the top peak of the barn's gable end. The light cascaded down onto a fine dusting of snow, clearly showing Helen's path into the barn.

The barn doors opened and the light from the floodlight illuminated the first few stalls, then petered out into complete darkness toward the back. Margaret stood in the doorway, the light casting a distorted silhouette with two heads upon the floor. She peered into the darkness in front of her as she stepped inside.

Chapter Forty-Five

THE UNWEAVING

As Margaret entered the barn, Helen kept within the shadows, waiting for her to falter into the hidden circle on the floor.

"Running and hiding isn't going to save you," Margaret called out.

"I wasn't running from you, nor was I hiding," Helen said, stepping out of the darkness into the light of the doorway, draped in her mother's cloak.

Margaret reached her hand up toward the rafters in an effort to cast a spell, but nothing happened. She took a step forward and was stopped by an invisible wall of energy that bounced her back with some force. She was trapped within the circle Helen had drawn.

"I was luring you into my trap," Helen said, walking around Margaret.

Margaret's aura turned from her normal shade of murky

brown to a deep ebony. Helen now had the undivided attention of her co-pilot. The demon had taken over Margaret's form in an attempt to save itself.

Reaching behind the grain sack, Helen pulled out her bag and began to set out the copper bowls on the four corners of the cross that still lay hidden under the hay. As she added the herbs to each bowl, the demon became agitated, casting any spell he could think of in a language that sounded ancient and evil. His failed attempts only added to his violent outbursts.

The first bowl to be lit was the bowl that represented north, full of boneset. The second was east and contained betelnut, the third south with cloves, and the last, west with chrysanthemums. After each bowl had been lit and the smoke began to fill the circle, Helen began walking in a clockwise direction, guiding the smoke as she went around the circle.

"Exardescat e tenebris lumen, neque rursus malum eiiciatur. Per ipsum dei potentiam ad infernum redeas," Helen said, with as much conviction as she could muster. *Let the light burn out of darkness, and let no evil be cast out again. By the power of God you can return to hell.*

"What are you doing you, stupid girl?" Margaret bellowed into the stillness.

"Exardescat e tenebris lumen, neque rursus malum eiiciatur. Per ipsum dei potentiam ad infernum redeas," Helen repeated, making her second loop around the circle. It was taking as much power as she could give to speak magic into the words.

As she spoke the incantation for the last time and completed the circle, she turned abruptly and walked counterclockwise, smothering the smoke in each bowl as she went, sealing the spell. As she did this, Margaret fell to the floor, her head tilted back and her mouth open toward the heavens.

Helen made her third and final loop, still spinning and pulling the smoke that lingered in the air, weaving it into a cage that contained Margaret. She stopped and looked at her kneeling there, with her head still tilted up, then made the symbol of the holy cross in the air.

"Let the light burn out the darkness and let no evil be cast out again. By the power of God, may you return to hell. Amen."

As Helen spoke, the black aura around Margaret began to pulse, pulling in and out of her body. Then in its final attempt, the demon spoke, his voice filled with a desperate kind of anger.

"You may purge me from this vessel but do not make the mistake of thinking I won't find my way back."

With that, the black aura pulsed out and spun up and over Margaret's body where she lay in a heap on the floor, then vanished into the darkness.

Helen stepped back and took a deep breath, then turned to see the yellow eyes of her wolf in the darkness. She smiled at him for the victory she had just achieved. *It's almost over, just one last spell,* she thought.

In that brief moment of victory, she let her guard down and before she could turn back around, something struck her with such force she was thrown halfway across the barn. With a loud splintering crack, she hit one of the barn's supporting beams and crumpled to the ground, the wind knocked out of her.

"Thank you. I've been trying to lose that guy for centuries. Nothing like a controlling man to weigh a woman down," Margaret said, as she kicked Helen forcefully in the ribs, once again knocking her free of breath. She then grabbed a fistful of Helen's hair and pulled her to her feet while she cried out in pain. "Ending you in this life will be far more satisfying than any of the others. Just when you thought you'd won, I get to crush you again," Margaret snarled, raising her hand to strike.

Storm sprang out from the shadows and sank his teeth into her right arm, making her let go of Helen's hair and freeing her. Margaret cried out as she struggled to shake the wolf from her arm.

It gave Helen just enough time to get her balance and head to the grain sack that held the rest of the items she needed for the final spell.

She heard the struggle come to an end as Storm let out a feeble cry that was followed by a large thud against the barn floor, shaking the boards all the way down to where she stood.

"Wretched beast! Why must you always have a wolf? Such vile creatures and so easy to kill. I don't understand why you insist on surrounding yourself with them," Margaret's voice echoed out into the barn as she walked toward Helen.

Helen scrambled to set up all the items for the time spell. She was pulling out the pocket watch and compass from the bag when one of Margaret's spells struck her. Helen fell forward, smashing her face onto the floor, leaving her with a broken nose and her head spinning. The blast of energy from the spell knocked loose a beam and it crashed down, missing Helen by inches and landing instead on the edge of her bag, smashing the mirror to bits.

Helen looked down. Her hopes and dreams lay shattered amongst the broken shards. How had a seemingly ordinary object destroyed all her hopes? In that moment she felt the ache of defeat creeping its way in, and the exhaustion she felt left her on the verge of giving up. She scavenged for a large enough piece of mirror to perform the spell but only managed to cut her hands.

Before she could regain her composure, she was struck with another blow, sending her plummeting to the floor in a broken heap. As she struggled to pull herself back up, she saw Margaret lift her arms in the air, crossing them as she brought them over her head. Helen knew what was coming next: an execution spell. She reached her arm out, frantically feeling for her staff, but it had been knocked too far out of her reach to get to it in time.

"Power of the north— " she began, calling on the winds to aid her, when she looked up and saw a shadowy figure standing by the barn door.

"Hey, you old bitch, why don't you pick on someone your own size."

Connor stood there with the shotgun from over the fireplace, pointing directly at Margaret. Standing weakly on one foot, he fired off a shot, just grazing her shoulder.

She swung her right arm forward and Helen watched as his other leg gave way beneath him, bending out at an unnatural angle. He fell to the floor, screaming and writhing in pain.

"No, Connor!" Helen cried out, moving toward him frantically.

"Love. That right there has always been your biggest weakness," Margaret said, moving her way to the front of the barn entrance. "You could have done so much with your powers, yet you waste it on these useless mortals. Why?"

"Margaret, I feel sorry for you that you think love is not worth fighting for. You truly have no idea what real magic is, do you?" Helen said as she bent down to try and ease Connor's pain with a spell.

She kissed his forehead, then took both her hands and charged a blue orb of light between them. She went to place it on his broken leg when Margaret cast a spell that sent the broken beam hurtling through the air, knocking Helen backward and crushing Connor where he lay.

Helen, bruised and broken, got to her feet as quickly as she could and tried to lift the beam off Connor with her powers. But she was waning, her power weakened from the energy it had taken to perform the exorcism. Connor saw her struggling and stopped her.

"No. Finish this," he said in a low, whispering voice.

Helen had crouched down in front of him, in an attempt to protect what little life he had left, as Margaret grew closer to them. "I can't, the mirror is broken—without its reflection, the spell won't work. I'm so sorry," she whispered back. Tears ran down her cheeks, leaving clean lines through the dirt and blood.

With Connor's last bit of life energy, he looked at her and pointed his finger toward an old chrome hub cap resting on a pile of grain sacks.

Helen's eyes lit up. She moved with as much speed as she could and snatched up the old hub cap from the ground. Reaching into her pocket, she pulled out the watch and compass, then spun around.

At that moment, the power of the Goddess broke free and filled every inch of her. A white light cascaded off her and fell to the ground. Her eyes were wild with rage. She picked up her staff, raised it over her head, and called to the winds.

A large gust rushed in through the barn doors and began circling around Margaret. Faster and wilder it spun, until she was trapped inside the vortex. She tried to lift her arms to cast, she tried to recite incantations, but the power of the wind bound her like a magical straitjacket.

Helen knew in order for this spell to work, she needed all her talismans and one of those was Storm. She walked over and knelt down where the body of the wolf lay. Her heart ached as she looked upon his body, resting cold and lifeless on the floor. She laid her staff down next to him and took off her hag stone, placing it on the wolf's chest. Instinctually, she cupped her hands together and laid them on top of the stone, as if the Goddess was guiding her movements. With the power of the Goddess inside her, she thrust all her energy forward and into the stone. As it hit the hole where the moonstone now lay wedged, it was amplified and the wolf's heart began to beat again. She let out a sigh of relief as he slowly moved his head up and looked around, then got to his feet and licked her face.

They walked back to the vortex where Margaret was still held. Helen stood there with her staff in one hand and an old hub cap in the other. She turned and passed the hub cap to Storm, which he held in his teeth, as she pulled out the watch and then the compass from her pocket. She opened the compass, walked up to the edge of the vortex, and began the incantation.

"With this compass, I shall find, the place to send you back in time. With this watch, I give you back, the years you stole within time's track," she said, spinning the hands of the watch backward.

As she spoke, Margaret's hair began to fade to snowy white and her skin wrinkled and sagged on her bones. The youth was being pulled from her and given back to the hands of time. Margaret tried to call out a plea, but the wind kept her words silent.

Helen grabbed the hub cap from Storm and held it up in front of Margaret's face.

"With this mirror, you have found, the magic wove has come unbound," she shouted, slamming her staff's point to the floor. "The power you so greedily tried to obtain by causing the death of so many was never even in your grasp. For the true power of a goddess doesn't lie within youth, beauty, or wealth. It lies within the power of love, nature, and a community that works together to protect one another. I am sorry that you let your heart grow so bitter that you were never able to know the true magic we all carry within us."

Margaret dragged in a long, rattling breath as the wind died down around her.

"If your inner light isn't strong enough to withstand the pull of darkness, darkness will always win," Helen said.

And with those final words, Margaret disintegrated, becoming nothing more than a fine ash softly floating to the barn floor and disappearing into the hay.

Helen rushed to Connor's side. He had taken his last breath and died without her. His body lay half in and half out of the barn, his face covered in a fine coating of snow as if nature had given him its own version of a burial cloth. She took off the hag stone and placed it over his heart in the same way she had done for Storm, and with all the power of the Goddess inside her, she pushed everything she had out through her hands and into the stone.

She waited, but nothing happened.

She tried again, channeling the last ounces of her strength and repeating the process over and over, but no life sprang back into him as it had done so easily for the wolf. She took off her mother's cloak and laid it over Connor's body in defeat and wept. Each tear slowly slid down her cheeks and softly landed on the cloak.

She looked out to where the sea split the land and saw a thin beam of red light begin to break the horizon. It was almost dawn, and her amplified powers would soon be gone. She lay down and curled close to Connor's body, speaking softly.

"We did it. She's gone and my curse is broken, but for what?

To live a life of grief and loss. This wasn't how it was meant to be. I can't do this without you."

She closed her eyes. The cold silence of the farmyard echoed back her loss.

"Well, I'm hoping you won't have to do that for many years," said a voice.

Helen opened her eyes.

There in the snow, Connor was sitting up with the cloak wrapped around him.

"Burr, it's cold out here. Can we go in?"

Helen knocked him over with the fiercest hug he had ever been given.

"You're okay? How?" she asked.

"Not sure, you tell me. Must have been something you did. The last thing I remember was being crushed and then passing out."

Helen looked down at the green velvet cape wrapped around his shoulders and smiled. Mary had been enchanting it with protection charms for years, intended just for this very moment. She had foreseen it. She had passed it on to Fionna who had kept it safe with her descendants until it had come into Helen's possession once again. It had taken a village to bring her to this point in time. Mary, her mother, and the community of wise women and healers were her triquetra. Without them, she would not have been able to defeat Margaret.

Helen took off running to the house with the cape in her hands as the sun broke the surface of the sea.

She flung open the door and there in the sitting room, resting in his chair, was Seamus. His body still lay on the floor, half in and half out of the hallway. Yet his spirit sat peacefully in his favorite chair, a pipe in his mouth. He smiled at her.

"You did good," he said to her as Connor came into the room. "This was the way it was meant to be. I was ready. It's been far too many years without my Katherine. I'm ready to go to her," he said, tilting his head in a gesture of farewell. They watched as he slowly faded away into the space between.

Connor took Helen's hand in his, lacing his fingers through hers, and they stood there in the quiet breaking of a new dawn.

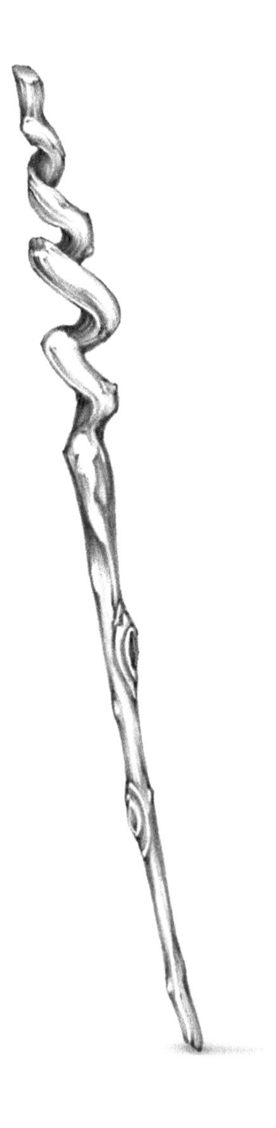

EPILOGUE

It was almost a year since the death of Connor's grandfather and the beginning of Helen's new life. Now that the spell had been broken, she finally felt as if she was truly living. She was grateful it was the last life she would ever have, and she didn't plan on wasting even a minute of it.

She had spent the better part of the year helping Connor on the farm and fixing up the cottage. Halfway through May she set up her own freelance marketing company and busied herself with several large jobs that kept her financially secure. Connor asked her to move in with him at the farm in the autumn, but she respectfully declined. Even though she was ready to take that next step in their relationship, she wasn't ready to let go of living at the cottage just yet. This was the first time she had inhabited Fernbeg without the threat of fear and destruction resting on her shoulders since she was a child, and she was enjoying the peaceful solitude of it.

That winter, a thin layer of snow coated the land and Fernbeg rested snugly in its camouflage as the winter winds blew in from the sea. A steady stream of gray smoke billowed from the chimney and a warm, inviting glow came through the windows of the cottage as the sun began to set.

Helen walked into the sitting room and looked upon the quaint little Scotch pine she and Connor had cut down earlier in the day. He was stringing lights around it, casting a cozy festive glow about the room. Storm looked on in amazement at there being an actual living tree in the house, and nosed at the branches with curiosity.

Helen handed Connor a tumbler of whiskey and kissed him softly on the cheek. Then she picked up a small box with a few ornaments in it from the coffee table. They had bought them at the holiday market where they sold their wool. There were four in total, a small wooden rabbit carved out of driftwood, an old antique thistle brooch that someone had turned into an ornament, a felted wool acorn, and Seamus's old pipe. Helen had found an old spool of red velvet ribbon and tied it around the bit so that it hung with its bowl facing outward. She handed the pipe to Connor. He took it gingerly and hung it in the center of the tree while Helen added the others. They stepped back to inspect their first tree together.

"It's a bit sparse and it definitely needs a topper," Connor said

"I completely agree about the topper, but it's not sparse—it's perfect. It gives us the room to gather things as we go and someday it will be full of all our adventures together," she said, pulling him in and kissing the whiskey off his lips.

She turned and left the room then, coming back a minute later with something in her hands. It was a wool hat she had knit with the wool shorn from the black lamb born the winter before.

On the front of the hat she had lovingly embroidered the triquetra in the white wool from the lamb's twin sister. It felt like the perfect symbol to top off their tree, with everything that had brought them together and led them to this very moment.

Connor smiled, shaking his head in approval. He lifted her up and she placed the hat on the top branch with the triquetra facing out toward the room. Then they sat on the sofa, whiskeys in hand, and looked upon the little tree as the embers of the fire began to die down. Helen rested her head on Connor's shoulder and with a snap of her fingers set the fire ablaze once more. Connor looked down at her and smiled. She was pure magic, in every way.

Printed in the USA
CPSIA information can be obtained
at www.ICGtesting.com
LVHW061202181223
766713LV00033B/380/J